A Book of
Boys' Stories

A BOOK OF
BOYS' STORIES

Written by
ROBERT BATEMAN
and
NICHOLAS MARRAT
Illustrated by
PAT NEVIN

HAMLYN
LONDON · NEW YORK · SYDNEY · TORONTO

ACKNOWLEDGEMENTS

Stories by Robert Bateman.

SKIN-DIVE, BEWARE OF FERNANDEZ!, SPECKLES, THE LAST TERM AT WILDMERE, THE DIZZYBOAT, THE ARROW AND THE TARGET, BILL'S BATTING COUSIN, CHARLIE BASSETT'S ROCKET TRIP, EDDIE'S SUMMER PROJECT, WAITING FOR ROGER, FEODOR'S LUCKY ACCIDENT, RUMPUS AT WESTLAKE, THE SECRET OF ZK 170, MATCH WITH A CATCH, THE UNEXPECTED TREASURE, TOO EASY FOR TIM, THE SCHOOL IN OUTER SPACE.

Stories by Nicholas Marrat.

THE PLANETOID GRID, BOY WITH A GUN, MURDER IS FOR MEN, CHAD STENSON — TV REPORTER, IMPERNO QUARTARO — SPECIAL AGENT, THE FIGHTING FLANAGANS.

First published 1964
Tenth impression 1978 by
The Hamlyn Publishing Group Limited
LONDON · NEW YORK · SYDNEY · TORONTO
Astronaut House, Feltham, Middlesex, England
© Copyright 1964 The Hamlyn Publishing Group Limited
All rights reserved. No part of this publication may be
reproduced, stored in a retrieval system, or transmitted, in
any form or by any means, electronic, mechanical, photocopying,
recording or otherwise, without the permission of The Hamlyn
Publishing Group Limited.
ISBN 0 601 07056 9
Printed in Great Britain by Butler & Tanner Ltd
Frome and London

CONTENTS

SKIN-DIVE

Sam Todhunter didn't care much for continental breakfasts in any case, so missing this one mattered very little. He'd been warned not to eat it. Diving was something best done on an empty stomach, Bill Maxted had told him the night before as they walked along the sands towards the cape. He'd told a few spine-chilling stories about people who'd gone down straight after a hearty meal, and then regretted it when they doubled up with stomach cramps while on the bottom.

He drank one cup of coffee, though. The morning was chilly; though the sun was already well up it had been an icy night, and it would be another hour before the heat began to make itself felt again.

'Where are you off to in such a hurry?' asked his father, laughing.

Sam avoided his eyes. 'Meeting Bill Maxted. We're going along the coast a bit.'

'You'll be back to lunch, won't you?' His mother looked vaguely anxious. 'I don't want you eating odd food in some café. Spanish food isn't like our own, you know. It could give you an upset stomach.'

He shook his head. 'Be back by one at the latest.' He ran down the steps from the hotel terrace, across the dusty road towards the bright gleam of the sea.

He'd read about skin-diving. He'd seen it on television, too, and longed for the chance to try it. So far the best he'd been able to do had been messing about a few feet below water with a breathing-tube, but Bill Maxted's father had the real thing — a boatload of gear: suits, oxygen masks, safety-lines, the lot. And Bill had already been down a dozen times, so he wouldn't have to learn without an expert.

He saw his holiday friend nearly a mile away, a black dot on the beach waving with one hand above his head. Both walked rapidly down towards the beached launch which lay between them, exchanging shouts of greeting when they came within earshot of each other.

'Where's your dad?' Sam called. 'Isn't he coming?'

'He had to go to Malaga for the day. But we've got José to crew for us.' He cupped his hands, and bellowed in the direction of the launch, 'Hi, José!'

There was an answering shout, and a small man in a boiler suit came out of the engine house wiping his hands on a rag. '*Hola! Como está?* A fine day for it, no? Which way we go?'

Bill and Sam put their shoulders against the bows of the launch, and heaved until she slid gently into the water. 'To the north,' panted Bill. 'Let's go up to the cape. There's water up there so clear you can see for miles along the bottom. How long will it take us?'

José shrugged his shoulders. 'Twenty minutes. Maybe thirty.' He started the engine, listened carefully as the diesel thudded into action and then increased speed with a roar, pushing the launch out across the bay, with the bow slicing cleanly through the clear blue water.

José's guess was a good one. Sam's watch showed that the trip took twenty-five minutes. He and Bill sat in the bow sorting out equipment, as the launch nosed into a tiny inlet beyond the cape. José picked his anchorage carefully, then let the hook go overboard with a grin. '*Magnifico!*' he exclaimed. 'Now you take your dive, while I clean the engine. When you come back I have hot coffee waiting for you. That is good, no?'

'That is good, yes,' grinned Bill. Aside, he whispered to Sam, 'My old man's got José trained to a fine art. Next thing he'll be bringing cups of hot coffee down to us on the bottom! Here, Sam, climb into this. It should be about your size.' He handed Sam a black flexible waterproof suit that covered him from his shoulders to his feet, then strapped the oxygen mask across his face. 'You've got enough there for ten times as long as we'll be under water,' he said reassuringly. 'Don't pull it into place until we go under.'

'What do we do? Climb in, or jump in?'

'Climb in. You don't want to get your head and mask under, or the mask gets wet inside. Watch, and I'll show you.' Bill Maxted hung a short ladder over the side, and lowered himself down it into the water.

'Cold?'

Bill shook his head. 'Wonderful! Just cool enough to be ideal with these suits on. Come on in.'

More cautiously, Sam followed him down the ladder. Now that he'd reached the actual moment of the dive he found he was nervous, with his heart thumping. Of course, up-to-date skin-diving gear was supposed to be foolproof, but just supposing something did go wrong? Would he be able to keep himself from getting into a panic?

'Now put on your mask.' Treading water, Bill Maxted helped him adjust it, then fitted his own into place. Suddenly, with a flip of his frogman flippers, he was gone. The foam and wavelets on the surface prevented Sam from seeing him for several seconds; then, looking down into the clear depths, he saw the outline of Bill's diving-suit against the sandy bottom, spread-eagled as if he were asleep there. He dived clumsily, and resisted the inclination to surface immediately when he felt the comforting stream of oxygen fill his lungs. Through the goggles he saw Bill Maxted rise from the bottom to meet him. Controlling his movements with the flippers, he lowered himself gradually to meet his friend, who then turned and swam slowly along about five feet off the sand and fronds of pale green seaweed. A shoal of tiny fish loomed up in front of Sam's goggles, whipping away at lightning speed to avoid him.

Bill swung round to the right, then pointed up. For a

11

moment Sam couldn't make out what the curious shape was above them, then he realised it was the underside of the launch. The outline of José's head and shoulders was visible at one side. He tried to wave, and saw an acknowledgement from above.

Bill Maxted now touched him lightly on the arm, and pointed towards a huge rock sticking up from the sandy bottom. They swam over towards it, side by side, and circled round, avoiding the long tendrils of weed that trailed threateningly from below it. Sam had been warned about these. The long ones were strong enough to hold you fast if once you became entangled with them, and it was a long and difficult job to get free again. Some skin-divers had failed to get free before their oxygen supply ran out, and he had no intention of adding to their number. He pointed, and saw an answering signal from Bill, who promptly rose three feet to dodge them.

Sam felt warm and comfortable. The exertion of swimming was enough to combat the cold of the water fifteen feet below the surface, and the view of the sea bottom was fascinating and new. Also fascinating was the experience of manoeuvring in the diving-gear, with the confidence given by the constant supply of oxygen, and no need to count the seconds as in a normal dive.

After five minutes they surfaced beside the launch. José grinned at them over the side. 'What? You not bring back no fish? What you expect to eat for my dinner, eh? Seaweed?'

'What d'you expect us to do?' spluttered Bill. 'Sneak up behind 'em and put salt on their tails?' Then, as José obviously didn't understand what he meant, he added, 'We can't catch them with our hands, you know.'

They swam round the launch, then went down again. Sam remembered only just in time to replace his mask, and followed Bill on a long head-to-toe swim which seemed to take them a great distance in a very short while — so far, in fact, that he began to feel just a little uneasy about finding their way back. Suddenly, in front of him, Bill came to a halt and stood upright on a narrow ledge of rock. Sam had no time to stop himself, and went crashing into his friend, dislodging him, so that they both rolled over and over on the sand beside what loomed up as a high underwater rock cliff. Bubbles of air told Sam that Bill was laughing inside his mask. Together they began to climb. It was only after they had climbed for some seconds that Sam began to realise they had swum much deeper, that, in fact, the sea bottom had shelved, and that at this point it was perhaps thirty feet or more below the surface of the water. It was dimmer, and he could see only a few feet on all sides.

The rock was smooth, with few footholds, and their progress upwards was partly a climb, partly a swim. Sam saw a wave from Bill, which seemed to indicate that he should take the lead. He thrust himself upwards, and caught hold of a jutting outcrop of rock, then paused, looking through a neat round hole to the far side. The hole was as smooth as if carved and rubbed down by stone-masons, but he knew it had been made by centuries of underwater currents sweeping in and out, slowly wearing down the rock. He put his head and shoulders into the hole, and wondered if there was enough space to wriggle through. Caution made him abandon the idea. He turned, to signal to Bill Maxted that here was something worth looking at, but Bill wasn't to be seen.

Sam looked up, then down, then all round him, wondering how in the world his companion had managed to disappear. Knowing Bill's capacity for mischief, he had a sudden misgiving. Had Bill swum back to the launch, leaving him to find his own way? That was the way the Maxteds — father and son alike — tended to think about beginners: just chuck 'em in and give them a tough test right from the start. Surely, though, that didn't apply twenty or thirty feet under water, a hundred yards away from a launch?

Panicking, he thrust out from the rock, swimming wildly away from it, hoping he'd remember the right direction —

then realising with relief that it didn't much matter, because if the worst came to the worst he could always come up to the surface to find his bearings.

It was a stream of bubbles from below him that caught his attention. He turned, and glided towards them.

And then he stopped short, first with relief, then with alarm. For Bill Maxted was there after all, farther down the underwater cliff. But he was trapped. In the climb he had somehow managed to dislodge a huge boulder, which had settled into a crevice, pinning his leg in a narrow channel below it. Bill was pressed against the rock, pointing downwards to his leg, and heaving at it to show that it was beyond his power to free himself.

Sam moved in closer. He found two precarious footholds, then tried to grip the surface of the boulder. It was slippery; his hands failed to get a firm hold, and so he moved them farther down, trying to shift the boulder from below. It moved, for he felt a definite grating sensation, but the movement was so minute that he was aware he had no hope of shifting it.

He let go, and turned towards Bill Maxted. Bill was now very nearly exhausted, as far as he could judge from the slow movements and the look of what parts of his face weren't obscured by the mask. He took Bill's limp hand, wishing he knew Morse code, so that he could communicate with him. All he could do was grip it firmly, encouragingly — though what there was to be encouraging about he had no idea. How *did* one set about shifting a boulder under water?

He stood still, his feet in the soft sand of the sea bed, his mind racing. Then, with a wave to Bill, he set out at right-angles to the cliff, swimming as fast as he could in what he hoped was the direction of the launch. He counted as he swam, planning to come to the surface after two hundred strokes. When the time came he rose gradually, remembering that he'd been under water some time, and that he should get used to the change in pressure by degrees.

He surfaced, and the glare of sunshine, even through his goggles, was almost blinding. He pulled them off, and looked round for the launch. He groaned. He'd come badly off course, and it was nearly a hundred yards away, farther out to sea; José was sitting in the stern, his eyes fixed intently on a fishing-line.

Sam shouted. There was no sign from José to indicate that he'd heard. A second shout brought José's head round slowly, and then he stood up, walked to the bows, and waved.

Sam returned the wave with both arms. For a few moments José stood apparently undecided, then he began heaving in the anchor. Sam lay on the surface, and waited while the launch moved slowly towards him at low throttle.

Sam signalled him to come closer.

'What all this trouble? Mr Bill — where's he gone?'

Sam caught the gunwale of the launch and hung on, spluttering. Between gasps for breath he explained. José's eyes rounded with astonishment and alarm. 'What we do now? You got ideas?'

Sam panted quick instructions, then replaced his goggles and mask, released his hold on the gunwale of the launch and swam under water in what he hoped was the direction from which he'd come.

It was difficult to find landmarks. He saw one huge forest of seaweed, ten feet across, trailing up in long tendrils from the bottom, but was it the same one he'd passed and vaguely remembered from the first journey? Were there dozens like it down there? He had to take that chance, for he had no idea how long Bill Maxted could hold out in his weakened state. What happened to a man under water if he became unconscious? Did the oxygen system still work efficiently? He swam hurriedly now, racing towards what he hoped would be the cliff.

It wasn't. It was a high ridge of sand, deceptive under water at any distance beyond a few feet. He hung on to the slippery weedy surface, wondering whether to turn left or right, trying to recapture in his memory the way they had come before.

He plumped for the right, and began working his way along, hand over hand, conscious now that he must avoid swimming any more for fear that when he found Bill he would be too exhausted to help. His arms ached from the heavy exercise, and even if his plan worked out there was a great deal of hard work to be done.

Suddenly the sand-bar ended. There was a deep channel beyond, and his heart sank. He groped his way across it, reached out into an extraordinarily dark patch ahead — and barked his knuckles against rock! Swiftly he brought his body vertical, and began scrambling along the rock face, blowing out huge cloud of bubbles with the effort.

And then his foot touched something soft. He looked down, and found his heel was kicking Bill Maxted's head, and that Bill's arms were reaching up towards him.

He lowered himself, grabbed Bill by the shoulders, and tried to instil confidence by a firm squeeze with both hands. He saw Bill's eyes, wide and staring; if he could see Bill's, then Bill could see his. He winked, and to his relief saw an answering wink.

He surfaced, and waved to José. Slowly the launch swung round and cruised towards him. José stood in the bows, holding the anchor as instructed. When he was only twenty feet away he lowered it gently over the bow, so that it hung level with the water-line, and then darted back to thrust the engine into reverse. The gear change, the sudden roar as the launch lost way, gave Sam new heart. He'd had doubts about José, whether his English had been accurate enough to understand his instructions.

But he need not have worried, for the launch came to rest a foot away from him, with the anchor easy to grasp. José raced back to the bow to help him, and as Sam carried it down José paid out cable steadily to make the task easier.

The weight of the anchor was difficult to handle, even

under water where weight counts for much less. Sam wrestled with it, holding it with one hand while he groped for the cliff face with the other. Then, inching himself down to the foot-hold beside Bill, he wedged one fluke of the anchor under the rock. He worked it back and forth until he was certain it was firmly in place, then gave two sharp tugs on the chain.

The next few moments were agony. He could see Bill's eyes, still wide and staring, then he turned away and watched the anchor, terrified in case it broke loose despite all his careful adjustment.

The roar of the engine above nearly deafened him. The water became cloudy. He laid one hand on the chain, felt it grow taut and begin to move.

Then, suddenly, there was a rending noise right beside him. The boulder rose up, teetered for a moment on one edge, and plunged down, grazing his side as it went. Bill's leg floated free; he grabbed Bill's arm, and guided him slowly and carefully to the surface.

It was that evening, at supper, that Sam's father said, 'How did you get on this morning, Sam? What did you find to do?'

'We went diving,' said Sam. He hoped there'd be no questions — tried to avoid the inevitable anxious look from his mother.

'Isn't that rather dangerous?'

Sam drew in a deep breath as he saw Bill and Mr Maxted walk into the hotel dining-room and come over towards them. There was no way in which he could signal his complicated message without being seen. Instead, he took the initiative. He stood up. 'Hullo, Mr Maxted. Did you have a good day in Malaga? We went diving.' He grinned. 'You might be able to reassure my mother for me. She imagines that it's dangerous.'

A smile flickered at the corners of Mr Maxted's lips. His eyes darted between Sam and his mother. Then he said,

'Dangerous? Don't worry, Mrs Todhunter. Diving's quite safe — as long as you work in pairs, and one man is a first-class rescuer.'

Sam laughed silently to himself. It wasn't exactly a lie, and it had the desired effect. And after the Maxteds had sat down nobody was able to see the firm, warm handshake of gratitude exchanged between Sam and Mr Maxted.

Each had good reason for it!

BEWARE OF FERNANDEZ!

'Hard-a-starboard!' shouted Mr Willerby, then raced down to the maindeck as the *Mary Blenheim* swung sluggishly to her helm. The gun crews, working savagely, were hurrying to get their weapons reloaded. Tom O'Hara, high on the poop with Captain Blount, watched as the lean black shape of the pirate ship cut her way nearer, gaining yards with every minute as her sails billowed on the nor'westerly breeze. With her extra speed it was easy for her to draw level and bring the full terrifying force of her broadside to bear on the lightly armed merchantman. Gun muzzles gleamed at the double row of ports, and swarthy figures were clearly visible man-handling powder and shot round the open section of the stern gallery. Tom tried to steady his musket on the rail and pick off at least one of the pirates, but Captain Blount put a hand on his arm.

'Save your bullets, lad! You'll never hit 'em with a musket at that range.'

The *Mary Blenheim* lifted on a heavy sea, then dropped into the trough beyond just as smoke puffed from every gunport along the flank of the pirate ship. The broadside, of solid shot, whistled across the decks, yards high; the only damage was to the chimney of the cook's galley, which leaped into the air, bent crooked, and fell over the side with a loud splash. From the port side the *Mary Blenheim*'s gun crew gave a gallant cheer of derision; then, as the ship rose on the next wave, came Mr Willerby's order to fire.

The worn timbers of the *Mary Blenheim* shivered as the six small cannon went off. Tom stood by Captain Blount, shielding his eyes from the sun and peering hopefully towards the pirate ship.

He heard a groan of despair. 'They're falling short, Tom. She can outsail us, she's got better guns, and ten times as many. We're done, lad.'

Tom took a firm grip on his cutlass. 'We'll fight 'em on deck, then, sir. Let 'em come alongside. We'll show them what cold steel feels like.'

Captain Blount shook his head. 'Mr Willerby!'

The Mate of the *Mary Blenheim* turned hurriedly from the guns. 'Aye, Cap'n?'

'Lower the flag!'

Tom's jaw dropped. 'Surrender, sir? To a pack of cut-throats?'

'That's Fernandez's ship, boy, I've heard tell of it. There's a hundred men aboard, and only twenty-five of us here on the *Mary Blenheim*. We couldn't hold 'em off for five minutes.'

'But...' Tom gasped. 'Surely they'll kill us?'

Captain Blount watched sadly as the flag was brought down. 'They'll certainly kill us if we don't! Get down on the main deck, boy, and help Mr Willerby.' He lowered his head. 'Tell every man to lay down his arms. Pile 'em on the hatchway where Fernandez's rogues can see 'em.'

'Aye aye, sir!' Tom clambered down from the poop and ran to pass on the orders to the Mate. 'What will they do, Mr Willerby? Put us along the plank?'

The Mate shrugged his shoulders. 'Don't take fright, Tom. Fernandez may have a black heart, but it's our cargo he's after, not our dead bodies. Lay your cutlass down, boy — and that musket. Look lively, lad, they're coming alongside.'

The lean, battered pirate ship was bearing down towards them, her sharp bows kicking up a white froth of water, her helm swung hard over so that she moved in without a collision and lay five feet away. Looking down, Tom saw men waiting at the touch-holes of the cannon ready to blow the *Mary Blenheim* out of the water at any sign of resistance.

Sullenly the crew lined up. Tom stared across at the heavily armed pirates as they swung into the rigging to leap over the gap.

And suddenly he made a decision. He slid out of sight behind the mainmast, darted along the port side, crouching low, and ducked into a hiding-place he'd known about for months, ever since he'd shifted a barrel of salt beef in the storeroom and discovered that the deck boards below were rotten with age and damp. Under them was a deep, narrow slot between two of the great oak ribs of the ship, and inside the slot, hanging in a bag, were his most valued possessions — his father's gold watch, and the money he'd saved from his first voyage. Clutching a lump of salt beef and a handful of biscuit he lowered himself into the hiding-place, and dragged an empty barrel over the hole just as he heard heavy footsteps pounding along the deck only a few yards away.

It was pitch dark, and the smell was indescribable, for the reek of the bilges came up from below. He jumped suddenly as a pair of bright eyes gleamed in the blackness only a yard away, then, realising that the rat had detected the food in his hand, he pushed it inside his shirt for safety.

Above, the heavy footsteps continued, then came the clatter of hatchboards being lifted, and the creak of the windlass.

There were shouts of triumph from the pirates as the bales of Indies silk were hoisted on deck. Sweating, and also boiling with anger at the loss of the cargo for which they'd sailed a year's journey, Tom shifted his position and munched fiercely at a lump of biscuit. Immediately, the gleaming eyes returned, and two more pairs beside them.

There was nothing he could do to frighten the rats away. Perched on a ledge, they remained absolutely still and silent; and as he stared at them, gradually he made out the outline of their crouching bodies.

He waited. The noise on deck continued, and though the windlass was silent there was now a chorus of singing.

A group of drunken men burst into the storeroom above him, and he heard them raiding the barrels for food, and cursing when they found nothing but salt beef. Tom retreated to the farthest corner of his hiding-place. What did they expect on a homeward-bound Indies trader? Fresh pork? Apples? He jumped as a barrel was flung on its side and began rolling with the motion of the ship. Then, with a heavy dragging noise, the very barrel that covered the hiding-place was pulled aside.

Tom held his breath as daylight poured down, lighting up the narrow space. There was a quick scuffling as the rats ran to safety. For a split second the toe of a shoe was in sight, only six inches above Tom's upturned face, then the barrel crashed back, dislodging lumps of rotten wood.

On deck the noise gradually died away, and then there was complete silence, except for the sound of the water lapping against the ship's sides.

Slowly, cautiously, Tom pushed the barrel to one side.

And then, through the hole, downwards to meet him, came a wisp of smoke.

Tom's heart hammered. The *Mary Blenheim* was on fire!

He scrambled out of the hole, and darted to the doorway leading on to the deck. Fernandez's pirate ship was a full three cables' length away, stern on, with her sails already filling with wind.

And the *Mary Blenheim* was deserted, with thin slivers of flame snaking up from the open hatchway of the hold.

Tom raced across the deck, no longer caring whether he was seen from the pirate ship. He seized a bucket on a rope, dipped it over the side, and then hurled the water into the hold. Smoke and steam billowed out, and he dashed back to the side for more water.

Then, to his astonishment, out of the depths of the hatchway climbed a blackened figure with scorched clothes. Quickly Tom changed his mind about the second bucket of water. He raised it above his head, shouted, 'Stand still!' and tipped it over the man's shoulders. Water streamed down the smouldering jacket, dousing the fire.

'Mr Willerby!'

'Aye, Tom. Thank you, lad.'

'But how did you ...?'

'Never mind that, lad. Get two more buckets and we'll work a relay.'

For two hours they fought the fire, until Tom's arms felt as if they were being drawn out of their sockets by the heavy weight of the buckets as he drew them up to the deck. At one stage it seemed hopeless, when the flames found the broken wooden boxes which had contained the cargo of silk. New tongues of flame rose shoulder high above the deck, and only by leaning dangerously far into the hatch and hurling water into the very heart of the flames did the Mate succeed in regaining control.

It was growing dark when they stopped, exhausted, and leaned against the bulwarks.

'Is it safe?' gasped Tom.

'I think so, boy. But we'll have to keep watch through the night, turn and turn about.'

'Where's Captain Blount? What's happened to the crew?'

The Mate's eyes flashed with anger. 'Fernandez took them aboard his ship.'

'What for? He won't be able to make them turn pirate.'

'No, but he can make them work the ship. They're all good sailors. And that leaves Fernandez's men free to man the guns and board the ships as they attack.' He frowned. 'It's better than walking the plank, or tasting a cutlass across your throat.' He paused. 'I didn't fancy any of 'em, so when they sent six of us into the hold to hoist cargo I slipped away and hid.'

'What do we do now, Mr Willerby?'

'We sleep on it, boy. Sleep's the best time for thinking. The brightest ideas come when your head's on the pillow. I'll take the first watch.'

Tom stretched out on his narrow bunk in the empty forecastle, and was asleep almost as soon as he lay down. The shots of Fernandez's men, and the tiny gleam of the rat's eyes, haunted his sleep, and he was almost glad when the Mate shook his shoulder and handed him a mug of hot soup. 'Drink this, Tom — it'll wake you up and warm the lining of your stomach. Put on heavy clothes — it's cold out on deck.'

Tom swung his feet out of the bunk, and sat up. 'Is the fire all right, Mr Willerby?'

'There was a flicker awhile back, but I gave it three buckets of water. Call me at dawn. You'll find more soup on the galley stove if you want it.' Then, as Tom stood up, the Mate rolled into the bunk, too weary to go back to his own quarters.

Tom drank the soup. Then, looking down at the exhausted face of his companion, he fetched an extra blanket from another bunk and laid it over the sleeping figure.

Out on deck there was a moderate breeze, and bright, cold moonlight. Tom patrolled the decks twice round, halting to peer into the open hatch in search of the slightest tell-tale gleam of smouldering embers, but there were none. Then he climbed to the poop and stood at the wheel, fingering the lashings which the Mate had made to keep the ship roughly on course.

So this was what it was like to have a ship under your command! The bows rose on the swell; overhead the sails billowed and the rigging creaked.

Command? He laughed grimly. There was no command any longer on the *Mary Blenheim*, when the two of them had no choice but to take the course set by the sails. A man and a boy couldn't alter sail. The only control they had was with the helm — and that would be of little use if the favourable wind were to shift. Whatever way it blew they'd have to run before it, and if it blew gale they'd have to watch helplessly while the force of it burst the stays and snapped the masts like sticks.

Except for their freedom, they'd almost have been better off on the pirate ship!

Tom made another circuit of the deck, then went into the galley and stoked the stove. He found a small barrel of salt beef, and put some of it to soak in fresh water to provide food for the coming day. What was it the Mate had said? Sleep's the best time for thinking? He couldn't imagine what any amount of thinking might do to get them out of danger.

Outside, he checked the wind again. Was it imagination, or had it increased in strength? Was the swell deeper and fiercer than before?

He examined the hatch again, and climbed down into the wet, squelching mass of rubbish to look for any signs of lingering fire. Then, back on deck, he propped himself up against the bulwarks and waited for dawn.

Crash! The great roar, like thunder, and the red flash which lit up the sky, brought him fully alert. He stared across the water, seeing a jumble of distant lights, then a long tongue of flame which crept upwards, lighting up a mast and the billowing white canvas of a sail.

'Mr Willerby!'

There was no response to the shout. Tom ran along the deck to the forecastle, and seized the Mate's shoulders. 'Mr Willerby! Wake up — there's a fight on!'

The Mate sat up, rubbing sleep out of his eyes. He looked at Tom dazedly, then jumped to the deck and ran outside just as another mighty flash lit up the horizon, followed by the deep rumble of guns.

'It's Fernandez again, mark my words!'

'Shall we change course and try to make a run for it, Mr Willerby?'

Before the Mate could reply there was yet another flash of gunfire. Startled, the Mate clutched the bulwarks and strained his eyes across the moonlit sea. 'That was the other ship replying,' he exclaimed.' 'Tis too soon for Fernandez — not even his rogues could have loaded the guns again so quickly.' He spun round. 'Tom, are you game to take your life in your hands?'

Tom looked at him, laughing. 'We're in a mess enough already, Mr Willerby. Nothing we can do could make it any worse.'

'Then unshackle the wheel, lad, and steer for the fight!'

Tom stared, aghast.

'We're going in, Tom. We'll surprise Fernandez from the blind side.'

'But we've no men to fire the guns!'

'I've time enough to load 'em. I can run down the line with a fuse. It'll be a ragged broadside, but we might save the brave lads on that other ship.'

'Aye, aye, Mr Willerby!' Tom ran to the poop, and wrenched the shackles off the wheel, then spun it and felt the *Mary Blenheim* heave herself round on to the new course. She rolled wildly as the seas met her broadside on, then steadied as she picked up speed once more.

'D'you want a hand below, Mr Willerby?'

'If you shackle the wheel again, then I could do with it. Bring me a barrel of black powder, and all the chain-shot you can find.'

'Chain-shot?'

'Aye, boy, we'll go for her sails and rigging. We haven't a chance of hurting her below waterline with small cannon like these.'

Tom raced to the storeroom, dreading that he'd find the pirates had taken away every ounce of powder and ammunition. But the lock was still on the door. He burst it with a violent twist of a belaying-pin, then slung one of the small powder barrels on to his shoulder just as a further crash of guns showed that the battle was not yet over. As he staggered under the weight of the barrel he glanced out to sea, and his heart jumped as he saw how close the *Mary Blenheim* had come. The lean hull of Fernandez's ship was clearly in sight, and beyond it, only a few cables' lengths away, a broad-beamed merchantman, heavy laden, with her mainmast hanging drunkenly and blazing like a Yule log.

He ripped open the barrel, and helped the Mate load the pathetic little line of guns.

'They're bound to see us, Mr Willerby! The moon's right behind us.'

'They won't be looking,' replied the Mate grimly, as he rammed a load of chain-shot down the muzzle of the last gun. 'Every man jack of 'em will be on the other side, standing by with grappling-irons ready to jump aboard. Get back to the wheel, Tom. Take her in close, then swing back to bring us broadside on.' He laughed deeply. 'We'll show Fernandez what it's like to be taken by surprise.'

At the wheel again, Tom watched as the gap between the ships grew narrower. Another broadside from the pirate vessel blazed in the moonlight, bringing down the foremast of the merchantman, but a moment later there was a gallant reply from a few scattered guns. And this time it was aboard Fernandez's ship that flames burst out. There was a sudden roar, as if a powder barrel had exploded, and the force of the explosion was so violent that he felt the surge of it come across the water and shake the strained timbers of the *Mary Blenheim*.

He swung the wheel.

The ship groaned as she felt the helm, then heaved herself over a huge swell and plunged into the trough beyond. Moon and stars moved in a swift arc above the masthead until the *Mary Blenheim* was broadside on to the black flank of the pirate ship.

And then her six cannon spoke.

The crashes came at intervals of five seconds, as the Mate raced from one gun to the next, thrusting his lighted fuse at the touch-holes.

Tom watched the pirate ship — and then gave a loud cheer as the mainmast collapsed over the side, carrying with it a mass of sails and tangled rigging. Across the water he heard startled shouts, and a few ragged musket shots, but the gap between the ships was widening again.

The guns on the merchantman spoke up once more, as if given new heart by the reinforcement. There was the unmistakeable rattle of grape-shot — the iron fragments that could cut a sail to ribbons, or throw a dozen men to the deck.

The Mate's face appeared at the head of the poop ladder. 'We'll give her another broadside,' he panted. 'Can you bring us round?'

'Aye, sir, I reckon so. You'll be using the guns on the other side?'

'No, boy, you'll never sail her smack into the wind. Go full circle and we'll come up just as before.'

Tight-lipped, his eyes on the great sheets of canvas that stretched overhead, Tom edged the *Mary Blenheim* off course, and began a gradual circle. He knew already that a real circle wasn't possible. It would have to be a course shaped like a flat-iron, with the straight line past the pirate ship as its end, then a gentle curve outwards to a sudden turn when he found he was trying to sail too close into the wind, and finally a similar curve back to the start of the run in which the Mate would set off his second broadside.

Salt spray burst up in clouds across the poop, drenching him and filling his eyes so that for a few seconds he was almost blinded. He felt the *Mary Blenheim* heel over, almost on her beam ends, as the wind caught her flank. With a full crew they'd have eased sail, but as it was he must risk having the yards stripped bare by a sudden squall.

The ship groaned with the strain, and he had to fight to hold his course. He slapped the helmsman's rail beside him. 'Come on, old lady, show your best! Just one more point into the wind and we'll make it.'

Shuddering, the *Mary Blenheim* came round, and lurched groggily forward to the point at which Tom decided to make his turn. He waited until the ship was in a trough of the waves, then swung the wheel hard over.

From below came a frenzied clatter, as pans cascaded off the galley stove. As the deck heeled Tom braced himself across the wheel, with his arms locked round the spokes. Seas burst up on to the poop, surging up to his waist, but glancing for'ard he saw that the Mate's guns, on the other side, were high above water. Could he complete the turn without a sudden roll back which would swamp them and make the powder useless?

The *Mary Blenheim* rose and seemed to hang on the edge of a tremendous cliff of water, then slid forward, bows swinging, into the new course. The Mate appeared again at the ladder, shouting, 'Well done, boy!'

Proudly, Tom sailed the *Mary Blenheim* in for a second salvo against Fernandez's pirate ship. The battle, he saw, was still going on, with both ships stripped of canvas by broadsides of chain- and grape-shot, and a thick cloud of smoke obscuring the decks though it was now almost full daylight.

And then Tom found that the *Mary Blenheim* refused to answer her helm!

Frantically he wrenched at the wheel, but couldn't move it. He looked down at the steering-chains, drawn taut in their deck runners, then looked up at the pirate ship looming up almost dead ahead.

He raced to the ladder. 'Mr Willerby! The steering's jammed!'

Pounding feet thundered up from the main gun-deck. The Mate took one brief look at the narrowing distance, put his shoulder to the wheel, and heaved until sweat burst out of his bare arms and forehead.

The wheel stayed firm.

'We'll pass within twenty feet,' he gasped. 'If she fires her heavy guns we're done. But we'll give 'em our broadside first. There's nothing you can do up here — come down below with me.'

His heart hammering, Tom followed the Mate back to the row of six loaded guns.

'Here, take this fuse. You know how use it? You've watched before?'

Tom nodded, and grabbed the smouldering fuse. He stood over the gun nearest the stern, and watched the Mate's raised hand. Mr Willerby was staring out through a gunport, choosing his moment.

The hand flashed down. Quick as lightning Tom held the fuse to the touch-hole and jumped back to avoid the recoil as the gun flung itself back on its iron wheels. The smoke and din were unbelievable; he darted to the second gun, then the third, and a moment later the Mate's hand guided him up to the ladder.

In the daylight above they looked across the narrow gap, at the mangled wreckage of the pirate ship's deck.

And then the Mate gave a cheer. He waved both arms, and shouted at the top of his voice.

Tom's jaw dropped. For surging along the deck, pushing aside the dazed pirates, were Captain Blount and the crew of the *Mary Blenheim!* Already three of them were at the davits of the longboat, dropping her gently into the water. Tom saw Captain Blount wave a cutlass at one pirate who blocked his path; the man flung up his empty hands in terrror and ran away across the deck.

Into the longboat piled the crew, and willing hands reached up to grab the bulky Captain as he jumped into the stern boards. Then swift cutlass strokes slashed the ropes, oars were unshipped, and with lusty strokes the boat pulled towards the *Mary Blenheim.*

The pirate ship was now well alight, and as another broadside of grape-shot from Mr Willerby swept across her decks there was a thunderous crash from the guns of the other merchantman.

Then, from the stern cabin of the pirate vessel, a fantastic figure strutted out on to the deck. Tall, black-bearded, he wore the looted uniform of a high admiral, complete with gold lace and cocked hat. In his hands was a brace of pistols.

32

Tom fired a single cannon

He mounted the poop and stood by the wheel, looking across the water at the retreating longboat.

Tom's hands itched for a musket. Then he started in alarm as he saw the pistols raised, levelled at the men in the longboat.

'Mr Willerby!'

'Aye, boy,' came the answering shout. 'I see the black-hearted rogue. It's Fernandez himself!'

His last words were almost drowned as Tom fired a single cannon.

And then aboard the pirate ship there was no longer a stern cabin, no longer a wheel above, no longer a dandified captain flourishing his pistols.

At the same moment men rushed to the one mast which remained, and hauled down the black flag in surrender. And the longboat drew alongside the *Mary Blenheim*.

It was only the beginning. For the next few hours the crews of both merchantmen fought to strip the two blazing ships of all that was valuable, and load it aboard the *Mary Blenheim* until she was weighed down almost to her scuppers. Twenty-five sullen survivors of the pirate crew watched, helpless in their chains. Not until late in the day, with the doomed ships almost sunk beneath the waves, did the *Mary Blenheim* with her double crew turn into the wind and begin the long run home.

Tom dragged his weary legs up to the poop and saluted his Captain and Mate. 'All snug below, Captain,' he reported. 'May I have your permission to turn in?'

The Captain looked at him expressionlessly. 'You may, boy. But you'll be called at eight bells.'

'Eight bells?' Almost too exhausted to stand, Tom could scarcely believe his ears. 'Why's that, sir?'

'The *Mary Blenheim*'s always been a one-mate ship, Tom — the Mate and I have taken watch-and-watch about. But today's made me see I'm an old man.'

'*You*, Captain Blount?' cried Tom in astonishment. 'But you led the escape!'

'Aye, after you and Mr Willerby had providentially blown the door off our prison with a round of grape-shot.' He sighed. 'It's time I stuck to my charts and my cargoes, and left the sailing to younger men. So you'll be called at eight bells.'

Tom's heart leaped. Could the Captain really mean that at sixteen he was to get the chance of a lifetime?

'D'you mean...?'

'I mean, go below and get some sleep,' grinned the Captain. 'Off you go, *Mr Second Mate O'Hara!*'

THE PLANETOID GRID

'Boys!' Com-controller Telfer snarled. 'Give me the good old days when there weren't any space-born kids.'

'In your young days there were only astronauts and cosmonauts flipping back and forth from Earth into space — being wondermen,' said Junior-com Dorlas. 'Then Earth Space Commission put the first manned satellite into orbit. Now, we've got a ring of satellites. As common as a new city is down on Earth. Cities in the sky, you might call 'em — and a new generation born in them. That's progress. And your generation did it, so why resent it?'

Telfer glared at his junior across the banked instrument console of Satellite Communications Control.

'Get well paid for your turn of duty up here, don't you?'

Dorlas shrugged. 'Fair enough — with bonus.'

'A fortune, they pay you. And chaps like me have to train you. Then you go back to Earth Base Seven X wearing your space-duty medal and act the big-shot. Plenty of money saved up, and a fat pension.'

'Why pick on me now?' Dorlas asked. 'You get paid three times as much. When you go back you won't ever need to work again. Don't know what makes you so resentful.'

'You do!' Telfer snapped. 'You and those space-born boys. Take it all for granted, you do. Where would you be without us?'

'You wouldn't get far without us either,' Dorlas grinned. 'The boys and others of my age-group have to be trained, don't we? If not, then who's going to man the satellites? Without us they'll fall out of the sky.'

'Which is just what you'll be doing if I have much more argument from you. I'll deport you back to Earth with a tag pinned on you — "Temperamentally unsuited to space conditions".'

Dorlas was silent for a moment. Then he nodded slowly.

'Guess you would too,' he said quietly. 'Just because I argue with you and stand up for the space-born boys.'

'And why not? You're senior to the boys, but junior to me. Your first loyalty is to me. We must have discipline up here on the satellites. Orders must be obeyed without question, or else space-ships could spin off into the void or a satellite go out of orbit. Hundreds of thousands of lives might be lost.'

'But I haven't disobeyed any orders,' Dorlas protested.

'You've argued against me. D'you call that good discipline?'

'It was only a friendly argument.'

'Friendly!' Telfer exclaimed. 'You're not here to be friendly. You're here to do a job of work.' He glanced at the computer-clock. 'Ten minutes and eighteen hundred miles back in orbit flight, two space-born boys on planetoid messenger-training told me to go swallow a spheroid! All you did was laugh. Apart from being bad discipline — d'you call that friendly?'

'No,' Dorlas admitted. 'But I knew they didn't mean it.'

'They meant it right enough,' Telfer retorted grimly. 'I told them to bring their space-scooter back into our orbital beam — and they told me to go swallow a spheroid.'

'Only one of them said it — that red-haired gimbo they call Bluey. He's a bit high-spirited. His co-pilot Tinder is top of his section in com-training. They make a good team.'

'There you go again,' Telfer snarled. 'Taking their side.' He manipulated switches and dials. Coloured lights faded from his section of the console and an equal number flickered to brightness on Dorlas's section.

'I'm due for a coffee break.' Telfer stood up, his lightweight transparent space-suit billowing in puckered ripples as a mixture of oxygen and diathene pumped out to counter his physical effort. 'I'll be in the airlock division, if you need me. If you have any trouble you can't handle, throw that auto-brain switch and wait for me to come back. Get it?'

'Yes, sir. Got it.' Dorlas spoke briskly, not smiling until Com-controller Telfer had left. Then he burst into laughter. 'Poor old Telfer,' he chuckled. 'Grows more touchy every day. Hope I don't get like that after years of space duty.' Dorlas moved a switch. 'Calling S. C. 9. Come in, S. C. 9. Poppa has gone for coffee.'

'Space-scooter 9.' A cheerful voice came through the speaker. 'S. C. 9 receiving you. Vision circuit link, please.'

Dorlas manipulated dials. The audiovisor screen flared to blue light, flickered, darkened before it cleared to show the head and shoulders of a red-haired boy, grinning, and beside him the face of a dark-haired, strongly featured boy. The scanner angle from the scooter's control panel wasn't aligned to cover the head and shoulders of both boys.

The scooter's audiovisor screen showed Dorlas's head and shoulders — his image shimmering slightly as light reflected from his space-suit. The boys wore their heavier suits, completely transparent except for the dark solar visor, but this didn't reflect light.

'Poppa doesn't like us,' said Bluey.

'Why should he?' Bluey's co-pilot Tinder grinned. 'You're always baiting him.'

'You do your share too, Tinder,' said Dorlas. 'He knows you call him Poppa. Is that being respectful? You're a pair of dopes.'

'How would you like a poke on the snoot?' Bluey's clenched fist loomed large on the screen. 'We're the brightest pair of space-scouts you've ever had on communications training, so don't call us dopes.'

Dorlas laughed. 'See what I mean? All that big talk. I understand it because it's how Earth-born kids behave. Used to myself. But not Telfer. He's a big man around the satellites. He and his generation helped to build this space empire.

They're proud of it. A lot of their mates died while discovering things that help you and me to live up here. I try to take your part, but when you forget all that — well, you are dopes, and it's you who'll get a poke on the snoot, young Bluey!'

Bluey groaned in mock despair.

'Are *you* picking on us now?'

'No. Just straightening you out on a few points.'

Tinder adjusted the scanner to bring himself more into focus, and said:

'We know that Telfer and the rest of the senior technicians are space experts, and have spent their lives building and manning the satellites, but do they have to ram it down our throats all the time?'

'Do you have to ram it down *their* throats all the time that you're the first space-born kids in the Universe?' Dorlas retorted.

'Whose side are you on?' Bluey demanded indignantly.

'More on yours, I suppose,' Dorlas admitted. 'I'm the generation between yours and Telfer's so I can see both sides.' He chuckled. 'And get kicked by both of you,' he added, and stabbed a warning finger at them. 'But Telfer has more rights than you two characters, even though you think you've inherited space. That doesn't mean you've got to be meek and yes-sir, no-sir all the time. It means that if you want respect, you have to give it too.' He grinned at them. 'Okay — lecture over.'

'Thanks!' said Bluey sarcastically.

'It made sense,' said Tinder. 'Dorlas is young enough to know how we feel, yet he has to work with Telfer.' He frowned as he gazed directly at Dorlas. 'But Telfer might have had the decency to listen to our theory before he cut the audovisor circuit.'

'I think he would have listened if Bluey hadn't told him to go swallow a spheroid. How can you expect technical co-operation when you snap out a silly remark like that?'

'Well — he was sneering at me,' Bluey protested. 'And he

wasn't really listening. Made it look as if no matter what we said, he wouldn't believe it.'

'You weren't able to see *your* ugly face either,' said Dorlas. 'I was, and you even made me want to tell you not to be so snooty. After all, Bluey — all you had was a theory that the Planetoid Grid was doubling-up on its memory tracks. That's a pretty far-fetched theory for anyone to state.'

'But it's possible, isn't it?' Tinder asked.

Dorlas shrugged. 'There's an old saying: "In space, all things are possible." But the Planetoid Grid's brain isn't human. It either works perfectly, or doesn't work at all. A human brain can be working in the wrong way and not know it because its memory may be faulty. The Grid can't behave that way.'

'We say it can,' Tinder insisted stubbornly.

Dorlas sighed gently. 'There you go again. You're still at school, yet you defy my experience as a fully trained communications technologist and Telfer with his thirty years of knowledge. Dammit, Tinder — he helped to build the Planetoid Grid. He's a right to treat your theory as crazy.'

'We're going to prove it's not crazy,' said Bluey. 'By going to the Grid.'

'No!' Dorlas cried sharply. 'No — you mustn't do that.'

'We're doing it,' said Tinder quietly. 'You haven't checked our course while we've been talking, else you'd see we're only a few thousand miles off.'

'Listen to me, Tinder,' Dorlas spoke urgently. 'The immediate area of the Planetoid Grid is banned to all space-craft. If you insist on going to the Grid to prove some crazy theory of your own, I'll have to orded you in.'

'You can't,' said Bluey. 'Provided we don't refuse to keep clear of the International Space Lanes, you can't order us off any voluntary flight.'

'You stupid young fools!' Dorlas snapped. 'You can't break International Space Flight laws and hope to get away with it.'

'We're not breaking them,' said Tinder. 'You read the

Flight Manual, Dorlas, and you'll see that satellite-based space-craft below a six-person capacity are exempt from Satellite Control unless operating on an actual Space Lane, or attempting to fly beyond a ten-thousand-mile perimeter of the satellite.'

'You're so clever,' Dorlas retorted sarcastically. 'Know it all, don't you? All right — so you may be technically clear, but you forget one thing.'

'Tell us,' Bluey grinned. 'We love to learn.'

'You can wipe that grin off your face. As communications officer in Satellite Control right now, I'm ordering you to return to base.' Dorlas moved a switch. 'I am now recording that order. Calling Tinder and Blue in S. C. 9. Return to base. Repeat: an order from Satellite Control. Return to base. You are heading for a prohibited flight area. Return to base at once.' He glared at them as he released the switch. 'That order is on tape. Turn back, or you'll be in trouble.'

'You're a pal,' said Bluey. 'A real pal, that's you — you addle-pated nit!'

'Don't be rude.' Tinder switched off the audovisor before the furious Dorlas could reply and turned to face his friend. 'Guess we're on our own now.'

Bluey nodded. 'Guess we are.'

'Dorlas will send out a space alarm.'

Bluey shrugged. 'It'll take them quite a while to find us now we've broken the circuit.' He focused the forward scanners and switched on the scooter's survey screen.

From out of the deep blue of space above Earth's green-glowed sphere an oblong object hung suspended like a silvery waffle-iron. Some likened it to an old-fashioned wire-mesh fly-swatter. Others said it was like a fisherman's net fixed to a curved framework.

Both these descriptions could apply, because few people, except authorised technicians, were allowed to approach the Planetoid Grid closer than three thousand miles from the space side. No space-craft was allowed to approach from the

Grid's Earth side, all repair or maintenance craft having to go way out on the Space Lanes, then veer back to the Grid.

As the distance lessened, so the Grid's appearance changed. At a thousand miles it shimmered like a huge mesh sail reflecting the sun. At five hundred miles it was a wide, glinting framework, as vast as a city of skyscrapers with millions of windows. At a hundred miles it seemed to fill the sky — a man-made structure spinning for ever in orbit with Earth.

Yet to the boys in the approaching space-scooter the Planetoid Grid appeared to be stationary — just as the satellites did. And because the boys adjusted the speed of their scooter to the same eighteen-thousand-odd miles an hour at which the Grid orbited the Earth, they also appeared to be stationary.

Tinder's skill as a space-pilot, and his ability to judge instruments and handle the power controls of his craft as fast and precisely as the top space-ship pilots, were well known among the space-born boys. But having grown up in space, flying through the void was as natural to Tinder as walking was to an Earth-born boy. Neither Tinder nor Bluey had visited Earth and therefore couldn't cope with gravity pull and other forces, but few boys could beat them in their own environment.

Tinder now changed the scooter's course, and opened the induction booster to spurt the speed up to the required level as the craft anchored itself in orbit alongside the Grid.

'Record a tape for our return readings, Bluey,' Tinder ordered. 'We'll feed it into the automatic brain, then nothing can go wrong.'

'Are you expecting something to go wrong?'

'Can't tell, can we? This Grid is a mighty fearsome thing when you get real close to it. Lots of static power in it too. Perhaps it could de-magnetise our instruments.'

Bluey shivered as he surveyed the enormous mass of the Planetoid Grid.

'I don't feel quite so clever now. Never realised it was so terrific. How can we hope to check our theory?'

'Don't let the size of it scare you. For one thing, it has a million and a half solar batteries. Those account for three-quarters of its size.' Tinder pointed upward. 'See that red-painted section? That's its memory. All the rest is the channel honeycomb containing a thousand million circuits.'

'Great sizzling meteors!' Bluey cried. 'The real working part isn't much bigger than our scooter.' He peered intently at the red-painted section. 'It glows, Tinder — it glows!' he exclaimed in an awed voice. 'Looks as if it's red-hot.'

Tinder laughed. 'You scare too easily. Surprised at you, Bluey. The red paint is meant to give a glowing effect. And if you look more closely you'll see that the paint is on the Grid structure, but each tiny hole contains a ruby. Rubies reflect the solar rays *and* the paint. So the whole effect makes the honeycomb of circuits look as if it's red-hot.'

'Yeow!' Bluey gasped. 'There must be all the rubies in the Universe fitted in there. Wish I'd paid more attention to my lessons.'

'Why?'

'Well, I know that the Ruby Ray is a miracle light which can transmit and receive sound signals so that sound can be made to travel at the speed of light. I know that the Ruby Ray system was perfected several years ago and made the Planetoid Grid possible. But I never realised just how many rubies the Grid contained.'

'Approximately a million,' said Tinder. 'And a thousand sound-carrying wave circuits can pass though each one.' He waved a hand to indicate the remainder of the massive structure. 'The rest of the Grid functions like the usual electronic communications system — like telephone exchanges and automatic relay circuits. The light-waves which carry the sound are projected through a ruby from the sending end and beamed on to a ruby in the Grid. This ruby is fitted into a sort of metering brain-box. The brain automatically directs the light-beam into a converter, which then relays the signal on the correct channel.'

Bluey grinned. 'Ain't science wonderful! But I still can't see how we can prove our theory. I wouldn't know the first place to look in this colossal thing.' Then he scowled angrily. 'I suppose I should learn to keep my big mouth shut. It's all your fault.'

Tinder looked surprised. 'Mine? Why?'

'You were the one who said you knew why we were picking up ghost voices from the Grid. You were the one who said you'd worked out how it might be possible to upset the Planetoid Grid's memory.'

'But you came with me when I said I could prove it by visiting the Grid,' Tinder pointed out.

'I just came along for the ride.' Suddenly Bluey chuckled. 'No, I didn't. I came because I'd do anything to help you prove you're right, so's those snooty technical experts like Telfer are forced to respect us space-born boys. But it seems pretty hopeless to me,' he added.

Tinder opened the scooter's canopy and announced: 'I'm going out. Coming?'

'What can I lose?' Bluey asked.

'Okay. Connect our life-lines and anchor cable to the magnetic clamps, and we'll climb around the Grid.'

'What are we looking for?' Bluey double-checked their life-lines and the scooter's anchor cable.

'Sabotage,' Tinder replied grimly.

'Won't the duty officers — Telfer and his mates — have thought of that?'

'I don't think so. In fact I'm sure they haven't else they'd have sent an inspection team to the Grid. These Earth-born space officers believe their equipment is one hundred per cent perfect.'

'It has to be, doesn't it? There's no margin for error in space.'

Tinder halted his floating-stride walk when they reached

the Grid structure, and signalled Bluey to use the closed-circuit radio in their space-suits.

'The equipment might be perfect,' said Tinder above the speaker unit's hum of typical closed-circuit feed-back impulses. 'But what some human beings assemble, others can take apart.'

Bluey's bewilderment couldn't be seen through the dark solar visor, but his voice expressed it.

'You're always one jump ahead of me in technics, but this time I'm not even close behind you,' he admitted. 'How can anyone take this Grid apart? And why the closed circuit? There's nobody near enough to pick up our conversation.'

Tinder pointed upward. 'There are human beings on the Earth side of the Grid.'

'How d'you know?' Bluey sounded scared.

'Watch the top right corner of the Ruby Ray section. Watch closely.'

They stood, arms linked, using the small portable gravity-ray generators to help them keep upright in the weightlessness of space. Then Bluey's arm gripped tighter when he saw a tiny movement high above them. A glint of light on a piece of metal — a strange movement of red colour, like a ruby eye rolling.

'Wh-what is it?' he stammered.

'Someone's working on the Grid.'

'B-but how did they get here? Why haven't we seen their space-craft? Why haven't they noticed our scooter arriving?'

'Simple answers, I think. They must be using one of the small maintenance space-scooters — the one that's based on our model, but adapted to carry two men and their repair or maintenance equipment,' Tinder explained. 'We couldn't see the craft because it's anchored on the Earth side of the Grid, and our instruments didn't pick it up because the Grid impulses would screen it. They haven't sighted us because they're working outside their craft and can't watch their own instruments.'

'That makes sense.' Bluey spoke in a relieved tone. 'But what are they doing? Control didn't report any maintenance-craft near the Grid.'

Tinder chuckled. 'I think they're stealing rubies. They'd hardly tell Control about that. Let's get back to the scooter.'

'Without trying to find out who they are?'

'Almost impossible from this side. Are you game for a fight?' Tinder asked.

'Any time,' Bluey declared enthusiastically. Although often slow on head-work, fighting was Bluey's speciality. 'Jumping meteors, Tinder! Are we going to capture them — just *us*?'

'We can try.' Tinder grinned. 'We'll have surprise on our side. Ready?'

'Aye — ready and willing!'

They returned to the scooter. Tinder zoomed the craft in a tight turn to circle over the great mass of the Planetoid Grid, then opened up full power to counteract the loss of distance as they flew at right-angles over the Grid. This was a complicated manoeuvre because, by the time they had circled above the Grid, the structure was ahead of them in its natural orbit of about eighteen thousand miles an hour.

Tinder had to pace the scooter up to some thirty thousand miles an hour in order to reach a position where he overshot the Grid. Then by ejecting gravity rays and compensator rockets he slowed the scooter, swung it to point midway down the Grid's structure and held course until Bluey could fasten the craft's magnetic anchor to one of the Grid's struts.

This took only a few minutes. Scarcely long enough for the boys to sight the small maintenance-craft anchored so close to the Grid that from any distance it was invisible.

Tinder and Bluey climbed from their scooter, and were only a few yards from two space-suited figures before they were seen. A man's voice, carrying clearly through his space-suit open-circuit radio, cried: 'Kaylor! Look — quick!'

Another voice snarled:

'You damn fool, Morson! What's up with you? Didn't

Tinder made fast time towards the man working on the Grid

I tell you to keep quiet while I refitted the contacts? You've made me miss —' The voice broke off when the man working in the Ruby Ray section saw the boys. 'What the hell's going on? Use your gun, Morson! Use your gun. Shoot first. Ask questions after.'

It isn't easy to use force in space. Heavy blows from a clenched fist land with the impact of a feather. A man with a small repeater ray-gun can keep an army at bay. But guns, like tools and any other equipment, have to be securely fastened to a space-suit, or else they work loose and float away. And to undo such a fastening takes time.

Earth-born people on space duty are taught how to move in space, although this is an unnatural action. But the space-born boys grew from babies with the daily familiarity of space movement.

Tinder made fast time towards the man working on the Grid. Bluey made even faster time to the gun-drawing Morson.

Morson's first and natural reaction when he saw Bluey practically on top of him, and before the gun came free, was to swing his fist at Bluey's head. Bluey parried the blow by easily brushing aside the man's arm.

'You're a silly little Earth-man, aren't you?' said Bluey cheerfully. 'Don't you know you can't fight here the same as you can on Earth?'

'Keep away, or I'll burn you up!' Morson's clumsy gloved fingers struggled to unfasten the ray-gun's holding-clips.

'You and what army?' Bluey sneered. 'Ever heard of space Judo? Like this.' He moved in close — swift and light in action, hands making fast, practised moves.

In seconds Bluey had pinioned Morson's arms and bound his wrists and ankles with the man's own life-line. Then he released the ray-gun and flung it away. The gun spun off in a floating arc — doomed to endless flight in the void.

'Let me free, you...' Morson's voice roared through the helmet-speaker. 'I'll kill you!'

'Aw shuddup!' Bluey jerked the life-line and dragged the helpless man after him as he moved towards Tinder.

Meanwhile Tinder had been experiencing a more difficult tussle, because the other man kept gripping the Grid's structure and space Judo works only if the body is entirely un-anchored. But after a few minutes of grim struggling Tinder loosened the man's grip and, with deft skill, had made him powerless.

'Couple of nice prizes for Telfer, eh?' Tinder chuckled.

'I'll say!' Bluey laughed. 'This'll show him and his snooty opinion of our theories.'

'Now listen,' Kaylor spluttered. 'If you let us free, we won't tell anybody we saw you near the Grid. We don't want to make trouble for you space-born kids.'

'Trouble is something we ain't got,' Bluey retorted. 'It's you who've got it — not us.'

'Looks as if they've replaced about a hundred real rubies with synthetic ones,' said Tinder.

'A nice little racket you chaps thought up,' said Bluey admiringly. 'Clever — and took a lot of courage too.'

'Dangerous though,' Tinder added. 'Synthetic rubies don't filter the rays properly. That's what caused the Grid's memory to go faulty.'

'Hey, Tinder! Honest — did you really guess that was what was happening?'

'No guess,' said Tinder. 'It was the only theory that made sense. But of coure I had to check it for myself.'

'Blast you!' Kaylor snarled.

'Thanks,' said Tinder, 'for nothing. Sorry to have upset your fortune hunt, but there are too many lives depending on the Grid's function to let you get away with it. But you certainly had a brilliant idea.' He paused. 'Let's see now. A hundred rubies worth about twenty thousand dollars each — less the cost of the synthetic ones.'

'They're not cheap,' said Bluey.

'About five thousand dollars each,' said Tinder. 'It still

leaves 'em a nice fat profit. Come on — let's get our prisoners back. I can't wait to see old Telfer's face when we report to Control.'

But Telfer soon got over the shock, and quickly turned the space-boys' adventure to his own advantage.

'Yes, sir,' he said to the Supreme Space Controller. 'I'll admit I took a risk in letting the space-born boys investigate the Grid, but no Earth-born person can beat them in space. I thought it would be worth the risk.'

Bluey and Tinder glared at Telfer, dumb and furious, yet knowing that severe punishment would be theirs if Telfer hadn't said he had sent them to the Grid. By doing this Telfer had made their own efforts official.

'Well, all's well that ends well,' said the Supreme Space Controller. 'I'll see that the boys are mentioned in space dispatches.'

'Thank you, sir,' they chorused.

Telfer switched off the audovisor, and said:

'So now you're heroes. I suppose that'll make you more impossible than ever.'

'Aw — go swallow a spheroid!' said Bluey.

'Make it two,' Tinder added. 'And I hope they choke you.'

The boys marched out of the control-room.

Telfer looked at Dorlas and sighed.

'You can't win, can you?'

Dorlas shrugged. 'I wouldn't know,' he said. 'But I sure wish I was a space-born boy. They have all the fun.'

SPECKLES

Speckles was a dreamer. One look at him made that perfectly clear — and also showed why he was called Speckles. Perched well down his nose, his glasses looked as big as frying-pans.

He pushed them down even farther, and glared over the top of them from the window of the Science Lab.

'Go away!' he shouted. 'Buzz off, the lot of you. I'm busy.'

But Calthorpe College was a cricket school with no place for dreamers. Anybody like Speckles, whose one interest in life was science and who dozed right through the rest of the school curriculum, was asking for trouble. A dozen hands reached up towards him, grabbed him by the wrists and the sleeves of his jacket, and hung on hard. Like an obstinate cork being drawn from a bottle, more and more of Speckles appeared over the window-ledge. His eyes bulged, and his neck went pink.

'Hey — leggo, you blighters!' he yelled. 'Leave me alone!'

The reply came in a chorus. 'Not until you come out for cricket practice.'

There was a spluttering sound from Speckles, balanced precariously on a ledge, with his legs kicking wildly inside the laboratory. A stream of halfpennies, toffees, notebooks and pens came tumbling out of his jacket pockets on to the grass oustide. 'No cricket practice for me,' he shouted. 'I'm busy doing an experiment.'

'So are we,' came a threatening voice from below. 'Pull him out another inch, fellows, and see if he'll slide the rest of the way.'

'*Yaaouch!* Pack it up!' Speckles wriggled even more wildly as the outstretched arms gave another heave and brought two more inches of him into view.

'Are you coming, then? I'm going to count three, and then we'll give you another tug. Ready, everybody? Then here goes. One ... two ...'

'All right!' bellowed Speckles. 'Push me back in and I'll come.'

'Mmm,' exclaimed a new voice thoughtfully. 'Seems a pity, now we've got him so far. Let's give him another heave.'

There was a yell from Speckles as the rest of him shot into view and he was lowered head downwards on to the grass. He picked himself up, groped for his glasses, and glowered at the white-flannelled crowd around him. 'Come on, then,' he muttered. 'Let's go down to the nets and get it over — but don't think I'll forget this. You wait! By the time I've finished there'll be no more cricket for the rest of the season.'

It sounded to Frank Dunton, Speckles's closest friend, like one of the hundreds of threats he'd heard in the two years they'd been at Calthorpe. But then, next day, when Frank went round to Speckles's house to see him, there was no answering call from the window behind which Speckles spent his spare time reading.

Could Speckles Brewster be sulking? Frank picked up a chip of granite from the path and tossed it up against the window, but there was still no reply. Then, puzzled, he went round to the back door and knocked.

'Oh it's you, Frank,' said Mrs Brewster. 'You'll find Speckles down in the woodshed where he messes about with his chemicals. He's been down there all morning.' She laughed. 'He's stuck a notice on the door saying "Danger—Keep Out: High Explosives" — so you'd better watch out.'

Frank strolled thoughtfully down to the woodshed, but as he approached, Speckles suddenly popped out and stood guard in front of the closed door. 'What d'you want?' he growled threateningly.

'Gosh, Speckles, I've just come on a friendly visit, that's all.'

'Friendly visit, my foot. You helped drag me out of the Science Lab yesterday, didn't you? Well, you can just turn right round and go away again. I'm busy.'

This was so unlike the usually amicable Speckles that Frank stepped back a pace. 'What's all this about high explosives?' He pointed to the notice on the door behind his friend. 'Are you making a bomb, or something?'

Speckles's face went scarlet, 'Go and get lost!' he burst out, and went back into the woodshed.

Frank went home frowning. What in the world could Speckles be doing with explosives? He scratched his head in puzzlement, then suddenly his mouth dropped open. Crumbs! Supposing that in a fury about what had happened he was planning some hare-brained scheme to blow something up? After all, he *had* threatened to end all cricket for the season. Supposing he was planning to wreck the pavilion or the pitch? You never could tell with scientists — they did all kinds of crazy things.

But he kept the idea to himself. It wasn't the kind of idea for spreading around; everybody else would pull his leg for months if nothing happened.

It was Saturday — no school, but a chance in the evening to go up to the playing-fields for extra net practice. He set off straight after tea, joining up on the way with three others in the First Eleven.

'Hey, look at that! It's old Speckles trotting along. Don't say *he's* turning up for extra nets.'

Frank followed the pointing finger and, sure enough, far ahead of them, striding along faster than ever before in his life, was Speckles.

'Come on, Frank, let's catch up and make him join in. You know how he hates cricket.'

Frank shook his head. 'You catch him if you want to. I've come up here for serious practice — not playing tag with Speckles.'

He hung back, while the others sprinted ahead and disappeared behind a hedge. He didn't catch up with them until he was level with the cricket pavilion, from behind which they emerged with puzzled expressions.

'What's up?' asked Frank. 'Where's Speckles?'

'He got away. We watched him through the window and he put something in his locker, then locked it up tight. When he saw us, he shot out of the back door and we couldn't catch up. *Whew* — old Speckles may not be any good at cricket, but, boy, can he run!'

Frank frowned. 'What did he put in his locker?'

'We couldn't see properly. But it was something small and round.'

Frank froze in his tracks. *Something small and round.* The recollection of that notice came back to him — the one on Speckles's garden shed which said: DANGER — KEEP OUT: HIGH EXPLOSIVES.

Was it a bomb he'd put in his locker?

All through net practive the thought of a small round bomb ticking away busily in Speckles's locker haunted him, and he missed more balls than he hit. He was glad when it was over.

What was the best thing to do? Go to the Head and tell him? He couldn't imagine doing that. The Head would just roar with laughter, and later on the story would get out and he'd look an absolute fool in front of the whole school. On the other hand, if he kept quiet and it really was a bomb, when it went off the pavilion would be wrecked and Speckles would be in real trouble.

He was nearly home when he turned round sharply and went back along his tracks, to Speckles's house. This time his shout from the gate brought Speckles hurrying down to the door. 'Come on in, Frank.'

Frank stood in the doorway. 'I know what you put in the pavilion,' he said.

'Uuh?'

'You'd better go and take it out again, double-quick.'

Speckles's huge glasses slithered down to the tip of his nose, and his eyes bulged. 'Won't *anybody* leave me alone?' he roared. 'Can't *anybody* mind his own business?' He backed into the hallway, and slammed the door so suddenly that Frank had only just enough time to move out of the way.

Next afternoon, when Frank took his dog for a Sunday walk, he hardly dared go past the school. Instead, he headed for a high hill from which there was a clear view down across the playing-fields. As he reached the summit and gazed down, he gave a gasp of relief.

The pavilion was still there!

It was still there when he arrived at school on Monday, and it still hadn't blown up after lunch when they went down to the nets. Speckles came too, not because he wanted to, but because Monday cricket was compulsory.

Frank changed quickly. Speckles was staring out of the pavilion window, as if waiting for everyone to get out of the way before he opened his locker; but Frank lingered on, and so did the three who'd been with him on Saturday evening.

'Come on, everybody!' shouted the Games Master from outside. 'Don't waste time in there.'

Reluctantly Speckles put his key into the lock, and opened the door of the locker just enough to pull out his cricket boots. He was about to slam it shut again when hands reached out over his shoulder and grabbed the door.

'Don't be in such a hurry, Speckles. Let's see what you're hiding in there.'

Speckles struggled in vain to close and lock the door. 'Let go, you blighters!' he yelled. 'It's nothing to do with you.'

But the yell was drowned by an even louder shout from Frank. 'Stop it! Leave that locker alone, or you'll all get blown to blazes — *there's a bomb inside!*'

Everybody stopped dead, staring first at Frank and then at Speckles.

Speckles blinked back at them.

'A bomb?' he muttered, as if he'd never heard the word before in his life. 'What on earth gives you that idea?'

Frank goggled at him. 'What *are* you hiding in your locker then?'

Speckles let out his breath in a long sigh, and then put his hand into the locker. 'I suppose you'll never let it rest until you know.' To everybody's astonishment he brought out the china head of a doll. 'That's what it is. The groundsman's little daughter was here the other afternoon, crying her eyes out because she'd broken her doll, so I took the head home to stick it together for her. I didn't want any of you to know — you'd only have said I'm softer than ever. So I brought it back last night when I thought nobody would be around. I was planning to take it back after you'd all gone this afternoon. Well, now you know — so have a good laugh.'

But nobody did — at least not for a long time. Then Frank started chuckling away to himself in a corner. 'I must have been crazy to think you'd blow up the pavilion, Speckles. But honestly, you did threaten to end all cricket for the rest of the season.'

'Gosh! Did I?' He rubbed the steamed-up lenses of his glasses. 'Did I really say that? But surely you didn't take it seriously?'

'Not until I saw the high-explosives notice on your woodshed.'

Speckles roared with laughter. 'That was in desperation. It took a long time to mend this doll's head. I had to keep you nosey lot out of the way. But I'll think of something less dramatic next time.'

'There won't be a next time,' grinned Frank. 'We've learned something out of all this — that just because you're mad on science, and don't like games, you're not automatically as nutty as a fruit cake.'

'Oh, I am,' chuckled Speckles. 'But not *that* nutty.'

BOY WITH A GUN

The Texas dusk lowered a curtain of purples, pinks, greens and blood-red slashes across the foothills. Mesquite rustled, and tumbleweeds rolled and bounced as the whispering breeze of advancing night swirled lazily over the ground.

Rocks speared, jagged black, against the sky, and between them the earth and stone piles around the mine-shaft clustered like dome-headed giants. From far away, borne on the soft breeze across a silent land, a coyote's call bayed and sobbed in fluting cadences.

Soon the rocks and fissured ledges began to creak and crack as they contracted in the cooler air, after a day of baking sun had heated them like a furnace. Small twitterings and squealings from the tiny creatures of the night, amid rock crevices and earth burrows, defied the apparent emptiness of the land. Busy they were, and intent upon their nightly foraging for food and mates, fights and fun.

The old man and the boy did not heed the sights and sounds of this Texas dusk. For months now they had been a part of it, day after work-filled day, week after heat-tortured week. For them the dusk meant ceasing work, preparing fire and food before sleeping deep until the dawn. Each day, each night, the same — except this night.

'Late,' said the old man. 'Late, eh, Clancy?' He cackled meaningly.

The boy squatted on his hunkers, kindling-wood poised before lighting.

'Yeah, late,' he agreed. 'Sure are late, Delaney. Worth it though, huh?'

The old man chuckled. 'More than enough, son — more than enough.'

'How much, Del?'

'That's the fourth time. You deaf?'

'Nope. Just like to hear you tell it.'

'Around forty thousand dollars. Could be more. I knowed it! All along I knowed it. Reckon Titus will be sore, huh?'

'He never did believe you, did he? He pulled out after a few weeks. Sure beats me why he ever came at all.'

'He ain't no prospector. Not Titus. But we needed his help. Leastways, I thought we did.' Delaney groped in the dusky light, slapped the boy's shoulder. 'Better'n a man — that's you, Clancy. Guts, it takes, and spirit — and a sort of faith. Sometimes you ain't nothin' else but them. I'm proud of you. Now git that pesky fire going.'

The kindling-wood flared, the dry-brush chips sizzled and spat. Orange flames set a circle glowing beneath the rock-face, raising a wall of light against the encroaching darkness. The old man and the boy busied themselves with camp chores, each to his own agreed portion. They worked with an unhurried speed born of much practice. The boy prepared the food, the old man cleaned tools, tended the burros, fixed the bed-rolls.

'Water's gettin' mighty low,' said Clancy, flattening dough mixture in small circles and dropping them into the baking-tin above the now red-hot fire. 'Do I have to make another trip to the water-hole?'

'Not if we can crush and separate that last batch of gold-bearing rock by noon tomorrow. We could be halfway to water by sundown.'

'Could work all night,' Clancy suggested.

'I don't favour it. Never have. To me, it means gold is your master. No man makes me work all day and all night — no siree! So why should gold? Got all our lives ahead of us, ain't we?'

'It makes sense. You allus make sense. Titus had you figured for a windy ol' coot. Not me, though.' Clancy turned the baking biscuits with a deft action. 'Say, Del.'

'Yep?'

'How come Titus is my cousin?'

'On account he's the son of my sister's daughter, and you're the son of my daughter.'

'Kinda confusing, ain't it? Him being so much older'n me.'

'Waal, you were sort of late arriving.'

Clancy rocked back on his heels, reached for the coffee-pot and set it on a stone built into the fire.

'Ain't many of us left, are there, Del? My ma and pa being dead, and Titus's ma and pa too, and his two brothers. Just you and me and Titus out of the whole Delaney family. It'd be good to take back all that money to a real family, wouldn't it?'

Delaney came to the fire and squatted beside the boy. 'We got Titus.'

Clancy laughed. 'He ain't got us. He done walked out on us way back. How d'you figure Titus?'

'For truth, son?'

Clancy nodded.

'A no-good hombre. Shouldn't say it of my own kin, but it is so. Two older brothers, he had, and wild they were, with likings for easy money. So they taught him young, and that's a bad time to be taught such things.'

'But they were hanged for robbing a bank and killing the cashier. Titus ain't hankering to follow them, is he?'

'Mebbe not, but could be he'll come to it. Got no stamina. Couldn't stick this, could he? Never sticks at nothin' for long. Not work. It's a funny thing, son, but these hombres who don't like work do sure enough work harder at not doing it.'

'How d'you mean?'

'Like Titus trailing all the way up here with us, working awhile, then pulling out and trailing all the way back to the border. If he'd stuck it, he'd have been rich.'

'But he didn't know that.'

'Nor did we. Not for sure. We struck pay-rock a few weeks ago. In another week we'd have had to give up. As it is, we ain't been eating enough for this last week, but now we'll make it. But what's Titus doing? I'll wager he's hanging around San Rosito, taking odd jobs, earning a dollar here, a dollar there — talking big and acting small. And every day worrying about how he can find some easy money.'

'Shall you give him some money if we meet up with him?'

Delaney shrugged. 'Why not? He's kinfolk, no matter what else he is. Sure, we'll give him a stake for him to use as he wants.' He dug a finger into Clancy's ribs. 'Then it's you and me for dreams come true — eh, son?'

'Sure is, Del! Our own ranch, and me raising palominos and you raising shorthorns. And a real fine house, and — and — geewickety! A *real* bed!'

'*And* a bath. Don't forget that,' Delaney chortled. 'Allus did hanker after having my own bath. Is supper ready?'

'Comin' up.'

'Then let's git to it. We got sleep and an early dawn to meet.'

They ate, frugally but sufficiently, cleaned all the dishes, stowed the packs, then stretched on their blankets and slept. The moon climbed up the starlit sky, shining greenish-white over the plain below where, close by the trail to the water-hole, a lone horseman rode his nightly vigil.

Before dawn he headed for the high chaparral, disappearing into its shaded, tangled depths. The tiny pinpoint of fire way up among the rocky foothills told him that the man and the boy would remain another day, or part of a day. So he waited and watched, half starving yet kept alert by his hunger for gold that might be his for the taking.

In the dark before dawn, as the moon paled and the stars lost their glitter, Delaney awoke the boy. Coffee was boiling as pearly slats shredded the eastern sky. They drank coffee, ate the remains of the supper biscuits. Then, leaving Clancy to clean camp, Delaney set to work on the crusher. Clancy soon joined him, and together they split and pounded the gold-bearing rock to a size small enough to extract nuggets before powdering the remainder to dust. A precious dust, carefully rammed into stout sacks, sewn tightly at each end and small enough to transport easily.

By noon they had rolled heavy rocks to cover the mine's shallow entrance, and thrown dirt and stones all around to hide traces of their camp. Such precautions wouldn't fool the searching gaze of a skilled gold prospector, but would prevent an ordinary trail-rider from knowing that gold had been found beneath these barren hills. No one would linger for long among these rocks, and gold prospectors weren't very numerous in this territory.

Two burros were loaded with the gold-filled panniers and ordinary packs, leaving the third to be shared as a mount. One burro normally carried all the gear, and Delaney and Clancy used the others as saddle-mounts. But the gold-dust was too heavy for just one of the sturdy little beasts to carry.

'Here — put this on under your shirt.' Delaney handed a money belt to Clancy, who took it with surprise.

'Why, Del? Thought we'd stashed it all in the pokes in the panniers? This belt will ride mighty hot.'

'Mebbe so,' Delaney growled as he stripped to fit a similar belt on himself. 'I ain't exactly pleased with the thought of it either, but there's a lesson for you to learn. Never keep all your cash in one pocket, nor all your grub in one pack.' He chuckled. 'Nor all your gold in one place. You can lose all your cash through one hole, or the crittur carrying your packs can run off or fall in a river and leave you to starve.' He tapped the belt. 'Got nuggets and a measure of gold-dust in these hyar belts. Only a small part of what we own, but if anything happens...' He shrugged. 'Waal — we got somep'n left to see for our weeks of work.'

'What can happen?'

'How should I know until it does? Heat might git us, or the burros run off. Or we'll mebbe meet up with a gang of no-good hombres. Never can tell. Now let's git moving. You ride first. I'll walk.'

'No. You ride, Del.'

'Quit arguing! I'll tell you when my feet are killing me so's I need to fork a burro to rest 'em.'

Clancy swung on to the burro's back.

'Just as you say, Del. You're the boss.'

'Sure am.' Delaney grinned. 'Real big boss of a boy and three burros!'

The old man was wise to make the boy ride through the late-noon heat. It takes years of experience to know how to walk over scorching earth and rock surfaces under a blazing sun. There are ways of placing the feet so that pressure doesn't come too often in the same spots. There are ways of lengthening or shortening the stride so as to avoid sweat-cramps. A way of leaning the body to ease the strain on shoulders and spine. Ways of keeping saliva in the mouth, and ways of breathing which cool the air passing into the lungs. All these things the old man knew from years of trailing and prospecting in fierce heat. Ways there was no time now to teach the boy.

So Delaney trudged beside the plodding burros, and Clancy rode loose-limbed, panting from the heat, and by late afternoon they had reached the haven of shade beneath the first section of tall chaparral. They stripped the burros of loads and let the little beasts roll their sweating hides dry in the dust. Making comfortable back-rests of packs and panniers Delaney and Clancy stretched, silent and weary, waiting for the sun to ease its torment of the day.

There was sufficient water only for a few sips each, and they feared to eat what little food they had in case it brought greater thirst.

'Sleep till moonrise,' Delaney croaked. 'Be cool trailing then. Should make the water-hole by dawn. Then one more day will bring us close to the Sonora Trail. Bound to sight a stage or wagon round there. Cleaned your gun, Clancy?'

'Not today.'

'Clean it now. Mebbe we'll sight somep'n worth shootin' for a meal as we git near to water.'

Delaney had bought the gun for Clancy, taught him well how to use it, and the boy could fire with equal accuracy from hip or shoulder. A light gun with carved walnut stock. A lady's gun, some called it. Good for killing a small crittur, with a big enough bang to scare a night prowler. Its tiny bullets would have to hit a man in just the right place to hurt him real bad. Clancy was proud of it — and of his shooting skill. He cleaned the gun lovingly, wrapped it in the oily cloth, then lay back and in seconds was fast asleep.

Delaney awoke the boy at moonrise, having already loaded the burros, and they set off without delay. This time the old man rode the burro, and, because he was fresh from his sleep and the night clear and cool, Clancy loped along afoot. They changed places at frequent intervals, and in this fashion trailed at a fair speed.

'Tain't so far now,' said Delaney, peering around him as he sat astride the burro. 'See that slope of pines yonder?'

'Yep, I see 'em.'

'We'll trail east of the pines, then take a sharp curve south.'

'Why not head straight?' Clancy asked.

Delaney chuckled. 'I'd sure like to. It'd save a mite of time. But this water-hole ain't like the one we used way north of the mine. This hyar water-hole used to be a regular watercourse from the hills before a rock-fall plumb filled it. Happened years ago — mebbe a hundred, mebbe more. Then sand and dirt silted up around the rock until it was deeper'n a horse and rider, but the water still bubbled underneath it. Now it's what you might call one of nature's death-traps.'

'How come?'

'Shifting sand — not really wet, not really dry, and it has weeds growing on it. Experienced trail-riders can spot it in daylight, but even they will ride clear around it at night.

There's more'n one place like it in this territory. Many a poor ignorant trail-rider has lost his life in it. Sunk without trace. Sucked right down.'

'Sounds a real dangerous place to find a water-hole. I'd have gone straight across it.'

'You wouldn't if you remembered what I taught you about reading signs. You forgot?'

Clancy thought for a moment. 'No — no, I ain't forgot, Del. You told me allus to follow critturs' tracks whenever I reached a strange water-hole.

'That's right, son. And in daylight you'd see there weren't no tracks at all on one side of the water-hole. Critturs have a way of knowing such things. Allus learn from critturs.'

'But I wouldn't see it at night.'

'So you'd wait for dawn — even though your tongue was plumb hangin' out — or you'd let a burro lead you.'

'Not a horse?'

'Nope. A horse ain't so quick on the scent as a burro. Some horses are, but some ain't got the sense they're born with — like some humans I know,' Delaney growled as he swivelled again to peer around him.

'Why d'you keep peering around, Del? Ain't no one trailing this territory but us.'

'Not as I know to,' the old man admitted. 'Ain't *seen* anyone, but I sure enough got the prickles.'

'The prickles?' Clancy questioned.

Delaney rubbed the back of his neck. 'Yeah — right here. A sort of prickle feeling. And a hunch too. Don't ask me which came first. Mebbe a fella grows a sixth sense after years of trailing, but I'll wager our gold to a bone button that there's another rider not far off.' He pointed to the pack-laden burros. 'Four times them critturs have cocked an ear and hesitated in their stride. They heard somep'n — that's for sure.'

'Mebbe a coyote?'

'Not around here. Any coyotes would be on the far side of

72

the water-hole, on account we heard 'em yelping awhiles back — calling a meeting up on the slopes, like they allus do.'

Clancy didn't argue any more, but saved his breath to concentrate upon keeping up a brisk pace. He didn't disbelieve the old man, but there were times when Delaney didn't make sense, and Clancy was never quite sure whether Del was acting a bit ornery, like so many old-timers did.

The moon was paling now, although the stars were still bright and shining with that strange incandescence so noticeable in the dark hour before dawn. In a little while they, too, would start to fade as the first rays of the new day began to lighten the eastern horizon.

It happened at the same moment that Clancy realised he was growing tired.

He heard Delaney shout. Heard the thud of hooves and sounds of something crashing through the tangle of brush on the far side of the burros. Then his foot snagged on a root or loose stone, and Clancy stumbled to fall heavily on his shoulder. He heard Delaney's voice yell: 'No, Titus, dang your eyes — don't! Wait, Titus, wait!' Then came the staccato bark of a gun, and another shot, small and flat-sounding, like the report of a six-gun.

Clancy's own gun, which he carried slung around his shoulder, had fallen, and in the confusion of noises he thought perhaps it had fired itself as it hit the ground. But a flash of memory assured him that the safety-catch was on, so it couldn't have been his gun that had fired.

In such moments when so many things appear to be happening at once it isn't easy to be sure of the order in which they happen. So quite naturally Clancy began climbing to his feet, aware that his knee and shoulder hurt and that his nose was bleeding and his eyes watering so much he could scarcely see. He soon realised he'd hit knee, shoulder and nose when he fell, and the result of this was his first thought.

He heard footsteps near him, and half turned, believing it was Delaney coming to assist him. Then something went clonk inside his head. Sparks flashed across his eyes, pain seared through his skull, and he was sinking down and down into soft black darkness.

Clancy's next thoughts were immediately concerned with pain and the throbbing thud of what felt like a hammer inside his head. He heard a familiar voice, as if coming from a great distance.

'Geewickety! Ooh ... I feel bad,' said the voice, and it was quite some seconds before Clancy realised it was his own voice.

He opened his eyes. The effort sent fresh stabs of pain through his head. He felt terribly sick. He lay quiet, eyes closed, face pressed on a pillow of coarse tufted grass. It was cool and spiky, and had an aromatic sage-like scent which was pleasant. So pleasant that Clancy breathed more deeply, and this seemed to clear his head and ease away the sick feeling.

Slowly he opened his eyes again. This time without so much pain, and the throbbing inside his head was dying down. Now he could think more clearly. Then, on a sudden, very clearly.

'Del!' he yelled, and sat up quickly. Dizziness made his vision blurred, and his head thudded again; but slowly these died away. 'By cracky,' he whispered, 'I was hit on the head. Someone sure enough clonked me.' His hand probed gently at the tender place behind his ear. He could feel the swelling. 'Titus!' Clancy exclaimed, and turned slowly to peer around him. 'Del? You called Titus. What —' Then he saw Delaney, stretched out beside the saddle burro.

Clancy scrambled to his feet, fought off the giddiness and .stumbled to the old man's side.

'Del — Del!' he called softly as he knelt down.

In the dim light he could see blood over one side of Delaney's face. He glanced up. The three burros stood gazing at him.

'Looks like he's dead, fellas,' Clancy muttered, and didn't

at first notice anything wrong. But when he moved to fetch a water canister he saw that the gold-filled packs were gone. He collected the canister and went back to the old man.

'It *was* Titus, wasn't it?' he whispered. 'You were right about another rider being near us. I should've listened to you. You're *not* a crazy old coot — you're wise and clever. And now — now —' Clancy clenched his fist — 'Titus has the gold. But your life was worth more. Ain't no gold can buy the likes of you, old pardner.'

'When you've quit buryin' me — will you pass me some dad-blamed water?' said a hoarse voice.

'Del! Del, you ain't dead!'

'If I am, then I'm a mighty thirsty ghost. Reckon I was knocked out. Hearing your voice sort of brought me out of it.' Delaney eased up on one elbow, then groaned. 'By cracky, my head's fair humming.'

Clancy held the water canister. Delaney drank gratefully, then Clancy swigged a good measure himself. The water refreshed them like wine. Delaney touched his head.

'Waal — guess I don't want it much closer than that,' he observed. 'Reckon the buckle on my hat mebbe deflected the bullet so's it just skimmed my scalp.'

'Was it Titus?'

Delaney frowned painfully. 'Yeah, son, it was Titus. It's coming back to me now. He bust out of that scrub yonder. Must've been trailing us all night, then circled to come up ahead of us. Moved faster on a horse, and by taking a wide sweep he knowed we wouldn't hear hoof-beats. Reckon he walked his horse up to this ambush point.'

'So he's been waiting on us — all this time?'

'Seems that-a-way, son. The gold's gone, huh?'

Clancy nodded, then yelped as his bruised head creaked.

'Oh no!' Delaney cried. 'The dirty coyote! He didn't shoot you too?'

'Clonked me on the noggin. I made it easy for him by falling over. How long ago, Del?'

'Can't be all that long. Dawn's a-comin' up. Mebbe twenty — thirty minutes.'

'Then he can't have got far.'

'Not with his horse carrying them loaded packs and him as well. Titus ain't no light weight.'

'I'm going after him.'

'You and me both. Help me up, son.'

Delaney struggled to his feet; stood swaying for a moment before he collapsed with a groan.

'I can't make it. Must've bust my ankle when I fell. Head's purty bad too.'

'Here's the water. That's all we've got,' said Clancy. 'I'll take the other canister. Stay here — I'll be back.'

'Now wait!' Delaney called after the boy. 'Wait, Clancy! Don't go after him. He's a killer.'

But Clancy had collected his rifle, spare canister, climbed on the burro's back and was moving off before the old man could finish speaking. He gave a cheery wave and urged the burro to a loping trot. The little creature seemed to sense its master's need and sped along without hesitation. Burros are notoriously self-willed, and usually prefer to halt if master says hurry, and speed up when he says take it easy.

'Good ol' Pico!' Clancy patted the burro's neck. 'Keep going, amigo, and mebbe we'll sight that murderin' Titus.'

Clancy's head was clear now and the pain had subsided to a dull ache. He was furious at the treachery of his cousin Titus. This anger gave him strength of mind and body, and cast off the tiredness of all-night trailing and the effects of a blow on the head.

An opaque light filled the land with swirls of eddying colour as dawn filtered over the hills, spreading swiftly across the valley to clear the night mist around the water-hole. Visibility became easier each minute.

Pico the burro stopped so abruptly that Clancy was almost pitched over its head.

'You fool crittur!' he gasped, and was about to urge Pico on again when, ahead of them, he saw a man and a horse. Clancy pulled the burro's flicking ears with an affectionate grasp.

'Clever ol' Pico,' he whispered. 'You sensed 'em even before I could see 'em, didn't you? His horse is lame, so he has to walk beside it — *and* carry one of the gold packs.'

Clancy slid to the ground, leaving Pico's head-rope trailing so that the burro wouldn't wander off, and, grasping his gun, sped on silent feet to the near-by trees.

Using these as cover, Clancy moved up until only a short distance behind the man. Then he stepped out, levelled his rifle and yelled: 'Hold it, Titus, or I'll drill you for sure.'

Titus whirled, but staggered because of the weight of the gold pack over his shoulder. He fired his rifle from the hip, but the bullet spanged harmlessly wide of Clancy.

'Don't make me do it, Titus,' Clancy called. 'Just drop that gold, leave your horse and mosey on. That's all I'm asking.'

'I should've killed you at the same time as that old fool,' Titus snarled. 'The gold's mine, see? All mine. Delaney ain't no use for it, and why should a kid like you have it? You asked for it.' He steadied himself, levelled the rifle.

Clancy trod forward until his own rifle would be in range. 'Delaney ain't dead,' he called. 'You don't dare shoot me — or you'll hang like your brothers.'

Titus squeezed the trigger. The rifle jerked as the mechanism jammed. He cursed and flung the rifle away, drew out his six-gun and fired twice. Bullets spurted dust some yards short of Clancy's feet. Titus was out of six-gun range.

Clancy raised his rifle, aimed and fired. Titus's hat flew from his head.

'Don't make me do it, Titus,' Clancy repeated. 'Just drop that pack and get moving. The next bullet goes through your arm. The next through your knee. Don't make me shoot at kin — even though you're a thieving, would-be murderer.'

Titus bellowed furious curses, raised his six-gun and emptied it in a staccato hammering of shots. A bullet plucked a hole in Clancy's shirt. The others whined into the distance.

'Come back, or I shoot to kill!' yelled Clancy

Suddenly Titus moved with desperate speed, pulled the other gold pack from the horse and, though burdened by its weight, set off towards smooth, weed-covered ground.

'No!' Clancy yelled as he realised where Titus was heading. 'Come back, you fool! Come back, or I shoot to kill.'

An idle threat, because Clancy knew that Titus was moving out of range. He fired two warning shots, but Titus kept moving. Then, as he began to run forward, Clancy saw him stumble, struggle up and stumble again.

The two heavy gold packs fell to one side as Titus struggled for balance. He lunged forward, his legs disappearing.

'Don't struggle, Titus!' Clancy yelled. 'You're in quicksand. Hold on — I'll get a rope from your horse.' He turned back, raced to the horse, grabbed the coiled lariat from its saddle-thong and turned again... halted and stared wide-eyed.

'Oh no, no!' he exclaimed. 'It can't be. Not like that — not so quick, so awful quick.'

But it was. Quicksand *is* awful quick. It closes over a stone, a stick — or a man. Just like that.

Clancy walked slowly to the edge of that smooth, innocent-looking area, searching in vain. It was as if Titus had never existed. Only the two packs of gold remained as evidence that he'd really been there.

These had fallen, by strange accident, on the one rock-hard patch before the quicksand began. Without the packs Titus would have found foothold and hand-hold to pull himself back. But the gold packs barred his way to safety...

Now, Clancy is a man, and a wealthy ranch-owner. His ranch spreads clear over the territory containing a water-hole named Pico's Place.

Near the water-hole is a large patch of real pretty-looking ground. A high iron fence surrounds it so that no man or beast can approach the water-hole from that direction. Folks around those parts call it Titus's Folly, but no one seems to know why. And neither Clancy nor an old, old man they call Del will tell them.

THE LAST TERM AT WILDMERE

I don't know what it was that first made me suspicious. But it was a bit odd for two masters to go sick in a week. Then, when the two who took their places turned out to be huge toughies who knew less than we did, I nipped out of the Fourth Form at mid-morning break and collared Stevenson in the corridor.

'Steve,' I said in a low voice, because one of the toughies was lurking only five feet away, 'come up to the dormitory for five minutes. I want to talk to you.'

He looked at me as if I'd gone mad. 'Look, Peters, if you think I'm going to miss tuckshop just to listen to you, then you've got another thing coming. You know it's only open for five minutes, and we don't get another chance until after tea.'

I grabbed him by the sleeve and hustled him down the corridor. 'If you'd stop worrying about your great fat inside for a minute, then you'd go a great deal further in this world.' At that point I stopped. Stevenson didn't need to go anywhere in the world — he was there already! If your old man's a millionaire, then you don't have to worry. And though Steve never swanked about all the money that would be his one day, it was impossible to forget it — especially when exams came round and the rest of us had to swot like demons to be sure of getting through.

'Oh, all right,' said Steve. 'I'll come. But this had better be something good. I've never missed morning tuckshop before in my life.'

I pointed at his bulging midriff. '*And* it looks like it!'

We went upstairs, Steve puffing and blowing like a whale because of the effort of heaving his great hulk from stair to stair. Then when we reached the dormitory, he sat down with a gasp on the edge of his bed. 'Now, let's have it. If you're quick enough, maybe I can get downstairs again in time.'

I grinned at him. It was funny — Steve made me furious with him for most of the time, but he'd always been my closest friend — ever since my first term at Wildmere. And it had nothing to do with his money, either. I'd made that plain from the very beginning when, on a day that I was flat broke, he'd tried to shove a pound note into my pocket. Sometimes I could still see the scar on my knuckles where they'd crashed into his chin.

'Steve — forget about tuckshop just for this once. This is important. It's about those two new masters.'

'What about them? They're a very odd pair.'

'Odd isn't the word for it. Have you realised that the one who's supposed to be the English master can't even spell?'

Steve shook his head, and chuckled. 'It's not a thing I'd have noticed. I can't spell either.'

'Well, take my word for it. He spells "premier" with two mm's! And the other one — the Geography chap. D'you know where he said Tierra del Fuego was? In the north of Italy.'

'Isn't it?' asked Steve in surprise.

'It's on the bottom corner of South America. The point is, they're a couple of duffers. I don't believe they're real masters at all.'

'Then what are they doing here?' said Steve vaguely.

'That's what I want to find out — and I want you to help.'

Steve straightened up, and his plump face became serious and important. 'Detection, eh? Oh, you can rely on me.'

I wasn't sure about that. Even in such a simple matter as bringing me back an ice-cream on a hot afternoon he'd let it melt on the way across the playing-fields. At least, that was what he'd told me. Whether it had melted in the sun or inside him, I'd never been able to find out.

But there was one thing one could rely on. Steve could keep his mouth shut — which was more than I could say about any of the others in the Fourth Form. 'What I want you to do is shadow that big chap.'

'The one called Rutherford?' Steve rubbed his hands together. 'Oh, I'll do that all right.' He looked out of the window, and smiled a far-away smile. 'You know, I've always fancied myself as a bit of a Sherlock Holmes.'

I had to shove my handkerchief up to my face and blow my nose hurriedly, to keep from laughing. Nobody in the whole world could have been less like Sherlock Holmes than Stevenson. Most of the time he was even dimmer than Dr Watson.

'Do I have to carry a magnifying glass?' asked Steve, wide-eyed.

'Now what d'you want that for?'

'Well, Sherlock Holmes did, I think. And it would be useful for clues.'

I let out a long sigh. 'All I want you to do,' I said patiently, 'is watch what he does. I'll be watching the other one, Simpson.'

'What for?'

I sat on the edge of the bed beside him. Obviously, this was going to need time and an even temper. 'Look, we're agreed that they're not proper schoolmasters, aren't we?'

'Yes.'

'Well, then, why are they here? How did they get the jobs? Even though the Head's a bit old, he's not a fool. He'd see through those two in half a minute, and the other masters would take only ten seconds. So why hasn't somebody done something?'

Downstairs the electric bell began ringing. Steve jumped up crossly. 'There, I knew you'd make me miss the tuckshop. Now I'll have to go hungry until this evening.'

'Never mind,' I said soothingly. 'Remember, there's always lunch.'

'Huh!' he snorted, then added scornfully: 'Lunch — bah!'

We went back to the Fourth Form room. It was Geography, and I listened in amazement while the master called Simpson told the class that coffee beans were grown mainly in Northern Australia. It was a hot summer's day so nobody argued about it, but I could see a few raised eyebrows among some of the brighter members of the Fourth Form. Steve's weren't among them. As usual in Geography he was asleep, with his hands folded across his bulging waistline.

'What's your name, boy?'

I looked to the front, briskly. 'Peters, sir.'

'Well, Peters, you'd better pay a bit more attention, see. This here's a geography lesson, not time for lookin' round the room. Where's China?'

I tried it on a bit. The worst that could happen was six of the best. 'I didn't know you'd lost it, sir,' I said very respectfully.

His face went red with anger, and I saw his fists bunched up. And the came clear proof that Simpson was no more a teacher than my Great-aunt Hildegarde. Whoever heard of a teacher coming down between the desks like a wild bull, with his fists up ready to snap your head off at the roots.

There was no room to run. My desk was up against the wall. I did the only thing possible — lowered my head, and then, as he swung his fist, brought up the desk lid with all the force I could muster.

He made a noise as if I'd hit him with a red-hot branding-iron, and leaped back from the desk, clutching his hand. I stood up, ready to jump past him and run for the door.

But then a curious thing happened. With a terrific effort he calmed himself, thrust his injured hand into his pocket, and went back to the front of the class without another word to me. He faced Meadows, a tiny little chap with horn-rimmed glasses. 'Perhaps *you* can tell me where China is?' he said in a voice as sweet as sugar.

As soon as class was over I collared Steve again. 'There, now do you see what I mean? These chaps are phonies.'

'What am I supposed to have seen? I was asleep.'

I took hold of my hair with both hands, and tugged. It's a wonder the whole lot didn't come out by the roots. 'All right,' I said wearily. 'Forget it. Just go and shadow Rutherford.'

I went off in the other direction, padding along like an Indian on the warpath, thirty feet behind Simpson.

Wildmere is full of corridors. The main building is hundreds of years old, and some say it used to be a monastery. Anyway, there are four quadrangles with cloisters round them, and at a junction of these I had to stop, for fear of getting too close to Simpson as he turned a corner.

I stepped back into a doorway.

A hand touched the back of my neck.

My inside turned to ice. I stood rigid, unable to move, breathe, or make a sound. Then a voice said, 'Oh, gosh, it's you. Did I give you a fright?'

I turned round slowly, and looked at Stevenson. He was hidden behind me.

'What are you doing there?' I asked. 'You're supposed to be shadowing Rutherford.'

'Well, I...' he stopped, and went red in the face. I looked down at a scattering of crumbs around his feet. His glance followed mine, and he said, 'I couldn't go shadowing on an empty stomach, could I? You wouldn't have wanted me to do that, surely? So I just nipped round to my locker for a lump of cake.' He nodded his head vigorously. 'Cake keeps your strength up, you know. And for jobs like shadowing, you need plenty of ... *ouch!*'

I lifted him up on tiptoe by the firm grip I had on the end of his nose. Then I wagged his head backwards and forwards, while his toes danced frantically to keep him from falling over. 'You great cake-eating idiot!' I growled. 'Where is Rutherford?'

'I . . . I . . .'

'*Where is Rutherford?*'

'I was going to look for him.' Stevenson's eyes rolled. 'Leggo by dose, Peters. You'll bust something.'

I released his nose. 'Well, where is he?'

He rubbed the tip of his nose with a fat hand. 'I don't . . . well, Peters, as a matter of fact . . .'

'As a matter of fact you haven't the slightest idea? That's about it, isn't it?' I flattened myself hurriedly into the doorway as footsteps approached. '*Sssh!*'

'Wassamatter?'

I clapped my hand quickly over Stevenson's mouth just as Simpson and Rutherford turned the corner together, deep in conversation.

'What about the old man?' Rutherford was saying.

'Don't worry about *him*,' said Simpson roughly. 'He's too scared to say a word. So are the others. That's the whole point, you see. They suspect — but they can't prove nothing. They can't get on to the cops, because if they was wrong then they'd look fools.'

'Good. Then I'll bring the car down to the quarry tonight, all ready.'

'Supposing somebody spots it before tomorrow?'

'Phew, mate, you don't half bring up difficulties, don't you? They won't spot it, because I'll hide it properly, that's why. There's bushes down by that quarry — lots of 'em. Enough to hide a hundred cars.'

'What about the plates? The kids will be sure to remember the numbers.'

'Stop *worrying*, I tell you. I've fixed all that, too.'

That was the last I heard. It was too dangerous to creep out of the doorway and try to follow behind them. In any case, Stevenson was tugging violently at my sleeve.

'What is it? What's the matter?'

Stevenson's eyes were bulging. He pointed out of our hiding-place. 'That... that was Rutherford.'

'Yes,' I said, 'of course it was Rutherford. What about it?'

'Well, you wanted to know where Rutherford was. I... I... just thought I'd better tell you.'

I closed my eyes, and thumped my bare fist against the wall. One thing was certain about Steve — he hadn't got his brains from his father. Nobody like Steve could ever become a millionaire.

The quarry? My mind was racing. What quarry, and why?

There were dozens of puzzling questions. Only one thing was certain — I was dead right about Simpson and Rutherford. They *weren't* masters, they were crooks! And all the staff were too terrified to say anything about them.

What could they be planning to do with a car at a quarry? What was supposed to be happening tomorrow? It was the end of term. Were they planning to pinch all the school cups, or something like that?

I looked at my watch. It was only two minutes to lunch-time, so there was no chance to do anything until after school was over for the day. But then, before tea, I'd be able to nip down to the police station and warn them.

But warn them of what? What could I say that wouldn't sound nonsense? What policeman would pay attention to the story of what I'd overheard in a corridor?

No, I had to get some real proof that they were up to something crooked.

My mind came back to the car. Hadn't one of them said something about plates? Number-plates, that must mean. He'd *fixed* them, he said — because the kids would remember.

It didn't make much sense.

The lunch-bell rang. 'Come on, Steve,' I said, but he didn't need any urging. Not for a lunch-bell.

It wasn't until the middle of the final class of the afternoon that I decided what to do. I shot down to the main gates as soon as lessons were over, and cut across three fields to the nearest quarry. It was big, open and overgrown with grass. There was nothing I could see that looked suspicious. Certainly no bushes where a car could be hidden.

I walked back to the school. What other quarries were there? I knew of one, but that was almost in the town, with houses all round it. There'd be no hiding-place for a car anywhere within half a mile of it.

Then I remembered one other. I'd never been close to it, but I'd seen it from the train at the start and finish of term. It lay about a mile beyond the town, and there were bushes all round it.

There was no time to investigate before tea. As I went in through the gates the bushes rustled beside me. The owl face of Stevenson popped out.

'Oh, crumbs!' he babbled in a high-pitched squeak. 'Peters, you did give me a start. I... I... thought it was Rutherford or Simpson.'

I stared at the plump midriff that hung from the bushes. 'What on earth are you doing there?'

'K-keeping watch.' He looked at me anxiously. 'Am I doing the right thing? I thought I'd better be doing something.'

I looked at him, puzzled. 'What exactly are you watching for?'

He looked even more puzzled. 'Well, you know,' he mumbled, and waved his hands.

It was fatal. With a tremendous crash of breaking twigs, Stevenson descended. It was like an airship crashing into a jungle. 'Ooch!' he yelped. 'Ouch!' A branch cought his trouser-leg and slithered up the inside. It was part of a holly bush. His face went purple.

Then he disappeared. There was absolute silence, except for a low moaning somewhere in the middle of the bushes. I pushed aside the leaves, and looked in.

What I saw was a shoe, upside-down. A large pink leg

90

stuck out of it in the direction of the ground. I gripped it tightly. 'Hullo!' I shouted into the bushes. 'Is there anybody on the end of this leg?'

There was. It gave a squeal like a pig, and floundered about in the depths of the bushes.

I heaved.

Nothing happened, except that my arms nearly came out of their sockets.

I heaved again: 'Hold on, Great Plump One,' I chuckled. 'Help is at hand.'

The shoe came off. The sock came with it.

I looked at the large pink foot that wriggled upside-down in the midst of the bushes. Pulling was getting me nowhere. There was only one possible answer to the problem of Stevenson.

I chose it. I plucked a handful of long grass with seed-heads on the top.

I tickled the foot.

There was a wild squeal from inside the bushes, and a heaving and thumping. Stevenson burst his way out, covered with small twigs and leaves. 'Peters!' he puffed and blowed, 'You're a . . . oh, blow it, I thought you were my *friend*.'

I brushed him down. It was a long job. There was a lot of him. 'You're on watch again after tea,' I said. 'But not in the middle of a jungle. All I want to know is if Rutherford or Simpson go out. If they do, then follow them.'

'F-follow them? I couldn't keep up. You know that.'

'Use my bike. No, on second thoughts I'll need that myself.' I looked at him, and wondered if anywhere in the school there might be someone mad enough to risk lending him a bike. I shook my head. There wasn't. That was one thing I could be sure of. 'You'll have to walk,' I said.

His eyes bulged. 'What, *me*?'

I hooted with laughter at him. 'It'll help to get your weight down.' But he was gone already, lumbering up the drive at the sound of the tea-bell.

After tea I set off for the quarry. It was a long ride, mostly uphill, and towards the end of it I began to wonder if I was wasting my time. Perhaps I hadn't heard correctly? Perhaps what I'd thought was 'quarry' was really something quite different?

I reached it at last. It was a desolate place, so overgrown that you could walk up to it and never realise that under all the bushes there was a huge chalk quarry. The only easy way in was through a break in the bushes where the old rusty railway siding ran down. I pushed the bike out of sight in the bushes, and walked down the crumbling wooden sleepers.

I don't know what I'd expected to find. Secret aerodromes, perhaps, or smugglers' dens. But there was nothing at all in the quarry. The rails came to an end close to the far end; beyond them were two old railway trucks lying on their sides and the rusty iron wheels of a crane. That was all.

I started back up the sleepers. Far away I heard the whistle of a train.

And then, unmistakeably, the engine of a car grinding its way along in low gear over the ruts and bumps of the track leading to the quarry.

For a moment the sound meant nothing to me. Then I jumped into the shelter of the bushes as the front of a car swung into the quarry entrance.

It was a big old sports car — one of those noisy low-slung machines with a huge engine and a top speed of about a hundred. It stopped, and the driver got out. He was too far away for me to recognise him, and the light was beginning to fade.

He disappeared into the bushes. Suddenly I remembered my bike. It was only a few yards away from the place where he'd vanished. Would he spot it? If he did, what would he do?

Then he came out again, and climbed back into the car. He backed it out, and began to turn it. I took advantage of the few moments in which his back was turned to move closer by about thirty yards. It was a quick sprint, and I just had time to fling myself into the long grass at the foot of the bushes as he finished turning the car.

I parted the grass with my hands, and peered through at him.

It was Rutherford!

So I had not made a mistake. But what on earth was it all about?

I watched as the car was backed into hiding in the bushes. Then Rutherford came out and walked up the sleepers to the entrance. I waited five minutes in case he came back. Then, keeping under cover as much as I could, I moved up to the car.

It was quite a job to find it. Rutherford had hidden it cleverly, even going to the trouble of pulling branches in front of the bonnet and tying them together with string.

I stood beside the car, listening carefully for any tell-tale sounds of movement that would mean Rutherford had returned and was sneaking up on me. But there was complete silence.

Why hide a car in the bushes at the edge of the quarry?

Could it be because it was stolen? I looked at the car carefully. It was older than I'd thought; the bottoms of the doors were deeply pitted with rust, and the chromium-plating was shabby. Surely it wasn't the kind of car anybody would steal? To begin with, it was unusual-looking and so the police would be able to spot it. Secondly, a lot of money would have to be spent on it before anyone would want to buy it.

No, I felt pretty sure that wasn't the answer.

But of one thing I was positive. Nobody would hide a car unless there was a crooked reason. And there wasn't much doubt that Rutherford and Simpson were crooks.

I opened the bonnet and looked at the engine. It was a massive eight-cylinder machine, with a carburettor for every pair of cylinders. Not much care had been taken of it, for the whole thing was covered with a layer of dirt and oil; but even so, I didn't doubt that it could pass most other cars on the road. It would be ideal for crooks as a getaway car.

Yes, but to get away from what?

I remembered suddenly what I'd overheard them say about number-plates. I went round to the front of the car. and bent down to look at them.

At a distance they looked quite normal. But at a range of twelve inches it was easy to see that they were faked. New white letters and numbers had been painted on to a sheet of gummed plastic, which had been stuck over the top of the original number-plates again; it wouldn't take ten seconds to tear off the plastic dummies.

I did it for them. I pulled them off the front and back of the car, screwed them up and chucked them into the depths of the bushes. Then I went back to the bonnet, pulled out the distributor of the ignition and stuffed it into my pocket.

Then I recovered my bike and rode back to school.

The plump moon-face of Stevenson greeted me over the supper-table. 'Well?' I asked him. 'Did you keep watch?'

He nodded vigorously. His double chin wobbled. 'Oh yes, Peters, I did just as you asked.'

'Did either of them go out?'

'Oh, not at all. They were both in their rooms. I sat out by the tennis courts. The lights went on in their rooms soon after tea, and they're still on.'

'Then I expect you'll be surprised to hear I've been watching Rutherford myself?'

He jumped. 'B-but you couldn't have. You were out.'

'Yes,' I said grimly. 'Yes, my fat friend, I was out. And so was Rutherford. So where were you?'

'I told you.' Stevenson's voice came in an anxious squeak, like a little pig on the way to market. 'I was sitting out by the tennis courts.'

'*All* the time?'

His eyes shifted uneasily. 'Well, p-practically all the time, Peters. I just went indoors once. It's a h-hungry job, sitting.'

'Luckily it didn't matter,' I said. 'I know where Rutherford was, and what he was up to. But just so that you'll learn not to be lazy, you need a lesson.' I turned sharply. 'Look, Steve, look over there!'

He looked. While he was looking I ate his poached egg. It seemed only fair. After all, I'd done all the hard work.

As always on the last night of term we were late getting to bed, but everybody woke early, and there was a frenzied last-minute packing of trunks, so that they'd be ready for the railway van after breakfast. Breakfast was early, too, and then there were cheers as the coaches arrived to take us down to the station. I piled in beside Stevenson. Rutherford and Simpson were in the same coach, sitting up at the front and paying no attention to the row going on all round them. If there was any further proof needed that they weren't real schoolmasters, then that was it.

At the station I grabbed an empty compartment and hustled Stevenson into it. Then I stood at the window shouting 'Full up!' whenever anybody came near.

The train pulled out. I didn't see any sign of Rutherford and Simpson, though. From the moment the coach reached the station they'd seemed to vanish into thin air.

The train picked up speed slowly. It chugged out of the station, past the church and the shops. I looked out of the window as we swung round the bend which would bring the quarry into view.

Then there was a sudden jerk and the train stopped. It was so violent that it threw me across the compartment. I landed with a thump on the seat, then bounced back again.

'Yaaouch! I say, Peters, that's my stomach you're sitting on.'

I climbed to my feet again, leaving Stevenson nursing his wounded middle with both hands. The school carriage was the end one of the train. Somewhere in front I heard a loud clanking noise, then there was a shout in the distance. I looked out of the window, and saw the engine-driver and fireman walking past the engine, carrying what looked like a huge log of wood.

'I say, Steve, I think somebody put a log on the rails!' He blinked at me. 'What would they want to do that for? Couldn't they *saw* it in half?'

'It would wreck the train, idiot, if we hit it.'

The engine whistled, then chugged hard to get the train into motion again. 'We're off,' I said.

But then I looked out of the window again. We *weren't*. I looked farther out.

And then I shouted. For the train had gone on — leaving our coach behind. 'Hey,' I yelled, 'come back!'

But the train was already speeding away into the distance.

And our carriage, left alone on a gentle slope, had begun to roll forward.

Heads were popping out of the windows of the other compartments. 'What's going on?' somebody yelled.

The reply didn't come from anywhere in the carriage. It was Simpson's voice, from beside the track. 'Keep calm, everybody. Everything's going to be all right.'

The carriage jolted violently. 'Ooooh! My breakfast,' gurgled Stevenson behind me. But the jolting continued.

And then I understood why. The carriage had gone round the points, and we were lurching down the old siding to the quarry. Creaking and groaning over the rusty rails, the carriage was gaining speed. Ahead I could see the gap in the bushes where the rails went down to the quarry bottom.

I could also see Rutherford. He was running across from the main line towards the quarry, waving his arms.

It was Simpson he was waving to. They disappeared through the bushes just ahead of the carriage. One moment we were in bright sunshine, the next we were scraping through the bushes, with twigs and leaves pushing through the open windows.

'What's happening?' asked Stevenson. He was sitting behind me, calmly munching potato crisps from a paper bag.

I couldn't give him an answer that would make sense. I knew *what* was happening, but I didn't know *why*. All I felt certain about was that Simpson and Rutherford had put the log on the line to stop the train, and that they had uncoupled our carriage and changed the points.

But *why*? What could they gain by running a carriage-load of schoolboys down into a quarry?

The coach was now nearly at the bottom of the quarry. Suddenly I wondered what would happen when we got there. At the speed we were travelling — about twenty miles an hour — surely we'd go sailing over the end of the lines, and into the old trucks and the sheer wall of rock ahead?

I pushed Stevenson over on his side. 'Lie flat!' I yelled.

'Ouch! I say, you ass, you've spilled my crisps!'

'Bother your wretched crisps.' He was trying to sit up again, and I had to grab his hair to force him to lie flat. I stretched myself out beyond him, and dug my free hand into the gap at the back of the seat, ready for the crash.

But no crash came. On the level ground at the bottom of the quarry the carriage slowed up, and came to a halt.

I jumped to my feet and flung open the door. But just as I was about to climb down, Simpson's voice came from close beside me. 'Stay where you are, Peters!'

I looked round. He was facing me, with a pistol in his hand. I backed into the compartment again.

'All right, everybody — keep calm.'

It was Rutherford this time. His voice was coming from the other side of the carriage. 'Nobody's going to get hurt. All we want is Stevenson.'

'Uuh?' The grunt came from behind me. 'Who wants me?'

'Shut up a minute!' I said quickly.

Rutherford spoke again. 'Where's Stevenson? If you'll come out here, Stevenson, everything will be all right.'

Stevenson stood up, clutching the remains of his bag of

crisps. I pushed him back into his seat before he could be seen from the window. 'He isn't here,' I shouted. 'He didn't come in the train. His father called for him by car.'

'I s-s-say, th-th-that's not true, you know.'

I jammed my hand over Stevenson's mouth. 'He went by car, I tell you.'

'It's no use bluffing,' came Rutherford's voice. 'We know he's in there with you, Peters. We saw him get on the train.'

I took my hand away from Stevenson's mouth. 'What do you want him for?'

'You'll be told, all in good time. Now hurry up, boy — otherwise somebody may get hurt. We haven't got all day to waste.'

I looked out of the window at Rutherford. He looked back at me. And then he raised his pistol, aimed it at the window beside me, and fired.

The bullet made a small, neat hole in the centre of the pane. 'That's for not hurrying,' shouted Rutherford. 'Now send Stevenson out.'

White-faced, Stevenson pushed past me. 'Wh-what do they want?'

'I don't know; but you'll have to go out and see — otherwise they may start shooting again.'

Stevenson opened the door, put his foot on the running-board, and looked down at the long drop to the ground. 'I c-can't!' he gasped. 'It's too far.'

'You'll have to,' I said. 'Close your eyes.'

He closed them, and groaned. Then he jumped.

He landed like an enormous blancmange dropped on to a stone floor. A grunt of terror and discomfort burst out of him; then he stood up straight and tottered towards Rutherford. 'I say,' he bleated, 'what *is* all this? Why do you want me, and what are we doing in this place?'

But Rutherford took no notice. 'Peters,' he called out. 'Come to the window.'

I looked at him again. 'Yes?'

'Why do you want me, and what are we doing in this place?'

'Your job is to take a message. Go to a telephone and ring Stevenson's father. Tell him that, if he wants his son back safely, it will cost him thirty thousand pounds. Tell him that we'll ring again to say where he should bring the money.'

Then, before I could reply, he seized Stevenson's arm and dragged him away up the quarry.

Instantly there was a buzz of excited conversation. Somebody put a head out of a window, warily. 'What do we do? Fetch the police?'

'No,' said a voice behind him. 'Better not do that. You know what happens when people are kidnapped and the police are called in.'

'Get the police,' I said. 'Somebody run back to the town and tell them.'

'But surely they'll have got Stevenson away by the time the police can get here?'

I felt the comforting outline of the car distributor in my pocket. 'I don't think so,' I said grimly. 'They'll be back in a minute, so send somebody quickly.'

A door on the opposite side of the carriage was flung open and someone landed with a thud, then raced away in the distance.

We waited.

It was a long wait. Far away I heard the whine of the car's self-starter. Round and round it went, briskly at first, then slowly and with an effort as the car batteries became exhausted. Then came clanking noises as someone tried to start the car with the handle. I leaned on the window ledge of the compartment, and listened.

Then footsteps pounded down the slope towards us. Simpson came into sight. Sweat was rolling down his face, and his shirt collar had been tugged open. 'Who's done it?' he screamed angrily, waving the pistol. 'Who's wrecked the car?'

Twenty-three grinning faces looked out of the windows towards him.

'Who's got the distributor? Must be one of you who knew about it all the time. Come on, or I'll start shooting.'

My heart thumped. He looked as if he meant it. I felt in my pocket. 'You mean this?' I called, holding it up.

'*You!* I might have known it would be you, Peters. Come on, hand it over.'

I held it up high.

'Chuck it to me. Quick!'

'All right,' I said. 'Catch!'

I threw it. But not to Simpson. Not for nothing was I the school champion at throwing the cricket ball. The distributor sailed high into the air, and came down in the thickest part of the jungle of bushes at the entrance to the quarry. There was a cry of anger and alarm from Simpson, then he raced back along the rails to search for it.

But he hadn't been gone two minutes when we heard the sound of car engines labouring along the rough road above the quarry. There were shouts in the distance, and then half a dozen police appeared. Simpson and Rutherford were handcuffed. Stevenson strolled along in front, still munching potato crisps.

It was over. I don't think Stevenson ever understood what had happened — or what was going to happen, but for the stroke of luck about the distributor. But his father did. Wildmere School closed down after the scandal, and Steve and I went to a new school next term. On our first day there a brand-new bicycle was waiting for me.

'Coo!' Stevenson burst out. 'What's the idea of my dad giving you a new bike? He hasn't given me one — and look how brave I was last term.'

'Brave?' I asked him. 'When were you brave?'

'What?' he said indignantly. 'Have you forgotten? I jumped from that carriage, right after breakfast, too.' Then, thoughtfully, he added: 'I was even braver than that. D'you realise all my food for the journey was in my case? And I left all that behind.'

THE DIZZYBOAT

Bob Larbery sighed. It wasn't that the *Kitty Susan* was a beautiful craft: she was old, stumpy, with a slightly lopsided look about her mast. But that didn't matter. She was a two-berth boat, Bermuda-rigged, with a hull that he knew was sound, because only at the end of the last summer he and his sister Betty had helped scrape, caulk and paint her — with old Mr Johnstone's firm promise that in return they'd have plenty of trips in her in the future.

Even the firmest promises go adrift. It wasn't Mr Johnstone's fault that his rheumatism had become so bad during the winter that he'd had to give up his job, retire five years early — and that meant he had so little cash that he'd been forced to put the *Kitty Susan* up for sale. And there she lay, in her usual berth, with a plywood notice tacked on the mast saying: FOR SALE — ALL FOUND — £150.

For all the money Bob Larbery had, it could just as well have been £15 or £1,500.

'You'd like her?'

It was Jim Rowfant, who owned the boat in the next berth, a neat, spankingly new thirty-footer called the *Ocean Ranger*. Bob nodded to him. 'I'd give my right arm for her. My left one, too, I think. But where would I get a hundred and fifty?'

Jim Rowfant grinned sympathetically. 'I know. I know just what you mean. If you've got boats in your blood, it's heartbreaking to see one like the old *Kitty Sue* up for sale when you haven't got a penny in your pocket.' He shook his head. 'You'll just have to wait until you're older. That's what I had to do.' He waved at his own boat. 'That's my fifth. I started off with a plank and two sheets of iron bolted together at the bow and stern to make the sides. That was thirty years ago, and the whole lot cost me about ninepence. What about taking on a job during the holiday? That way you could save up enough to buy a dinghy next year.'

Bob smiled ruefully. 'I suppose so. But what I really want is the *Kitty Susan*.' He walked away down the boardwalk between the lines of moorings, looking at each boat as he passed, waving to the people he knew, and eyeing with expert judgment the boats that hadn't been trimmed up yet for the new season. One or two of the older ones were down by the head; their nail-weary planks had opened during the long winter months, letting a dribble of water into the bilges every time the tide lapped against the hull.

But not the *Kitty Susan*. He looked back at her through the forest of masts; she rode high and proud, with last summer's paint still bright and new.

A hundred and fifty pounds. *Phew!* Ah well, he might as well forget it, unless the sky suddenly started raining money. He went back to where Betty was squatting on the pierhead, jerking the tip of her rod in a vain hope of tricking the small fish swarming in the water below.

'Well?' he asked.

Betty screwed up her face. 'Not a bite. All you can catch up here is a howling cold.'

'I know.' Bob took the rod from her chilled hands. 'What we need is a boat.'

'Oh yes,' she said scornfully. 'And a million pounds, and a big car, and a castle in Spain.'

'Old Mr Johnstone's *Kitty Sue*'s up for sale.'

'*What?* Oh no, don't say that!' Betty climbed to her feet. 'You're kidding, aren't you?'

'I'm afraid not. He needs the money, you know.'

She nodded. 'Yes, I know.' She looked down at the stone flags of the pierhead. 'How much is he asking?'

A hundred and fifty, sister dear,' replied Bob bitterly. 'So it's no use raiding your piggy-bank to buy her. I don't expect we could raise one pound between us. I was talking to Mr Rowfant. He said I ought to take a summer job during the holidays, and save up to buy a dinghy.'

'A dinghy? What use is that?'

'Better than nothing at all, Betty. Better than what he started with.' He stopped suddenly, staring into space. 'Crumbs!'

'Crumbs! What?'

'I wonder if we could do it?' Bob put down the rod, and whistled softly to himself. 'Where can we get some old sheets of galvanised iron?'

Betty looked at him blankly. 'I've no idea. Ask me another.'

'There's a junk-yard up at the back of the town. I've seen it — full of old cars and oil drums. Come on — and bust open that piggy-bank of yours on the way there!'

He set off at a run, leaving Betty to pack up the fishing-tackle. On the way he called in at the post office, and drew out the seventy-five pence he had in the savings bank. Then, at top speed, he raced up to the yards behind the railway track, where the top of a huge pile of abandoned cars could be seen sticking out above the coal trucks. The gate was wide open; he stood looking at the mountain of old junk and scratched his head in puzzlement, wondering where to begin.

'You want something, son?'

'Maybe,' said Bob cautiously. He eyed the bald-headed old man who popped up beside him as if from nowhere. 'But I bet you haven't got it. I'm after some galvanised iron.'

'Corrugated?'

Bob shook his head. 'Ordinary flat stuff. Strong, but it doesn't matter about sizes. Smaller the better, probably — it'll be easier to carry.'

The old man stroked his chin. 'There's a heap of it some-where around, if I can lay my hands on it.' He shaded his eyes, and stared at the pile of cars. 'Now where would it be?' Slowly his gaze travelled downwards, and he chuckled. 'You're on it, son. Twenty sheets of it. How much d'you want?'

Bob calculated feverishly. He hadn't got down to details as far as that. He tried to imagine the finished job, and himself alongside it, to compare the sizes. Then he glanced down at the heap of odd-shaped pieces under his feet, and back at the old man. 'How much are they?' he asked cautiously.

The old man shrugged his shoulders. 'Depends whether you want 'em delivered. If not, you can have 'em for ten pence each.'

Bob looked over his shoulder, desperately searching the road behind him for any sign of Betty. Not until she arrived would he know how much he dared spend. 'I shall need a bit of timber, too,' he said. 'Two long planks, strong and thick, and a lot of short bits.'

The old man looked him up and down. 'There's more old timber here than I've space for. Tell you what I'll do — I'll make you an offer. Have you got a handcart?'

Bob shook his head.

'I'll lend you one. Load it with as much of this old sheeting as you want, with your timber on top, and we'll call it an even quid. 'Ow's that for a bargain?'

A grin came bursting out on Bob's face. 'Done! It's a deal — and very generous of you.'

'Hullo, there!'

Bob turned. It was Betty, puffing and panting from a long run to catch up with him. 'I've got my money,' she gasped, 'but I'm not parting with a penny of it until I know what it's for.'

Bob stepped off the heap of galvanised-iron sheets. 'This, for a start. And some timber. We're going to build a boat!'

Betty's eyes bulged. 'You must have gone off your rocker. We can't build a boat out of this.'

'Are you willing to take a chance on twenty-five pence? I've got seventy five, and I need another twenty-five.'

Betty looked at him doubtfully. 'You honestly believe we can do it?'

'Look, sister dear, have you ever seen me throw away good money for nothing? I may be wrong, but so far I think I'm right. Come on, make up your mind, so that we can start loading the handcart.'

Half an hour later they were staggering back into the town, pushing a handcart that threatened to fall over at any moment, so high was it piled with planks and iron sheeting. Their faces were beetroot red with laughing, for all the way through the outskirts they'd kept on meeting friends, who'd stared at them and asked if they were setting up business as rag and bone merchants. They were thankful to reach their own driveway, and to wheel the handcart as quietly as they could past the back door and down to the old shed at the bottom of the back garden, where nobody minded what kind of mess they made.

Then, for five long and exhausting days, they made a mess such as nobody had ever seen in all the years they'd lived there. People walking on the shingle beyond the end hedge peered over in curiosity at the sound of hammers thumping the iron sheeting, and the squeal of the old hacksaw with which Bob hacked it into shape.

Gradually the boat grew. The two planks formed the keel, and scrap timber from the back of the shed became a series of ribs on to which they tacked the sheeting. They caulked the leaks with a sticky mixture of tar and sawdust, and then laboriously wheeled it out through the back gate, one end supported on a wheelbarrow, the other on the chassis of an old pram.

There were hoots of laughter from those who watched. Bob felt his cheeks growing red with fury, and he glanced at his sister. Hers were the same. 'Pay no attention,' she muttered. 'If we don't take any notice, they'll soon lose interest.'

She was right, of course. There's no fun in teasing if the person who's teased doesn't respond. They set the boat up on the sand, and then stirred up in a big can every scrap of paint they could find in the bottoms of old tins long forgotten in the depths of the shed. That was mainly Betty's job; she sat with the can in front of her, pouring in oddments of green, white, grey, pink, blue, black and a vivid yellow which had once been used with absolutely disastrous results for painting the cupboards in the kitchen. It looked like proving a disaster once again, for though there wasn't very much of it, it seemed to dominate all the other colours when she stirred them all together in the can. She was busy for the best part of an hour, while Bob worked his way over the boat with a file and emery paper, rubbing the rough edges down in readiness for painting.

'Ready?' he said at last.

Betty nodded. 'Here you are.' She glanced into the can, and made a face. 'It's a terribly unattractive colour... in fact, it's utterly horrible, but it'll have to do.'

Bob took the can, and peered inside. 'It's a sort of — well — really a kind of...'

'Dead seaweed?'

'Well, yes, I suppose that's about it.' He dipped his brush. 'Anyway, here goes!'

With two brushes in action it took them three hours to slap on a first coat. It dried quickly, and they were able to put on a second one later in the day. Then, exhausted and grubby, they stood back to look at the results.

Their eyes met, and both of them grinned.

'She doesn't really look too bad, does she?' said Betty.

'At least she looks like a boat. The colour doesn't much matter.'

'If she's dry, we'll launch her in the morning. Tonight let's have a rest.'

Bob shook his head. 'Mast and sails. And we'll need some kind of tiller to steer her. Let's have another look in the woodshed. There ought to be an old car tarpaulin in there. We can cut that up for sails.'

And so there was still no rest for either of them. While Bob constructed a mast and an oar, Betty stitched the heavy canvas into sails. It was the longest day since the work began, and they fell into bed so tired that they both woke late for breakfast.

But after breakfast they were all ready for the great moment. Unfortunately, as soon as they slipped out of the back gate on to the beach, they discovered half the town was also ready. There were crowds standing round the boat, pointing at her and laughing, and a great guffaw went up as they approached.

'You're not going to put *that* thing in the water, surely?' yelled somebody.

'You'd better call her the *Flying Saucepan*,' shouted another. He thumped his fist on the side, and the sound boomed and echoed through the hull.

Bob gritted his teeth, and remembered what Betty had said the previous day. He put his shoulder to the stern, and shoved. The boat moved gently down towards the water, now supported amidships by the pram chassis. He signalled to Betty, who clambered aboard. He'd remembered to secure the pram chassis on a long rope to a peg in the sands, and suddenly he felt the boat go free. He was standing in the water up to his ankles; he gave a final shove forward, then hauled himself over the gunwale. The boat rocked wildly, and there was another burst of laughter from the crowd.

'Quick!' shouted Bob. 'Grab the oar and keep her on course while I put up the sails.' He began hoisting them up the mast. The old oil-stained tarpaulin was heavy, but he got it to the masthead, and then secured the end of the heaving line to the foot of the mast. A gust of wind promptly filled the sails, and swung the bow of the boat in a rapid half-circle.

'Straighten her out!' he shouted to Betty.

'I can't.' Betty was wrestling with the oar in the stern, fighting to bring the frail boat back on to her course, but though they were moving farther out from shore they were still going in a circle. At each turn Bob had a moment's glimpse of a row of laughing faces on the beach, and over the top of the hedge his mother and father looking anxiously out to sea.

As well they might: for the circles were getting faster and faster, with the sails picking up gusts of wind from every direction at once, it seemed. Bob jumped to the stern and took over the oar. 'There's only one possible name for this tub,' he muttered.

'What's that?'

'The *Dizzyboat!*' He managed to smile as he said it, but he didn't feel like smiling. For there was no doubt about it, the boat was a failure. You couldn't build boats out of sheet-iron and scrap wood — otherwise everybody would be doing it, and the real boat-builders would all go out of business.

Wearily, he began fighting to bring the *Dizzyboat* back to the beach. It took an hour of hard labour, with Betty raising and lowering the sail according to which direction the boat was facing in her wild circles. He only gained real control when he was able to thrust the oar down and touch bottom, which served not only to steady the *Dizzyboat* on what he laughingly called 'her course', but also enabled him to push the boat along as if she were a punt. Finally, willing hands grabbed the bows and held her secure while he found the pram chassis, and wedged it under the keel. A dozen of the spectators helped to haul the *Dizzyboat* up the beach. One of them was Jim Rowfant. He shook his head admiringly. 'Hard luck, Bob! But it was a brave try. Better luck next time.'

'I don't think there'll be a next time,' said Bob gloomily. 'I haven't any money left to rebuild her. Anyway, I've learned my lesson. You can't go sailing on the cheap.'

Jim Rowfant looked from Bob to Betty and back again. 'Would you like to crew for today — both of you? It might take your minds off your troubles.'

'Gosh — yes, please! When do we start?'

'Right now. As soon as you've made this thing secure. We don't want her getting carried off by the tide, or she'll be a menace in the harbour. Right? All fixed? Then off we go.' He set off for the moorings, with Bob and Betty following close behind.

When Bob saw the *Ocean Ranger* again he had to swallow hard. She was such a beauty. He wondered if he'd ever manage to make enough money to have one like her. Still, he wasn't really all that ambitious. He'd settle quite happily for the *Kitty Susan,* lying forlorn in the next berth with the FOR SALE notice still tacked to the mast.

'Nobody's been to buy her yet, then?'

Jim Rowfant shrugged. 'Not that I've seen: It takes a long time to sell a boat. They're not like cars, you know, or houses. Plenty of people wouldn't even want a boat.'

Bob felt his eyes go glassy. 'They must be mad.'

Jim Rowfant threw back his head and laughed merrily. 'Now that's what I like to hear. You'll make a good sailor, Bob, if you think that way. The only man who's worth his salt on a boat is the kind who can't bear to be anywhere else.' He jumped aboard the *Ocean Ranger.* 'Come aboard! Betty, you take the tiller — only you're in luck this time: it's a wheel. Bob, you give me a hand with the sails, then fend her off gently as we move out.'

It was the start of a wonderful day. The *Ocean Ranger* handled beautifully, skimming across the sparkling water out of the bay and along the coast past the town. Bob glanced at Betty as she spun the wheel, bringing the *Ocean Ranger* on to a new tack towards the fishing-grounds where Jim Rowfant was hoping to bring up a few mackerel on a light line. She was smiling to herself; he could guess the daydream she was having, because he was having the same one himself.

The only trouble about the day was that it ended too quickly. Good days always did that, Bob thought ruefully as they came back to the moorings and made the *Ocean Ranger* secure for the week. Jim Rowfant put fifty pence into Bob's hand. 'Be a good sport and pop down in the evenings just to see she's all right.'

Bob returned the money. 'You don't have to pay me to do that.'

'But it would help in a small way towards saving for a boat. Every little bit counts, you know.'

'Look, Mr Rowfant, this won't be a job — it'll be a real pleasure.'

Slowly Jim Rowfant replaced the money in his pocket. 'Don't forget, then, that there's fifty pence a week whenever you want it. There's no boatman in charge here now, so to me it's a big help to know that someone's keeping an eye on the *Ocean Ranger.*'

Bob kept a very close eye, morning and evening. He adjusted the mooring-lines, moved the fenders when there was any risk that a change of current might chafe the *Ocean Ranger*'s sides against the *Kitty Susan* alongside. He took the job seriously, which is probably the reason why he jumped up in bed in the middle of the night when the wind suddenly howled round the house.

He sat bolt upright, listening. And then, above the noise of the wind, he heard the thunderous crash of waves against the breakwater outside the yacht basin.

He jumped out of bed and went to the window. Clouds were racing across the pale moon, but there was enough light to see the big white-topped seas smashing against the timber lock-gates that blocked the entrance to the yacht basin. Already one of the timbers — huge old railway-sleepers — had been knocked out of position.

He called Betty, then dressed hurriedly. They ran down to the beach, and looked out to sea.

'The breakwater's smashing up!' gasped Betty. 'Look, the whole of the top part has disappeared.'

She was right. The great seas thundering in from the Atlantic had shaken the breakwater so much that the concrete was beginning to crumble away, foot by foot, letting the waves crash over the top and race onwards towards the yacht basin.

Bob wiped the wet spray from his face. There was nothing they could do about the breakwater, but was there any way in which they could strengthen the lock-gate before the waves knocked away any more of the timbers? Fighting his way down the beach, he looked towards the rows of yachts at their moorings. Already those nearest the gate were beginning to pitch and roll; he heard them grinding together, and one began edging out to the limits of its mooring-lines.

'Quick!' he shouted. 'Help me to get the *Dizzyboat* into the water. Quick as you can!'

Betty looked at him in alarm. 'We can't take that thing out in this weather. You must be crazy!'

'Crazy or not, we've got to. There's fifty thousand pounds' worth of yachts lying out there, and if the seas break through they'll all be turned into matchwood.' Already he was wrenching at the rope which held the *Dizzyboat* in place on her pram chassis. It ripped out of his hands, and the wheels shot away down the beach, with the *Dizzyboat* rocking wildly on top.

The whole contraption hit the water with a crash; and they had barely time to leap aboard before the boat shot away from the beach, carried by a fierce current towards the lock-gate. There was no need to row; moving in rapid circles the *Dizzyboat* hit the lock-gate with a loud crash of crumpling sheet-iron. Water spouted up through holes in the side.

'Climb on to the gate!' yelled Bob, as he stumbled into the stern, with water already halfway up to his knees. And as Betty was straddling the gate, with waves up to her waist, he flung her the mooring-line. She heaved at it, and took a double turn round one of the railway-sleepers. Bob scrambled up beside her. Betty's eyes were wide with fright; he managed to grin at her. 'Water's cold, isn't it?' he said with forced calm, as if they'd just been in for a swim from the beach on a chilly day.

115

Feebly she smiled back, but her teeth were chattering. 'T-t-too c-c-cold. What do we do now?'

Bob wasted no time on words. He was already wrenching at the end of the sleeper which had been knocked out of position by the waves. Each time the seas fell back he shoved it an inch farther forward, then hung on grimly until his muscles cracked as the next wave tried to thrust it back again. 'Give me the end of the mooring-rope!' he shouted over his shoulder.

Betty pushed the wet rope into his hands, and he lashed the top of the sleeper to the one next to it: just in time, as a huge wave — the biggest yet — came thundering in towards them. He heard it before he saw it. 'Look out!' he bellowed. 'Hang on as hard as you can.'

The wave struck at shoulder height. Bob felt his grip on the sleepers wrenched loose, and he began to fall off the top of the lock; then Betty caught hold of the soaking wet shoulder of his jacket and hung on like a limpet. He could hear her gasping with the strain, but slowly she hauled him back into position as the wave ebbed back.

'*Phew!*' Bob blew out a lungful of water. 'Bless you, my little sister. Where did you get all that strength?'

'Eating up my crusts,' she spluttered. 'Bob, could we pull a few bits off the *Dizzyboat* to wedge in the top of the lock? They might help to keep the water out.'

'Good idea.' He looked down at the waterlogged hull dragging on the mooring-rope, then slid down the line until he was astride the bows. He took out his clasp-knife, and levered at the nails which held the iron sheeting to the timbers. The blade snapped at the first attempt and tore a lump out of his thumb, but with the broken blade he ripped out six nails, and was able to rip the metal away for a length of several feet. He kicked at the overlapping joints on which he'd spent so much time and trouble until they came apart, then lifted up a piece of sheet-iron four feet square. 'Grab it!' he called out, and pushed it into Betty's outstretched hands.

Then Betty caught hold of the soaking wet shoulder of his jacket

He wriggled back into position beside her, and they pushed the sheeting into the gaps between the timbers, bending it and twisting it to help support the lock against the pounding seas. Bob's shoulders ached with the effort. Betty, her wet hair streaming out like rats' tails in the wind, was white with exhaustion.

Another huge wave hit them. The lock-gate shook and the timbers rumbled, but they held in place.

'Hooray!' said Bob feebly. 'I think she's going to last the night.'

'Yes, but are *we*? How do we get ashore again?'

Bob looked at the narrow concrete catwalk which led up to the wooden gate on either side; as he looked, yet another wave crashed against it. Anybody trying to wriggle along its smooth surface wouldn't stand a chance if a wave came. 'We don't,' he replied. 'We stay here. We'll have to.'

And so began a long battle against the cold and exhaustion. They clung on, too tired to talk, too tired to do anything except fight each new wave as it came. They heard the church clock in the distance strike four o'clock, then five, then six. In the east the sky became gradually lighter.

It was a quarter to seven by the clock when they saw a policeman riding his bicycle up the rough road at the top of the beach. They waved frantically, and shouted. Bob tore off his shirt and held it high above his head, using one arm as a flagpole.

The policeman stopped, and got off his bicycle. He shaded his eyes against the wind, and peered out towards them.

'He's seen us!' gasped Betty. 'Look, he's waving his arm.'

They watched as the policeman mounted his bicycle hurriedly and pedalled towards the town.

Five minutes later two cars came to a halt on the rough road. People were running behind them, and then came a lorry with a big inflatable pontoon. Dozens of willing hands helped to carry it to the water; three men climbed aboard, and began rowing it towards them as others on the beach paid out a securing-line. Nearer and nearer came the rescuers, until finally the pontoon bumped against the foot of the lock-gate.

Bob helped Betty scramble down, then jumped in beside her.

Ten minutes later he was waiting for his turn in a hot bath.

They stayed indoors, resting, all day — though the rest was interrupted by a constant stream of visitors. It was at teatime that Jim Rowfant turned up.

'Thanks,' he said, shaking them by the hand. 'I ... well, I just don't know what to say.'

'Is the *Ocean Ranger* all right?' asked Bob anxiously.

'No damage that a spot of paint won't fix. In fact, every boat in the harbour is safe, thanks to the pair of you.' He reached into his pocket, but Bob shook his head.

'No,' he said, 'I told you already — I don't want that fifty pence.'

'*Fifty?*' Jim Rowfant threw back his head and laughed. 'This isn't fifty pence. It's a cheque — from all of us who have yachts in the basin.'

'But...'

'No buts,' said Jim Rowfant firmly. 'This time I insist. You saved all our boats — thousands of pounds' worth.' He took the cheque out of his pocket. 'There's a funny coincidence about this.' He handed Bob the cheque.

'Gosh,' exclaimed Bob, 'it's for a hundred and fifty pounds!'

'Yes, that's what I meant by the funny coincidence.'

'I don't understand.'

'Surely you do? Isn't that exactly the price that's being asked for the *Kitty Susan?*'

Bob looked at Betty, and Betty looked at Bob. They were both thinking the same thing. The *Dizzyboat* hadn't been exactly a success, but she'd done one thing. She'd earned them the *Kitty Susan!*

MURDER IS FOR MEN

Insurance companies, doctors and the police are familiar with the term 'accident-prone' — when applied to people who just can't help being involved in accidents.

Policemen, especially those in the detective branch, are also familiar with a similar proneness which can be called a form of accident. Most crooks will claim it to be an accident when they are arrested. Crooks gamble on not being caught. Some crooks are more clever, or more lucky, than others. A very few are never caught. Others are caught every time they break the law. Well, that's the way of it, and nobody has worked out just why it should be so.

A lesser-known form of proneness is that of becoming accidentally involved with crimes — usually as a witness. The police know all about this and every experienced officer can recite examples. These unlucky witness-prone people often go through a period of being suspected of committing a crime — or being concerned in one — merely because they were there when it happened.

Chad Stenson was witness-prone. To begin with, his first name of Chadwick was given him in honour of a supposedly wealthy uncle, who had promised to make the boy his heir. Unfortunately, Uncle Chadwick spent a lot of other people's money, stole a few thousands more and was killed in a car smash while trying to escape from the police at a border post. So even Chad's name was linked with a criminal.

During Chad's last months at school he witnessed the theft of a car — solely because he was interested in cars and had been observing an expensive model when the thief drove off in it. Chad's first job in a shop — which he hated, so soon departed — enabled him to witness some neat shoplifting. His evidence caused a whole gang of expert shoplifters to be caught.

Chad's next job was on a local newspaper. Interesting work which sent him running around town on errands instead of being shut inside a building all day. On one of those errands Chad saw a child hit by a car driven by a very important local resident. The car didn't stop, but owing to Chad's quick thinking and good memory the police overtook it and forced the driver to halt. The very important resident was good and drunk, and the case created a lot of fuss — Chad being a key witness. Once again his proneness was observed by the police. There was no suggestion that Chad personally had had anything to do with these three crimes. He just happened to be there when they occurred. Other people go through a lifetime without even witnessing a car accident.

After a couple of jobs Chad began to develop an ambition to work in television. Through the influence of the newspaper editor Chad was taken on at the local studios, Skyway TV. During his first week, leaving the studios late one night, Chad fell over a ladder. Nursing his injured knee he went to the night watchman's office for first aid. The watchman checked the ladder and found burglars had entered the administration offices on the second floor. Chad helped to capture them, and thus was a witness yet again.

These experiences do not explain why Fate singled out Chad Stenson as a witness, but they do explain why he developed a keen interest in police work. Not that he wanted to be a policeman. He was more keen than over to remain in television work. But having made so many statements as a witness, appeared in court to give evidence and observed police procedure at a crime, Chad became a student of crime. Not as a reader of crime books but as a worker-out of crimes.

He pondered a great deal on the ways different people

committed crimes. Not spur-of-the-moment crimes, like drunken driving, although Chad wondered why a man who was supposed to be intelligent could ever risk driving knowing he was drunk. Chad classed that sort of man as a fool.

But the crimes committed by professional crooks puzzled Chad even more. Many such crimes weren't carried out because of hunger but just to get as much money for as little work as possible. Yet most of these crooks were caught, and often by making silly mistakes. The man who'd stolen that flashy new car, for example: why had he ignored a boy standing only a short distance away? He might have known the boy — Chad himself — would be a witness. And why steal a distinctive-looking car like that, anyway? Why not a new, but more ordinary model?

Same with smash-and-grab crooks. Chad thought they chose the wrong times. And those shoplifters — well, they'd been too greedy. If they hadn't tried to lift so much stuff Chad wouldn't have noticed them. Stupid, they were, Chad thought. All of them — just plain stupid.

Same with the burglars. Why leave a ladder standing at a place where obviously no ladder ought to be? And at that time, too. Had they waited another half-hour, all the TV technicians and staff would have been gone. No one would have fallen over the ladder. If *I* ever commit a crime, said Chad to himself, I'll plan everything to the last detail.

He was thinking about crime and the stupidity of most crooks when he fell over the body in the studio driveway.

Experience stopped Chad from panic. The man was huddled up close to the hedge, well off the smooth-surfaced car section. Chad remembered police advice. 'Never touch anything,' Inspector Dooly had told him. 'Never pick up an injured person. Wait for a doctor. You might kill them by moving them. In other words — keep off and contact the police.'

Chad ran up the driveway to Reception, and did just that. Inspector Dooly groaned when the call came through.

Detective-Sergeant Duff looked sympathetic.

'Trouble, sir?'

'That was an old friend of yours. The boy wonder-witness himself!'

'Not Chad Stenson?'

'It was indeed.'

'Don't tell me he's witnessed something else?'

Dooly reached for his hat. 'He's found a body. Let's go.'

'A body?' Duff muttered disbelievingly. 'The boy wonder is getting ambitious, isn't he?'

'My very thoughts,' the Inspector agreed as they headed for the car park.

The police car drove up the long driveway and swung into the circular parking-space. Chad stepped forward.

'Well?' the Inspector snapped. 'What fool's moved it?'

Chad gulped, coughed. 'Moved what, sir?'

'The body, of course.'

'Er — no one, sir. When I went back after phoning you — the body had gone.'

Inspector Dooly sighed gently.

'How kind of it!' Gimlet eyes glared at Chad. 'You're sure it really was there, Chad?'

'Yes, sir.'

'Couldn't have been, could it?' said Sergeant Duff softly. 'I mean — a body stays put. So it couldn't have been a body.'

'It looked like one,' said Chad, wishing he was in two other places. 'A man — all huddled up, not moving. I didn't touch him, though.'

The Inspector nodded. 'Notice what he was wearing?'

'Brown overcoat, ragged at the sleeves, creased across the back. I couldn't see the front because he was lying half on his face. I thing he had black and white check trousers and black elastic-sided shoes.'

'Very observant, aren't you?' Then Dooly added quickly: 'Yes, we know that from experience, don't we?'

'Photographic eyes,' Duff added.

126

'Sarky,' said Chad, stung to anger. 'I notice things. Is that a crime?'

'Giving false information can be a crime,' Duff retorted. 'Making a public mischief, wasting police time —'

'All right, Sergeant,' the Inspector interrupted. 'I think Chad acted in good faith.' He paused to glance back down the driveway. 'Pretty dark down there. How could you see colours?'

Chad pointed to a building — three-storeyed, flat-roofed — standing apart from the main studios.

'The top floor is Brian Foxglove's apartment. He's onstage now, but when I came up the drive all the lights were on. He'd be getting ready in his dressing-room — that room at the end. Uses very bright tube lighting.'

'No curtains?'

'No, sir. The light streamed across the drive. That's how I could see.'

The Inspector nodded. 'All right, Chad. Better safe than sorry. But just be more careful next time. G'night.'

The policemen stepped into their car and were driven away. The studio doorkeeper said: 'You've got three minutes before the red light goes on.'

Chad spun around. 'Thanks, George!' and bolted into the building.

'Ur!' the doorkeeper growled. 'Bodies! Got some imagination, these kids 'ave.'

One minute left as Chad stumbled into the studio, hopped and skipped over writhing trails of power cables, ducked under the sound-boom trolley and reached the first caption board.

'I'll murder you!' the studio manager hissed. 'Forty seconds, and you just arrive. Who d'you think you are — Sweet Lily?' He grinned. 'Go on — grab your board!'

A brassy-voiced loudspeaker spoke urgently.

'Twenty seconds!'

More lights flared on. Blue-glow filled the backdrop.

Shadows over the unlit sets, glare over the opening interview set where two figures sat miming. Cameras tracked up, hiding the figures from Chad's view.

A camera facing him edged in, zoom lens peering.

'Ten seconds!' said the disembodied voice. 'Turn profile on the intro, Bob; we'll take you on three.'

The announcer, poised amid tangling cables, didn't query the order. 'Will do.' He turned slightly.

The studio manager, earphone cable trailing, came crab-like on his knees past Chad to crouch under camera B.

'Live!' said the voice. 'Let's go!'

Music flowed up, filling the dark cavern of the roof above the sets — faded down. The motionless announcer began to work at his smile, watching the monitor.

Chad ducked down as the camera facing him relayed the captions, lens angle changing slightly. Chad watched his monitor.

Skyway Presents . . .
The World in your Day
People who Matter
What Matters to People

The monitor showed captions off and close-up of announcer. 'Tonight we are glad to be able once again to present Brian Foxglove interviewing people who matter . . .' His voice ambled on, flowing honey-and-buttered words.

Chad scarcely heard it. He was busy changing captions, checking the script. When all was ready for the next shot of his caption board he crouched down, watching the action in his monitor.

Brian Foxglove — relaxed, immaculate, suave — was interviewing a personality, feeding in the right questions, eyes moving cleverly to watch monitor, studio manager, his notes and his victim all at the same time. A great art — so they said. Looked so easy, but that was all part of the skill of this new profession. The Interview Man.

Chad wanted to be an interview man. He knew what everyone thought about Brian Foxglove. Sweet Lily, they called him around the floor. So he was. Sweet-smelling, silk-suited, every hair casually arranged, make-up shaded just right, hands manicured, tie a wee bit out of line to show he really hadn't bothered to dress well. Voice softly warm, eyes crinkling a little around the corners. They said he sucked a lump of sugar soaked in some kind of spirit ten minutes before he went on-set, so that his eyes shone. The women loved him. He received hundreds of letters every day. The studio hated him. They cut him out for a week, but women callers jammed the phones, shoaled in letters of protest, even queued all day in the drive to voice personal protests at losing 'their Brian'.

That was why the announcer had to lard it up on the intro with his 'glad to be able once again to present Brian Foxglove'. The studio had given out that he'd been overworking. Actually the big chiefs had been fighting all week, up there in the flat overlooking the driveway. Skyway TV had fourteen directors. Ten cared only for profits and audience ratings. Four cared for quality and culture. Brian Foxglove played four against ten — and won.

Bob Andrews moved past Chad on his way to the next announcing spot. He winked at Chad, jerked his thumb in the direction of Skyway's gift to gasping womanhood, and whispered: 'Witless nit.'

'Phooey!' Chad whispered. 'You're jealous.'

Bob grinned. 'Why should I be? He only gets two hundred a week more than me. At least I get a pension. He won't live that long.' Bob straightened, walked behind a set, and then reappeared in front of a camera on the other side of the floor.

The first interview closed. Chad's camera swung in on the captions, faded up for six seconds, then trundled away to position for its next shot. Bob Andrews spoke his piece. Silent but urgent movement at another set as Brian Foxglove crept into his seat to face the next apprehensive victim. Cameras slithered and shunted around him.

He glanced at the monitor, using it as a mirror, and carefully coaxed a tendril of hair out of place. It took a little coaxing because the casual hair style was set solid by a spirit spray, but Brian Foxglove liked to appear slowly more dishevelled as the programme continued. He looked more natural that way.

'Works so hard too,' quoth his admiring viewers. 'Looks fair exhausted by the end of the show, he does, poor dear.'

The studio grew hotter under the lights. Make-up experts with their loaded trays pattered softly over cables, wiping shiny foreheads and noses and eartips with spirit, dabbing on powder, wiping eyebrows. Sweating eyebrows gleam like frosted half-moons under top-lighting.

The cameras never ceased their restless shunting back and forth. The cables slithered and stretched and coiled. The sound-boom trolley trundled in and out, its mast dipping and rising as the mike was winched highed or lower. The auto-cues fixed below each camera's eye moved obediently at the touch of a man sitting way back in the shadows, watching script and remote-control auto-cue, synchronising with the camera so that not a line was muffed or a cue missed.

On the skeleton walks above the flare and bustle, technicians reset lights, raised or lowered backdrops. Watching all the time — not people, but machines and switches and gear.

Somewhere behind the tall 'flats' upon an iron staircase, the long low control room squatted, bug-eyed, filled with noise and flickering screens above a console of dials and knobs and switches. Here the producer, his secretary and technical assistants worked amid a seemingly chaotic tumult of sights and sounds.

Roy Eden, the producer, was linked by microphone to his assistant on the studio floor — the quiet-voiced man who slithered, crouching, between cameras, cables, sets and participants in the programme. Through this link came Roy

Eden's directions to: 'Close up on two, take back one, tell that fool to smile less. Spread it — we're four seconds under,' and so on.

And from out of the apparent confusion there emerged on to the transmission screens the easy-moving sequences of presenting 'people who matter', and 'what matters to people'. The brief pauses in live transmission, while the natural break beamed out its gabbling advertisements, were used to reposition cameras, mikes, caption boards; soothe nervous personalities whose camera appearances were yet to come; adjust make-up and grapple with some technical fault which refused to become apparent during rehearsals. Technical faults, from blown fuses to cut cables, seem always to wait for the live transmission.

Each camera-man, sound-technician, lighting-engineer and his respective assistant concentrated on their own task, oblivious to sweatingly nervous guests fidgeting on the sets and more sophisticated professional performers who flicked over script pages and cursed the cuts in their juiciest lines.

This packed jungle of men and machines fascinated Chad, and he sped through his share of the behind-the-cameras work so that he could watch how everything was done. He didn't have a lot to do, and part of his job was to watch and listen and learn what went on around him. He'd learned how not to rush and tear about, even though the slave-driving stop-watch flayed his efforts, as it did all who took part in putting a live programme on the air.

As far as the personalities were concerned, the show was unscripted. That is — they didn't see a script, but were fed questions by the interviewer. All they had to do was answer in as natural a manner as possible. Brian Foxglove did the rest. It was he who held his script below the camera angle and glanced at his 'feed' lines and notes on each guest. It was he who watched the crouching man with the earphones who signalled 'speed to close' if the merciless seconds had been overrun.

Each camera had its allotted timing for tracking in and back, for zooming to close-up, for panning to some object held in the interviewer's hands. Of three cameras bunched around a set, one would pull out a few seconds before that interview finished and position itself on a caption board holding material for the next shot. Each camera-man had his own script and sections of the floor marked with what looked like mystic symbols made by chalk — to remind him of the various positions for his camera.

Brian Foxglove used every opportunity to dominate the screen, often forcing an extra shot on himself by over-speaking his victim. Roy Eden would curse softly through his sound link, but his assistants in the control room had to switch Brian's close-up to the transmitting-screen. They couldn't hold a shot on a silent personality. Brian knew this and hogged every camera angle he could make them use.

This hidden battle in the rat-race of TV personalities went on grimly throughout all Brian Foxglove's appearances. Afterwards, at the get-together for drinks on the house, he always apologised profusely for over-speaking, or ignoring camera cues. He did this with a pathetically boyish air of fatigued bewilderment which fooled all but the hardened producer and his equally hardened and cynical staff.

If Brian Foxglove had come right out and complained that he wasn't receiving enough screen time they could have fought him and won, because, after all, he was there to interview people who mattered. But the sweetly cunning Brian never made an open fight of it — he merely sabotaged everyone he could while the show was live.

At first Chad admired Brian Foxglove and reckoned him tops in the interview racket. But after a few weeks on the programme he didn't admire Brian quite so much: when Chad grew to know the men and women who worked hard for long hours to put the programme on the air, he found them more skilled, more honest and certainly more reliable and human. He even began to resent the tricks Brian Foxglove played to boost himself at the expense of the producer and technicians. Sometimes Brian made trouble for those people by fouling their directions so that it appeared they hadn't carried out their orders properly.

Chad was sensible enough to realise that some of his studio associates were perhaps slightly jealous of Brian Foxglove. They were all highly skilled employees of Skyway TV, and it was human to resent one person receiving about eight times as much pay as they did, and for considerably less work. Stage and film stars, experienced actors and others who were paid high fees for TV appearances were different, because most of them had had a long, hard struggle to reach the top of their profession.

Brian Foxglove had not. In fact, nobody knew where he'd come from when Adrian Fellowes introduced him to the programme. He talked big about his travels — presumably he'd been all over the world — and spoke casually of films he had produced and directed. But no one had ever seen these films on the screen. When faced with this he explained airily that they had been made abroad. Thus the image of Brian Foxglove impacted itself in two extremes each side of the cameras.

Each night, twenty million pairs of eyes goggled at him on the viewing-side of the screen. Women's magazines ran competitions, with first prize including dinner and escort to a theatre with Brian Foxglove. Old ladies loved him like a son. Young ladies pinned his likeness above their beds. Teenage lads copied his hair style, his suits, shirts and ties. Grown men, for some reason, hated his guts — as did most of the people on the transmitting side of the screen. It was an explosive situation, but worth thousands in advertising revenue to Skyway TV's directors.

The lull in activity on the studio floor when a filmed sequence splits the live show has a weirdly suspended appearance. The first few seconds are consumed by the usual regrouping of people, cameras, sound booms, caption boards and monitors, ready for the next studio relay. But after that, everyone more or less 'freezes' in his anticipated position.

Nearly all key personnel stand, sit or crouch — silent and motionless, watching the monitor screens and listening to the sound-track feed-back so that on the exact second when the film ends they are ready for the studio again becoming 'live'.

Assistants and junior personnel, like Chad, the trolley-handlers, prop-men and make-up girls, stay more or less motionless, but exchange whispered conversation or mime at one another by grins, nods, winks and other facial contortions. Some merely gaze around, some stare at the floor, lost in their private dreams. Most are bored, because probably they've seen and heard the film insert run through five or six times during rehearsals.

Having completed his own tasks Chad checked his script to see all was correct, received the thumbs-up sign from his camera-man, then gazed at the poised tableau of the studio. His gaze wandered up into the cavernous shadows above and beyond the lighted floor.

Chad couldn't see anything overhead because the banked rows of limes and arcs flooded down in blinding intensity, although he knew men were up there in the cable galleries — poised and waiting as were those on the floor. But ahead of him stretched the new studio extension; and, above that, he could see ghostly arms spindling to the floor. These were the partially completed girders and struts of the upper section of galleries and stairways.

A canted portable floodlight etched a path of light upwards, its beam fading into the blackness. Chad could see the big notice at the head of the stairway leading from his end of the studio: HIGH VOLTAGE — DANGER . He knew the words by heart, for they appeared in many places around the studios, where power cables snaked and writhed to and from main fuses and switch-boxes.

Behind Chad, two make-up girls chattered in whispers.

'You're a fool, Brenda,' one was saying. 'You might know *he's* not the type to mean anything he says.'

'He'd better mean it.' The other girl spoke in a harsh voice. 'Or I'll kill him — that's what I'll do. I'm telling you, Phyl — I'll kill him!'

The producer's floor assistant turned his head, raised a finger warningly and pursed his lips in a 'sh-sh'. Chad heard the girls move away. The man winked solemnly at Chad, who winked back. Then Roy Eden's voice in the assistant's earphones said:

'If Brian pulls it again on the pistol-man's spot, I'll cut to the pistols and hold it until he finishes, so keep number two on those pistols, chum. Got it?'

The man nodded and spoke close to the mike hanging on his chest. 'Got it. Will do!'

'Okay, Ernie — stand by. Ninety seconds to run.'

The assistant moved away. Chad resumed his upward gaze. He barely restrained a yelp of surprise as he saw, clearly focused in the beam from the canted floodlights, the figure of a man. A slightly familiar figure wearing an old brown overcoat, black and white check trousers. The shaft of light against the blackness illuminated the figure as if on a photograph. Then the man moved into the gloom, passed the danger sign and disappeared.

Seventy of the ninety seconds had passed and the studio began to stir from its poised suspension. Brian Foxglove eased another strand of hair out of place and started to mime with the pistol-man across a low table covered with a collection of guns.

'Ten seconds!' A voice overrode the fading sounds of the film.

The announcer glanced up at the control room.

'Five seconds!' said the voice.

'Hey up!' said a new voice. 'One of me guns is missing.'

'Quiet!' the producer's assistant hissed, and hurried towards the set.

'Pistols,' said Bob Andrew. 'They go bang. Or do they? Tonight we have Mr Anetone Marcos, whose collection of most unusual pistols is world famous. Brian Foxglove will let you into the mystery . . .'

The announcer's camera swung away. Chad's camera flashed the name of Anetone Marcos. Control mixed the caption so that it became superimposed under the man's head and shoulders.

'Call me Annie,' Marcos boomed. 'Everyone does.'

Brian Foxglove crinkled his eyes, warmed his smile patronisingly into the zoom lens and opened his mouth to speak.

'They have, y'know,' said the completely unembarrassed Annie. 'Pinched the ruddy thing, they have. The big 'un.'

'It will be found, my dear Annie, never fear,' Brian cooed, making furious hand gestures under the camera. 'But what a fascinating man you are. A lifetime's experience with guns has enabled you to produce what I believe you call a fluid gun.' Brian beamed into the camera. 'Such an intriguing name.'

'Aye — but never mind about that,' said Marcos. 'Who's pinched the ruddy big 'un?' He glared around the cameras. 'Which of you lot's got it? Come on now!'

'Lovely, lovely!' Roy Eden's voice came through the earphones. 'This is real punchy stuff! Whoever finds that flaming gun is sacked.'

'Now, Annie, whilst our friends are looking . . . Brian fought to regain control of the interview.

'I ain't fooling,' Marcos interrupted. 'Are you sitting on it? Hoist yourself and let's have a look.'

'Well, really —' Brian began, but the remorseless monitor reflected his suddenly harassed expression. Swiftly he put his smile back on and stood up. His script and notes cascaded to the floor. The studio buzzed with titters of laughter.

Then abruptly came a harsh hissing — a flash of blue-white light, a puff of smoke above Brian Foxglove's head.

Slowly, almost gracefully, his body arched, spun and fell.

A woman screamed. The set blacked out. The relay circuit was cut.

Roy Eden's voice called: 'Don't panic! Cut to trio. Step in, Bob. Ad-lib until the cameras cue in.'

A few seconds of disorder before discipline took over. The cameras lurched across to the jazz trio. Bob Andrews ad-libbed with cajoling skill.

'A fuse blew out.' He grinned. 'Now wouldn't you know that would happen to us. Never mind . . .'

'He's dead,' said the spectral voice of Anetone Marcos. 'He is, y'know. Ruddy well dead, he is.'

* * *

The studio was a sad, drab ghost of its previous self. Cameras were cold, shrouded pillars of steel — inert electronic boxes. Microphones were mute buds of metal spiked on spindle-shanked stalks. The sets were cubby-holes of sham, with tatty curtains hanging in grimy folds across artificial windows. Faded blue backdrops reflected bare-bulbed lighting, like the inside shells of gutted refrigerators.

Massive pilot lights seemed to lose three-quarters of their power and gave only minimum reflection — accentuating instead of decreasing the black-folded sound insulation below the cable galleries. Two portable floods shone a fan of light across one side of the studio, where police detectives worked around the chalked outline on the floor.

The programme's guests, as well as the body of their late host, had departed, after giving names and addresses and statements to patiently inquiring policemen. Now it was the turn of the production staff and technicians.

Inspector Dooly was assisted by Sergeant Duff and more detectives than Chad Stenson had ever seen assembled in one place. He'd been among the first to be questioned.

'Well, at least we didn't receive the phone call from you,' Sergeant Duff observed.

Inspector Dooly looked at Chad.

'But you were here, weren't you?'

'Yes, sir.'

'Were you a witness to what happened?'

'Well, I —' Chad began when the Inspector interrupted him.

'Now listen to me, son.' Dooly dug his finger into Chad's chest with stabbing prods of emphasis. 'You've been a sort of boy-wonder witness, and we've tried to be kind to you in the past because we realised you were witness-prone. Know what I mean?'

'Yes, sir.'

'Right. Then let's make this perfectly clear. If you *actually saw* what happened, then tell me every detail. If you did not see what happened, then don't waste my time. This isn't a case of car stealing or shoplifting — it's a case of murder. And murder is for men. Not boys who *think* they saw bodies, or heard this or that. I want facts. Understand?'

'Yes, sir.'

'Did you see what happened?'

'No, sir. I was behind a caption board. I heard a hissing noise and saw what appeared to be an extra bright light. I thought perhaps a bank of lights had fused. I looked around the board, saw some smoke in the air near number one camera, and Brian Foxglove falling.'

'But you didn't see anything else?'

'No, sir. But before then, while the film was being run, I saw —'

'No, thank you,' said Dooly firmly. 'Apart from the fact that we've already experienced the results of your vivid imagination once today, I want answers to my questions — nothing else.'

Chad shrugged. 'If you say so, sir.'

'I do so say. Did you see the missing pistol?'

'I saw the pistols on the table during rehearsals. I picked several up to look at them.'

'Including the largest one?'

'I saw it, but didn't touch it because it looked heavy.'

'At what time did you see it?'

'On my way out for the break af five o'clock. We had an hour's break after rehearsals. I was coming back from the break when I saw the body.'

'You mean the body that never was,' said Sergeant Duff. Chad flushed angrily, but kept his mouth shut.

'So you last saw the large pistol at five o'clock?'

'Yes, sir.'

'As we have witnesses who saw it more than an hour later, we shan't need you as a witness.'

'That'll be a change,' said Sergeant Duff.

'And phooey to you too!' Chad retorted childishly, although perhaps naturally in the circumstances. 'Anyone would think I made up stories just to be a witness.'

Sergeant Duff chuckled. 'I bet you'd just love to make one up now. This case is a lulu. Think of the publicity you'd get. A witness to a murder in front of twenty million people.'

'How d'you know he was murdered?' Chad asked.

'He had a singe and haircut,' said the cold-blooded sergeant. 'Electrocuted right through his little noddle.'

'Electrocuted!' Chad gasped. 'I thought he was killed by the missing gun?'

Inspector Dooly shrugged. 'I've heard of a few unusual murder weapons, but I've never known anyone killed by a water-pistol.'

'A water-pistol!'

'Well — a rather special high-powered one. It's been designed for use by bank guards and cashiers. Tonight it was charged with ordinary water, but normally it would fire a stream of special liquid dye. The bank thief or robbers couldn't wash it off. The liquid might even temporarily blind them. We'd like to find the pistol, but it certainly couldn't kill anyone.' The Inspector frowned. 'Why do I always feel I have to explain things to you? Go on — hop it, but don't leave the building.'

'I can't help any more?'

'I doubt it.'

'Okay,' said Chad. 'G'night.' He moved out of the fan of light into the shadows where others waited, uneasily.

'What a mess,' said Bob Andrews. 'Poor old Brian certainly went out in a most spectacular fashion.'

'Are you sorry?' Chad asked.

Bob looked surprised. 'Naturally I am.'

'I thought you hated him?'

'I thought I did too. But it didn't go very deep. For me, he was a man who lived but wasn't loved. Death earns a respect which life denies us.'

'Sergeant Duff said that Brian was electrocuted,' said Chad. 'How could that happen?'

Bob shook his head. 'I don't know, laddie. Doesn't seem possible to me. I think the sergeant was wrong to tell you that.'

'Why?'

'Because I heard the police doctor say he *thought* that Brian died as a result of electrocution, but he'd know more after his autopsy.'

'What's an autopsy?' Chad asked.

'A sort of medical examination after a person had died in mysterious circumstances. A doctor may say that death appeared to be caused by high-voltage electricity, or shock, or poison, but he cannot be certain until he's made a thorough examination. Brian could have suffered a brief shock from a loose cable, or something like that, but he might have died from a weak heart. It's very tricky, to be sure.'

'But if he died of a weak heart, it wouldn't be murder, would it?'

Bob shrugged. 'If somebody deliberately caused a loose high-voltage wire to touch Brian, then it might well be attempted murder or manslaughter.'

'The viewers must have had a shock,' said Chad.

'They didn't see it. The cameras were on the pistols and

on that Annie character. Then the producer cut the whole set. so at present no one outside the studio will know Brian is dead.'

Chad suddenly remembered something.

'Excuse me, Bob. Got to rush.'

Bob grinned. 'Don't go farther away than the toilet, old son. The Inspector has sealed off all exits. I've tried, but it looks as if we're here for the night.'

'Thanks for the tip.' Chad circled behind the sets, slipped out of the studio by a door which led into the passage to the offices. There was no policeman stationed by this almost hidden exit from the studio floor.

Chad entered one of the secretaries' offices and closed the door quietly. He switched the phone to an outside line, dialled a number and waited.

'*Morning News,*' said a brisk voice.

'Hullo, Gertie. Chad Stenson here.'

'Hi, Chad! How's TV treating you? Are you a producer yet?'

'Not yet.' Chad grinned. 'Gertie, is Dick Tarrant in the building?'

'I expect so. That man almost lives here. Our chief reporter and permanent boarder! You want?'

'Yes, please.'

'Hold on.'

Chad heard the telephonist ringing through to several departments before she located the chief reporter.

'Canteen, as usual,' said Gertie. 'Here he is, Chad.'

'Thanks.' Chad waited.

'Tarrant here. That you, Chad? What's up? Been witnessing some more smash and grabs?'

'Something like that.'

'Got anything useful for me?' Dick Tarrant asked.

'Very useful. As big a scoop as you'll ever have.'

'Talk, brother, talk!'

'You've got to promise me something first.'

'All my blood — and as much of the paper's cash as they'll let me pay you.'

'More than that.' Chad chuckled.

'Shylock! Okay — what?'

'I want fullest co-operation any time I phone or call for information. There's a certain person whom I've only seen once — no, twice,' Chad corrected himself. 'I've just remembered that he looked very much like someone who figured in a feature story you did when I worked for the *News*. I might want to check back in a hurry.'

'Who is he?'

'Don't know for sure. I'm only guessing at present. But you'll have photos.'

'Then his picture will be in the morgue, and we'll check through back numbers for you. Co-operate all the way. That's a promise. Now give, brother, give!'

'This hasn't been released to anyone as far as I know, Dick. You'll have to handle it carefully — it's red-hot.'

'And keep you out of it? Okay, shoot.'

'Brian Foxglove is dead.'

'*What!* How?'

'The police think it's murder.'

'Oh, brother — *broth-er!*' Dick Tarrant's voice grew tense. 'Right — pencil poised. Give out, Chad — fast and true.'

Chad gave out. His experience of how reporters worked helped him to explain all the facts without rambling. Dick Tarrant was duly appreciative when at last Chad said:

'That's all the facts as I know them, Dick.'

'Enough for us to get a beat on every paper in the country. We won't forget this, young Chad. You got theories, suspects — studio gossip?'

'No,' said Chad firmly. 'I work here. It wouldn't be loyal if I gave you gossip. You can dig that yourself. I've got a theory right enough, but I've given you the facts and that's all you're getting from me.'

'Okay — I won't push you. You'll be seeing me up there

soon. Contact the paper whenever you want help. We'll be your slaves. For a couple of days, anyway. Bye now.'

Chad left the office, ran on tiptoe along passages to the toilets, then back to the studio. A policeman halted him and asked:

'Where d'you think you're going?'

'Into studio A3. The Brian Foxglove show.'

'What's your name?'

'Chad Stenson.'

The policeman referred to a list of names.

'How did you get out of the studio?'

'By a door. Now I'm going back.'

'Don't get funny with me,' the policeman growled. Then probably realising he'd be in trouble for allowing Chad to leave the studio without being seen by him, he added gruffly: 'Go on, then — get back in there.'

The studio now blazed with light, most of it directed on to the cable galleries and iron stairway high up in the building. Inspector Dooly and a group of detectives stood below the HIGH VOLTAGE — DANGER sign. Dooly was holding the missing pistol. Anetone Marcos was explaining how it worked. Chad edged closer to eavesdrop.

'No — don't touch it,' the Inspector was saying as he held the pistol suspended by the trigger guard.

'How can I tell if it's been fired if I can't touch it?' said Marcos.

'You say there is a gauge to register the amount of liquid in the reservoir?'

'Yes, but it's on the other side.'

'Then I'll turn it,' said Dooly impatiently. 'Now can you see?'

Marcos peered closer. 'Yes. It's three-quarters empty,' he replied.

'And you are certain it was full when you brought it into the studio?'

'I am.'

'A number of people played about with the guns during rehearsals. Perhaps it was fired then?' Dooly suggested.

'It was — several times. I fired this and three of the others to demonstrate them. But I refilled all of them with plain water from the wash-basin.'

'Before or after the studio break?'

'After.'

'You're sure of that?'

'Of course I'm sure. D'you think I'm daft or something? And those guns never left my sight after I refilled them.'

'This one did,' said the Inspector drily. 'You lost it, didn't you?'

'Aye — that was during the couple of minutes between me walking on to the set and one of the prop-men following me with the table.'

'They moved the table after rehearsals? Why?'

'Because it was splodged with water.'

'All right, sir, thank you. That is all now.'

'Can I go home?' Marcos asked.

'Not yet, sir, if you don't mind.' Dooly beckoned to Sergeant Duff. 'Fetch those prop-men, and tell the studio floor manager I want the names of every single person who was behind the sets after they returned from the break.'

Chad eased away, found himself next to the make-up girls. Brenda looked strained and nervous. Phyl had been crying.

'Sorry about Brian,' said Chad awkwardly.

'Why?' said Brenda nastily.

'Well — I thought you girls sort of liked him.'

'Thought wrong then, didn't you?' Brenda snapped.

'Don't take it out on the kid,' said Phyl. 'He was only being polite.'

Brenda stretched a tight little smile.

'Sure. I'm sorry, Chad.'

'That's okay. I'm sorry it all happened.' Chad paused, before asking casually: 'You remember that chap in the brown overcoat and black and white check trousers? He was back-stage while the film was running — must have been near you. D'you know where he is? I wanted to speak to him.'

'Who?' Brenda didn't sound interested.

'Oh yes, I remember,' said Phyl. 'Scruffy-looking character. Well, his coat was scruffy anyway. Looked as if he'd slept in it. I've seen him somewhere before. Can't remember where, though. Who is he?'

'I forget his name,' said Chad. This was a lie, but he'd only just that second been able to link his memory of a face with a name. 'Where did he go?'

Phyl shrugged. 'Search me. I don't keep tabs on all the odd characters who float around here.'

'Thanks, anyway.' Chad hurried off.

After all, he *knew* where the man went. And Chad was pretty sure that the pistol had gone with him — up to the cable gallery.

Chad climbed into the studio control room. A blonde, smartly dressed girl was sorting some papers.

'Hi, Jane! Saw you through the window. May I come in?'

The producer's secretary waved a casual hand.

'Why not?' She glanced at him. 'Shocking business, isn't it? Or did you hate him too?'

'Me? No, I didn't hate him.'

She sighed. 'Poor Brian. He did that to so many people. They loved him or hated. You just couldn't be indifferent to him.'

'You didn't hate him then?'

She smiled gently. 'No, Chad. Why should I?'

'I dunno. Most of the women around here were loopy over him.'

She nodded. 'I was one of them.'

'Oh, I'm sorry.'

'Why should you be? I wasn't in love with him. I'm married, you know. I just thought he *could* have been one of the greatest things in television. He tried too hard, he lived too hard, he used people too ruthlessly, but he was learning slowly how to give more of himself instead of taking from others. Now he's dead, and it was all for nothing. Poor Brian.' She seemed suddenly to remember she was talking out loud, because her head jerked up and she stared directly at Chad. He saw that her eyes were filled with tears.

'Well — something you want, Chad?' She asked in a business-like tone which contrasted strangely with her sad eyes.

'Wondered if you had the studio ticket list for tonight.'

'M'm.' She flicked through some papers. 'It's here somewhere.' She pulled out a sheet of foolscap. 'Here it is. Does the boss want it?'

'No. I'd like to see if a friend of mine got in,' said Chad.

She waggled a finger at him. 'Bad lad! You know how the boss feels about friends and relatives of the staff. Their place is at home, not in the studio.'

Chad scanned the list. 'No — I can't see his name.'

'You didn't apply for a ticket.' Jane was mildly suspicious. 'I issue them for the boss to initial, so I know.'

Chad grinned. 'Because I know how the boss feels, especially as we don't have an audience.' He tapped the list. 'But two staff tickets were issued. Perhaps my friend got one of those?'

'Cunning, that's what you are, my lad. As a matter of fact, one of the staff tickets was for Judy Marsh. She's joining us next week and came in to see how we did it.'

'And the other staff ticket?' Chad insisted.

Jane frowned. 'Oh lawdy me — I can't remember. Request from O.B., I think.'

'Do Outside Broadcasts usually ask for a studio ticket?'

Jane snatched back the list. 'Now listen, my bright and bonny junior — less of the questions. It's none of your business anyway. And if you've wangled a ticket through a pal on O.B., I'll see you don't do it again. Got it?'

'Got it.'

'Then take it and cut off. Go and play games with the police. I'm not in the mood.'

'Sorry, Jane. Didn't mean any harm.'

She smiled weakly. 'That's okay, Chad. It's been a nasty, nasty day and little Janie has just about had enough.'

Chad walked quietly from the control room, leaving Jane staring sad-eyed into the row of blank screens.

He turned back along the catwalk, moving into the shadows and resting against the guard rail, watching the floodlit scene spread over the far half of the studio.

Chad was rather surprised to see the Skyway news cameras were set up and the news-team boys dodging around, some with lip-mikes, some with portable sound-recording gear. Then he realised how natural it was for the news team to be there. Who had more right to film and record such a dramatic event than the company's own TV news reporters? Right in their own backyard, so to speak.

Now, for the first time since the dramatic exit of Brian Foxglove, there was a moment for quiet thought. Chad had been quick enough to think of his old pals on the *Morning News,* but that was mainly tied in with the query he had over remembering those elusive facts about the stranger. Like having a word on the tip of your tongue and not being able to say it.

But fragment by fragment it had come back. The staff ticket issued to the O.B. unit had, on a sudden, welded those useless fragments of memory into one very useful pattern in Chad's mind. He didn't need to check the newspaper files now. He knew who the man was. The man who had been dead, then missing — then very much alive.

It all happened before Chad joined Skyway. Dick Tarrant had done a special feature write-up. Skyway TV directors had threatened libel action. The story had been 'killed'. The story of Adrian Fellowes — Skyway TV's top announcer and creator of the 'People who Matter' programme.

Adrian Fellowes had put it on the screen, nursed it and grafted at it until the programme reached the top-ten rating. Day and night, he'd worked — worked so hard that his wife left him because she claimed TV meant more to Adrian than she did. Overwork made him ill. He took drugs to keep going. But the show he had created became a Frankenstein's monster which slowly crushed him.

Then to save himself, he introduced a protégé — a newcomer called Brian Foxglove. Adrian Fellowes schooled and trained the unknown Brian, paid him more than the studio would pay for a try-out man. Loaned him large sums of money to buy exclusive clothes, a car, a fancy address to live at and a special publicity agent. Adrian Fellowes had been in TV since the very early days of its invention, had spent years in radio broadcasting, knew all the angles. With Adrian Fellowes behind him, Brian Foxglove couldn't go wrong.

Yet few people knew just how much Adrian Fellowes was behind this new star of the goggle-box. Not until Brian Foxglove wangled and schemed and twisted him out of his job. Then, broke and ill, Adrian sued Brian, claiming back the money loaned him. Adrian also claimed an agreement with Brian, that he would remain producer as well as personal agent.

Brian denied the agreement. Adrian admitted it was a verbal agreement of honour. In court the judge had made some pointed remarks which showed he believed Adrian; but, there being no written evidence, it was one man's word against the other's.

Adrian Fellowes lost the case. The *Morning News*, feeling he'd been wronged, began a series of articles written by Dick Tarrant. Skyway TV stepped in — and that was that. Adrian Fellowes disappeared.

Chad stared unseeingly across the studio, his mind filled with these thoughts and memories. Then abruptly he jerked upright as he remembered something else.

Adrian Fellowes had a nephew who worked in the O.B. unit. This was Chad's last link in how the ticket had been obtained.

No security check at an atomic research station could be

148

more efficient than the check on who entered studio A3 when 'People who Matter' was in residence. It was a standing joke that if even the producer lost his entry card, he wouldn't get in without it. But Adrian Fellowes had got in.

Chad tried to remember who had been in the studio. This wasn't too difficult once he had eliminated all the crew who were inside the perimeter of the sets. Then take out the programme guests. That left the auto-cue man, the prop-men, the two 'fill-in' interviewers and the make-up girls — all of whom would pass in and out of the actual shooting-arena.

By this method Chad remembered Judy Marsh — a girl in a green dress who sat well back in the shadows, watching all that went on. No one else. Chad was sure of it. Certainly no one from O.B. He knew most of the Outside Broadcasts unit on sight. So the last ticket had been held by Adrian Fellowes. But he couldn't have got into the studio once the red light went on. Chad himself had nearly missed it. No — the man must have entered only a few seconds before the show went 'live'. Adrian Fellowes would know every foot of the studio, know just where to stand so that nobody noticed him. He'd know how to reach the cable galleries, and all about the high-voltage cables — even know which one was most dangerous.

Chad began to feel slightly sick as the evidence against a man for whom he had learned pity built up into the pattern shaped for murder. What was it Inspector Dooly had said? Murder is for men. Chad shivered. On a sudden it was grown-up and ugly.

Chad imagined himself in the position of that lonely, des-perate, ruined man, lurking in the shadows, climbing to the galleries, gazing down on the floodlit idol of millions — and wondered how *he* would have felt. This made him feel more sick then ever... this glimpse of life as lived by a grown man. Up to now Chad's feelings had been those of a boy, enjoying a serious but not too desperate game.

Now it became clear as a picture of ruthless ambition, treachery, dishonoured friendship, leading to revenge and violent death under the blue-white lights.

But one piece of the pattern still eluded Chad's searching mind. How was Brian Foxglove killed? How could a high-voltage current be joined to his body? How could it be done without affecting others who were only a few feet away from Brian? The camera-men, the producer's assistant, the prop-men — all standing just off-set, waiting to strike it when the interview with Anetone Marcos ended? And, most important of all — where would Adrian Fellowes go?

Could he have slipped quietly back to the studio floor and left? No. He couldn't do that because the exit doors were locked during live transmission. Nor could he have mingled with the studio staff, even allowing for the confusion which followed, without being noticed. The producer had faded out after the trio, and 'programme continuity' had taken over from another studio, announcing the usual apologies for technical breakdown. The pilot lights in studio A3 at once came on, so that Adrian Fellowes couldn't have stayed in the gloom beyond the sets — he would soon have been noticed.

Chad worried at this problem. The thought occurred to him that he should go down on the floor and tell Inspector Dooly how he'd worked everything out. He was still deciding whether or not to do this when he heard his name spoken angrily from below. He peered over the guard rail and saw Dick Tarrant and a *Morning News* photographer arguing with the Inspector.

'That Chad Stenson!' Inspector Dooly stormed. 'If I get my hands on him there'll be another death around here.' He waved his hands furiously. 'No, Tarrant — don't tell me you came here on a hunch. Someone tipped you off. And Chad's the only one who's left the studio. One of my men saw him coming from the toilet. He sneaked into an office — all the phones are switched to outside lines after the offices close. Only an employee of Skyway would know that, so

150

Chad saw the huddled figure of Adrian Fellowes

don't tell me you've not heard from him. He once worked for you. He'd know a tip-off would be worth money.'

'Now, Inspector — per-lease!' Dick Tarrant, big, jovial but shrewd, boomed cheerfully. 'I'm not a criminal just because I try to do my job. This is news — big news — and I'm entitled to be here. As for Chad ... well, I haven't seen him in weeks.'

'Maybe not seen him,' Dooly growled. 'But I'll wager you've heard from him. Come over here — I want a private word with you.' The two men moved away.

Chad exhaled a deep breath. That was a near thing! Now he daren't go down on the floor. Neither had Adrian Fellowes. So where else could he have gone? Chad pondered on this, surveying the labyrinth of cable galleries.

Suddenly he remembered the emergency exit for the upper half of the studio structure. Only the technicians knew about this, but Adrian Fellowes and some of the older producers who had been here when the studio was built would know about it. Chad knew because, being naturally curious, he'd asked a friendly engineer to show him around.

He moved along the gallery, crossed a narrow iron bridge to another gallery close to the wall, and groped his way around the outer section until he came to a fireproof door. Chad swung the heavy handle, eased the door open and stepped into a sloping concrete passage, eerie with blue light from a low-powered bulb. This form of lighting was used in case a sudden opening of the door sent a shaft of light to cause top reflection on a camera.

The slope levelled out, and the warm sweetish smell of diesel oil became marked. The floor vibrated gently from the engines of the auxiliary power unit, housed in great steel-mesh cages away to the right. Chad trod softly towards them. A few yards from another fireproof door which led to an outside iron stairway he saw the huddled figure of Adrian Fellowes.

The man's shoulders were supported by a corner of the

steel-mesh and a concrete pillar, his head bowed forward, chin on chest. One hand moved in small plucking actions against the lapels of his coat. The other hand lay palm upwards across his knees.

Chad knelt down and spoke quietly.

'Hullo, Mr Fellowes. Can I help you?'

The head lifted slowly until Chad could see the eyes surveying him, without surprise, almost with relief. The once-smart moustache was straggly, and a stubble of beard shadowed the gaunt cheeks below dark-circled eyes.

'My God!' the voice was husky. 'Don't tell me someone recognises me.'

'Sure I do. You're famous.'

'Was, my dear boy — was. Are the hounds of justice running at your heels?'

'There's only me,' said Chad, feeling he had to speak as if to a child. 'I can't lift you myself, but I'll make you more comfortable, then go for help.'

A flicker of interest appeared in the man's eyes.

'You're a kind infant. Who are you?'

'Chad Stenson.'

'You work in the studio?'

'Yes.'

'That is how you knew me?'

'No. I remember you from when I was at school and when I worked in a newspaper office. I always thought you were super.'

'How nice. How very nice. He always thought I was super. That would look well on my tombstone, wouldn't it?'

'You shouldn't talk like that,' said Chad sharply. 'You look ill, but you're not going to die.'

The straggly moustache twitched in a tired smile.

'I am, dear boy, I am. I had one attack on my way here. Fell down in the drive. I've just had another. The doctors told me it would be like this. Funny — but I don't feel all that ill. Just very weak.'

'I saw you in the drive. Thought you were dead, but when I went back you'd gone.' Chad took off his jacket to make a more comfortable head-rest. 'Did your nephew in O.B. get you a ticket for the studio?'

'That is not a fair question. Let us say a friend got me a ticket.'

'Why?' Chad asked fiercely. 'Why did you do it? I know he'd played dirty tricks on you, but wasn't there another way of getting your revenge?'

The bleak eyes stared had. 'So Brian is dead? He's really dead?'

'Didn't you know?'

'I feared he was. But I didn't know for sure.'

'Then you didn't mean to kill him?'

Adrian Fellowes moved his head slowly from side to side.

'Death was too easy for him. I knew a better way to make him suffer. Ridicule — he hated ridicule. He didn't have a sense of humour. Today was going to be the first of several tricks to make him look silly in front of the cameras. Good friends in the studio were going to help me with others. Now it's all over. It's all gone wrong — and so have I.'

'How could you plan a trick with a water-pistol?' Chad asked. 'Marcos came here at short notice — how could you know?'

'He's an old pal of mine. I put him on a show some years ago. Gave him his big chance. He obtained a fat contract for his special guns because of it. Annie always vowed he'd repay me. He kept his word too. That's why he fooled about with Brian when the show was live. It wasn't what Brian had rehearsed. It was beginning to make him look silly, wasn't it?'

'Yes,' Chad agreed. 'Especially when Annie made him get up. But then —'

'Ah yes! But then — I had to do my bit. So simple, but always effective — like the old custard-pie-throwing gag. I was going to spray Brian with water. Only that. Does it sound silly?'

154

Chad laughed. 'It *sounds* silly. I bet it would have been a great joke.'

Adrian Fellowes nodded. 'The best jokes are always simple. Then Annie would have made a scene—accused Brian of stealing his gun and generally wrecked the show.'

'And you'd got other tricks arranged so that Brian would be made a laughing-stock?' Chad smiled grimly. 'That would have been a fair sort of revenge for what he did to you.'

'Yes indeed. We had it all worked out,' said Adrian Fellowes eagerly.

'Oh gosh!' Chad exclaimed. 'What a mess. The police say he was murdered by being electrocuted. But how could he have been?'

'So simple,' said Adrian Fellowes in a tired voice. 'So very simple. A powerful jet of water caught the end of a high-voltage cable. Some fool of a workman left it hanging bare. But normally no one would have been in that gallery, would they?'

'Wait a minute!' Chad grew excited. 'D'you mean that the jet of water from the pistol carried a charge of high-volt current on to Brian's head? Is that how he was electrocuted?'

'I'm afraid so, dear boy. Water is an extremely good conductor of electricity.'

'Then why didn't it jump back to the water-pistol and kill you too?'

'It nearly did, but the pistol grip was made of rubber. That saved me. The voltage kicked the gun out of my hand. You'll find it lying around the gallery somewhere.'

'But you see what this means?' Chad cried. 'It was an accident! You didn't kill Brian. You only fired water. It *was* an *accident!*'

Adrian Fellowes gazed squarely at Chad.

'Maybe so, but in my heart I am glad he is dead. That makes me a murderer.'

'You didn't — ' Chad paused — 'you didn't aim the water deliberately on that cable, did you?'

There was no answer. Adrian Fellowes's head had sunk lower. He appeared to be sleeping.

'I'll fetch help.' Chad sped back to the gallery.

The police were searching along that end of the studio. A few minutes later and they would have reached the emergency door. Chad's message was relayed to Inspector Dooly.

An hour later the ambulance had departed for hospital with the semi-conscious Adrian Fellowes, and Chad was alone with the Inspector.

'Well,' Dooly sighed. 'I suppose with your record for being witness-prone I should have known the final and most important evidence would come from you. I wonder what it is that forces you to be involved in cases? You're a nice lad, really, but you're a terrible nuisance.'

'Why?' Chad grinned. 'Solved your case, didn't I?'

'I'll admit you helped,' said the Inspector grudgingly. He turned as Sergeant Duff came close to whisper a message. 'So that's it,' the Inspector declared. 'Adrian Fellowes died ten minutes ago.'

'Oh!' said Chad. 'I'm sorry.'

'So am I,' said the Inspector. 'I really am. And — d'you know something, Chad? No one in this damn studio has yet told me they're sorry Brian Foxglove is dead.'

'He'd like that,' said Chad softly.

'Who'd like what?'

'Adrian Fellowes — on his tombstone. "They said they were sorry." He'd like that.' Chad glanced around the eerie now deserted studio. In the dim light the caption boards looked like tombstones.

He said goodbye and walked out into the reality of the night.

THE ARROW AND THE TARGET

They rode together through the forest paths, back towards Redcliff Castle — John's pony bumping along behind the big black charger of his father, and the men-at-arms clattering along a dozen yards behind. John thought miserably of the many times they had ridden together before, and of the tales his father had told as, in the sunset, they came towards the grey walls of the castle up the sloping meadows where he'd played when he was younger.

But, now that he was fourteen, there was no more playing. There had come the day when his father had walked into the room where he sat practising upon the lute, and had taken the instrument from his hands, saying: 'Your horse is waiting, John. It is time you learned to help defend this castle and the estate which will one day be yours.'

Unwillingly he had gone out and climbed into the saddle, but for a whole year the rides had been fun — gallops across the open fields, meetings with other boys of his own age who rode at their father's sides. But then had come the day when his father, Sir Harry Redcliff, had brought out a crossbow, bright, new and shining with highly polished metal fittings, and presented it to him. 'You have learned to ride,' he had said. 'Now it is time to learn to fight.'

John had held the crossbow clumsily, and had nearly broken his thumb by letting off the trigger too soon so that the taut cord whipped sharply past his other hand, rapping his knuckle so hard that he dropped the crossbow with a yell of agony. Sternly, his father had ordered him from the saddle to pick it up again, to reload and fire at a target pinned to a tree twenty yards away. John had not only missed the target, he had even missed the tree — and the heavily weighted arrow had sped away and been lost in the dense woods.

'Come on, boy,' Sir Harry had shouted angrily, 'you can do better than that. Every Redcliff in history has been an expert with the bow. I cannot have it said that my son is a weakling and a simpleton.'

White-faced, John had tried again, day after day, even practising in secret with the help of one of the men-at-arms. But though he had learned to support the weight of the crossbow, and draw back the cord to load it, his aim had not improved. His arrows went yards wide of the target; or rose, soaring high into the air, to fall so far away that there was little chance of recovering them. 'John's darts' had become a joke; every day people from the village brought them back in handfuls, knowing that there would be a small reward.

Finally today had come — the day of the Tournament, and to the roars of laughter of the crowd he had finished last in the crossbow competition, beaten not only by the sons of other knights but also by the lads of half a dozen villages. As soon as the competition was over his father had sent for their horses and galloped away, leaving him to follow and not saying a word all the way home.

As the castle came in sight John edged his pony closer to his father's charger, dreading the moment when everyone who had stayed behind would also learn the story of his disgrace. But there was not a sign of relenting on his father's face. As soon as the drawbridge had clattered down Sir Harry marched the huge charger across the planking into the courtyard beyond the portcullis.

There were shouted orders among the men-at-arms; grooms dashed out to lead away the horses and in the confusion and noise John tried to steal away to his room unobserved. But at a turn of the spiral stairs he found his father

160

John saw the figure topple from the parapet

standing at a window, staring out at the red glare of the sinking sun. He turned, and his face was no longer stern.

'All right, John — do not be afraid of me. Go up to your room; there is a place for lute-players in the world as well as fighting men.'

John hung his head. Then he repeated, bitterly, the words his father had said to him so often: 'Every Redcliff in history has been an expert with the bow.'

Sir Harry laughed sadly. 'History will have to change, John. Perhaps in years to come they will look back upon a century of Redcliffs who have been expert with the lute.'

John turned away blindly, and stumbled up the stairway to his room. He tossed the crossbow on to the table beside his lute and flung himself upon the bed, burying his head in the pillow to shut out the fading daylight and the sounds from the courtyard — anything which would keep alive a day he would spend his life trying to forget.

But the jeering voices of the crowd at the Tournament, and the sly grins of the village boys as he missed the target over and over again, would not go away — not until sleep came. And even then it was sleep filled with dreams in which as a grown man he was taunted by his fellows, challenged to duels which he dared not fight; his honour and the name of Redcliff made a joke throughout the length and breadth of England.

What woke him he never knew; but he sat bolt upright, conscious of a tiny scraping sound, repeated over and over again. The room was dark, except for a pale shaft of moonlight crossing the end of the bed. For a moment he thought the sound had been made by a mouse, then he realised that it came not from inside the room but from somewhere beyond the window.

He rolled from the bed, crossed the room to the window, and peered out into the night.

Then he froze.

Below his window was a narrow parapet, running twenty

162

feet above the battlements, past rows of dark windows — from one of which gleamed the flickering light of a lamp.

And in the light of that lamp from his father's room, John could see a figure outlined on the parapet, facing the window, with a crossbow raised to take aim!

Icily calm, though his arms and legs felt weak, John reached round to the table behind him and lifted his own crossbow. Placing the loader on it he pulled back the cord, slipped an arrow into place and raised it to his shoulder.

The recoil jerked him back sharply. He heard a cry from the darkness, then saw the figure topple from the parapet, hang by one hand for a moment on the edge, then drop down to the battlements, and totter a few paces before falling forward with arms outstretched.

Clutching the crossbow, John raced to the door and down the stairs. In the passage leading to his father's room he crashed headlong into a man-at-arms, nearly sending them both to the ground. The soldier steadied himself against the wall. 'What is the matter, young master?' he gasped.

'An attempt upon the life of my father! I shot the man, but he may still have enough strength to get away. Search the battlements!'

John raced on, and flung open the door of his father's room. Sir Harry was at the window, leaning out; as John ran towards him he spun round, sword in hand.

'Oh, 'tis you, John! Good shot, boy — you saved my life. I saw the fellow a second before you fired.'

'I have sent men to search the battlements, Father. He cannot have got away.'

Sir Harry shook his head. 'He was not alone, John. There were two others with him; they lifted his body over the battlements and down a scaling-ladder across the moat.'

John slammed his fist down upon the table. 'Lend me your sword, Father. Any man who would come by night to kill you must not get away.'

Sir Harry put the sword back into its scabbard. 'Too late,

John.' There was a curious light in his eyes which John had never seen before. 'There will be other times, though, so tomorrow I will have the blacksmith forge you a blade of your own. No man can rule these hills and guard his people from harm without making enemies.' He looked over John's head. 'Sergeant, did you find aught upon the battlements?'

'Not a thing, sir. But one thing is certain — Master John's arrow is still in the man, for there was no sign of it.'

'Then back to your duties.' Sir Harry waited until the men-at-arms had backed from the room. 'John, come with me to the armoury, and we will choose a breastplate and armour for you.'

Proudly, John followed his father into the next room.

'Here,' said Sir Harry, lifting down a gleaming iron breastplate, 'this was mine when I was your age. Will it fit you?'

John tried it, then shook his head. 'It is too small, Father. What about that one upon the table?' Before his father could stop him he reached out and picked up the bigger breastplate. His eyes widened.

'Father, what is this?'

Red-faced, Sir Harry took the breastplate with the crossbow arrow embedded in the side. 'I am sorry, John,' he said. 'Yes, I was the figure at the window. There was just time to climb back in from the battlements and take this off before you arrived. The man-at-arms did not delay you as long as I had hoped.'

'But, Father ... !'

'Yes, it was a deception. But it proved what I had thought — that if there was good reason to shoot straight you would be as good a bowman as any. Tonight, John, you proved yourself to be a man. Now I have a son who is not only a good lute-player, but also a fighter who will one day take my place.'

BILL'S BATTING COUSIN

It was one hour before the first big match of the season that Bill had two surprises. The first was the arrival of his cousin Roland from New Zealand, to stay for an indefinite length of time while his parents were away on a world tour. The second was when Tony McPhee burst into the house with the doleful news that they'd be one batsman short because of 'flu.

In any other match it wouldn't have mattered much, because one of the usual reserves could have filled the gap. But Romsey Village always had to turn out its strongest side to avoid heavy defeat at the hands of their deadly rivals, the Bondford Secondary Modern School.

To Bill the news was disastrous, mainly because he'd been boasting for weeks how this time Romsey were going to win by at least fifty runs. Now, as likely as not, they'd lose by a hundred. 'What are we going to do?' he asked Tony in desperation.

'What *can* we do?' Tony threw up his hands. 'We'll have to use a reserve and hope for the best.'

It was then that Bill's cousin Roland chipped in. 'I used to play a bit of cricket in New Zealand,' he said, his nose in the air. 'But I've never played *village* cricket.'

Bill made a face at Tony, but the Romsey skipper wasn't taking any notice. His eyes were on Roland as if he was the answer to a prayer. 'What team did you play for?'

'Oh, various teams,' murmured Roland. 'Senior teams, of course,' he added.

'Of course,' echoed Bill acidly. He'd never liked Roland

before he went to New Zealand, and he liked him even less now he'd returned.

'Would you ... I mean could you possibly ... ?' Tony fawned on Roland in a way that revolted Bill. 'Do you think you'd be willing to play for the village this afternoon?'

'In a little local game?' inquired Roland condescendingly. 'Yes, it might be quite amusing. Of course, I have no gear with me. I forgot it would be summer in England.'

'Oh, we can attend to all that,' said Tony eagerly. 'I've no spare white flannels, but my dad is about your size. His would fit. As for a bat, I'm sure we can fix you up. When do you like to go in?'

Roland studied his fingernails. 'In a game of this kind it doesn't matter much, does it? First wicket down, I suppose.'

Now Bill had intended to interrupt this before it really got started. What Roland didn't know was that for the past three years he'd been exchanging regular letters with Roland's sister Marjorie, and that one of Marjorie's biggest jokes was about Roland's appalling cricket.

But now, after Tony's exhibition of hero-worship, he decided to say nothing. Let Tony stew in his own juice for once. It would teach him not to take people at their face value.

It was with some satisfaction, therefore, that when the game began he watched Roland buckle on his pads and wait for the first wicket to fall. Against the Bondford fast bowlers that didn't take long. A short-pitched ball that rose almost shoulder-high had one of the batsmen floundering: he touched the ball with the tip of his bat, and sent it straight up in the air for an easy catch by the Bondford second slip.

A yell of delight went up from a batch of Bondford boys sitting on the bank to the left of the pavilion. Bill caught Tony's anxious eye. 'Don't worry,' he said. 'Don't forget you've got my marvellous cousin going in next.'

Something in his voice made Tony's forehead become furrowed. 'What d'you mean? Why d'you say it like that?'

168

'I just happen to know that he isn't marvellous at all. He's hopeless.'

Tony's eyes went as blank as jellies, as though everything had suddenly gone right out of focus. 'Then why didn't you tell me at the time, you silly ass?'

'Because you didn't ask me, that's why. Because you were too busy making a fool of yourself, begging that stupid cousin of mine to play.'

'Oh, crumbs!' Tony looked gloomily out across the field towards the wicket, where cousin Roland was now taking centre. Hopefully he swung round. 'You're pulling my leg, aren't you?'

'Have you ever known me pull anybody's leg?' murmured Bill. 'I'm a serious-minded chap, as you should know by now.'

Tony nodded his head miserably. 'Yes, I know.' He stared again at the centre of the field, and watched the Bondford fast bowler walk back to his mark.

Bill grinned, and let out an ecstatic sigh. 'Well,' he said with a certain smug satisfaction, 'here goes.'

Then he sat up abruptly, unable to believe his eyes as Roland raised his bat and brought it down with tremendous force, lifting the ball high over the bowler's head, soaring upwards towards the sun. Bill strained his eyes to follow its flight, then saw a quick scattering of people beyond the boundary, and heard a gasp from the crowd by the pavilion.

It was a six! Not only the first of the match, but first of the season for Romsey.

Tony swung round on Bill, his face alight with excitement. 'You *were* pulling my leg, you crafty rascal. He's a first-class batsman.'

Bill blinked at him, too bewildered to speak. Had Marjorie written all about Roland's bad cricket just as a joke? It hadn't read like a joke.

Tony grabbed his arm. 'Here comes the next ball. See if he'll do it again.'

The Bondford bowler was at his mark, turning, and beginning his run. He came up to the wicket faster than ever, and delivered a sizzling full toss.

Exactly what happened Bill couldn't see, but his cousin Roland was on the ground, twisting from side to side and clutching his knee. This time the 'Oh!' from the crowd had a different sound to it, and there was a groan as two of the Bondford team picked Roland up from the turf and carried him between them to the pavilion.

Bill and Tony were already at the pavilion steps. 'Is it bad?' asked Tony anxiously.

Roland screwed up his face into a look of agony. Tight-lipped, he said nothing — too gallant to let out a sound of complaint.

Or so it seemed to everybody except one.

Bill had known Roland on and off for fifteen years, since their prams stood side by side in the park. The others hadn't. Only a cousin or a brother could have detected that faint gleam of triumph in Roland's eye, or spotted the fraction of a second's smile before the dramatic show of agony.

'Poor old Roland,' he said, joining in the chorus.

After that it was a walk-over for Bondford. They won by three wickets, with an hour to spare.

But nobody in Romsey seemed to care about that. To Bill's annoyance all they seemed to be worrying about was the condition of Roland's knee. It was Club evening at the village hall; everybody fussed round him with ice-cream, cold drinks, and promises of drives to all the local beauty spots because he couldn't get to them himself.

'What's the highest score you ever made, Roland?'

'It's a wonder they've never picked you to play for New Zealand.'

'Are you going to be a professional later on?'

'In that six of yours — can you show me the foot movements? On paper, I mean.'

It was sickening. It would have been so even if Roland

had been genuine — because, as Bill said to himself, he's a nasty creepy bit of work anyway. It was doubly sickening in reality, certain as he was that Roland's left knee was no more injured than his right.

How could you get a hard knock on the knee when trying to play a full toss? Oh yes, there were ways — but pretty improbable ones, about as likely to happen as bowling six men in one over, or playing the ball right over the main road into the horse-trough.

No, it was phony! Bill felt he'd never been more certain of anything in his life.

'May I have another iced lime?' Roland was asking.

No sooner had he asked than it arrived, cold and dewy in a tall glass. Bill reckoned it was about Roland's sixth. He nursed the small glass of lukewarm orange in his own hand, and scowled at it. The sight of his cousin holding forth to the whole village was more than he could bear.

'Test matches?' Roland was saying. 'Yes, I suppose they'll come later. I'm in no hurry. I want to strengthen my strokes on the offside before they pick me for a Test series.' He winced, and clutched his knee. 'Pity about this. It'll mean no more cricket for me in England.'

'Rotten luck,' said someone. There was a chorus of 'Never mind, there'll be plenty more seasons,' and 'Anyway, we can't offer you much in the way of bowling down here in Romsey.'

The final straw that night came when somebody found a wheel-chair, and Bill found he had the job of pushing Roland home. When they reached the darkness of the lane up to the house he felt strongly tempted to take Roland by the hair, lift him up, and make him walk the rest of the way. That would teach him!

Only he didn't. That wouldn't teach Roland at all. If Roland was to be proved a liar, then the proving had to be done in front of witnesses — plenty of them.

He lay in bed that night, staring at the ceiling, his mind

turning over one idea after another, rejecting every new scheme for one fault or another.

But finally, as the church clock was chiming midnight, he let out a deep sigh of satisfaction. He went to sleep with a smile on his face.

He was up early, fussing around in the kitchen before breakfast, and refusing to explain to any of the family what he was up to. Then, straight after breakfast, he checked up that Roland was still in bed with a tray on his lap. Satisfied about that, he picked up the telephone.

'Hullo?' he said quietly. 'Is that you, Tony? Look, let's have a conference this morning. We've got to find a way of making the team stronger for next Saturday's game. Will you bring them straight round here afterwards?'

He put the phone down, and went upstairs. 'Roland — may I come in? How's the knee?' he asked sympathetically. 'It's a wonderfully sunny day, so I've rigged up a deck-chair with a footrest. It's all ready, out in the garden. Come on, let me help you get dressed.'

Twenty minutes later, with contortions of pain as he went, Roland descended the stairs, supported by Bill's arm. At the bottom he climbed into his wheel-chair, and Bill pushed him round the house to the spot he'd picked carefully for the deck-chair, at the far side of the lawn just out of sight of the French windows. Beside the deck-chair lay a pile of magazines; over the top of the canopy was an extra sunshade of brightly striped canvas. Nothing had been forgotten.

Roland let out a luxurious sigh, and allowed Bill to transfer him from one chair to the other.

'Comfortable, Roland? Anything else you want?'

'I'll call if anything occurs to me,' murmured Roland, his face already buried in a magazine.

Bill clenched and unclenched his fists, fighting down the impulse to seize the magazine, tear it up and stuff it page by page down Roland's throat. Instead, he smiled. 'Then that's all right. I'll be out presently with some drinks. What do you prefer?'

Roland lowered the magazine. His eyes lit up greedily. 'Iced lime,' he said, licking his lips. 'I can't do without iced lime when the weather's hot.'

'Then iced lime you shall have.' Bill went back indoors, and checked up on the ice-cubes he'd been freezing in the refrigerator. He found two tall glasses, a packet of straws, and the bottle of lime juice. The church bells, ringing for the start of the service, came to an end.

He sat down at a window, from which he could see the gates of the churchyard. After a while he poured himself a glass of lime and added two cubes of ice. He was a firm believer in mixing pleasure with business.

He sat there with pencil and paper, working out ideas for next Saturday's team, until he heard the final notes die away from the church at the end of the closing hymn. Then he stood up, arranged the tall glasses of iced lime on a small tray, and set the tray on a folding-table.

He pushed open the French windows, and began to walk down the lawn.

'I should think it's about time!' Roland greeted him indignantly. His face was the colour of a boiled prawn; the sun, Bill realised, had been hotter than even his wildest hopes. He reached a point about thirty feet from Roland and then stopped, with his head thrown back.

'Well, come on,' said Roland irritably. 'What are you waiting for?'

'It's the phone. I can hear it ringing.' Bill set down the table, still thirty feet from Roland and ran back to the French windows.

He closed them behind him, and waited. Within thirty seconds the front-door bell rang. He sprinted along the hall, and opened the door wide.

'Well come in, Tony — and all the rest of you! I expect you're hot? We'll have drinks in a minute, as soon as we get the meeting going. Come in here — it's the coolest room in the house.'

They followed him into the drawing-room, and stood in a group by the French windows. 'How's Roland?' asked Tony anxiously.

'Oh,' said Bill vaguely, 'as well as can be expected. You'll see him presently.'

And indeed they did! A smile of ecstatic pleasure spread across Bill's face as suddenly across the lawn came Roland, running towards the table. He stopped, picked up a glass and held it to his lips. And then, above the glass, he saw the astonished faces at the French windows.

Even though it was a hot day, they chased him for two and a half miles. But afterwards they had to admit that, even if he was a poor sport and a third-rate cricketer, he was the fastest runner the village had ever seen.

CHAD STENSON - TV REPORTER

'What type of news do you cover?' Chad Stenson asked.

'Everything is news,' said Mark Venner. 'Everybody is news. News of any description is interesting to somebody, somewhere, even though you may not think it is. Newspapers and magazines can use more news than our TV newscasts. All our news must be visual. Does that answer your question?'

'Yes, thanks,' Chad replied.

'Then forget it, because it's wrong,' Mark Venner snapped. 'I was giving you the "policy" answer. That is what our fat-faced, profit-greedy directors declare to be the policy of Skyway TV's news service. But getting news costs money, and advertisers aren't very interested in news, so we're the Cinderellas of this outfit. We're supposed to be on the spot to film and report fires, floods, havoc and any dramatic event of human interest. But they don't happen every day, so our money allocation is just plain stupid. We've got an old truck and even older gear. Occasionally we get a new camera, but most of my lads use their own.' He glared at Chad. 'Why you asked to be transferred to my squad from a nice cushy studio programme I'll never know. You must be bonkers.'

'They call you the action squad, don't they?'

Mark Venner smiled grimly. 'Some call us the suicide squad. So you want action? Got tired of working in a nice warm studio?'

Chad nodded. 'That — and other reasons.'

Mark Venner glanced at the inter-office memo.

'I see that your previous producer thinks you're a lively

lad — quick, intelligent, hard-working. Also that you once worked in a newspaper office. I suppose you fancy yourself as a reporter?'

Chad shrugged. 'Not at first.'

'That's big of you.'

'What job will I be doing, Mr Venner?'

'Call me Mark — everyone does. Your job? General dogsbody. If the truck won't start, you're the one who'll push it. If a cable has to be put over a dirty, muddy stream, you're the one who'll wade across with it. If you're the one who has sandwiches when we're stuck ten miles from a café, you're the one who'll go hungry. We're mean and rough and full of dirty tricks designed to make life difficult for you. Still want to join us?'

Chad grinned. 'Why not? I've met a lot of nice people in TV. I might as well meet the other sort.'

'Okay.' Mark scrawled his signature on a card. 'Here's your press pass. Keep it with you at all times. It'll get you past police, fire-pickets and other obstructions, if our squad is operating there. Sometimes we cover race meetings — horses, cars, dogs, auto-cross, things like that. You'll have a free view, *if* we give you enough time to watch. But we don't do many of those jaunts. They're usually the O.B. boys' privilege. You can take it we generally get sent on the sticky ones. When you're not working outside with the squad, you'll stay in or close to the Call Room. When we leave — we leave in a hurry. If you miss a call you'll be sacked. Okay?'

'Okay.'

'Right. You'll find Digger Blake — he's an Aussie — in the O.B. shed across the yard. Say I sent you. Now hop!'

Chad hopped. His reception by Digger Blake was no more encouraging than his interview with the boss of the news-team camera crew had been.

'Flamin' heck!' said Digger. 'So you're the new scrub-boy. You ain't dry behind the ears yet, mate. What use are you going to be?'

178

'Thanks,' said Chad. 'Great welcome.'

'Yeah? What d'you want then — a flamin' band? See that shoulder-harness? The buckle-end's snapped. Take it to stores, get a new strap, fit it on and bring it back here. Right?'

'Right.' Chad took the harness, inspected it, then asked: 'How do I fit the new strap?'

Digger stared coldly. 'Funny thing. That's the same question I asked when I was first given the job.'

'What's the answer?'

'Flamin' well find out. Now hop!'

Once again Chad hopped. 'Hop' seemed to be the operative word of the news action squad.

The first call came an hour later. There were four beside Chad in the crew. Mark and Digger on cameras, doubling on sound-recording. 'Bleep' Jensen, sound-recording engineer. Ruff, truck-driver, aerial-erector, cable-operator and 'stand-off' man. Ruff was an ex-racing car driver, ex-cowboy, ex-boxer — a quiet, tough man who was expert at standing-off crowds of inquisitive onlookers whose interference might spoil camera shots or on-the-spot interviews.

Chad soon began to wonder why he'd chosen to apply for transfer from static studio work, especially at this time of year. He wanted to gain as much experience as possible in all departments of TV, but to change to outside work in mid-winter was slightly crazy. Yet there were good enough reasons, and Chad had reckoned he stood a better chance of a transfer at this time. Everyone liked to work outside in summer. Wintertime wasn't so attractive. So he got the transfer without any competition.

Ruff drove the truck with a nonchalant sort of concentration. He didn't speed along busy streets leading from the studio, but nipped through every opening, judged every traffic light, overtook other vehicles and avoided pedestrians without losing time. Once clear of traffic he built up the engine revs and sent the truck bowling along at top speed.

'Route okay, Ruff?' Mark queried.

'Okay, Mark. What's the griff?'

Digger laughed harshly. 'Flamin' cat up a flamin' tree?'

'How right you are!' Mark grinned.

'Oh no!' Bleep protested. 'Not again.'

'Human interest,' said Mark. 'Snow and ice, lonely, empty house, cat up tree, heroes to the rescue — ta-ra!'

'All this for a forty-second clip run-off between two blue-nosed politicos,' said Bleep.

'I don't get it,' said Chad.

'Bleep means it'll probably take us and the fire brigade about nine hours of slog to get there, do the job and get back,' Mark explained. 'But all the public will see will be forty seconds of our film slipped in between boring studio shots. Hey, Ruff — you got weather news?'

'Yup. Not good.'

'How bad?'

'Main roads clear — side roads full of snowdrifts.'

The truck lurched in a skid, skilfully corrected by the driver. Ruff chuckled. 'Oh yes, I forgot — icy road warning too.'

'Flamin' wonderful,' Digger exclaimed. 'That bit he forgets!'

'Listen,' said Mark. 'Let's make this easy. Long shots and zoom in. If we can't sight the kitty, fuzz up the negative and tape a patter about frost-covered fur. With me?'

'With you,' said Digger.

'Hold everything!' Ruff called.

The experienced crew grabbed bracing-supports and kept their seats. Chad wasn't quick enough. The truck slid on a sharp turn, rocked, swayed, then straightened in axle-bumping progress. Chad was shot to the floor, rolled and bounced back and forth. The crew let him find his own feet.

'Flamin' energetic, ain't he?' said Digger.

'Ah — youth!' said Bleep. 'Can't even sit still for two minutes.'

'Next time,' Mark snarled, 'when Ruff says hold — you grab a strut and do just that, see?'

'Thanks for telling me,' said Chad, nursing his bruises.

Mark clipped him on the ear. 'I'm the sarky one around here, so cut out the clever bits.'

Ruff called: 'Trouble up ahead.'

Mark peered from the truck interior over the top of Ruff's shoulder.

'Set 'em up,' he snapped, half turning his head so that the others could hear. 'Watch your light meters — this snow has top glare. Take the portable, Bleep. Get shovel clangs, thuds, engine revs. You know the drill.'

Digger and Bleep worked with astonishing speed. Digger slid cameras from cases in the special carrying-racks, fastened them around his person, together with light meters. Bleep pulled on the tape-recorder harness and earphones, strapped the recorder in place, fixed a button-mike on his coat and took a larger mike in his hand. In seconds both men were ready. Only then did Bleep ask:

'Is the kitty-cat digging itself out?'

'No,' said Mark. 'The firemen are.'

'Flamin' idiots,' said Digger. 'Supposing there's a real fire somewhere?

'What's insurance for?' said Bleep. 'Stop worrying.'

The truck slowed to a halt. They all piled out and struggled through the snow to the fire-engine. Digger and Bleep went to work. Angle-shots of the fire-engine rammed into a snow-drift — shots of spinning wheels. Bleep's external mike waved around picking up a mixture of sounds. Then he called to Chad:

'Grab this mike — get high up on that drift and hold it facing the wind.'

Chad struggled upward, found support on a gatepost buried beneath snow and held the mike aloft. The bitter wind howled around it.

'Enough,' Bleep called. 'Come down.'

Chad stepped forward, slipped and went up to his neck in snow. It took long minutes to haul him out.

'Why?' Mark demanded of Bleep. 'Haven't we got enough library recordings of howling wind?'

'Realism,' Bleep grinned. 'For my private collection.'

'Not in company time,' Mark snapped. 'Pack up and let's be off — the engine's nearly free.'

'Are they going on?'

'No. They're following us when they've dug clear. Ruff's going to try across the field. The house garden backs on to one corner.'

No one sympathised with the snow-soaked Chad. He trudged miserably to the truck, climbed inside and was sent rolling when it started off without warning.

The truck was a German-made, rear-wheel-drive vehicle, and under Ruff's skilled and experienced control it crossed the field as if designed especially for such work. After the initial bumping and sliding the journey was moderately smooth, until Ruff skidded the truck in a semicircle and declared: 'All change. This is as far as we go.'

The field sloped down to a hedge. This slope was piled high where snow had drifted, and impossible to cross. The drift extended beyond the hedge, sweeping up to cover the small house as far as its upper windows.

They climbed from the truck and surveyed the scene.

'What flamin' idiot phoned in the call about the cat?' Digger asked.

'Driver of a milk-collection lorry,' said Mark. 'His was the last vehicle to get through before drifts blocked the lane to the farm, two miles away. He couldn't reach the tree without ladders. And anyway, he daren't stop, else his lorry would have got stuck.'

Ruff pointed across the field.

'Circle around there with the longest nylon rope we have.'

'The one with the claw-clamp attachment?' Bleep asked. 'Then what?'

'Rig it to that tree beside the house. It's a good stout tree. Should stand the weight of a pulley and tackle.'

'Good!' Mark slapped Ruff on the shoulder, then poked Digger in the ribs. 'Get set up.'

Digger went back to the truck for his cameras. Mark turned to Chad. 'You're the lightest, so you're elected to take the rope through. Ever seen a claw-clamp?'

'No.' Chad began to wonder even more why he'd been crazy enough to transfer to the news squad.

'Show him, Ruff,' said Mark. 'While Bleep and I set up the other gear.'

Ruff led Chad to the truck. From a side locker he pulled a massive coil of rope.

'Looks heavy, but it's surprisingly light.' Ruff hefted it in his hands, then held up the metal attachment at one end. 'You throw this over the thickest branch you can find. Its weight will carry it so it hangs down. Then by just flicking the rope you'll be able to run it through the open clamp. One good pull on the rope and the clamp will snap shut — dead easy. Look, I'll show you.' Ruff demonstrated the simplicity of it.

'Releasing it is more tricky,' he added. 'But it's easy to climb up the rope and move this small lever. The claw won't open until you give at least three pulls on the rope. So you can climb down to the ground, give a few heaves on the rope and the clasp will come free. Watch out it doesn't bop you on the head when it falls,' Ruff warned Chad. 'That's the only danger. Got it?'

Chad nodded. 'Got it. Seems simple enough.'

'Right — then let's hop.' As they joined the others Ruff said with a chuckle: 'Now I'll be able to try out my trick gun.'

'Gun?'

'Yes. I've rigged up a gun to fire a thin rope — like life-boats use. Once you've attached the nylon rope to the tree I'll fire the thin rope across to you. Tie it to the end of your rope and I'll haul it across.' Ruff pointed to the ladder-rack on top of the truck. 'I'll fix the rope to that, drop on a light-weight pulley, and we can swing across the drift.'

'Oh, I've got the idea now!' Chad became enthusiastic. 'Couldn't work it out at first.' He looped the coiled nylon rope over his shoulders.

'Ruff told you what to do?' Mark asked.

'Yes. I'm to circle around the deeper drifts, get into the garden and fix the rope to the tree.'

'That's the idea. Now hop!'

Chad stumbled and floundered more than hopped, but he managed to circle the deepest drifts without plunging higher than his waist in the snow. It was hard going, and he began to appreciate why Mark Venner chose this method. It would be difficult to keep valuable cameras and sound-recording equipment out of the snow while struggling through it.

This exercise warmed Chad to a tingling glow, making him feel much more energetic. He also felt happier about the new job. He might be given the dirtiest tasks, but someone had to do them and this particular one was important. Mark had been right. A heavier person would have sunk much deeper into the drifts — probably wouldn't have got through.

At last Chad circled until he reached a rise of ground level with the garden tree. He trudged across, skirted a deeper drift where the banking sloped downward, and with a final heave clambered over the almost hidden fence of the garden. A few minutes later he stood beneath the tree.

'Oh my gosh!' Chad exclaimed, looking upward. 'You poor wee thing. I thought they were joking about a cat.'

Chad wasn't especially fond of cats. He liked them. He liked dogs, too. Some people are crazy about cats — but you didn't have to be a cat-lover to feel sorry for the poor frozen-looking creature crouching on one of the upper branches. Its fur was so thickly covered with frost and powdered snow that only its eyes and a faint twitching of its pointed ears betrayed the cat's presence in the tree.

For some reason, probably known only to cats, this one

had climbed the tree, become paralysed with fear and clung to the branch, unable to move. Particles of snow and ice blowing around the cat had turned it into a small crouching white statue.

Chad uncoiled the nylon rope, judged the distance to the strongest branch and flung the metal claw-clamp towards it. His aim was bad. The metal fell back, almost hitting him on the head. He tried again, and again. The cat's eyes watched him intently, but it didn't move. At his fifth attempt Chad sent the claw-clamp cleanly over the branch.

As the rope swung gently he flicked the main length so that it looped itself around the metal. He pulled downward in a swift tug. The clamp sprang closed, trapping the rope securely. Chad swung on it a few times to test it. Then, trudging up to the highest point of a snow-covered garden shed, he signalled to Ruff and the others. Ruff waved the line-firing gun. Chad yelled that he understood the gun was ready to fire.

He heard a faint plop and saw an object snaking through the air above the deep drifts. It arched upward to fall slowly in a long, curving trajectory above his head until it dropped about three feet from the tree. Chad clambered back, tied the line to the rope-end, then signalled Ruff to haul in the line with the rope attached.

While the rope was being stretched across Chad moved carefully along the slippery branch towards the cat. He was halted by Mark, shouting furiously.

'Stay where you are, you dope! We want rescue shots before you touch the cat.'

Chad waved to show he understood. The cat surveyed him solemnly.

'You'll have to wait, puss. Got to take your picture first.' Chad rubbed chilled fingers as he balanced himself in the tree. 'They'd better take mine too. I feel like Tarzan — a deep-freeze Tarzan at that.' He giggled at his weak joke and glanced towards the house.

No smoke rose from the chimneys and the house looked cold and deserted. Then Chad realised that from his perch in the tree he was level with the bedroom windows and could see something small and white moving in one of them. He thought at first that the window-glass was reflecting a snow-covered tree branch, but a longer scrutiny made him think differently.

'Oh my gosh!' he muttered, and struggled farther up the tree to get a better view.

There was no mistaking what he saw this time.

Chad glanced down as the tree creaked and swayed. Bleep was swinging along the rope, gripping a block and pulley in one hand and operating a camera with the other. He landed gently, waved a signal and the pulley was hauled back.

'Stay there,' Bleep ordered Chad, and aimed his camera upward. 'Okay, I've got the cat. Now climb slowly towards it. Make it look real hard. Miss your footing and slip once or twice. That'll please the customers.'

'D'you want me to break a leg?' Chad inquired.

'Can you?' Bleep grinned. 'You'll get compensation. But don't fall until I've got you sighted.'

'Stop kidding!' Chad was annoyed.

'Who's kidding?' Bleep retorted. 'Intrepid TV news reporter breaks leg to save life of cat. The customers will love it.'

'I'm not a reporter yet.'

'Make a good job of this and you'll be promoted. Not to worry. A broken leg heals quickly.'

'You're crackers!' Chad exclaimed. 'And anyway — the cat can wait.'

Again the tree creaked and swayed as Digger swung across and dropped beside Bleep.

'Go get the flamin' thing!' Digger called. 'And let's all go home. Who d'you think you are — Tarzan the snowman?'

'There's something more important than the cat.' Chad pointed to the house, slipped and went slithering down the branches. He grabbed the first hand-hold he could find. But

'Now grab the flippin' kitty!' Digger shouted

this small branch snapped. Chad fell astride a lower branch, flung his arms around it and held on.

'Wonderful!' Bleep cried.

'My angle too.' Digger had dashed to the other side of the tree. 'Now grab the flippin' kitty!'

Chad realised the cat was right under his face. He raised his left arm, cradled it around the now shivering animal and drew it to his chest. Suddenly the cat seemed glad to be there. Its fur crackled as the ice layer stuck around it moved.

'That's great!' Bleep called. 'Now edge backwards to the trunk. I'll reach up and take it from you. Hey, Digger, cover Chad from your side.'

'Will do.'

Chad eased back, grateful to reach the firmer support of the tree-trunk. He passed the cat down to Bleep.

'Okay — cut!' said Mark, who had arrived on the pulley without Chad noticing. 'Nice work, Chad.' Mark grinned at Digger. 'A sweet little four minutes, I think. Ruff's taking shots of the fire-boys as they cross the field. Is the cat okay?'

'Think so,' said Bleep. 'Half froze.'

'Jump down, Chad,' Mark ordered, and waited to steady him as he landed. 'Now take the cat in your arms. Hold its face to the camera. Run a few close-ups, Ruff.'

'Won't someone listen to me?' Chad yelled. 'It's important.'

Bleep finished filming. 'Okay, now talk.'

'Up there,' said Chad, 'there's a baby in a cot — waving its arms. I think it's crying.'

'Babies do,' said Bleep. 'All the time.'

'Shouldn't peep in windows, said Digger. 'Not bedroom windows. It's naughty.'

Mark waved them to silence.

'The house is supposed to be empty. Go on, Chad, tell me what you saw.'

'I could see the baby clearly, but there's someone else in the room too. Looks like a young woman. She's lying on the floor — sort of huddled up. She didn't move at all.'

'You're sure about this?'

Chad nodded. 'Quite sure.'

Mark turned, signalled to Ruff, then yelled instructions. Ruff waved acknowledgment.

'The fire-engine's reached the field,' Mark told Digger and Bleep. 'They'll probably make a ladder bridge over the drifts once they know there are people stranded in the house. Get all the shots you can.'

Chad left them and ran to the house. The cat began moving. Chad unzipped his windcheater, stuffed the now partially thawed-out cat inside, and hurried on.

Snow had drifted high up the back of the house. Chad struggled through heavy drifts to reach the front, where snow lay less thick. The front door was locked. Chad thumped on it and called 'Anybody home?' through the letter-box flap. When he opened the flap and listened he heard a baby crying. But the sound was only faint.

Three windows fronted the lower part of the house. Chad pushed at them. Two were locked, but the third slid open. He climbed into a small room, sparsely furnished, went from there into a hallway. He unlocked the front door, leaving it partly open, then called again loudly: 'Anybody home?' The cries of the baby came from beyond the stairs.

Chad pounded up them. The cries became louder and from left of the stairhead. He hurried along the landing, paused, then quietly opened a door and stepped into a small room. Obviously a nursery, judging by the bunny-rabbit wallpaper, the cot and baby toys scattered around.

The baby stood in its cot, chubby hands grasping the rails, weaving on sturdy-looking but unsteady legs. Its face was tear-stained, its hands and arms blue with cold. The baby gazed at Chad, wide-eyed but silent now.

'Hullo,' said Chad softly. 'Where's your mum?' His foot stubbed against something on the floor. Chad looked down on a young woman, lying very still, as if in deep sleep.

He heard Mark's voice calling.

'Up here!' Chad called back.

Feet thudded on the stairs.

'Don't you know better than to break into —' Mark began, but stopped when he saw the woman.

Meanwhile Chad crossed to the cot, pulled up all the blankets he could find, wrapped them around the baby and lifted it in his arms. The cat stirred and stuck its claws into Chad's shirt.

'Ouch! I'd forgotten about you.' Chad moved the baby to the other side.

'I think she's alive,' said Mark, kneeling on the floor. 'Must have collapsed. Lucky you saw them. What fool said the house was empty? Have a look in the other —' Mark flashed a grin at the burdened Chad. 'No, I'll do it. You've got your hands full.'

Mark returned with a pile of blankets. He covered the woman carefully. 'She's due for hospital. How's the baby?'

'Asleep,' said Chad in surprise.

Mark nodded. 'Exhausted, poor little mite. The blankets warmed it, so it slept. Maybe just as well.'

'The firemen are coming over.' Chad looked out of the window.

'Take the kid downstairs. Tell them that we shall need a stretcher.'

Chad met the fire officer in the hall. From that moment the fire-brigade men took over, but not before Digger and Bleep had a number of shots of Chad with the baby cuddled in one arm and the struggling cat in the other.

'D'you *have* to keep taking photographs?' one of the fire officers complained. 'You TV chaps are a damn nuisance. Why don't you leave people in peace?'

Chad grew suddenly furious.

'Listen, chum — if it hadn't been for us going to the trouble to take photographs this kid and its mother would still be without help. A few pictures aren't going to harm them. So why don't you belt up?'

190

'Good on yer, cobber,' said Digger. 'Now hand over that baby to the big bad fireman and let's hop.'

Chad was still fuming as he struggled back to join Ruff.

'Forget it,' said Ruff. 'Our job is to go out, record the news in pictures and sound, then get the heck out of it. I expect Mark will leave Bleep to cover the fire-engine's trip back. They've radioed for an ambulance to meet them on the main road.'

Mark and Digger returned. 'Pull out, Ruff,' said Mark 'Let's get this stuff in the can. Bleep will do the follow-up.'

They climbed into the truck. Ruff sent it bouncing back over the field.

'What happened?' Chad asked. 'Why were they alone? Is the baby's mother very ill?'

'Enough!' Mark snapped. 'Bleep will sew it up and get the reasons. Then we'll fit it on to your tape. You'll have to get used to this, Chad. We've got a deadline to meet. All our film has to be processed, then cut and edited. We dub the sound-track on later. That doesn't take long. One of the announcer staff do it from our facts.'

'Some flamin' cutting to do,' said Digger. 'I over-shot. So did Bleep.'

'Couldn't do much else,' said Mark. 'Too many angles. We might get four minutes.'

Ruff laughed scornfully. 'Bet you we only get three.'

And that was all they did get.

'A tragic result of heavy snowstorms was averted today by our news team,' said the news reader later that evening. 'Here are scenes from their hazardous journey through the snow to rescue a mother and her baby. Firemen were also at the scene.'

Chad watched it on the monitor. No shots of the fire-engine being dug out. No shots of him struggling with the rope. One brief shot of him holding the baby, several shots of firemen handling the stretcher over a snow bridge made of ladders, then the transfer to an ambulance.

'Seven hours it took us,' said Chad. 'They didn't show half of it.'

'Why should they?' said Mark. 'The whole damn news only gets seven minutes. You'll get used to it.' He left them.

Chad looked doubtful. 'But who was the woman, and what was the matter with her? Why —?'

Bleep halted the flow of questions.

'Someone else is on that angle. There might be a follow-up — human tragedy and all that blah. We went out for a cat-up-a-tree shot. We stumbled on the other. Got to be careful. Might be some family row. Her old man may have tried to murder her. So all we do is film the facts — sick woman, crying baby in lonely house cut off by snowdrifts, cat up a tree, fire-engine stuck in snow. Quick, slick human drama. Not our business to pass opinions on it. That's the studio boys' job.'

'Flamin' frustrating, ain't it? said Digger. 'But you did well, cobber.'

'From him, that's a compliment.' Bleep grinned at Chad.

Mark came back, a slip of paper in his hand.

'Fire at the docks,' he announced. 'Cargo ship — might blow up any minute. Let's hop before she does.'

'Ah well,' said Bleep, 'it'll be warmer down there.'

Chad grinned. He was beginning to get the hang of the job. Film the facts, Bleep had said. Let's hop.

Chad hopped.

CHARLIE BASSETT'S ROCKET TRIP

The trouble with Charlie Bassett, Jim muttered to himself, was lack of imagination. He stuffed three rather tired-looking doughnuts into a paper bag, and crammed this into the food locker of *Uranus 1*. He slammed the door so violently that the handle came off; angrily he bolted it back again and then walked back across the dump with an instinctive feeling down near his belt that it must be about time for lunch.

It was, and he had second helpings of both courses. That was sheer common sense; ruefully he had to admit that three doughnuts might be rather too little to last two space travellers on a journey of millions and millions of miles. True, *Uranus 1* didn't rely on old-fashioned propulsion by solid or liquid fuel. Not for nothing had he spent three days out in the garage developing the Jim Corbett Space-Wasp, specially designed to alter the whole idea of getting from one planet to another.

But even with a Space-Wasp, three doughnuts was risky. He wished he hadn't needed to spend all this week's pocket-money on extra wire and dry batteries — and wondered first if there'd be a chance to raid the larder after lunch, and, second, if Charlie's lack of imagination would prevent him from adding at least a couple of apples or a bottle of lemonade to the rations.

The larder raid proved to be impossible. It was almost as if the whole family had got wind of Project Uranus and were hanging round the kitchen deliberately to prevent it ever being carried out.

Mentally, he tightened his belt. It was better to arrive

hungry on Uranus than not at all. He set off again for the dump, and was relieved to see Charlie Bassett beside *Uranus 1,* waving a paper bag in greeting.

'What have you got, Charlie? Sausage rolls?'

Charlie looked shocked. He clutched the paper bag tightly — but not too tightly — to his chest. 'No, I've got my golden hamsters. You didn't think I'd leave *them* behind, did you?'

Jim's eyes bulged. 'Golden hamsters? What use d'you think golden hamsters are going to be on Uranus?'

Charlie looked at him blankly. 'I don't understand. They aren't actually any use here on Earth.' He clutched the neck of the paper bag, opened it carefully, and peered affectionately inside. 'But I'm fond of them. I couldn't leave them behind.'

'Huh!' Jim put a wealth of feeling into his snort of disgust. 'What about food? I suppose you brought some food?'

'Oh, yes,' said Charlie brightly, 'I've brought some food. Enough to last them a week.'

'Them?'

'The hamsters, of course. It's good of you to think about —'

Jim interrupted him violently. 'I didn't mean food for the hamsters, you fathead! I meant food for us.'

'Oh!'

'Well, did you bring anything for us? I've got some doughnuts. What have you brought?'

Charlie Bassett put the paper bag down beside him. Inside it something moved, and a small paw stuck out at the top. 'Actually, no,' he said, avoiding Jim's eyes. 'I mean to say, I meant to, but I kind of forgot.'

'I suppose that means I'll have to share with you,' grumbled Jim. 'But we're going to look pretty daft if something goes wrong and we don't get there quickly.'

Charlie frowned at him anxiously. 'It won't take more than a week, will it? You see, Araminta's all right — she doesn't eat much, but Hercules has a terrible appetite. I can't bear to think of him being hungry.'

196

Jim gulped. Of all the stupid asses in the world to pick as partner for a space voyage, why did he have to choose Charlie Bassett? Still, there wasn't much he could do about it now. 'We're leaving in ten minutes,' he said. 'Better synchronise our watches.'

'I haven't got a watch.'

'You haven't got *anything* much, have you? Except golden hamsters.' Jim snorted. 'Keep the door closed while I nip back to the house. With any luck they've all gone out and I can get us something more to eat from the larder.' He climbed out of *Uranus 1* and stamped angrily back across the dump.

He halted at the garden fence, and peered cautiously through a knot-hole to see if there was anybody visible inside the kitchen window. There wasn't, so he pushed open the back gate and moved silently along the grass path between the vegetable-beds towards the back door. It was closed, and so was the window beside it. On a warm summer day that could mean only one thing — everybody had gone out. Relaxing his caution, he went round to the front door, rummaged for his key, and let himself in. 'Hullo!' he called out, as a last precaution, but there was no reply. Selecting a large paper bag from the shelf in the kitchen, he opened the larder door.

'Whew!' It was as if they'd *known* he was off to Uranus and would need a good supply of food. There was a tin of freshly made buns, two packets of biscuits, and a small meat pie. On the other shelf above these he found a tin of sardines, and another of corned beef. When he'd crammed all these into the bag there was no room for any more. He closed the larder door and sneaked out of the house, with his heart hammering at the possibility of meeting someone on the front path as he let himself out.

He was in luck. He shot round the house and along the path to the back gate without being seen by anybody, including the neighbours whose windows overlooked the garden. He glanced at his watch and then started running, realising that twenty minutes had gone by since he'd left *Uranus 1*, and that Charlie was expecting him back in half that time. He climbed up to the top of the ridge of old tins, broken bicycles and half-bricks that surrounded the dump, and looked across to the other side.

His heart stopped beating. *Uranus 1* was gone!

Staring wildly at the spot where the rocket had been he scrambled across the dump towards it, wondering if it had fallen over, or if his eyes were deceiving him.

But they weren't. In the place where *Uranus 1* had been there was now nothing but a large ragged hole — just as if something terribly powerful had blown up.

He looked up into the clear blue sky, shielding his eyes with one hand, straining to see anything up there. But there was nothing to be seen. *Uranus 1* had gone — gone beyond recall. He thought of Charlie, sitting alone with his two golden hamsters, Charlie the silly ass who must have started fiddling with levers and controls while he'd been away.

His throat went dry. That was the last of Charlie. Charlie didn't know how to steer the rocket, or how to land it, and there was nobody up there to help him.

He sat down. Absent-mindedly he opened the paper bag and ate two of the buns, then suddenly realised this was hardly respectful to the late Charlie Bassett. He reproached himself; it was hardly kind to sit munching while your best and oldest friend sailed off to his doom in the unknown wastes of outer space.

No, there was no doubt what he had to do next. There'd be a horrible row about it, but he'd have to go round to Charlie's parents and tell them what had happened.

His feet dragged reluctantly as he set off across the dump towards the road. He'd always been a bit afraid of Mrs Bassett, and it seemed likely she might be quite angry about losing Charlie. Charlie was the only son she had; and though he was a bit of a fathead, at heart he wasn't such a bad chap.

He walked slowly along the pavement towards the cross-roads. Ahead of him, where the old cinema had been pulled down, men with pneumatic drills were busy working on the foundations for a new building. He stopped to watch them. Alter all, there was no hurry about telling Mrs Bassett. Arriving ten minutes sooner wouldn't help to bring Charlie back. He leaned against the wall overlooking the building site. Come to think of it, he was doing Mrs Bassett a good turn by postponing the moment when she'd have to hear about Charlie. And, anyway, what was going on down among the new foundations was too fascinating to miss. On one side three men were drilling their way through an old brick wall, and on the other a row of concrete-mixers were turning, and pouring out a thick stream of grey cement into troughs dug deep into the ground. Farther off, lorries were bringing rubble and tipping it into a huge hollow, where a steam-hammer was thumping it down to make a firm surface. He watched one lorry pull up, reverse, then raise its back in readiness to tip a heavy load of bricks, old metal pipes and ...

Jim gripped the top of the wall tightly with both hands; gliding down from the back of the lorry into the hollow was *Uranus 1*!

Jim shouted. He waved to the men down below; they grinned cheerfully, and waved back, then went on with their drilling. To his horror the steam-shovel moved along on caterpillar tracks towards the place where the lorry had tipped *Uranus 1*.

Jim ran along beside the wall, looking for a door. When he found one he hurled himself against it, but though it shook, it refused to open. Panting, he raced along another side of the building site, until he was directly above the steam-hammer. 'Stop!' he shouted frantically, pointing at *Uranus 1*. 'Wait a minute, I've got to talk to you!'

But though the driver turned his head and waved a greeting, obviously he didn't hear above the noise of his machine.

The huge hammer rose, right above Uranus 1

His hand went out to a control lever and the huge hammer rose, right above *Uranus 1*. Jim looked from left to right and back again. Surely somebody must notice the big letters, saying URANUS 1, painted on the side of it? Yes, of course it looked like an old water-boiler, because it had been an old hot-water-boiler until he converted it, but all these men must have heard of space-ships — must know the meaning of the words 'Uranus 1'.

Crunch!

Jim covered his eyes. He thought of Charlie Bassett and the two golden hamsters, all flat as pancakes, doomed for ever more to be part of the foundations of the new block of council flats. And all because nobody would *listen*!

He didn't want to watch the hammer and the drills any longer. His mind went back to Mrs Bassett. She might as well know the worst. Nibbling another bun (there was no question at all of having to share them with Charlie now), he trudged along until he reached the corner of the road in which Charlie lived. *Had* lived.

The blame, he supposed, would all fall on him. It wasn't as if he could claim that *Uranus 1* was a genuine space project, to outdo everything the Russians had done. He'd been *thinking* of it as genuine, of course, for all the weeks since he began it, but in his heart of hearts he'd always known the rocket was nothing but an old hot-water-boiler, and the Jim Corbett Space-Wasp nothing but a bundle of bits and pieces out of broken radio sets. It wasn't as if he could report that Charlie Bassett had died gallantly, five hundred miles out in space, with a last heroic radio message back to Earth. Charlie had died under the horrible impact of a steam-shovel, cooped up in a water-boiler.

His footsteps dragged up the steps to the front door, and he rang the bell. His stomach turned as he watched it swing open, and the severe face of Mrs Bassett appeared.

'I've ... I've come to tell you about Charlie.'

'I should certainly think so! And about time, too.'

He looked at her in surprise. How could she have known so soon? 'I didn't mean it to happen,' he said lamely.

'I should hope not. White dust all over his suit just back from the cleaners! You should know better than to let him play inside an old boiler.'

Jim stared at her blankly, then his eyes travelled downwards as Charlie Bassett looked out from under her arm. 'I'm sorry, Jim — really I am. But the golden hamsters got fed up, and I was bored waiting.'

'You were under orders to remain at your post. Next time you'd ...' The words died away on Jim's lips. 'Never mind.' He nodded. 'Goodbye, Mrs Bassett. Goodbye, Charlie.'

He went home by way of the building site. There was now a broad wet sheet of concrete where the steam-hammer had been working. He looked at it for a moment, but his mind was already on something else — an enormous metal drainpipe lying in a field behind his house.

Stood on its end, with a ladder for getting in and out, it should do splendidly — as the body of *Uranus 2*!

EDDIE'S SUMMER PROJECT

There'd been the summer of the butterfly collection, and the summer of the Eastsea Angling Festival — but the latter was one Eddie Mathers would rather forget, because of its icy climax, with six of them clinging on for dear life to the side of an upturned dinghy while a motor-boat came out from shore with what seemed incredible slowness to rescue them. Earlier there'd been athletic summers, when he'd been up at the crack of dawn to practise sprints down at the recreation ground in the hope of carrying off the County Junior Prize; and gardening summers, when he'd tended and watered a patch of greenery in the hope that by July it would be a sea of bright colour.

There'd always been a summer project; but now, moving away from Eastsea, the whole pattern seemed to have been upset. In a strange northern industrial town, where he knew not a single boy or girl, life promised to be thoroughly drab and uninteresting. Even at school he'd failed to make any friends. He supposed it was his southern voice which caused the trouble. 'Ee,' said Charlie Moyes, 'tha sounds a bit stook oop, tha does.' He'd pushed Eddie hard in the stomach with his fist. 'Ah don't take mooch to fancy talk — and ah reckon you'll not make pals easy, not while you're oop on your high horse.'

He'd tried coming down off his high horse, but as he'd never been conscious before of being 'stook oop' it wasn't easy. He'd even tried talking with a Bradfield accent, but there was no doubt about it — you had to be born up in the North to talk that way. 'Ee,' he practised in front of the mirror in his bedroom. 'Ah sound real daft wi' a Bradfield accent!' And he had to admit that was right. He did.

It wasn't much encouragement at the start of the summer. It looked as though this would be the Summer of the Solitary Cycle Rides — but at least there were plenty of places to explore, if you didn't mind a lot of pushing up steep hills. Bradfield lay in a cleft between high moors of such poor land that not even sheep grazed there. Once you had climbed well above the town you were well away from the smoke of the cotton mills, with not a house in sight — nothing, in fact, except the stump of a distant stone Folly, begun by one of those eighteenth-century eccentrics trying to build a tower up to heaven.

One sunny afternoon he set out to reach it. The last two miles had to be ridden over thin and bumpy grassland, with a wary eye kept on the route to avoid sudden boulders. Eddie was red in the face and wet with perspiration by the time he reached the Folly, and the moment he leaned his bike against the mossy granite wall he wished he hadn't bothered to come, for the Folly was little more than a shell of stonework, ten feet high. The rest had fallen — perhaps after two centuries of high winds the stonework had become undermined. The trimmed granite blocks lay scattered for fifty yards in every direction. He picked one up. Whoever had originally chipped it to size had been a conscientious workman, for the surface was smoothly finished. He put it up on the nearest heap of blocks, and then stood staring first at the Folly, then at the fallen ruins.

It was a funny sort of summer project, but at least it would give a purpose to his cycle rides. He scratched his head. Why not? Rebuilding the Folly would be more fun than touring the lanes and wishing fruitlessly that he were back at Eastsea once again.

No sooner decided, than begun. He heaved stone after stone into position, until by the time for returning home he'd replaced more than twenty. His hands were scratched and sore, and his mucles ached from wrestling with the big chunks of granite, but there was no doubt about it — he'd made progress.

He stopped only when he heard the mournful note of the hooter over at the prison. That meant five o'clock; over in Bradfield they didn't bother to use factory whistles at the start and finish of the working day, for the distant hooter was loud enough and accurate enough. He looked across the valley at the dark grey walls of the prison, and shivered. Now that the sun was going in the hills it looked bleak and sinister; he was glad to pedal down the slope towards the road and the way back into town.

His hands had plenty of time to recover before the next visit. One thing about Bradfield was its weather. Eddie had always thought of Manchester as the place with the wettest and gloomiest climate in the country, but he was willing to place a hefty bet that Bradfield had twice as many inches of rain every year. Most of them seemed to be concentrated into the next five days. The gutters ran like rivers, and even the ride to and from school was enough to soak through any but the thickest raincoats.

Five days indoors was enough to make him thankful to get up to the Folly again when the sun came out once more. He set out early, determined to put in a full day's work and raise the height of the walls by at least a foot before the light faded.

With him he took his lunch and tea, in a haversack over his shoulders. As he pedalled hard in bottom gear up the slope of Bradfield he was halted suddenly by Charlie Moyes, 'Ah see tha don't care mooch for Bradfield,' he grinned.

'I've seen better places,' admitted Eddie. 'It's a good place to get out of on a sunny day.'

'Ayo, but wheer to? There's nobbut moors and hills for miles.'

Eddie looked at the open, friendly smile. He wondered if he'd simply be laughed at if he explained about the Folly.

'I've found a place worth going to,' he explained. 'It's a tough ride, but I like it.'

He rode on, and pushed the bike briskly up the steep inclines, eager to reach his target. There was a cooling breeze across the hills when he left the road, and his wet, perspiring face dried quickly. The grass track was easier for cycling now that he knew the worst patches to avoid, and he made good progress on the long two-mile stretch up to the Folly.

He dismounted, and sat down on a heap of granite blocks to get his breath back. Whew! It was a gloriously clear day. The sky was bright blue, with just a few wispy clouds to the east; the hillsides were lit by the bright sunshine; far away to the south a tiny train, like a toy, puffed its way across the high viaduct. To the north, the direction from which he'd come...

Eddie stood up, frowning. He'd begun to think of the Folly as a private place, to which nobody else ever came. But far down on the grass track, pedalling laboriously towards him, was a figure in a bright red shirt and khaki shorts. Head bent, bottom high in the air, the newcomer was thrusting hard at the pedals, swinging the bike between tussocks of grass, and climbing steadily, not sparing himself in determination to reach the top without dismounting.

Eddie went round to the far side of the Folly, hoping not to be seen, hoping that whoever it was would take one of the side paths which skirted the summit. He sat at the far side for a full five minutes before remembering the bike, bright yellow and visible a mile off. He'd left it standing against the stonework, in full view from below.

Sighing, he heaved himself to his feet, and walked round the Folly — to crash headlong into Charlie Moyes!

'What on earth...?'

Charlie grinned at him. 'Thought ah'd find out about this woonderful place of yours,' he puffed. He raised one eyebrow, and looked up at the Folly. 'Can't say ah see mooch that's woonderful about this old thing. What d'you do oop here? Bird-watching, or flying kites, or somethin'?'

Irritated, Eddie said, 'If you must know, I'm trying to rebuild the Folly.'

Charlie looked at him as if he was mad. It was exactly the reaction Eddie had expected, and he supposed that it was a reasonable enough attitude to take. 'What for?' asked the North-countryman.

'I ... I don't know. Not really. Just for something to do,' he said lamely.

'Aye.' Charlie said it slowly, thoughtfully, then the corners of his mouth twitched. 'Ah always thought you was a bit daft. Now ah knows! But as ah'm here, ah'll give a hand wi' it.' He looked up at the work Eddie had done the previous week. 'Ah'll tell you one thing, mate — and that's about yon wall. It don't stand oop straight. Time tha've got anoother row of stones oop there, it'll be tumblin' down again. Tha's needing a ploombline.'

'A what?'

'Ploombline.' Charlie looked at him scornfully. 'Tha' don't know mooch, does tha? Got a bit of string?'

'Aye.' The North-country word came out before Eddie could stop it, and he felt himself going red in the face as Charlie laughed.

The 'ploombline' — a length of string with a small stone tied to the end — showed that Charlie was right. The wall was badly slanted, and had to be taken down and rebuilt. By the time they'd done this they were hungry enough for lunch. Luckily Eddie had brought plenty, so there was enough for them both.

Afterwards the new work went with a swing. Eddie brought the granite blocks up to the Folly, and Charlie Moyes, stronger and more skilful, wedged them into place. The wall rose swiftly, until Eddie had to build a platform below in order to reach up and hand further blocks to his companion. Every journey for more was longer than the last.

He reached down for one lying on the grass without looking at it, lifted it an inch, and was surprised when it slid suddenly out of his hands. His fingers felt sticky and slimy; he looked down, and saw they were covered with something white and treacly. He sniffed it, and frowned in puzzlement.

'Hey, Charlie! Come here a minute!'

'What's oop?'

'Come here and I'll show you.'

He waited, while Charlie Moyes scrambled down from the top of the Folly and joined him. 'This had better be good,' panted Charlie. 'If tha's brought me all the way down to show me a clump of bootercups or summat, ah'll shove tha teeth down tha throat, ah will!'

For answer Eddie held up his hands, covered with the sticky white substance.

'What is it?'

'Paint, Charlie. Fresh white paint.'

'Where did it coom from?'

'Off this stone. Who'd come up here painting stones?'

'Ah don't know, mate. Who'd come oop here rebuilding Follies?'

Eddie laughed. 'Yes, but this is even dafter! And look, there's a whole row of stones, leading down the slope, all covered with paint.'

Charlie walked the few yards to the nearest stone, and touched it with his fingertip. 'It's wet.' He tried another. 'Reckon they're all wet.'

'And over there — see? There's another row of them.' He stared down at the grass. 'They've all been arranged there for some reason. Look, here's a yellow patch, and a couple of bare patches, where they'd been lying before.'

Charlie scratched his head. 'Reckon it's a stupid kind of joke, Eddie. Ah don't see why anyone would bother.'

'Nor do I.' Eddie screwed up his eyes, and looked right down the line of whitened stones for a hundred yards. 'Could it be something to do with sheep?'

210

'Sheep? There's no sheep oop here. Not enough grass for grazing.' He turned back towards the Folly. 'Reckon it's not our business, anyhow. And we've got plenty of stones without having to use yon painted ones.' He climbed up into position at the top of the wall. 'Right, mate, let's have some more!'

They worked until evening, by which time the Folly had risen a full five feet. Charlie had worked cleverly, interlocking the granite blocks as neatly as the original builders, so that from a distance it was almost impossible to tell where the old work ended and the new work began.

'Come on,' said Charlie eventually. 'Ah vote we head for home.' He straightened up, and massaged the small of his back. 'Ee, ah've discoovered mooscles ah didn't know ah had!' Comically he staggered down to the ground, and sat astride his bike. 'Tell tha what! Ah'll coom oop again tomorrow.'

'So will I! And we'll get it finished.'

'Aye, but what about all yon white stones? Ah don't like to shift them, in case they're for a purpose.'

Eddie shrugged his shoulders. 'We'll worry about that tomorrow.'

As they rode home Eddie whistled softly to himself. Maybe he'd been wrong about North-country people. Charlie Moyes wasn't so bad after all — and best of all, he seemed to have the same kind of crazy ideas as his own. How many people could you hope to find who'd jump at the chance of spending days on end repairing a Folly just for fun? Not many!

'Good night, Charlie! See you in the morning.'

'Ten o'clock, mate. Ah'll race you to the top!'

Back home, he settled his aching bones in a comfortable chair in front of the TV set. His mother looked at him curiously. 'You'd better get cleaned up before supper. You look as though you've spent the day working on a building site!'

'I *have!*' He explained what he and Charlie had done.

'What a funny idea! What's it for?'

He grinned. 'Goodness only knows! It's just that — well — before it was blown down the Folly must have been visible for twenty miles across the hilltops. Part of the scenery. It's worth putting it up again, just for that alone.'

There was no response to that. He hadn't really expected one. Ideas like rebuilding Follies seemed to baffle most people, and his own family were certainly no exception.

The programme ended, and the news began. Eddie watched, listening only vaguely to the day's accounts of the comings-and-goings of politicians, and his eyes were starting to close when suddenly he jerked into wakefulness.

'...from Bradfield Prison just over an hour ago. Police with tracker dogs are searching all the roads leading southwards off the moors. The escaped man, George Malleson, is serving a five-year sentence for smuggling, and the fact that a rope ladder was used in getting over the prison wall leads the police to believe it was placed there by outside accomplices as part of a prearranged plan. A car is reported missing from a village two miles south of the prison.'

Into Eddie's mind came the gloomy grey outline of the prison. It remained there all through supper, and when the next news bulletin was due he was ready in front of the TV set five minutes in advance.

'...and it is known that Malleson had confederates on the Continent, who may be aiding his escape. Police are guarding all East-coast ports and checking the passenger lists of all steamers for Belgium and Holland. So far police have not traced the car stolen from near the prison shortly after Malleson escaped.'

Eddie frowned. He felt certain that something in the back of his mind was eluding him. He said goodnight to his parents and went upstairs to bed, trying to push the thought of the prison out of his brain.

But he couldn't. It remained there, persistently, while he fought to get to sleep.

Then, just as at long last he was dozing off, it came to him. The stones! He sat bolt upright, staring into the darkness, then switched on the bedside lamp and looked at his watch. It was nearly midnight; through the open window he saw a bright moon high in the sky.

He rolled out of bed silently, and began to put on his clothes. His brain was whirling now, testing out one plan after another, rejecting each in turn as impracticable.

He scratched his head. Whatever plan he used, he'd need help.

Charlie Moyes!

He was the obvious one. If he went to the police, they'd say he was crazy. Maybe he *was* crazy — but it all seemed to fit so neatly that he simply had to find out.

Silently he went downstairs, and let himself out by the back door. He wheeled his bike out of the garage, then went back inside for a coil of rope. As an afterthought he picked up a long coil of steel cable that his father used for making tow-lines for canal barges operated by his company. He strapped that on to the saddlebag, and looped the rope over the handlebars. Then he wheeled the bike into the road, switched on the dynamo, and pedalled round to Charlie's house.

Outside he stopped, wondering how on earth to wake Charlie without rousing the rest of the household. He didn't even know which was Charlie's bedroom, and there wasn't a single light showing in the whole house.

There was only one way to find out! Alongside one wall of the house, stretching up thick branches to within a few feet of the windows, was an elm tree. He put a handful of gravel from the path into his pocket and scrambled up the trunk of the tree, then felt his way cautiously along a thick branch, pushing through thick masses of leaves. A thinner branch, swaying slightly, bore his weight reluctantly; at one moment he lost his grip, slid sideways, and hung head downwards towards the lawn, lit up by the moon. The noise he made in regaining his seat on the bough seemed tremendous, and at any moment he expected to see angry faces at every window, or worse still a policeman's torch flashed in his face from the pavement beyond the hedge.

He wriggled as far along the branch as he dared, then pushed aside a last cluster of leaves.

He sighed with relief. His calculations had been right; the branch had brought him to a point between two sets of windows, with a view into two bedrooms. The one on the left — the larger one — had a double bed. The one on the right, into which shone a broad band of moonlight, had a single bed. To confirm that it was Charlie's, a heap of cricket bats and pads lay in the corner beyond the bed.

Clutching his precarious branch with one hand, Eddie groped in his pockets for the gravel. He threw two pieces; one missed the window, but the other hit it with such force that for a second he thought he'd cracked it. He waited impatiently.

'Great fat snoring hippo!' he grunted to himself, when the figure under the blankets made no movement. He took two more pieces of gravel, and lobbed them across the gap between branch and window.

This time he was successful. Charlie sat up with a jerk, rubbing his eyes and staring across the room. Quickly Eddie flung two more bits of gravel. Charlie leaped out of bed, and crossed to the window. He flung it open and looked out.

'Pssst!'

'What the ... ? Who's out there?' Charlie's voice came in a loud stage whisper.

'Me — Eddie — I'm up here.'

Charlie looked at him sleepily. 'Fine,' he said, yawning. 'Very funny. Very funny indeed! Now perhaps tha'll get down and go home to bed.'

'Get up, Charlie,' whispered Eddie urgently. 'I want to talk to you.'

Charlie's expression was extraordinary. '*What?* In the

middle of the night? Tha' must be stark staring bonkers, mate. Ah'm going back to bed.'

'Charlie!'

Charlie Moyes turned back to the window. 'Aye? he queried patiently.

'Look, Charlie, I'm not doing this for fun. I'd rather be at home in bed. Come on down — it's something serious.'

Charlie scratched his head. 'Oh, all right then!'

Ten minutes later they were both pedalling furiously out of Bradfield towards the hills. Charlie had seen sense quickly enough, once he'd come downstairs and Eddie had had a chance to explain the idea in the back of his mind.

They reached the point in the road where the path forked off across the moors to the Folly. 'We'll ride up as far as we can,' said Eddie. 'Better push the last bit, though.'

It was when they were two hundred yards from the Folly that he called a halt by raising his hand. 'Leave your bike here,' he whispered. 'It's a good one.'

'What does tha mean by that?'

'Never mind, Charlie. Just do what I ask. Look, stick it here out of sight, where the grass is long.'

They continued until they were within fifty yards of the Folly, then Eddie again called a halt. 'You go over and start shifting the stones,' he said. 'Quiet as you can. I'll be with you in a minute.'

Charlie sighed. 'Are tha sure we're not just being plain daft? Ah bet there's not a living soul for two miles except us two crazy idiots. Anyway, what will tha be doin' while ah'm shiftin' stones?'

'I'm going up for a closer look. No sense in both of us going — that would mean twice as much noise.' He slipped away, pushing the bike, leaving Charlie at one end of the long row of painted stones. By the time he arrived back Charlie had already moved about twenty of them; the remainder took them only half an hour, and they left them fifty yards away in a hollow, face downwards.

By now Charlie was openly rebellious. 'By gum, Eddie, tha'll look right daft when all this gets talked about. At school they'll reckon tha's proper dopy.'

'You're going to tell them, then?'

'Aye, if nothing comes of all this. Aye, ah'll have a right good laugh.'

'They'll have a good laugh at *you*, too, Charlie!'

'Huh?'

'You came, too, remember?' He tried out his Bradfield accent again. 'That makes tha just as right dopy as me!'

Charlie gripped his shoulder suddenly. 'Look, mate, it's gettin' light!'

Across to the east the first signs of dawn were starting to appear. The cold grey light showed the faint silhouette of the prison in the distance; nearer, it revealed the outline of the Folly on the hilltop just above them. Charlie caught Eddie's arm again. 'He's there!' he whispered excitedly. 'By gum, tha was right!'

Eddie swung round, and stared at the Folly. For a moment he could see nothing, then he made out a dark shape beside it, moving round the stone tower back to the doorway.

'What do we do, Eddie? Rush him?'

'No. We stay right here.'

'But...!'

'Look, Charlie, if my guess is right, we shan't have long to wait.' He pricket up his ears. 'Listen! Hear anything?'

Charlie raised his head. 'Huh! Nobbut an aeroplane far off.'

'That's what I thought I heard. It's coming nearer.'

Charlie was searching the grey sky. 'Aye, there it is! Small one — just one of those single-engined planes from the flying-club.' He screwed up his face. 'Funny time of day to go flying for fun.'

'It's not for fun, Charlie. Why d'you think we shifted those stones?'

'Ah dunno.' Charlie scratched his head. 'That's one of the daft things that's been puzzling me half the night.'

They leaped out of their hiding-place and sprinted towards the Folly

'Just wait another minute and you'll see. Look, she's coming in closer.'

'Aye. Circling round like, as if she didn't know where to land.'

'Now d'you understand about the stones? You're not any too bright this morning.'

Charlie thumped his forehead with a ham-like fist. 'They were there to mark a landing-path!' he muttered. 'Why didn't ah guess that?'

The plane was now very low indeed, skimming the top of the hill so close that its undercarriage must have missed the Folly by only a few feet. The figure beside the tower had emerged again, and was waving frantically with both arms.

'Do we rush him now?' demanded Charlie impatiently.

'All right, then!'

They leaped out of their hiding-place in long grass, and sprinted towards the Folly. They'd run thirty yards before the man saw them, so intent was he on trying to signal the aeroplane. Then, when they were only fifty yards away, he realised what was happening, and turned to run round to the far side of the tower. A moment later he appeared again, scrambling into the saddle of Eddie's bike.

'Tha daft fool!' shouted Charlie. 'Tha left the bike there. We'll never catch him now!'

But Eddie kept on running, though the bike was quickly drawing away, heading swiftly down the grassy slope towards the road.

And suddenly it happened. The bike seemed to rear up on its back wheel, the rider flung out both hands to save himself, but was flung off, landing heavily on his shoulders.

Eddie ran up, grabbed one arm, and twisted it into a half-nelson. Charlie arrived, panting. 'Lucky he hit a bump,' he gasped.

'Bump?' Eddie laughed. 'Why d'you think I left my bike up there?' He reached down, and untied the thin steel cable from the cycle frame just below the saddle. 'The other end

218

of that's tied up beside the Folly. Now it'll do to tether the legs of Mr George Malleson. Charlie, ride my bike over to the prison and let them know.'

'What about the aeroplane?'

'Let them know about that, too. I reckon they'll find it was pinched. They'll probably find the stolen car parked at the airfield. All they need to do is warn every airfield — that pilot has to land *somewhere.*'

'Where d'you think he hoped to land?'

'On the Continent. Malleson's got pals over there.' He looked down at the prisoner. 'Haven't you, Malleson?'

Sitting beside his tethered prisoner, Eddie watched while Charlie rode across the bleak moor to the prison. Presently he saw two small vans leave the gates and head back across the heather towards him.

He grinned. It had been a different kind of summer project than usual, but it had gained him his first friend in Bradfield. Charlie Moyes might be a bit slow on the uptake, but 'tha durstn't have to be a genius to be a right good pal.'

He grinned again. His Bradfield accent was improving!

WAITING FOR ROGER

Sam sat on an upturned orange-crate, and took the mug of steaming tea from Mrs Carrots. It drowned the sensation of icy cold horror inside him, and made him conscious once more of what was going on around him — the noise of Marty Rheinbaum's steam-organ, the sharp crack of the rifles at the shooting-gallery, and the shrieks of the girls riding on the Sooperdooper Overhead Railway.

The only place silent was the Wall of Death. There was no roar of Roger's engine from inside the great round wooden bowl, and there was no line of heads peering down from the top with excitement to watch him work the motor-cycle higher and higher up the side, exhaust thundering, handle-bars flashing in the sun, until to the hundreds who'd paid their money it seemed impossible that he could avoid crashing.

Well, today he'd proved their point. He'd crashed. Nobody would ever know why, as like as not: whether the sparking-plug had failed, or whether the carburettor had been blocked by dirt, or whether ... There were dozens of possible explanations, but none of them would bring Roger back out of the ambulance.

'Come on, luv, drink it up. I allus says a cup of tea does more good than anything else you can get. Takes away the shock, it does.'

'Thanks, Mrs Carrots.' He heard his own voice, faint and muffled as though far away. Odd, unimportant things fluttered into his mind: how green the grass was underfoot, and the effort to remember what Mrs Carrots's real name was.

The name everybody called her had come from her stall, where big fat carrots hung in rows on strings, swaying in the breeze, and anybody clever enough to throw darts into three of them won a prize. It was a dull game, but new, and novelty mattered more than anything else in the fairground.

He stood up.

'Wot you goin' to do, Sam?' Mrs Carrots scratched the back of her neck. 'You could get another rider until Roger's back on 'is feet again. Tell you wot, my 'usband might know of someone. 'E's good, that way, is George. Knows more'n you'd think.'

Sam shook his head. 'Thanks, Mrs Carrots. But it's too soon to start thinking about that. I'm all mixed up at the moment — and I must get up to the hospital to find out about Roger.'

'George'll take you up there. 'E'll want to 'elp, just you see.'

'But what about your stall?'

'If I can't run that single-handed, then I oughter be out of the business! You wait 'ere. I'll send 'im over with the van.'

She was as good as her word. Within five minutes Mr and Mrs Carrots's ancient van was grinding its way across the hummocky grass towards him. He went to meet it, and clambered into the seat beside George.

'Don't look so upset, Sam.' George gave him a friendly smile. 'He'll be all right, mark my words. They're marvellous in these hospitals nowadays. Patch a man up from a sack of pieces, they can.'

The smile vanished. 'Sorry, I shouldn't have said that. Anyhow, Roger's not all that badly hurt, is he?'

'I don't know.' Sam clenched his fists. 'I saw it happen — the engine cut out when he was right on the top edge. When he fell the bike came down on top of him. They ... they wouldn't let me go near him.'

'Well, we'll soon find out.' The van lurched on to the road, and George put it into top gear.

The hospital was a huge, bleak, forbidding building. 'D'you want me to come in with you?' George asked.

'Thanks, but I'd rather go on my own. You'll be needed back at the stall.'

'There's a bus runs back from here every half-hour. Stops right by the fairground.'

'That'll do me fine. Thanks for the lift.'

'It's little enough.' George frowned, thoughtfully. 'Maybe I can help a bit more when we know what's what.'

Sam went up the broad steps to the main entrance. The clerk at the reception desk phoned the ward for him, then shook his head.

'I'm sorry, but you can't see him just now. He's still unconscious.'

Sam gasped.

'After the operation, I mean.' The clerk leaned across the desk. 'But the doctor's coming down to talk to you. He'll be able to tell you more than I can.'

Sam sat on a hard chair, thumbing his way through a magazine without reading a word.

'Are you Roger's brother?'

He looked up, flustered. The doctor had come in silently, and was standing right in front of him. 'Yes, that's right,' he said huskily.

The doctor pulled up a chair to face him. 'He's had a bad time. Oh, he'll pull through all right, but there's one thing I think I'd better tell you right now.'

Sam gulped. 'What's that?'

'He'll have to learn another way to make a living. He'll never ride again.'

The words haunted Sam all the way back in the bus. It was difficult to imagine Roger doing anything else but ride the Wall; he'd been doing it for five years, ever since he was sixteen. Dad had done it for twenty years before, and but for his eyesight Sam would have been taking over as co-rider on his sixteenth birthday.

The fairground was busier and noiser than when he'd left, for now it was warming up for the evening's big crowds. He walked back to the deserted Wall, and went inside. Roger's bike lay where it had fallen; the handlebars twisted, and a pool of oil underneath it. Automatically he began cleaning up the oil, remembering Roger's warning that oil on the timber of the Wall was one of the deadliest dangers a rider had to face.

What rider? He sat down beside the bike. Pity there couldn't be an accident — lighted match in the oil, then a big flare-up and a cheque from the insurance company. It would be so easy, and he had matches right there in his pocket. The money would tide them over until Roger was out of hospital and they could start hunting for another way to make a living.

Another way? Roger wasn't going to like that! He shrugged his shoulders. There wasn't much choice, really — though what they could do instead of running the Wall of Death was a puzzle. Living with it from the day they were born, there wasn't any other trade or business they knew.

He pulled the matches out of his pocket, lit one, and held it down towards the pool of oil.

A strong hand gripped his wrist, and wrenched his arm upwards. The sudden movement put out the match.

'What the...?'

'Forget that idea, Sam! That isn't the way.'

'It's none of your business!' Sam said angrily.

'Roger wouldn't thank you for it. Anyway, it's dishonest. You wanted the insurance money, is that it?' George shook his head. 'The insurance companies aren't complete fools, you know.'

Glumly, Sam sat down on the floor. He spread out his hands hopelessly. 'What *can* I do? There's ten pounds in the bank, plus the bike, and the Wall. That's the lot. I warn you — soon as you've gone I'm going through with this.' Sam rattled the matches in his pocket.

226

A strong hand gripped his wrist, and wrenched his arm upwards

George heaved a sigh. 'Don't be a fool! Look, give me until morning. I'll think of another idea, somehow.'

'Well, I...'

'Agreed? Then that's settled.' George moved towards the way out, then slapped his forehead. 'I clean forgot what I came for. My missus says come over for supper when we close for the night.'

They talked ideas all through supper, but none of them were any good. Mrs Carrots was the final judge of each one in turn. 'Coconut shies? There ain't money in 'em. Everybody knows that. You got to be modern, see. Ain't no use bringing out old games, they're all tired of it. 'Ow many d'you see on the roundabouts? Not many — they're all on the Sooperdooper Overhead Railway. Am I right?'

'You're dead right,' groaned George, then his eyes lit up. 'What about Dodgems?'

'You gorn barmy or something?' Mrs Carrots looked scornfully at her husband. 'Where's Sam goin' to get the money for Dodgems? Them things cost thousands. You know that as well as I do.'

And so it went on. It was still going on between George and Mrs Carrots when Sam stumbled back sleepily to his own caravan. He avoided looking at Roger's empty bunk, put out the light quickly, and tried to imagine he was somewhere thousands of miles away and not a mere twenty feet away from the place where Roger had fallen.

He slept heavily and late, waking only when the knocking on the door grew so loud that sleep became impossible.

'Who's there?' he called out, yawning.

'Me. George. Can I come in?'

Sam rolled out of his bunk and put on his dressing-gown. He opened the door. 'What's the idea? What time is it?'

'Eight-thirty.' George grinned at him. 'And I've rung the hospital — Roger's doing fine.'

That brought Sam out of his daze. 'What did they say?' he demanded eagerly.

'Only that. But they think he'll be able to walk again in about six weeks.'

Dizzily, Sam clutched at the door. Only now did he realise that secretly he'd been expecting the worst — that Roger would die, or be a helpless cripple.

'Are you all right?'

'Sure. Sure, George, it's just that I... thanks. Thanks for ringing up and getting the news.'

'That's not all. I've had a busy morning. Is that bike all right?'

Sam blinked at him in surprise. 'It looks all right to me. Roger got all the damage — he was underneath it. But what's the game? Have you found another rider?'

George's face was blank. 'Yes and no. Don't start getting ready for a crowd, because there isn't going to be one. Just a few of our own people. And there'll be only one ride.'

Sam frowned at him, puzzled. 'I don't get it.'

'You will. Just leave it to me, and be expecting visitors at ten o'clock.'

Try as he might, Sam couldn't get any more out of him. Gorge shut up like a clam, and went back to his own caravan.

Sam dressed and had a quick breakfast. Then, with an hour to spare, he went into the Wall and looked at Roger's bike. He lifted it, tried the steering, and then kicked the engine into life. He twisted the throttle, gunning it up to top revs, then slipped it into gear and cruised slowly round the base of the Wall.

No, there was nothing wrong with the bike — except for whatever mystery had caused the accident. And if another rider was going to use it, he'd better find out about that double quick!

It didn't take much searching to discover the intermittent blockage in the float-chamber of the carburettor which had suddenly cut off the supply of fuel to the engine. He stripped it down, cleaned it thoroughly, and then gave it a severe test, leaning the bike far over on its side while he pushed up the engine revs to full throttle with a deafening roar that echoed up and down the sides of the Wall.

At the sight of George and two strangers he cut off the engine and set the bike on its stand. One stranger was unmistakeably a rider; Sam could tell them a mile off, and this one was no exception. He took the bike by the handlebars, swung it back and forth, testing the balance, and then put one leg over the saddle.

But it was the other man who intrigued Sam. He was bending over the handlebars, holding a curiously shaped metal bracket with wing-nuts at the base. He was humming quietly to himself, touching the bracket to the handlebars first on one side, then on the other. Finally he chose a point almost at dead centre, and fastened the bracket on tightly with the wing-nuts.

Sam opened his mouth, but George held up one hand before he could even begin to ask any questions. He stood watching dumbly as on to the bracket the stranger screwed a cine-camera.

'Okay?' snapped the rider.

The photographer moved round the bike, and peered through the viewfinder of the camera. He made two or three small adjustments, then nodded. 'Go ahead!' He pressed a button, and the camera whirred softly.

The engine roared into life. In went the clutch and the bike moved off, beginning the first circle and gaining speed, starting to mount the sides of the Wall.

Sam looked up. To his surprise the rim of the Wall was lined with faces. He made out Mrs Carrots among them, and realised they were all people he knew — people from the Dodgems, the roundabouts, and the dozens of stalls in the fairground. 'What's it all about?' he spluttered, catching George by the elbow. 'I don't understand what..'

'You will!'

But he didn't; five minutes later, when the rider brought

the bike back to its stand, the photographer packed his cine-camera back into its case and the row of faces vanished from the rim of the Wall. He understood still less when the rider said, 'I understand from George that you want to sell. Is that right? Well, I own a small fairground down in the south. I could do with this lot.' He waved his hand round the Wall. 'I'll give you three hundred for it — and another hundred for the bike.'

Bewildered, Sam started to say 'Done!' but George stopped him. '*Five* hundred for the lot, you old ruffian!' he grinned. 'The boy wants five hundred. Don't you, Sam?'

Sam nodded his head. He was hopelessly out of his depth, but his whirling brain was still clear enough to understand that five hundred was better than four.

'Four-fifty!' countered the rider. 'I won't go a penny more than that. It's not worth it.'

'Four-seventy-five.' George leaned patiently on the bike.

'Four-fifty,' repeated the rider firmly.

George heaved himself upright. 'Pity. I'd hoped to get it settled today, but this means I'll have to wait until tomorrow.'

The rider looked at him sharply. 'Tomorrow? What happens tomorrow?'

'Tomorrow we'll be selling to Bransby's Monster Circus. Mr Bransby's coming down in person, specially to look at it.'

The rider's face fell. He stood silent for a moment, then smiled craftily. 'I don't believe it. It's just a bluff!'

'Believe what you like,' said George. 'It doesn't matter to us who buys it as long as we get our price. And that's four-seventy-five.'

'Oh, all right!' The rider growled and muttered — but got out his cheque-book all the same.

Sam waited until he was alone with George. 'I've never heard of Bransby's Monster Circus.'

'Nor have I,' replied George airily. He waved the cheque. 'Put that in the bank. But first of all, pack a suitcase and lock up your caravan.'

'Uuh?'

'You don't want to travel round the country with the fair while Roger's stuck here in hospital. So I've fixed up for you to stay with my wife's aunt — here, in the town. She'll keep an eye on your van. Just let us know when Roger's coming out. Then you can both join up with us again.'

'But...' Sam paused. 'Thanks very much for all you've done, George. But what's the use of us joining up with the fair again? We'll have to get jobs, both of us. We have to make a living, remember.'

'Leave that to me,' said George.

So Sam did. For the next six weeks he stayed with Mrs Carrots's aunt, and to avoid making a hole in the four hundred and seventy-five pounds he took on a job with a garage, cleaning and servicing motor-bikes. It wasn't a job he much cared for, because every time he looked at a bike he thought of Roger's accident, but at least it earned the money to pay for his board and lodging.

He didn't tell Roger abouth selling the Wall. Whenever Roger began talking abouth the future he changed the subject quickly, thrusting the apples and grapes into Roger's hands, or putting in a hurried question about the bandaged leg which lay stretched out like a ramrod under the bed-sheets.

The secret became harder to keep, however, when Roger was up and walking about on crutches. 'Who's *got* the Wall?' he kept asking. 'Is it properly stored?'

'Everything's all right,' said Sam vaguely. 'Just stop worrying.' Instead, he did the worrying himself. It was all very well to trust George and believe everything would turn out well in the end — but, he reminded himself, how well did he really know George? He'd been kind, and so had Mrs Carrots, but people in fairgrounds weren't saints, any more than they were in any other place. His worry grew daily, until on the morning they set off together by train to rejoin the fair he was so tense he could hardly speak.

'What's up?' asked Roger.

Sam shook his head. 'Nothing,' he gulped.

'You're scared, aren't you? Scared George and his wife have done a bunk with the Wall and the bike?'

Sam shook his head again.

'Well, you're certainly scared of *something*!'

Roger looked at him intently. 'There's some kind of secret about all this. What is it?'

Sam met his eyes, then looked away. 'I've sold the Wall and the bike.'

'You've *what*?'

'Roger, I had to. The doctor told me you'd never be able to ride again. And it's no use with a hired rider — we wouldn't make a profit. I've got all the money in the bank, safe and ready. And George...'

But Roger had stamped out of the compartment and was standing in the corridor out of earshot, his face black with anger.

He was silent when they got out of the train and walked through the streets to the fairground. Even the familiar sound of Marty Rheinbaum's steam-organ drew no response from him, and as they began to press through the crowds round the stalls Sam saw that his fists were clenched so hard that the knuckles gleamed white.

'Roger, what are you going to do?'

'Do? Keep hunting until I find George. You didn't sell it all on your own, I know that. He was behind it. It's a swindle.'

'How can it be a swindle when I've got the money? Four hundred and seventy-five pounds.'

Roger halted, and blinked. 'As much as that? And you're *sure* you've got the money?'

Sam nodded. Then, raising his eyes, he gasped and pointed. 'Look!'

Roger turned.

Ahead of them was a stall gleaming with bright new paint. Crowds surrounded it, pushing forward towards the pay-box.

Suddenly George came to them as if from nowhere, and

was between them. 'Leg better, Roger? That's good. What d'you think of it?'

'What's that roaring?' said Roger dazedly. 'Sounds like a motor-bike engine.'

'It *is* a motor-bike engine. D'you know what's inside that booth? An old bike, with the gear locked in neutral. They pay their money, sit in the saddle, and rev up the engine, and in front of them there's a film.'

'What?' asked Sam. 'The film you took when the bike went round the Wall?'

'That's right. Look at the sign over the top: THRILLS AND SPILLS BY THE MILLION — RIDE THE WALL OF DEATH *Yourself!*'

Roger turned to Sam, laughing, then grabbed George's hand. 'I... I just don't know how to thank you.'

'Thank me? That's easy; just settle up the bills. That lot' — he waved his hand towards the booth — 'cost just about four hundred and seventy-five.'

Roger turned to Sam again. 'You're *quite* sure you've got that money? Then we're all right.' He raised his head, soaking up the noise and the smell and the colour of the fairground he'd known all his life. 'We're in business again!'

IMPERNO QUARTARO
SPECIAL AGENT

Father William Byrne — known to all the residents on the shanty hovel hill as Father Billum — surveyed the boy with a shrewd yet compassionate gaze.

'You will not tell me, so —,' Father Billum opened a small black-covered book — 'so I will have to tell you how, suddenly, out of dreadful poverty and hunger, you have acquired food, clothes and money.' He slowly turned the pages, gazed once more at the silent figure, then began to read aloud:

'Imperno Quartaro — domiciled in shanty 1783 on eighth ridge of Immigrant Hill. Eldest of nine children. Father and mother now dead. Has scavenged and begged in city streets to obtain food for his family. Has great pride in the traditions of the Casanas, from which district he was brought when younger. Doesn't run with a gang, as do other boys of the Hill. Is a lone wolf and possibly a dreamer.'

Father Billum looked at Imperno.

'You see — I know all about you.'

Imperno shrugged. 'Such things are easy to know.'

'That is true,' Father Billum agreed. 'It is no more than a rough sketch of who you are. The police have the same information. But here is something they don't have — listen ... "By enlisting the aid of Gorgo, a gang leader whom he fought and beat, Imperno obtained money from a foreign visitor. Gorgo pretended to be hurt by her car. Imperno promised her they would not go to the police if she paid him compensation. The lady paid an unknown sum to Imperno — possibly fifty dollars. He paid Gorgo ten dollars".' Father Billum closed the book with a snap. 'Do you deny that?'

Imperno shrugged again. 'Why should I?'

'It was fraud.'

Imperno chuckled. 'The police would have taken more in bribes.'

'There was no need for the police. The accident was faked.'

'For the foreign visitor there is always the police.' Imperno grinned.

'But you knew it was fraud?'

'No more than the police way.'

Father Billum tried another line. 'The people of the Casanas have always been honourable. Your father didn't teach you such ways.'

Imperno's eyes flashed angrily. 'The city taught me. The city killed my father and my mother. For seven hundred years our people lived in the Casana region. Then the Government sold our lands to rich foreigners and drove us to live on the Hill, without work or food. An empty belly makes a quick brain. I learn from the city.'

'There will be work soon for all of you.'

'When, Father Billum — when?'

'That I do not know, my son. Will you promise me you'll never commit this fraud again?'

'I promise.'

Father Billum was suspicious of this quick reply.

'Promises are easy to make. Do not promise me something you won't do — because then you will be a liar too.'

'I am not a liar to you, Father Billum. I do not use that trick again, so it is easy to promise.'

Father Billum sighed. 'But you have other tricks in your mind?'

Imperno nodded, smiling. 'Plenty.'

'I may be able to find you a job. Not very much perhaps, but a job of work.'

'Cleaning out lavatories? Or sorting garbage at the city dump? All for a dollar a day!' Imperno was scornful. 'Not enough for food for myself, and I have eight bellies to fill.'

'But at least you won't be a thief and a fraud, like Gorgo and the other gangs.'

'I am not a thief,' Imperno denied angrily. 'And the Government is a bigger fraud, because they drive us from our land and leave us to starve on the Hill. You tell me who is the bigger fraud, Father Billum.'

'I wish there were no truth in what you say,' said Father Billum sadly. 'So many things are wrong. There is greed everywhere. There is bribery in high places — aye, and in low places too.' He moved to put his arm around Imperno's shoulders. 'Tell me, why haven't you joined a gang like Gorgo's?'

'Because they are thieves.'

'And you believe that thieving is wrong?'

'They have to live. But me — I have to live with myself too.' Imperno thumped his chest. 'In here. To steal makes me feel sour inside. Besides — they are fools. The things they steal, they sell to men who pay too little. They steal to make others rich. They are sheep.'

Father Billum laughed softly. 'It is a sad reason for not being a thief; but even so, I believe there is great worth in you. I will try very hard to obtain good work for you.'

'It must pay well, Father Billum, because I have many young mouths to feed. For me to work like a scavenger and still not earn enough for food is no good.'

'You are so young to speak so strongly. A boy you are, Imperno, yet you accept the duties of a man.' Father Billum lifted his hands in a despairing gesture. 'This country is running with rivers of wealth, drawn from the lands of the people. The Government is so dazzled and bewitched by the invading hordes of speculators that they have no time to think of you and your people on Immigrant Hill. Tomorrow, they say — tomorrow and tomorrow and tomorrow we will clear the shanty hovels, build houses, schools, hospitals for the poor. Always tomorrow — never today. What can I say to you, my son, except have faith and live as best you can? I, too, am waiting for money promised me for schools and a new orphanage.'

'While we wait, we work,' said Imperno cheerfully. He pointed to the black-covered book. 'But I don't like my work to be written there, because I do what I have to do, not always what I wish to do.'

'You must be trained. Such a clear mind in one so young, such character and dignity must be educated properly. When I start my school you will be my prize pupil.'

'I may go now, Father?'

'Go, my son, but come to me at any time if you are in trouble and I will help you.'

'There are too many already for you to help.' Imperno waved a hand in the direction of the yard. 'Out there, they wait all day to see you. Some sleep on the ground all night. It is you who need help.'

Father Billum smiled. 'You are an arrogant young puppy, and you yap too much. Go now.' He paused as Imperno turned towards the door. 'Wait — there is something else.'

Imperno halted. 'Yes, Father?'

'The lady in the white car. The one you defrauded. She wishes to see you.'

Imperno laughed scornfully. 'But naturally! And to see me she waits with the police.'

'No, no — I give you my word she won't put the police on you.'

'You pleaded for me?'

Father Billum shrugged. 'A little, but not too much. You impressed her, and later she saw you drinking coffee on the plaza. We met, and she told me of you and asked my help to find you. Your new clothes made it easy.'

'Where do I see her?'

'Her car will be parked near the fountain in the Plaza del Torro at six this evening.'

'Salut!' said Imperno with a wave of his hand. 'I will be there. Adios, Father.'

240

'Adios, Imperno.'

He waited in the shadows of clustered palms — a small, still figure, poised like a drinking deer ready to speed away at the first sign of danger.

The white car was empty. No police were in sight, not even the special police in plain clothes. A big joke that, because all the special police wore cream suits, blacks shirts, white ties and wide-brimmed straw hats. They all strutted rather than walked. They all had the bulge of an automatic pistol under one arm. They all assumed the same hard-eyed unsmiling expression. These special — and secret — police were more easy to recognise than uniformed patrolmen, because other uniformed workers, such as bank guards, armoured-car drivers, were similarly dressed. But nobody dressed like the special police.

Imperno didn't know why there were special police, or what was so special about them, but he did know they were feared by all grown-ups on Immigrant Hill. Scary stories were told of how cream-suited men descended on a particular hovel and took away all the men. Political enemies, so it was whispered. Communists or agitators who spoke too loud their protests against having to work for starvation wages. But the cream-suited men didn't bother with boys, or the gangs of sneak-thieves. Even so, Imperno was watchful in case this lady with the white car was trying to trap him.

The carillon across the plaza belled a musical fanfare, proclaiming it was six o'clock on a warmly scented evening. In a few moments the plaza was a bubbling river of people as workers poured out from skyscraper offices. Cars sped in a solid phalanx, locked together by a coat of paint, rocketing around the one-way circle of the plaza. Hooters blared, tyres squealed, pedestrians leapt, and overloaded buses swayed and lunged like monstrous mechanised ant-heaps, with passengers clinging to backs and sides. The normal daily dash-for-home hour had begun.

When Imperno first witnessed this spectacle in the Plaza

del Torro he had been almost paralysed by the noise, the speed and the whirling mass of men and machines. Now he felt a part of it. Yet he hated it, because he knew that the inhuman pace and thrust of the city jungle had killed his father as surely as if a juggernaut of a bus had run over him.

Far from the mountains and plains of his beloved Casana lands the city had killed Imperno's father's spirit, and broken his will to live. Imperno's hatred of the city gave power to his defiance of it. A fierce, coldly calculating defiance, with an inner voice echoing in Imperno's mind, saying, You will not kill me. I am not afraid of you!

He saw her standing by the white car, gazing around before she opened the door and sat behind the steering-wheel. She was younger than he remembered at their first meeting. Imperno shrugged. Who can tell the age of a woman in the city? The girls dress like women, and the women dress like girls. Why should he care?

He sauntered from the shade, edged along the side of the car, and had climbed over the door and into the passenger seat before she realised he was near.

'If this is a trap, and the police come, then my friends will kill you,' said Imperno quietly but clearly.

She swivelled to face him. Cool in a pale blue dress, her blonde hair a golden halo above her sun-tanned face, her eyes grey, expressing a mixture of surprise and humour, red lips smiling.

'Well, well — the boy wonder himself! So Father Billum found you?'

'I wasn't lost. What do you want?'

'Perhaps I want my money back.'

Imperno shrugged. 'It is spent.'

Her fingers flicked his gay new shirt. 'On this?'

He nodded. 'And on food.'

'You really fooled me.' Her eyes were angry, but her voice held a hint of admiration. 'You know that? You really did. You're a good actor, Imperno Quartaro. For one so young,

242

you have great talent. Or perhaps you've pulled that fake accident trick on many visitors?'

'No, only you.'

'Is that the truth?'

'I am not a liar.'

'No? You lied to me.'

'That was business.'

'So it's all right to tell lies if it's business?'

Imperno gazed directly at her, smiling.

'You should know. You are grown up. Grown-ups tell lies all the time.'

She saw the smile, but saw also the fierce accusation in his bright unwinking stare. For some strange reason she couldn't meet his gaze, and turned away.

'That's as may be.' She felt curiously embarrassed. 'No sense in us discussing things like that,' she continued briskly. 'The fact is that you tricked me out of fifty dollars. Now it so happens that I believe you can do a small task for me. I'd be willing to pay fifty dollars. You carry out this task and we'll be quits.'

'Meaning that you will not pay me any more money?'

'Meaning just that.' She shrugged. 'Oh well, perhaps I'll give you a couple of dollars for expenses.'

'What is the task?'

'Then you agree to my terms?'

It was Imperno's turn to shrug.

'That depends on the task.'

She flashed an angry glance at him. 'Imperno, don't fool with me.'

'Who is fooling?'

She drew a deep breath, then exhaled very slowly — as if counting up to ten in case she lost her temper. She opened the car's glove compartment, drew out an envelope and extracted two photographs.

'Father Billum said you were very intelligent and learned quickly. Have you a good memory?'

'I think so.'

She passed him the photographs. 'Study these men's faces. The dark man is short and rather fat. The fair-haired man is tall, square-shouldered and walks with a slight limp.'

'The dark man is Boroturo.'

'Well, well!' she exclaimed, surprised. 'You're a well-informed young rascal, aren't you? How is it that you can recognise Boroturo?'

'He is a fixer. A five-per-cent man. He was head of the special police, but now he is head of Massine Developments. Massine is his wife's name.' Imperno glanced at her. 'She is very like you, Señora. Not so pretty — and small, like a doll.'

'What a character you are,' she declared. 'How many of you urchins from Immigrant Hill know such things?'

'Not many. They are too busy stealing and fighting.'

'Have you ever met Boroturo?'

'Once.'

'I don't believe it!'

'It is true.'

'Where?'

'In the offices of Massine Developments.'

'Ah. And I suppose you were there to buy an option on some gold or emerald mine way out in the mountains?' she retorted sarcastically.

'No,' Imperno replied calmly. 'I was cleaning the lavatory. He gave me a dollar. He wears all silk. Silk underclothes, silk socks, silk shirt, silk suit. He goes splursh-splursh when he moves. One day, I will have a silk suit. Why should I study these men?'

'So that you'll recognise them when you see them.'

'So?'

'You'll recognise the fair-haired man?'

'Yes. Where will I find him?'

'He hasn't arrived in the city yet. He's due on a morning plane. He'll go straight to his hotel. That has already been arranged.'

'Which hotel?'

'The Aconda.'

'I know it.' Imperno pointed. 'It is across the plaza. Small, but very expensive. They say the Aconda has gold seats in the toilets.'

'Let's forget about toilets, shall we?'

'As you wish, Señora.'

'I want you to watch for this man to arrive at the hotel. There's only one entrance or exit for visitors, so you won't miss him. You will watch all day if you have to, and follow him when he leaves.'

'He may hire a car or a taxi.'

'Then you'll wait for his return to the hotel. But I don't think he'll travel around the city until he has made contact with Boroturo. He can walk to Boroturo's offices from the hotel. On the other hand, Boroturo may call at the hotel. All I want you to do is to telephone a number I shall give you. You can use the phone?'

Imperno nodded. 'Father Billum taught me.'

'Good. You will phone this number, and to whoever answers you will say "Ajax and Atlas are meeting". You understand?'

'Perfectly. If Boroturo visits the Aconda, or if the man with the limp enters Boroturo's offices I phone and say "Ajax and Atlas are meeting". That is all?'

'That is all for now.' She fumbled in her purse. 'Here's some change for the phone. Meet me here at six tomorrow evening, and perhaps there'll be a few dollars for you.'

'Twenty-five, please,' said Imperno firmly.

'Now wait a minute —'

'And twenty-five now, please.'

'You've got a nerve!'

'It is a necessary thing to have in a big city.' Imperno smiled. 'My price is really a hundred dollars. I owe you fifty, so you will pay me fifty. Twenty-five now, and twenty-five when we meet tomorrow.'

'You —' she drew a deep breath — 'are an ungrateful, thieving, cunning, arrogant little twister!'

'And you are no fool,' said Imperno calmly. 'If you pay cheap, you get cheap goods. You pay well, and you receive good value. I am Imperno. I give the best.'

She was silent, tight-lipped, angrily drumming her fingers on the steering-wheel. At last she said briskly:

'Very well, I agree. But I warn you that if you fail me in this simple task I shall see that you're taught a lesson you'll never forget.'

Imperno remained silent. He had won his point, so why argue?

She handed him twenty-five dollars and a card with a telephone number written on it.

'You understand what you have to do?'

'Perfectly, Señora.'

'You can remember the message?'

'"Ajax and Atlas are meeting",' Imperno quoted. 'Do I need to know your name?'

'No.'

'How shall I know if I am telephoning the correct number?'

She nodded slowly. 'That's a good point. I expect I shall answer your call — or it may be a woman friend of mine.' She paused. 'I think you'd better say "I have a message for Karen". Then whoever answers will ask you "Who is Karen?" And you will say "My eldest sister". How's that?'

'Very good. "I have a message for Karen",' Imperno repeated.

'Who is Karen?'

'"My eldest sister."' Imperno chuckled. '"Ajax and Atlas are meeting"'.

'You're very quick. Remember to be quick to give the message. Run to a phone immediately you're sure that Boroturo and the fair-haired man are meeting.'

Imperno opened the door and slid from the car.

'Until six tomorrow, Señora.'

She nodded. 'Yes — six o'clock.'

Imperno returned to the shadows, waited until the white car moved away, and watched it out of sight across the plaza. Then he went to a seat near the fountain, sprawled on it and closed his eyes.

Think now, said the voice in his brain. Think, Imperno, think!

I will think, said Imperno to himself. I will close my eyes. That helps me to think, and also people will believe I am asleep. People don't expect a young boy to sit and think. But people are not surprised to see him asleep on a seat. The city has taught me to appear as people expect you to appear. They don't like you to be something they don't expect you to be.

Like the lady in the white car. She says to use the name Karen. Why? Because it's her name. She thinks I am just a thief from Immigrant Hill. Father Billum has told her I am perhaps a little brighter than some. But not bright enough to read the registration disc on the steering-post of her car. It had the name and address of the car owner. All cars in the city have these discs. She should have covered it, but she didn't, because she thinks she is very clever and I am just an urchin of the streets.

The name and address on the disc was K. Schulberg, Hotel Ambassador, Plaza Forino. It was printed in red. This tells me it's visitor's permit. If she were staying for longer than six months, it would be printed in black. So?

So why does Karen Schulberg need to pay a boy to watch a man ho is going to arrive at an hotel close to her own? Because she doesn't want the man to know she is there. At least, not until she knows whether he is going to meet Boroturo.

There are many private detectives in this city. Father Billum has told me about them. Mostly they are ex-special policemen, who now work for mining and property companies as spies to find out secret plans of other companies.

Why doesn't the lady employ one of these? Why didn't she

throw me out of the car when I asked for more money? Why does she even consider using a boy for this task? Because she thinks I won't be known to any friends of this man. Many boys hang around hotels to pick up tips for carrying luggage or running errands, so no one will be suspicious of me. Because the task she sets me is more important than it seems? Why is it important? I don't know the word Ajax, but I do know the word Atlas.

Boroturo is a big fixer. He buys and sells properties and leases and options, which, according to Father Billum, can be very important things to big companies and rich foreigners.

Options mean rights to buy land which may hold oil or emeralds or gold, or things they call raw materials. A man can hold an option on land without having to pay the whole price. Then he can sell his option to someone else and make much money. Boroturo deals in options, and one of Boroturo's business companies is called The Atlas Trading and Mining Company. But who is Ajax?...

Imperno changed position on the seat, as if stirring in his sleep. Where can I learn about Ajax, he pondered. Atlas is a business company. Isn't it possible that Ajax is a business company too? I will guess that it is. So why does Karen Schulberg want to know immediately Atlas and Ajax meet? I cannot guess that, but it must be worth money or she wouldn't pay money to find out. Perhaps Boroturo would pay money to know about the fair-haired man?...

Imperno opened his eyes, stretched, yawned and peered across at the clock on the carillon tower. Nearly seven o'clock. At seven each evening Boroturo came from his apartment and usually stopped for a shoe-shine, for which he paid five dollars.

Boroturo had started his working life as a shoe-shine boy and was sentimental about this matter, so always a row of shoe-shine boys waited beneath the entrance awning of his apartment block. Boroturo had an amazing memory for their faces and would choose each in turn — a different boy every time. Imperno had shone Boroturo's shoes twice. It was the one time in the day when the great man was alone. From the shoe-shine he walked to his car and drove to one of the rich men's clubs.

Imperno jumped to his feet and sped away, weaving in and out along the crowded sidewalks. He reached the apartment block as Boroturo was placing his foot on the shoe-shine stand. The other shoe-shine boys were scooting off in search of customers.

Boroturo was short, fat — a shining roly-poly of a man in silken clothes. A thick stubby cigar canted up from one corner of his mouth. He surveyed the street scene with the amused gaze of a man who owned the city. Some said he did. He twiddled a five-dollar note between manicured fingers, sunlight glinting from a diamond ring on his left hand.

'A word, Señor Boroturo.' Imperno stood close, his head almost level with the fat man's shoulder.

Shrewd eyes assessed Imperno.

'Ah!' said Boroturo. 'Two shoe-shines and one dollar in the toilet at my office block — yes?'

Imperno beamed. 'Señor remembers everything. A most wonderful brain.'

Boroturo loved flattery. What successful man doesn't?

'Of course,' he admitted modestly. 'Well?'

'Señor would pay for information?'

The shrewd eyes narrowed. 'Perhaps.'

'Does Ajax mean anything to Señor?'

'It might.'

'If Ajax is visiting the city very soon, would Señor wish to know?'

Imperno's arm was gripped with such force that it hurt, but he made no sign.

'Who sent you, boy?'

'No one, Señor. It is something I hear.'

'You know what it means?'

'No, Señor.'

'Then why come to me?'

'I hear talk of people watching for Ajax. And talk of Ajax and Atlas.'

'Where did you hear this talk?'

'Near the gardens of the Plaza del Torro,' Imperno replied truthfully. 'Between a visitor and one other person.'

Boroturo gazed long and hard. His eyes glittered with menace, showing the steel within the podgy silk-clad body.

'When does Ajax arrive?'

Imperno shrugged. 'The Señor is a business man. From him I learn not to sell until one is paid.'

'I am hurting your arm?'

'Yes, Señor.'

'But you don't struggle.'

'Pain is nothing.'

'I might break it so you would tell me without payment.' The grip tightened.

Imperno smiled into the hard eyes. 'If you hurt me, Señor, I shall kick you in the stomach and forget all about Ajax.'

'Good! Good! You have nerve.' Boroturo released his grip. 'Your name?'

'Imperno.'

'There are many Impernos.'

'Imperno Quartaro.'

'And you know about Ajax? Well, what *you* know I can find out.'

Imperno shrugged again and bluffed.

'Perhaps, Señor, but not in time.' He didn't know what he meant by this; but guessed that if time was important to Karen Schulberg, then probably it was important to Boroturo. Anyway, he had nothing to lose by bluffing.

'How much?'

'Ten thousand dollars.'

Boroturo laughed, coughed on cigar smoke, then laughed again.

'Bravo! You are a real city man. Five hundred dollars.'

'A thousand dollars.'

'You will never earn it.'

'How do I earn it, Señor?'

'You bring Ajax to me before he sees or speaks to anyone. You prove this, and I pay. You are a smart boy, but you try to bluff Boroturo. It is amusing, but not a game. You understand?'

'Yes, Señor. How do I pass the many doorkeepers at your offices?'

Boroturo whipped out a card and a gold pen. He scrawled *Admit,* signed his name and passed the card to Imperno.

'If you come without Ajax you will be beaten and thrown to the police. Adios.' Boroturo turned away, stooped, patted the shoe-shine boy on the head and let the five-dollar note float to the ground. 'Very good. Do your work well and you will be a rich man one day.' He strutted towards his car, climbed in and was driven away.

Imperno ignored the shoe-shine boy's curiosity and hurried from the apartment entrance. He had some more thinking to do. A bubbly, exciting feeling filled him. He'd been right! Ajax must be another company, and the fair-haired man must be somebody connected with it. Boroturo would never have listened if Imperno's words hadn't made sense to him.

A thousand dollars! It seemed impossible. But why? The special police and the private detectives in the city received big money for information supplied to one party or another. Much more than a thousand dollars. Father Billum had told Imperno stories of how spies and informants worked. There had even been a government inquiry over the selling of secrets, such as which new parts of the country were going to be offered for option to foreign money men.

Quite innocently Father Billum had fired Imperno's ambition to learn and understand more about this fascinating part of life in the city. To him these matters were of much more interest than running around with a gang of boys, thieving and begging and doing menial jobs to obtain a living.

Imperno spent several hours asking questions of various men he knew, particularly taxi-drivers and doormen at clubs, hotels and garages. Many of these men had once lived on Immigrant Hill and knew Imperno well enough to answer his questions helpfully. Imperno then bought food in the all-night market and returned to his hovel on the Hill to feed his family of brothers and sisters.

He slept only until one hour before dawn, needing no alarm clock to awaken him, and reached the city airport before any aircraft had arrived.

He waited three hours, until the passenger offices and lounges opened. Then, armed with knowledge gleaned from friends the previous evening, he checked all incoming flights for this day. The first three interested him particularly; and by adopting an air of smiling innocence, nicely mixed with shy bewilderment, Imperno endeared himself to certain airline officials.

From one of these men Imperno learned that the second incoming aircraft carried a passenger whose seat had been booked by the Ajax Projects Company Incorporated. The advance passenger list radioed through included a passenger with the name of Carl E. Schulberg. This was a surprise to Imperno, but he tried not to show it.

'Thank you very much, Señor,' he said to the official. 'That will be my uncle. I shall know him from his photograph, but he hasn't seen me since I was a baby.'

'He's an important man,' said the official. 'Obviously representing a big company. You are lucky to have such an uncle.'

'Thank you,' said Imperno seriously. 'I will see that he knows how you have helped me.'

The official beamed, sensing a large and grateful tip from Imperno's 'uncle'. 'I will show you where to meet him quickly.'

In this way Imperno carried out the plan he had so carefully conceived. His last act, whilst the aircraft circled to land, was to find a taxi-driver he knew in the airport taxi-park, pay him and so reserve the cab for immediate use.

The glistening plane hissed to a halt. The passengers descended the portable steps. Imperno watched closely from his favoured position, his mind holding a clear picture of the fair-haired man. This was the biggest gamble. Everything so far had worked out, but the fair-haired man *had* to be Carl E. Schulberg for Imperno's scheme to succeed.

A tall man, walking with a slight limp, was now crossing the tarmac. His fair hair was bright in the morning sun.

Imperno rushed forward.

'Señor Schulberg, please?' he spoke low-voiced.

'Yeah. Who're you?'

'Just a messenger. It is urgent that I escort you at once to a certain person. Shall I just say Atlas, and show you this?' Imperno held out the card Boroturo had given him.

The tall man studied it carefully.

'D'you know any reason for the rush?'

'No, Señor. Only that it is urgent.'

'Why send a boy to meet me?'

Imperno smiled engagingly. 'Perhaps because I would not attract attention. You might even be my uncle.'

Schulberg laughed. 'It makes sense.'

'I have a taxi waiting.'

'Real little organiser, aren't you? Okay — wait for me to clear customs, and I'll be right with you.'

One reason for the advance passenger lists was to sort out important visitors so that they could be cleared through customs and immigration without delay. Visitors with big money to spend were whisked through. Others took hours to pass the official scrutiny. A wearying, maddening process. Schulberg got through in ten minutes. Imperno rushed him to the taxi.

'This is what I call service,' said Schulberg as the taxi sped towards the city. 'How much did it cost you to bribe one of those airport boys to let you meet me on the tarmac?'

'Fifty dollars,' said Imperno without shame.

Schulberg took out his wallet, extracted the money.

'Always reckon to pay my own bribes.' He chuckled.

'Thank you very much. It was not expected,' Imperno added truthfully, then whispered: 'Drivers have ears, Señor. Perhaps we don't talk any more?'

'Oh, sure — sure.'

Imperno heaved a silent sigh of relief. He didn't want to be asked too many questions. The taxi raced into the city as if the driver thought he might die before he reached there. Imperno was familiar with this type of driving, but Schulberg hung on to the strap as if he were praying for a parachute.

They crossed the Plaza del Torro with a fanfare of squealing tyres, shot into the Avenue Presidencio and rocketed to a halt in front of the skyscraper offices. Imperno paid his friend — generously. Schulberg paid Imperno. So far, so profitable!

The showing of Boroturo's signed card had magical effects on the doorman, receptionist and liftman. In minutes they were zoomed to the penthouse offices of Boroturo.

'Just one little moment, Señors,' said a glamorous secretary, and disappeared through a green leather door — to reappear in about ten seconds short of a moment. 'Señor Boroturo is available now,' she announced.

Suddenly Imperno felt sick, shivery and afraid.

The luxury around him overawed even his unbounded confidence. The speed with which he had reached this impregnable domain of the great Boroturo had left him no time to think of his next move. Imperno liked to have time to think.

Then the bulk of Boroturo faced them.

'Greetings, Señor Schulberg! Welcome to our country!'

They shook hands in the manner of old friends.

'A very neat and quick welcome too, if I may say so, Mr Boroturo.'

'I made arrangements immediately I learned you were arriving a week earlier.'

'Make the chit out for one thousand and twenty dollars.' Boroturo
slapped Imperno's shoulder

'Huh?' Schulberg looked surprised. 'Oh, that. I was only aiming to take a few days' vacation before I got down to business. Just a personal reason, y'know.'

'Of course, of course,' said Boroturo smoothly. 'But if we conclude the business first, then your — h'm - personal reason will be so much more enjoyable, won't it?'

Schulberg nodded. 'Guess it will at that.'

Imperno coughed gently.

'Ah! Imperno Quartaro. My good young friend.' Boroturo beamed; then, grasping Imperno's shoulder, propelled him through the open doorway. 'One moment, Señor,' he said to Schulberg before he pulled the door closed.

'So you do not bluff,' said Boroturo. 'And I do not ask questions. The result is sufficient. Boroturo never forgets a good turn. You have done well, amigo.' He looked at the glamorous secretary. 'Give Imperno one thousand dollars. Make out a cash-chit for market research expenses and I will sign it.'

'The taxi cost twenty dollars, Señor,' said Imperno, recovering his confidence.

Boroturo roared with laughter. 'Make the chit out for one thousand and twenty dollars.' He slapped Imperno's shoulder. 'Adios, amigo — we shall meet again.' He turned, opened the green leather door, bounced through and slammed it shut.

'One thousand and twenty dollars,' said the secretary, handing Imperno the money. 'Good morning.'

'Yes,' said Imperno. 'Very good, I think.' He sauntered from the penthouse, defying an urge to yell and jump with glee.

In the reception hall he entered a phone-booth, dialled the number. He recognised her voice.

'I have a message for Karen,' he said.

'Who is Karen?'

'My eldest sister. Ajax and Atlas are meeting.'

He heard her give a sort of long drawn-out gasp. Then she said happily: 'Imperno — bless you!'

'Bless you too,' said Imperno politely.

'You're much earlier than I expected.'

'Ajax went straight from the airport!'

She didn't query this. Imperno said:

'Will you answer me a question, please?'

'Yes, if I can. What is it?'

'Ajax is Carl E. Schulberg. Is your name Schulberg too?'

'Yes, it is. I'm his wife.'

'Oh!' said Imperno. 'Well, it is none of my business, I suppose.'

'It is now.' She laughed. 'I was what they call a jealous wife. I thought my husband was coming here to meet — well...'

'Another lady?' Imperno suggested helpfully.

'Yes, I'm afraid so. But I knew that if he went straight to Boroturo, or if Boroturo came straight to meet him, then it really was business. I expect you think I'm awfully silly.'

'It is your business,' said Imperno. 'And ours is now finished.'

'Oh, but I owe you twenty-five dollars.'

'You know where Father Billum's mission is?'

'Yes — he took me there.'

'Give him the twenty-five dollars, please. Adios, Señora.' Imperno replaced the phone.

He went to a cafe and ate a huge breakfast. Then he bought some more clothes. Next he went to the house of a taxi-driver friend who had a room to rent, and paid him one month's lodging in advance. At noon he was at the mission.

'Back so soon, Imperno? And smarter than ever. What mischief have you been up to?'

'Just business, Father.'

'It must be good business for you to turn down twenty-five dollars.'

'The lady has seen you?'

'She has. And she added another twenty-five dollars. I am suspicious of your generosity, Imperno.'

Imperno sighed. 'I thought you would be. I would like to be trusted, Father Billum. Not to tell, but be trusted because I do not tell. This much you would grant to a man.'

'You are still a boy. But, very well — I will trust you as a man. What is so important that I must trust you?'

'Remember how you told me there is what you called an endowed orphanage? Each child must have one hundred dollars when it is brought, and that at least ten dollars a week must be guaranteed to be paid towards its keep.'

Father Billum nodded. 'That is so. Soon, perhaps, we shall have funds to do more for those with no money.' He shrugged. 'But until then, it's the best we can do.'

Imperno drew money from his pocket. 'I have eight brothers and sisters. We live in a hovel on Immigrant Hill. Here is eight hundred dollars.' He took more money from another pocket. 'Ten dollars each is eighty dollars a week. Here is one hundred and sixty dollars for two weeks in advance. I will guarantee the money each week.'

Father Billum stared at the money, then at Imperno.

Suddenly, before his eyes, the gay, arrogantly young and confident face of Imperno changed. The bright urchin eyes were now the pleading eyes of a young man. Tears brimmed over. The smiling mouth quivered. The hands were half raised, as if to pray.

'Please, Father, please,' he whispered.

In that gesture, Father Billum saw the reason why Imperno wanted to be trusted — needed to be trusted. Eight human reasons were good enough to trust any man.

Father Billum nodded slowly.

'Bring them to me, my son. We will trust each other.'

FEODOR'S LUCKY ACCIDENT!

Spring was just beginning. Feodor went from door to door, thumping on them, shouting, 'Come on, come on, everybody, it's time we started practice! The field is clear of snow.'

The sun was shining low on the horizon; all round the little town the tractors were being brought out of the barns and made ready for the spring ploughing. A man on a motor-cycle had ridden into the main street and stuck up a brightly coloured poster which said, 'Russia needs more wheat. It is up to *you*!'; and a lorry had come with stocks of seed corn ready for planting. Everybody was busy, and Feodor didn't want to be left out of the noise and commotion. Furthermore, he had a good reason for getting on the move. On the wall of the school gymnasium there was a blank space — for the shield held by the winners of the annual soccer match between the senior forms of Brashevsky School and their rivals over at Talinin, fifteen miles away across the steppes.

When he thumped on the door of Grigor's house, Grigor came out into the yard dressed as if for January. He was loaded down with woollen sweaters and leather jackets until he seemed twice his normal width. Feodor looked at him for a moment, and then burst out laughing. 'You can't play soccer in *that* rig-out!' he hooted.

Grigor looked dolefully down the road, at the thin layer of ice that still coated the town pond, and the heaps of snow at the roadside which had not yet melted. '*Brrr!*' he shuddered. 'Can't we wait another week?'

'By that time Talinin will be in full training,' retorted

Feodor. 'This year we're going to *win,* for a change. I want to see that shield up on the wall before I leave school and start my engineering course.'

'Oh, all right,' muttered Grigor reluctantly, and went indoors to change. Then, stumping along with his hands in his pockets, he followed Feodor on his rounds to the houses of all the other members of the school first eleven. 'Anybody would think we were Moscow Dynamo,' he grumbled. 'But even they do some of their training indoors.'

'That's because they keep in training all the year round,' said Feodor with a grin. 'Maybe if we win the shield this year it would be worth doing the same to hold on to it.'

'Ugh!' Grigor pulled his scarf a little tighter round his neck. Then he pointed. 'Look, that's Mikhail's house, isn't it? Well, I bet we shan't get *him* out for practice. He'll be sitting in front of a hot fire, with a good excuse that he's swotting for his examinations.'

'He can swot later,' said Feodor bluntly. He hammered on the door, won the argument that followed, and thus brought his training group up to three.

He had all eleven by mid-morning, and they jog-trotted out to the soccer field with the ball passing clumsily from foot to foot. It was as if their legs had forgotten all they'd ever learned about ball control. 'Don't worry,' said Feodor. 'It'll all come back to us. That's the trouble with this long Siberian winter — the sports season is far too short. We're all fat and breathless. A brisk run for five miles every morning will soon have us back in trim again.'

Grigor shuddered again. 'In the grave, you mean! I couldn't run five miles for the honour of being one of the men to go to the moon.'

'Nobody'd think of asking you,' yelled Mikhail. 'With a great fat stomach like that, they'd have to build a special rocket.'

The scrap that followed warmed both of them, even if it delayed progress down the road. Feodor began to think they'd go on wrestling all morning, and was about to step in and break it up, but a fast lorry racing towards the town with a load of farm tools reparated them with a blast of its horn which made them jump into the ditch in panic.

'What's it like down there?' laughed Feodor.

'Muddy!' said Mikhail, looking down in distaste at his boots. 'Smelly too. Give me a hand, somebody, I'm stuck.'

They heaved him out, and then dragged Grigor up in turn. 'Keep to windward of those two,' chuckled Feodor. 'They're a bit too fruity to be pleasant.' He kicked the ball hard along the road, and the team went after it at the double, each racing to be the first on to the soccer field ahead.

They played five a side, with Feodor as referee. It was a slow game; everybody was still creaky in the joints from lack of exercise, and Feodor grew angrier and angrier at the poor passing and the missed chances. He was so busy watching the play that he never noticed the huge gleaming saucer-shape that sailed overhead and landed half a mile beyond the soccer field; nor did he see the long column of trucks loaded with troops and guns that moved cautiously down the road towards it.

It was Grigor who called his attention to what was going on. Feodor looked in amazement. He'd seen soldiers before, but only in ones and twos when men of the town came home on leave from the Army. But these very clearly weren't on leave. The men had machine-guns, and ahead of the front truck in the line men were setting up heavy artillery beside the road, with the muzzles pointing towards the silver saucer.

'It's one of our space rockets!' shouted Grigor. 'I expect we'll see one of the space travellers get out of it in a minute.'

Feodor shook his head. He felt uneasy. 'Why would they bring all those guns if it was one of our own people? No — d'you know what I think?'

Grigor looked at him blankly. 'Go on,' said Mikhail, 'let's hear what you think. I bet it's a daft idea.'

'Have you ever heard of flying saucers?'

'Flying *what?*' muttered Grigor, but Mikhail said, 'Yes, *I* have. I've read about them in a book at school. Aren't they supposed to be space-ships from another planet? But surely nobody really believes...?' He looked again at the great shining saucer in the distance, and his jaw dropped open. 'I see what you mean, Feodor.'

'Our people were the first to go into space,' said Feodor slowly. 'Doesn't it make sense to you that people from another planet would choose our country to land in?'

'But...' Mikhail looked at the guns and the soldiers. 'Is there going to be a battle? How do we know the people in the saucer aren't friendly?'

'It wouldn't do to take any chances, would it? Suppose they aren't friendly, and they have weapons which could kill thousands of our people?'

'Look!' said Grigor. 'The soldiers are waving to us.'

Feodor followed his pointing finger. From the top of one of the trucks two soldiers were waving their arms rapidly, and pointing back along the road towards the town.

'What do you think they want?' asked Grigor.

'There's not much doubt about that. They want us to get out of the way, in case there's a battle. They want us to go home.'

'Right!' said Grigor, and started off briskly.

'Where are you going?'

Grigor rolled his eyes. 'If there's going to be a battle, then home's the best place to be. I don't mind fighting if I know what it's all about, but catch me squatting in the middle of *this*! We'd be shot at by both sides.'

Feodor looked at him scornfully. 'You'd miss the chance of seeing the first man from another world?'

'Fat lot of good that's going to be to me if I don't stay alive afterwards.' Grigor moved a little farther away. 'You stay if you want to.'

But Feodor wasn't paying any attention. He was listening

to a curious humming noise that was coming across the fields from the direction of the saucer.

'Look,' shouted Mikhail, 'it's moving!'

The saucer had lifted itself gently off the ground, and was skimming along, only a few feet up, like a hovercraft.

'It's coming nearer!' yelled somebody. 'Grigor's right. I'm off home.'

'You're too late.' Feodor stopped where he was, for the saucer was now only a hundred yards away, and still coming closer. Out of the corner of his eyes he saw the artillerymen on the road frantically swinging their guns round to the changed direction.

'I hope they don't start firing,' muttered Mikhail. 'They're pointing straight at us.'

The saucer suddenly came to a halt, right beside the goalposts. Feodor saw Grigor's eyes open wide in panic as the top began to open on some kind of hinge.

Over on the road more men were pouring from the trucks and taking up firing positions, with their machine-guns pointing at the saucer.

Feodor felt his heart hammering. He couldn't keep his eyes off the slowly rising top of the saucer, as he waited for whatever it was that might appear. His mind was filled with all the worst horrors he'd ever had in nightmares: creatures with ten heads and forty arms, death rays, rolling waves of poisonous weed that choked and strangled.

What came out, quite suddenly, was a thing with two arms, two legs and one head. The only unusual features about it were that its skin was luminous, and that it moved stiffly and jerkily as it stepped over the side of the saucer and slid down to the ground.

It looked down at its feet, and tested the firmness of the earth by stamping.

'Look,' said Mikhail in a croaking whisper. 'What's that thing it's holding?'

Feodor switched his attention to the creature's right hand,

in which there was a long pale blue tube. 'It's a gun of some kind,' he said quietly.

'What are they waiting for?' bellowed Grigor suddenly. 'Why don't the soldiers shoot?'

'Shut up!' barked Feodor. He was watching the gun. The creature from the flying saucer was moving it about uncertainly, and looking from the boys to the troops on the road and then back again.

'D'you think it's going to shoot?' quavered Grigor.

Feodor ignored him. His eyes were still fixed on the gun.

And then he saw that the creature was staring straight at him, with a penetrating look which made him feel most uncomfortable. He shifted uneasily. As he did so his foot touched the ball which lay in front of him. It shot across to Mikhail, who automatically hooked it and began to move forward. Soccer came to him so naturally that not even men from space could take first place in his mind.

Mikhail passed the ball back again. Feodor, with one eye on the ball and one on the space-man, pushed it across to Grigor, who jumped in panic, then let fly with a terrific aimless toe-punt.

The ball sailed up into the air, and came down right beside the space-man.

There was a puzzled silence all round. The space-man looked at the ball suspiciously, and bent down over it. For a moment he even aimed the long blue gun at it, then appeared to change his mind. He moved a step or two away, then ran towards it again.

On the road every machine-gun muzzle came up. The artillerymen jumped to their guns.

Then there was an astonished cheer as the man from space kicked the ball neatly back to Feodor!

Excitedly Feodor ran forward to meet it, and punted it back to the space-man. The space-man trapped it neatly on the inside of his foot, turned round, and kicked it towards the road.

Watching, Feodor saw a tremendous battle between discipline and human nature. He heard officers bark orders to stand fast, but an oncoming football was too much for one artilleryman. He jumped from behind his gun, ran out to meet it, and shot it back to the space-man again.

From the hatch top of the saucer came three more space-men. Two fell into line with the first, and the other man automatically slipped into defence.

More soldiers deserted their guns. Feodor ran forward with his hand held out towards the nearest of the space-men, who dropped his gun to grasp the hand with one that was cold, scaly but obviously friendly.

It was the beginning of man's friendship with other worlds. It was Feodor who took the first of the men from space to the United States and Britain. But for him, there might have been a space war which would have lasted for ever.

But there were many who never forgave him. They were the leading soccer players in Russia, Britain and the other rivals for the World Cup.

For none of them ever won it again. Nobody could play soccer as well as the men from space!

RUMPUS AT WESTLAKE

Nobody at Westlake School could remember anything like it. Not even old Mr Prettyman, the janitor, who claimed he'd been there sixty years. Of course, there'd been cycling crazes before, just like every other kind of craze from cameras to spinning-tops, but this time it was different. 'Very different,' as Mr Gootch, the maths master, remarked sourly to Form III when, in the middle of Geometry, young Aldis Minor turned pale green and had to be sent out of the class.

Usually if anybody turns pale green it's a matter for surprise, but nobody in Form III showed the slightest astonishment. You can't keep on being astonished about something when it happens three times in three days. It was Wednesday; on Monday the victim had been Carrots Jackson, and on Tuesday it had been Waldo Mokasie — though, because he came from Nigeria and was dark-skinned, he'd turned a peculiar greyish colour instead of green.

What caused it all? 'Well,' as Mr Gootch summed it up, 'if you *must* ride round and round in circles, you have to expect unpleasant results. And,' he went on, spinning round to catch Carrots Jackson dozing over his geometry book, 'talking of circles, what do we mean by the word "tangent"?'

It was a nasty habit of Mr Gootch's, and it caught Carrots on the hop. 'It's a ... well, sir... it's a kind of orange, only rather smaller.'

There was a deathly silence, broken only by a muffled choking noise from a far corner of the classroom. Carrots looked round him uneasily. '*Much* smaller?' he tried, hopefully.

There was a yell of laughter from behind him as Waldo exploded. Mr Gootch blinked rapidly. 'All right, Waldo,' he said sternly, 'if you're so amused by your friend's dull-wittedness, perhaps you can tell us the right answer?'

It was Waldo's turn to blink. 'What — me, sir?'

'Is there anybody else here named Waldo?'

'No, sir. I mean .... well — no, sir.' Waldo swallowed a lump in his throat so loudly that the curious noise was audible right at the back of the room. 'A tangent, sir? It's a sort of... a sort of geometrical term.' An anxious frown appeared on his forehead.

'A fairly obvious conclusion,' said Mr Gootch acidly, 'since this happens to be a geometry lesson. Can you go further than that?'

'Uuh?' Waldo looked round him desperately, hoping for clues among the blank faces at the neighbouring desks. Then his shoulders slumped. 'Isn't that enough, sir?'

'If you had done your homework yesterday you'd know what the word means.' Mr Gootch strode back to his table at the front of the room, and perched himself on the edge of it. 'But you didn't do your homework, did you, Waldo? Nor did you, did you, Jackson? Shall I tell you why? It's because you spent all afternoon and evening riding round that cycle-track of yours behind the tennis courts. Am I right?'

Waldo looked at Carrots, and Carrots looked at Waldo. Then they turned to face Mr Gootch. 'Yes, sir,' they said in chorus.

'Fascinating!' murmured the maths master. 'Two big boys with nothing better to do then go round and round a little circle of grass on bicycles. Perhaps you'd like us to put up some swings for you — and a slide? Or a sandpit, so that you can play sand-pies?'

Carrots's face went a beetroot shade. 'N-no, sir!'

'Riding round in circles makes you sick, doesn't it? Do you *like* being sick?'

'N-no, sir!'

Mr Gootch sighed heavily. 'Then why do you do it?'

It was Waldo who spoke up. 'It's a championship, sir, you see,' he gabbled. 'We take the time on a watch, and each chap has five minutes, so the one who gets round the track most times is the winner.'

'I see.' The gloomy look on Mr Gootch's face made it very plain indeed that he did *not* see. 'It must be great fun,' he said sadly.

Waldo's eyes lit up. 'Oh, yes, it is, sir! Tremendous fun, sir. I'm glad you see it that way.'

An excited babble of conversation broke out all over the classroom, with Carrots's voice rising above it in almost a shout. 'You go whizzing round, cornering like a dirt-track rider, sir! Faster and faster and faster, until you think the whole world's spinning round.'

'QUIET!' bellowed Mr Gootch. He waited until the hub-bub died away, then looked inquiringly at Carrots. 'You were saying, Jackson...?'

'Well, sir, it all gets faster and dizzier and...'

'...and the following morning you turn green? A most pleasurable pursuit.' Mr Gootch stared for a moment at the ceiling. 'Unfortunately, however, it seems to interfere with homework.'

'Y-yes, sir.'

'We can't allow that, can we, Jackson?'

'N-no, sir.'

'We shall have to find an answer, then, shall we not?'

'I suppose so, sir. Yes, sir.'

'And I think I *have* an answer! We will *combine* your cycle racing with homework.'

There was a curious, mystified gasp from the whole class. Waldo stared at Mr Gootch in cross-eyed mystification.

The maths master smiled — a small, rather grim smile which tightened a knot in Waldo's stomach. 'Square roots,' he said mysteriously. 'No — better still, cube roots. A little arithmetic should mix very well with your cycle championship. Shouldn't it, Waldo?'

'I don't understand, sir.'

'You will. Your homework will be to work out the cube root of the number of circles you ride.'

'Oh, crumbs!' Carrots Jackson's jaw dropped.

'Not crumbs, Jackson. Cube roots. *Accurate* cube roots — to three places of decimals.'

It was four o'clock when most of Form III gathered round the track, leaning on their bikes to watch the championships continue. It was Waldo's second turn. 'What have I got to beat?' he asked.

'Twenty-five,' shouted Aldis Minor. 'That's what I got yesterday. And you'll never beat it in five minutes.'

'Huh!' Waldo grinned, showing a flash of gleaming white teeth. He ran his fingers through the tight black curls on the top of his head. 'It's a matter of national pride,' he added. 'Don't forget, my country's quite a new member of the Commonwealth. We Nigerians have got to prove ourselves.'

'Ready?' Carrots held the watch, and waited while the second-hand crawled up to the top of its circle. 'Go!'

Waldo shot off with a powerful thrust of his foot on the pedal. For a moment it looked like a disaster, for so violent was the forward thrust that the rear wheel skidded on the slippery grass and the bike wobbled, nearly flinging him off. Then he was away, with the bike canted over gently to the left, bringing him round only inches from the white chalk line which marked the inner limit of the circle.

'One!' chanted the crowd as he shot past the starting-line and raced away into his second circuit, legs pumping hard, head well down over the handlebars, and the wide grin seeming to split his face in two. He was leaning the bike further inwards now, more confident of the grip of the tyres, and his speed was gradually increasing.

'Two!'

The shout seemed to spur Waldo's legs to even greater

speed. Taut muscles thrust downwards at the pedals, and his head dropped even lower towards the handlebars. The spokes of the wheels were a blur of shining chromium. Round he went again, with the bike held over as far as he dared.

'Three!'

Aldis Minor leaned forward, with a worried look on his face. Then he straightened to his full height and stared at Waldo in a very superior way. 'Of course he can't keep that up,' he snorted. 'Nobody could. He'll be dead-beat after the first ten rounds.'

'Four!'

'Come on, Waldo!' shouted Carrots Jackson, with a sidelong glance at Aldis Minor. 'Come on, you're doing fine!' There was a long-standing feud between Carrots and Aldis Minor, and when Carrots's record of twenty-three had been beaten by his rival's twenty-five it hadn't made their relationship any closer. Carrots screwed up his face in concentration, and his legs moved up and down on the grass, as if he were trying to add a little extra to Waldo's pedalling by remote control.

'Five!'

There was a broad band of perspiration across Waldo's forehead as he sailed by — but if anything, his feet were moving faster than ever.

'He's cracking up!' gloated Aldis Minor. 'Look at all that sweat. It's rolling off him by the bucketful. You watch — he'll have to stop in a minute.'

'Six!'

The grin on Waldo's face was as fixed as if carved in ebony. His eyes were bulging with concentration as he swung the bike into the seventh circuit, skidding his rear wheel over the dips and bumps of the grass track, and dodging the muddy grooves chewed up by the wheels of the previous competitors.

'Seven!'

Carrots stared hard at the fast-moving finger of the stop-watch, then gave a yell. 'He's way ahead! He'll do a twenty-six at least, if he keeps this up!'

'Eight!'

Aldis Minor's eyes flickered between Waldo's flashing figure and the stop-watch clenched in Carrots's hand. 'Let me see. Hold it still for a minute, Carrots, so that I can look properly.'

'You don't need to look, Aldis Minor,' replied Carrots with sudden dignity. '*I'm* doing the timing. All you have to do is keep your eyes on Waldo, and watch your record go down.'

'Nine!'

The suspense was terrific. Inch by inch the spectators were moving forward, until now the tips of their shoes were only just short of the path made by Waldo's flying wheels. Carrots waved them back.

'Ten!'

Carrots studied the watch again. 'It's fantastic!'

'It's suicide,' replied Aldis Minor, more in hope than faith, for there was no sign of Waldo's speed slackening.

'Eleven!'

'Three cheers for Nigeria!' yelled somebody at the back, and the chant was taken up by everyone except the scowling Aldis Minor, who was now squatting down with his eyes on Waldo's rear wheel as it missed a muddy pothole by a fraction of an inch.

'Twelve!'

'Oh, crumbs!' muttered Carrots. 'This is going to be really hard to beat. I've never seen anybody ride like that in my life.' He watched in silence as the rounds were reeled off — thirteen, fourteen, fifteen, sixteen.

'He's slowing up!' shouted Aldis Minor in jubilation. He turned to Carrots. 'There you are — I told you so.'

Carrots nodded glumly. It was no use arguing about it, for it was plain to see. As Waldo went into his seventeenth circuit his front wheel was wobbling, and to keep up the steady rhythm of his legs he was having to pump with the full length of his body.

'Seventeen!'

The smile on Waldo's face had changed. Sweat streamed down his cheeks, and his shirt clung wetly to his body.

'Eighteen!'

Carrots looked at the stop watch again. He wasn't much good at rapid calculations, and the second-hand now told him practically nothing, but the sight of Waldo labouring to hold the bike on course was an even more accurate guide to the situation.

'Nineteen!'

'Keep it up, Waldo!' he shouted desperately. 'You're doing fine.'

Waldo's head turned for a split second, and the weary look vanished. He grinned at Carrots, then wriggled his shoulders as if shaking off his tiredness. He came into the home stretch looking more relaxed.

'Twenty!'

And then came a gasp. For Waldo's speed was building up again. It was fantastic, but there couldn't be any doubt about it. From the moment he heard Carrots's shout he seemed galvanised into a new burst of energy and determination. The grin had returned — not quite as brightly as in the first few circuits, but with a clear indication that there was more strength left in him than everybody had imagined.

'Twenty-one!'

Aldis Minor bit his lip. His forehead was set in a deep frown, and his eyes flickered back and forth craftily, as if he was plotting some way of safeguarding his record by foul means. Carrots didn't see this for a moment, but as soon as he turned and spotted it he signalled silently to two of the other Third-Formers, who closed in on the record-holder, one on each side, ready to grab his arms if he made any sudden attempt to ruin Waldo's chances by thrusting out a foot in front of the scudding tyres.

'Twenty-two!'

Waldo pounded past them, head down, his breath coming in great noisy gulps.

'Twenty-three!'

'So this is how you do it? Most interesting.'

Carrots turned sharply, almost pressing the stop-button of the watch in his astonishment and dismay. Mr Gootch stood at the back of the small crowd, his arms folded in front of him, watching Waldo over the tops of his spectacles.

'Y-yes, sir. It's Waldo, sir.'

'Even I, with my fading eyesight, am still able to deduce that from those gleaming black curls and triumphant grin. Explain to me once again, Jackson, precisely what he is doing. You must forgive the short memory of an elderly man.'

'Er — yes, sir. Of course, sir.' Carrots looked round him wildly, in search of help, though what kind of help he hoped to find would be difficult to say. In the background a voice said softly and uneasily, 'Twenty-four!'

Carrots closed his eyes and concentrated. 'We have five minutes on the stop-watch, sir. The record's twenty-five circuits — by Aldis Minor.'

'Indeed! And Waldo is trying to beat that?'

'Twenty-five!' said the faint voice again.

Carrots stole a quick glance at the watch. 'He has beaten it, sir! He's still got a few seconds to go.' Then he looked up at Mr Gootch, and his jaw dropped with surprise as he saw the eager expression on the maths master's face. 'Come on, Waldo!' boomed Mr Gootch in a deep, throaty shout of encouragement.

Puzzled, the Third-Formers stared at him for a moment, then turned back towards the track, to watch Waldo's flying figure complete another circuit.

'Twenty-six!'

Carrots Jackson jumped up in the air with uncontrollable excitement.

'Don't forget he has to give me the cube root tomorrow

Mr Gootch was watching as Waldo scudded round one last time

morning,' said Mr Gootch, with curious satisfaction. 'How many seconds has he got left, Jackson?'

'Just a few, sir.'

'Come on, Waldo!' repeated Mr Gootch. 'You're only at twenty-seven. You can do better than that.'

Waldo completed the circle. 'Twenty-seven!' announced the voice in the background.

And then, from immediately behind Carrots, came a whoop of dignified but extreme delight. Mr Gootch was watching Waldo with a look of utterly blissful enjoyment as the rider scudded round one last time before Carrots clicked the watch and shouted: 'Stop!'

A dozen hands helped Waldo from the saddle. He was wringing wet from head to foot, and he staggered slightly as his feet touched the ground.

'Have I won?' he gasped. 'How many did I do?' Then he spotted the maths master, and goggled. 'Oh, crumbs!'

'Well may you say "oh crumbs," Waldo. A very splendid performance. Congratulations on beating twenty-seven.'

'T-twenty-five, sir. I only had to beat twenty-five.'

'For *your* purposes, yes, Waldo. But for mine, you had to beat twenty-seven.'

Form III became suddenly uneasy. It was Carrots who broke the silence. 'I don't understand, sir.'

'You *seldom* understand, Jackson,' said Mr Gootch sadly. 'That's one thing I can depend on year after year — that you seldom understand. Waldo will understand, though, when I remind him about the cube root.'

'I have to g-give you the cube root of whatever number of circuits I did, sir?' Waldo's face went blank.

'That's right. And twenty-seven would have been *far* too easy, wouldn't it, Waldo? What *is* the cube root of twenty-seven?'

'The c... oh, that's easy, sir. It's three.'

'Correct, Waldo! But what you have to bring me tomorrow morning is the cube root of *twenty-eight*!'

Waldo's eyes flickered. 'Oh, gosh!'

'Well may you say "gosh".' Mr Gootch looked round the uneasy circle. 'And for all those who hope to try for the record on other evenings, may I point out that the next *easy* cube root is the one for sixty four!'

'Uuh?' gulped Carrots.

'So there's one thing certain, isn't there, Jackson?'

'Uuh? I mean, what's that, sir?'

'Either you'll have to cycle a great deal faster, or learn a great deal more about working out cube roots!' Mr Gootch smiled blissfully, and strode back towards the school.

Carrots Jackson raised a bunched fist and thumped it hard against his forehead. 'Come on, chaps, pack up the cycle track,' he said. 'We're finished. He's done us again!'

THE FIGHTING FLANAGANS

'It was an accident.' Tim Casey backed away. 'He ran into my fist.'

'Oh yes?' Danny Flanagan advanced quickly. 'Like that, no doubt?'

'Oof!' Tim expelled air and sat down heavily. 'I'll tell my pa.'

'You do that.' Danny waved his fist. 'And your uncles and your brothers and your grandpa! The next one of your family that lays a knuckle on our Tich will rue the day — mark my words, Timothy me lad. He'll rue the day.'

Danny grabbed the arm of his youngest brother and hustled him away. Later, he held a conference.

Danny, Mike, Pat and Sullivan — commonly called Tich — Flanagan. All for one and one for all. Tich nursed his black eye with pride. He'd wanted one for a long time. It was a badge, a medal.

'Tich baited him,' said Danny.

'I did not,' Tich protested. 'Fought Tim Casey, I did. Bomp, biff, bomp!'

'What matter?' said Mike. 'It had to come.'

Pat nodded. 'Them Caseys — been asking for it, they have.'

'War,' said Danny. 'That's what. Family honour, no less. Them Caseys been getting uppity since Sean took to working in a bank. Clean collar and all.'

' 'Tain't decent,' said Pat. 'No Casey ever had brains before. That sort of thing goes right through the family. Tim Casey picked on Tich. Why Tim?'

Tim shrugged. 'Sean was at work. Bill was on an errand.

Rabbit was riding his bike. Rabbit's too small,' Tich added derisively.

'He's your size,' said Mike. 'So you did bait Tim?'

Tich twinkled a grin. 'A little,' he admitted.

'Tim shouldn't have clobbered him, though,' Mike insisted. 'It's a matter of honour. Each Casey matches up with a Flanagan. Always have.'

'The clay-pit,' said Danny decisively. 'That's the place. Settle it once and for all.'

Mike nodded. Pat asked: 'When?'

'Saturday.'

'Sean works mornings.'

'Afternoon then. Agreed?'

They all nodded. Danny drew out paper and a stub of pencil, and wrote: *Challenge you. Clay-pit. Two-thirty Saturday. No show and you are chicken.*

He folded the note, passed it to Tich.

'Deliver it,' said Danny. 'Be polite. Let's do this properly.'

Rabbit took the note. He smiled his toothy smile. His ears stuck out more rabbit-like than ever.

'I'll shine the other eye for you, come Saturday,' he said cheerfully. 'I can ride a bike. Can you ride a bike?'

'Sure I can,' said Tich. 'Two bikes. Both at once. Finest trick-rider in the world.'

Rabbit looked doubtful.

'Good morning,' said Tich.

'Polite, aren't you?'

'M'm. Us Flanagans always are.' Tich ran off, the winner of words.

Rabbit went to Tim, who read the note.

'It had to come,' said Tim. 'Them Flanagans are too uppity. Ever since Danny bought a car.'

'Sean has a motor-bike.'

Bull puffed towards them, carrying a load of groceries, and asked:

'What's to do? Saw Tich Flanagan. Has he been here?'

Tim gave Bill the note to read.

'Saturday's fine for me,' said Bill. 'Who gave Tich the shiner?'

'Me,' said Tim. 'He asked for it.'

'Oh! So that's why we got this. You shouldn't have done it, Tim. Tich is Rabbit's job. Sean won't like it. Makes us look bullies.'

'I'll shine the other one Saturday,' said Rabbit. 'I was busy this morning.'

Sean came home from work. The Caseys held a conference.

'We'll meet 'em,' said Sean. 'Settle this once for all. Have to watch out for police though.'

'Police!' Bill exclaimed.

'At the clay-pit?' Tim questioned.

Sean nodded. 'They might be dredging the water for that safe stolen from the post office last night. Tracker dogs led the police to the pit today.'

'We'll have to chance it,' said Bill. 'We can't put it off now. Rabbit's accepted the challenge.'

Sean nodded. 'We'll go.'

Saturday dawned damp and steamy. The sun gave up the struggle and stayed hidden by vapoury clouds. The mist thickened into white swirls, then lifted above the roads. But the clay-pit remained patchy—laden with fog, thickening towards afternoon.

The Flanagans arrived first and laid ambush for the Caseys. Small soggy lumps of clay, light as murky-yellow snowballs, splattered in a fusillade. The Caseys yelled in fury at such treachery.

Ignoring the gooey clay oozing over their clothes, and running down from heads which had ducked too late, the Caseys rushed to the attack.

Age against age, size against size, it was a right royal battle. The tension of months broke loose. The joy of at last expressing the long-restrained desires to settle the feud between the two families gave zest to each boy's efforts.

Tich and Rabbit grappled and wrestled, rolling over and over in the mud.

Danny and Sean punched and grunted, each pausing if the other's foothold slipped. Honour and fair play were given a lead by the eldest.

Bill and Mike swayed back and forth. Both had begun to study Judo, and now was a testing-time for newly acquired skills in combat. It didn't amount to much of a demonstration, because neither boy had learned enough to produce a winning hold or throw. But both enjoyed it mightily.

Tim and Pat circled warily, rushed to the attack, slithered, fell, rolled on each other — pummelling and struggling, well matched in size and strength.

Then suddenly two men were seen to grab the youngest boys — Tich and Rabbit.

'Yo-ho! Up the Flanagans!' Tich yelled the family battle-cry.

'Wahoo! Up the Caseys!' Rabbit's high-pitched squeal reached the older boys.

Sean, Danny, Mike and Pat stopped their battling when they saw their young brothers being yanked apart, and, feuding forgotten, closed their ranks and charged the two intruders.

The men fought hard, but pretty soon were being rolled in the mud — breathless and sat upon by two lads.

'You young fools!' one man spluttered. 'Gerroff my neck! Oooch!' His voice cut off as his face squelched in the mud.

His companion was bigger. He heaved upward, flinging Tim and Pat away from him.

'Hold it!' he shouted as they prepared to rush him again. 'We are police officers. Stay where you are. Let's have no more of this nonsense.'

Sean and Danny eased off their victim.

'Are *you* a police officer too?' Danny asked him.

The man raised up, wiping mud from his face. His eyes glittered with anger, but his voice was quiet.

'I am. And believe you me — you're in trouble. Real trouble.'

'How did we know you were coppers?' Danny protested.

'You were attacking our kid brothers,' said Sean. 'And you're not wearing uniforms, so how were we to know?'

'Too busy fighting,' said the bigger man. 'I know you lot. Always at it, aren't you?'

'None of your business if we are.' Danny retorted. 'We don't harm anyone.'

'Only each other.' Sean dabbed at his nose and grinned.

'Time you learned sense.' The second man climbed to his feet. 'I am Detective-Sergeant Crain. He is Detective Horser. We'll deal with you lot later on. But right now we're after three men. We lost them in the fog on the far side of the pit. There're more police around there, but we don't want to shout. Have you seen any men between here and the road?'

'Hah! Some hopes,' Horser sneered. 'Too busy scrapping, they were.'

'We saw you, didn't we?' said Mike.

'Nothing else but,' said Bill, and glanced around at the others.

'I saw one,' Rabbit squeaked. 'Over by those bushes. He wore a funny hat.'

Horser groaned. 'So now it's a party.'

'Wait a bit.' Sergeant Crain looked at Rabbit. 'A funny hat? Sort of shiny?'

Rabbit shrugged. 'Dunno. It was red. Had like a peak back and front.'

'Yah!' Tich scoffed. 'Some hat. Bet you made it up.'

Rabbit punched Tich on the nose. The other boys separated them. Rabbit jumped up and down with glee.

'I did it — I did it! I've given Tich a shiner!'

'When I wasn't looking,' said Tich reproachfully.

'Cut the capers,' Sergeant Crain snapped. 'Did you see which way the man went?'

Rabbit shook his head. 'No. I was busy.'

'Come on — make yourselves useful,' said Crain. 'Three men. Two medium height, one tall. One man wearing a red hat. It's a crash-helmet. He's got a motor-bike hidden somewhere.'

'The other two are wearing belted raincoats.' Horser added. 'They must have a car near the road. We were waiting on them coming for the safe they dumped here after they stole it.'

'I've got a car,' said Danny. 'Drive up the road to check on parked cars, if you like.'

'Soft, he is,' Tim gibed. 'Helping the police. It ain't decent.'

'Stow it,' said Sean, remembering he worked in a bank. 'I've got a motor-bike. We'll be pleased to help the police too.'

His brothers stared aghast at this traitorous offer. The Flanagans and the police — the police or the Flanagans — always were natural enemies of the Caseys.

Then Mike Flanagan said:

'Anything them Caseys can do, we can do better.'

To which Bill Casey retorted:

'You couldn't catch a cold — let alone a crook.'

Bedlam broke loose as the Flanagans and the Caseys vied with each other to prove their worth as good citizens in assisting the police.

'Quiet!' Detective Horser roared. 'Quiet — the pack of you. Listen to Sergeant Crain.'

'Okay,' said Crain, mopping the last of the mud from his face. 'Get you up to the road. There'll be some plain clothes officers in private cars, but I've no knowledge of exactly where they'll be patrolling. They might be along the side roads. If you see any, tell them you met us here. We want the man in the red helmet and two men in belted raincoats.'

'There's many who wear such raincoats,' said Danny.

'Would these boyos be having any other way of telling them?' Sean asked.

Sergeant Crain grinned. 'They're both short and stocky, and will probably be wearing worried expressions. That's all I can tell you. Stop any who look like 'em — we'll apologise afterwards. Send a message back here if you sight 'em within the next half-hour.'

Eight eager sleuths pounded away into the mist, which now was clearing on the roadway but still hanging over trees and hollows around the clay-pit.

Sean and Bill Casey leapt on the motor-bike, leaving Tim and Rabbit forlornly at the roadside. Danny yanked open his car door to let his brothers scramble inside, paused, grinned at the Caseys, and with a grand gesture of co-operation cried:

'Pile in, you two.' He pushed Mike and Pat. 'Make room for a couple of Caseys.'

'An insult, that's what,' Mike grumbled as Rabbit climbed over him on the rear seat.

Pat said: 'Sit on my knee, you rabbity nit.'

Loaded car followed roaring motor-bike, eight pairs of eyes scanning the road ahead and open land each side. Pat yelled:

'See that bike parked off the road?'

'Too late to stop now.' Danny kept his foot down.

The speed edged up, the car swayed under its load. Then Danny braked. The rear-seat passengers slid on to the floor.

'There's a parked car!' Danny pointed. 'No one in it.'

'Get your knee out of my neck,' cried a furious Mike.

The car sped on — some distance back from Sean's motor-bike. Then the bike swerved and cut speed. Danny saw Bill Casey signalling.

'They're overtaking a car ahead,' Danny yelled. 'Two men in it. Hold on, lads!'

He sent the car zooming on, then braked, changed gear and swung at an angle as he drew level with the other car.

Sean cut in front, slowed, then stopped. Danny braked harder and halted slantwise across the road.

The car carrying two men rocked to a halt to avoid a collision.

The Flanagans and the Caseys piled out, swarmed on to the car, pulled open the doors and grabbed the two men. One wore a belted raincoat.

Above the yelling confusion one man shouted:

'We're police officers! What d'you think you're up to?'

'Oh, begob!' Danny exclaimed. ' 'Tis two more of the breed.'

As the boys eased away Tich cried:

'Look out!'

They turned to see a car roaring down on them, followed by a motor-cyclist wearing a red helmet.

'It's them!' Pat yelled.

'They can't stop in time.' Sean dragged Rabbit from the roadway.

The oncoming car's tyres screeched in protest against jammed-on brakes as the driver fought to swerve around Danny's car. But he only partially succeeded. The car slithered broadside, skidded back the other way, shot out of control across the road and mounted the banking.

The motor-cyclist slowed almost to a halt before he hit the back of the policemen's car.

'After 'em!' Danny cried, and led the way across the road.

The two policemen jumped out and ran to the motor-cyclist in the red helmet — apparently unhurt, but now sprawled in the roadway.

Two men clambered from the car reared lopsidedly on the banking. They began to run. The Flanagans and the Caseys hared after them. In short minutes both men were smothered by leaping boys.

The policemen arrived as two puffed and frightened men were being sat on respectively by the Flanagans and the Caseys.

'Let 'em up,' said one policeman, pulling handcuffs from his pocket. 'We'll take over now. Thanks for your help.'

In short minutes both men were smothered by leaping boys

Danny grinned at Sean. 'Who won?'

Sean shrugged. 'Make it a draw this time. We had you licked, of course, but we'll leave it at that.'

'Yeah?' Mike jeered. 'You and what army?'

'Who gets the reward?' Tich asked.

'Ah! That's a sound question,' said Tim.

'Good citizens do not expect reward for helping the police,' said the second policeman. 'You only did your duty.'

Later in the day the evening papers carried the story: BOYS AID POLICE IN THRILLING CHASE OF SAFE ROBBERS.

Pa Casey waved the paper at his assembled sons.

'Traitors!' he bellowed. 'The lot of yez. Since when have the Caseys helped the police? *And* the Flanagans. 'Tis an insult! It's ashamed I am.'

Back at the Flanagan home, Mrs Flanagan stood large and forbidding at the head of the supper-table.

'Fine sons I have to do their duty — 'tis a widow-woman's blessing,' she observed quietly and sadly. Then her voice hardened and her eyes flicked each boy with a derisive glare. 'But you challenged the Caseys and couldn't even lick 'em. A draw, y'say? Shame on yez! And did I not tell you I'd have no more fighting and brawlin?' She moved swiftly for a woman of her size and dealt each filial head a well-judged box on the ears.

'That's for disobeying me,' she declared. 'And for not even winning at that.'

Danny winked at Mike. Pat nudged Tich, who peered up at his mother through one gorgeous black eye. Each of them was saying, without words:

'Wait till next time!'

THE SECRET OF ZK 170

'Good luck, Robbie. Have a good time.'

Robbie Hanson looked anxiously at his father. Professor Andrew Hanson had aged over the past few weeks. You had to be his son to be sure of it, but there were certain signs that Robbie hadn't missed: a stoop in the once erect bearing, and a tinge of grey in the mop of brown hair. The Professor's glasses, perched well down on his nose, revealed deep lines of worry round his eyes.

'Dad, if you'd rather I didn't go...? I mean...'

His father put down the folder of papers he was holding, and turned his swivel chair. 'Thanks, Robbie.' He gave a tired smile. 'If there was anything you could do to help, then I'd ask you to stay. But there isn't. The whole thing's a mystery.'

Robbie sat down on the edge of a chair. 'Can you tell me about it, Dad? Sometimes it helps, if you can get a secret off your chest.'

The Professor ran his hand through his hair, then shook his head. 'You wouldn't understand, Robbie. I know you're keen on science and you're learning fast, but this is terribly complicated stuff, far above your head.'

'Try me. I'll stop you if it starts making nonsense.'

'Well, I suppose it can't do much harm. It's an official secret; but if I can't trust you, then there's nobody in the world I can.' He leaned back in his chair and lit his pipe.

'Have you ever heard of Blaydon Rays?'

Robbie shook his head, then grinned. 'I've heard of Blaydon *Races*!'

'I wish these were as simple. Professor Blaydon lived years and years ago — right back in the 1970s. He died before I was born. In those days, of course, scientists were still muddling along, but he did make one important discovery — a ray that could stop any kind of mechanism.'

'You mean watches, cars, aircraft, and so on?'

'That's it. But it worked up to a distance of about five feet, and nobody could find out how to extend the range, so it was never developed. Then, about five years ago, the Government asked me to have a go at it.'

'Crumbs, Dad, I can see why. With a thing like that we could stop any kind of enemy attack except rockets.'

'It even stops those, Robbie. I found that out, because I was successful. It took a long time, and a hundred and sixty-nine failures, to find the answer, but now I have it. The new ray — ZK 170 — has a range of a thousand miles.' His face darkened. 'But there are two snags — desperately serious ones.'

'What are they?'

'The first one was discovered yesterday, when two government scientists came down to my laboratory. One of them had a dog. It slipped its lead while we were testing the ray on a target engine a hundred yards away.'

'What happened, Dad?'

'It ran into the path of the ray. Robbie, we made a frightful discovery that I should have reckoned with before. The heart of a living creature is just as much a mechanism as any engine.'

'You mean the dog...?'

The Professor nodded. 'Yes, I'm afraid so. Imagine what that means — a ray that can kill everything within a thousand miles.'

Robbie stared at him, round-eyed. 'Gosh, what a horror weapon! Thank goodnes it's safe, and nobody but you knows the secret of how it's made.'

The tired face seemed to go grey with strain. 'That's the

trouble, Robbie. It isn't safe. We were so busy after the accident with the dog that we didn't get back to the lab for twenty minutes. I hadn't locked up all the papers, because my assistant was there to guard them.'

'Well, didn't he?'

'Oh yes, he guarded them all right! When we got back he'd disappeared — so had the papers, and so had his car.'

'Phew!' Robbie's mind raced through the appalling possibilities that this could open up. 'But, Dad, just one man with this thing could terrify the world.'

'I know. One man — or one country. Every port in Britain is being guarded, and every policeman now has a photograph of Sherrill. But he's no fool.'

'What about airports?'

'Every air passenger is being checked. They're keeping a close eye on private flyers, too.'

'Then I don't see how he can escape, Dad. They'll track him down eventually.' He stopped, as a chilling thought struck him. 'Unless Sherrill doesn't need to get away? Couldn't he simply put the plans into the post to some other country?'

The Professor shook his head. 'From yesterday afternoon onwards every letter sent abroad was opened.'

'Then what about radio? Could he send all the details, using a private transmitter?'

'Luckily, no. Another scientist would need weeks of work studying my notes before they made sense.' He stood up. 'Anyway, it's not your problem, Robbie. Have a good week, and don't get drowned.'

'Thanks, Dad. And...' he paused. 'Dad, don't let this get you down. They'll catch him all right.'

But the frightening possibilities of what might happen were still very much in Robbie's mind as he stowed his rucksack into the old Rob Roy canoe which had served him well on so many holidays in the past. Exploring old canals was his hobby. Neglected, overgrown with weed from a hundred years of disuse, they were marked on modern maps by nothing more than faint dotted lines in blue. It was his dream to open them up again one day, for sailing and canoeing — but that was in the future. At the moment it was hard work to make twenty miles of progress in a day, for every few hundred yards a bank of reeds or a mudflat meant dragging the canoe out of the water, manhandling it along the bank, and launching it again on the other side.

He kept his canoe in a boat-shed at the bottom of the garden, on the river bank. The first half-mile of every journey was a hard pull up-river, to the silted entrance of the old Grand Inter-County Canal. Once past that, within a few miles came the choice of three different routes, all of which later developed additional branches heading to different parts of the country. Most of these he'd already explored, but one for which he'd allocated his holiday week this year was unmarked on all but the oldest maps. He'd never even spotted the entrance on his trips up and down the main canal, but he knew that if it existed it must lie behind a great bank of scrub and low bushes where he'd sometimes camped for the night.

He reached the spot, dragged the canoe on to the mud and clambered up the bank, pushing away the quickthorn which barred an old sheep path. For twenty yards it was slow progress, and though he wore long dungaree trousers and a heavy shirt he was scratched in a hundred places. Then he grinned triumphantly, for straight ahead was a mound of crumbling brickwork and the rusted remains of a huge cogwheel. It was all that was left of a canal lock. A moment later he was looking down into clear water running between stone-lined banks.

It was almost too good to be true. He'd been quite prepared to find the canal blocked and useless — but instead, here was an open channel, running beneath a covering of bushes. Why, it might even be possible to launch the canoe where he'd left it, and paddle through into the branch canal!

He went back, and shoved off from shore, swung the canoe round to face the bushes and covered his head with a piece of canvas for protection. Then, forcing the bow under the bushes, he thrust forward with the paddle, hooking it among the branches rather than attempting to use it over the side.

The canoe moved forward inch by inch. With one hand Robbie fended off the sharp points of the quickthorn, while with the other he manipulated the paddle. It was hot; midges and a host of other buzzing insects swarmed round him, and the sweat ran down his face. Though outside the sun was blazing down, the thick bushes shut out almost all the light and he had to grope his way forward, judging his distance from the bank on either side by the slap of the water against the stonework.

Then, ahead, appeared a lighter patch, and with a fierce thrust of the paddle he was out of the worst of the bushes, and into the section he had seen before from the bank. There, on his left, was the ruin of the lock machinery and the place where, a few minutes earlier, he'd had his first sight of the clear water ahead.

He was now able to use the paddle in the water once more, and he made good speed beneath the tracery of branches, through which sunlight dappled the water in front of him. The canal twisted and turned, came out for a few moments at the foot of an open field with cows grazing in it, then plunged once more into dense undergrowth.

He paddled for what seemed hours. Once he heard the sound of cars on a near-by road and the roar of a helicopter overhead, but otherwise it was a silent journey. When he reached a place where a huge tree had held back the creeping undergrowth, he pulled in to the bank and ate his lunch. Munching sandwiches in the pale sunshine that filtered through from above, he felt incredibly remote from the grim story which had begun the day. It was almost impossible to believe that two such different things could be happening in the same world at the same time. He thought of his father, sitting dazed and dismayed at his desk, wondering if he had let loose upon the world a horror worse than any which had ever been known before. If Sherrill sold the plans of the ZK 170 to an unfriendly country, within a few weeks that country could produce weapons which would bring every nation to its knees.

Paddling gently along an old canal seemed an odd thing to be doing when he knew such a grim secret, but he supposed his father had been quite right when he'd said there was nothing that he, Robbie, could do.

He slid the canoe away from the bank once again, and headed onwards. He no longer had any idea where he was, for the rough indications of the canal's course on his map had extended only for the first few miles.

Suddenly ahead of him there loomed a darker patch. For a moment he assumed it was simply a section over which the trees and bushes made a much thicker screen against the sunlight; then he realised, as he paddled into it, that he was entering a brick-lined tunnel.

He stopped the canoe and caught hold of the brickwork beside him. He stared into the blackness beyond with a mixture of excitement and uneasiness, for at long last he'd found what he'd always hoped to discover — one of the old underground canals which centuries ago had carried barges for miles underneath towns and cities, propelled by poles which the bargemen used as if driving punts.

Would he have room to use his paddle? Without any light, would he be in danger of crashing into jagged islands made by fallen masonry from the roof? If he wrecked the canoe a mile down the tunnel his chances of swimming to safety wouldn't even be worth thinking about.

Should he bring the canoe out of the water and attempt to track down the other end of the tunnel on foot? Or should he carry on, taking extra care, in the hope that the tunnel was still clear?

What had happened that morning influenced his decision.

The days of safety first were over and done with; a few more weeks might be the end of the world, so it didn't matter if he took a few chances.

He thrust forward gently with the paddle, and the canoe glided along in the dense blackness. The luminous dial of his watch told him the time was now half past two.

He paddled slowly and steadily, using the tip of the paddle every few moments to test his distance from the walls of the tunnel. The slap of water against the bricks echoed in the roof of the tunnel; it was an eerie sound, and he tried whistling to keep up his spirits, but the sound of that was even worse.

When he stopped he was surprised to discover that the silence was not as intense as it had been before. There was a distant rumble, and he wondered if the course of the canal was running immediately below a road or a railway. He quickly ruled that out — the sound was too regular; it was as though he were gradually drawing closer to some piece of machinery.

But that was ridiculous. If there had ever been machinery in use in the tunnel, it had been two hundred years ago, in the days of the first primitive steam engines! This was more like the throb of a diesel motor.

And in that same moment he realised that he had been wrong. He was not gradually approaching the source of the noise: the noise was aproaching him — from behind.

It was much louder now, and echoing from the roof of the tunnel. Whatever it was, it was coming along the tunnel rapidly; and he paddled furiously, in the knowledge that his frail canoe would collapse like a match-box in any collision.

His relief at seeing a faint light ahead was so great that he did not stop to wonder what it was. The light showed that the canal suddenly widened, with a landing-stage on its left side. He just had time to haul the canoe close in to the side when from behind came the beam of a small searchlight, missing him by barely a foot and lighting up the tunnel for a hundred yards ahead. The light came nearer and Robbie gasped with astonishment, for it was mounted on the conning-tower of a midget two-man submarine!

The sleek hull shot past him; then the engines changed their note as it slowed up and pulled in to the landing-stage. Keeping his head well down out of sight, Robbie watched incredulously as the conning-tower opened and a man clambered out. He heard an exchange of greetings on the landing-stage, and in the faint light he saw two figures leave through a door in the side of the tunnel.

He sat in the canoe, shivering in the damp and cold, but with his mind racing furiously. For the words of greeting had come as a tremendous shock. There wasn't a shred of doubt about it — the speaker had been his father's assistant, Sherrill.

And now the pattern of what had happened was becoming clear. Police and security forces at the airports and quaysides throughout the country would never catch Sherrill! The plan for smuggling his father's secrets about ZK 170 was diabolically clever. While the police searched every passenger going abroad, checked every plane, and examined every letter and parcel, Sherrill would sail out through the midst of them — in a midget submarine!

He swung the canoe round in the tunnel, about to begin a frantic paddle back the way he had come.

Then he halted. There was no way of knowing how long it would be before Sherrill and the pilot of the submarine came out again to begin their journey. If they caught up he wouldn't stand a chance in the narrow tunnel.

Could he sabotage the submarine? He propelled the canoe along the landing-stage, hand over hand, until it was alongside the black hull, and reached over towards the conning-tower; but in the poor light, whatever locking mechanism it had defeated him. Baffled, he moved away into the shadows, thinking furiously.

And then an idea came to him. The mooring-painter of the canoe was a good twenty feet long. Hurriedly he lashed one end to a ring-bolt on the stern end of the midget submarine and led it along on the side nearest the landing-stage, so that when the submarine turned it would not tangle. The other end he tied to the bow of the canoe and then settled down again, thankful that the grubby khaki of his shirt and trousers made them almost invisible in the gloom.

He waited until his bones ached with the cold and the cramped position in which he sat. He felt hungry; his watch told him it was now six o'clock, by which time his original plan had been to rest at a café and eat a leisurely evening meal.

There was a grating sound on the landing-stage, and the door opened. From his new position Robbie could see nothing, but the murmur of voices told him that Sherrill and his companion were coming closer. He crouched down out of sight as he heard the sound of the conning-tower being opened. A moment later the diesel engine rumbled into life.

The next half-hour was a nightmare. The canoe shot forward alarmingly as the submarine turned, and he had to paddle wildly to prevent it crashing into the flank of the sleek hull as it swung broadside on. Then there was a fierce forward pull, and the journey through the tunnel had begun.

Robbie could only guess at the speed. The canoe raced along, shipping water so fast that he could scarcely bail out rapidly enough with his drinking-mug, and at each bend he had to fend off with the paddle to keep the frail hull from being pounded against the rough walls of the tunnel. The cold and the damp were forgotten; sweat streamed down his face and arms. Ahead, the rumble of diesel was deafening, making it almost impossible to think; yet he knew he had to think, and quickly, for his plan so far had been no more than a desperate measure to ensure staying with the submarine. What happened after that he had no idea.

Suddenly the rumble died away to a murmur, as the midget submarine came out of the end of the tunnel. The daylight, dim though it was, seemed almost blinding to Robbie after his many hours in darkness. He saw the submarine clearly for the first time — a squat, gleaming metal shape, not more than twelve feet in length, sticking up two feet above the surface of the water and with its propeller only a few inches down, clearly visible as the top of the blades emerged, trashing the water of the canal into a foam.

But what was immediately clear to him was that the rear of the tiny conning-tower had a thick glass panel — in fact, he could see the back of a man's head. At present there was no reason why the man should turn to look astern, but sooner or later it was inevitable that he would glance back. And that would be the end of the journey for Robbie!

There was nothing he could do about it. Crouching low in the canoe was useless: as useless as an ostrich burying its head in the sand in the hope of escaping detection. He ducked only when the canoe was drawn rapidly under the thick curtain of bushes at the junction of the branch canal and the main one.

And then he realised what must be coming next. Along the main canal there were houses, villages, towns. A midget submarine could not hope to travel down in unobserved; obviously, now that there was enough water, it would submerge. Unless he cut the wire-rope painter, the canoe would go down with it.

It was at that moment, as he contemplated cutting loose from the submarine and trying to reach shore in time to give a warning, that a desperate scheme formed in his mind. It was so hare-brained that, if he'd had time to consider it, he would certainly have gone back to his original intention; but the decision had to be reached in a split second. He wriggled forward into the bow of the canoe, moving cautiously to avoid speeding up the rate at which water came in. He seized the painter, and began to haul the canoe closer to the submarine with his right hand, holding the loop of spare painter in his left until he was only a foot behind the thrashing propeller. He reached out and caught hold of the ring-bolt to which the painter was fastened on the afterdeck of the submarine.

Hanging on, though the forward pull seemed to be dragging his arm out of its socket, he lowered the loop of painter back into the water and jerked it forward, letting go hurriedly as he felt it hook round the blades and draw tight. The canoe raced forward and bumped hard against the stern of the submarine. Only inches from his chest he saw the propeller churn its way through the bottom-boards, and then splinters of wood shoot off in all directions. Water gushed in, drenching him, but as he prepared to leap overboard and swim to the bank there was a sudden change in the note of the submarine's engine. A moment later the propeller stopped with a scream of tortured metal, and looking down into the suddenly stilled water Robbie saw that round it, and the end of the shaft, the wire-rope was twisted in a hopeless tangle.

The canoe was sinking fast. The submarine, which now seemed small and frail without its motive power, pitched and tossed, even on the tiny waves of the canal. Robbie was now thinking and acting on impulse alone. He saw the lid of the conning-tower start to open, and leaped on to the stern of the submarine just in time to sit on the lid and hold it down. Blows thundered from below, and he heard muffled shouts from Sherrill. Robbie's weight, unevenly distributed, had tilted the submarine over at a sharp angle; and he now began to lean back and forth, slowly building up a steady rolling of the whole midget submarine, which steadily increased with each jerk back and forth of his body.

From inside there was now a constant chorus of angry, frightened shouts, but he paid no attention. He knew quite clearly what he had to do. Sherrill and his companion, by stealing plans of a deadly weapon, had lost all rights to mercy. Heaving back and forth, he was now going up to his knees in the water with each downward movement, and the lid of the conning-tower was touching the surface. With one final stupendous heave he brought the submarine rolling over once more, and as the conning-tower dipped beneath the surface he pulled open the lid.

There was a roar as the water rushed in. The submarine swung back again with the lid wide open, but the two men within had no time to clamber to safety before another great heave brought it back, with the open hatch even farther below water level. The thunder of the water crashing into the hull was deafening. Robbie lowered himself into the canal, still hanging on to the lid of the conning-tower, but this time the submarine did not lift. She began to settle lower and lower in the water, and soon he had to let go.

He moved away a few yards, and trod water. Not until the gleaming flank slid below the surface did he swim to the bank.

Dripping wet and running to keep warm, he reached a phone-box. His money was still intact in the pocket of his trousers, and he thrust the two-penny pieces into the slot.

Dad? Is that you, Dad?'

'Yes, Robbie? Your voice sounds odd. Is anything the matter?'

Breathlessly, Robbie told his father what had happened.

There was a pause when he had finished. When his father spoke, it was with tremendous relief. 'I'll have the canal dragged,' he said. 'Well done, Robbie — and I'll get you the finest canoe in the world to take the place of the one you've lost. Now — so that I can get the plans back quickly — where did it happen, and where are you now?'

Robbie closed his eyes. Suddenly there flooded back into his brain all that his father had told him about the plans for ZK 170, and how it could be the most terrible weapon of war the world had ever known.

'Dad,' he said, 'wouldn't it be a good idea if those plans were *never* found?'

There was a moment's silence. Then Professor Hanson said:

'Yes, Robbie, perhaps you're right.'

'Then in that case, Dad, I've forgotten where it happened, and I don't know where I am.' He laughed. 'In fact, I'm leaving here now, this very moment — before I remember.'

MATCH WITH A CATCH

Ted Ruthers strolled down towards him from the Prefects' Room.

'Hey, Johnny! Johnny Alban, you've been picked for the First Eleven.'

Johnny felt his mouth gape open. 'Me?' he gasped.

'Well,' said Ruthers patiently, 'unless there's another Johnny Alban in Larchmont College, it must be you.'

'Gosh! But I'm not good enough for the First Eleven.' He jammed both his hands into his trouser-pockets, and frowned at the prefect. 'Why did they do it, Ruthers? Sure, I know I hit fifty for the Juniors against Flensted House — but we've beaten Flensted every year since Noah. It doesn't mean I'm fit for a senior game.'

Ruthers shrugged his shoulders. 'Ask them yourself. I'm no cricketer. Oh, by the way, there's a letter for you in the Main Hall.' He continued on his way towards the tuckshop, leaving Johnny scratching his head in puzzlement.

'Why pick me?' he puzzled aloud — but he already knew the answer. Mallory, the cricket captain, was crazy about making experiments. Before every match he had a great new idea that was going to lift Larchmont cricket out of the doldrums. For days he'd be up in the clouds, scheming some bright tactical plan to outwit their opponents, but the trouble about all his notions was that he played cricket as though it was chess. He expected that while Larchmont made a crafty move the other fellows would just stand still.

Johnny Alban crossed the open patch of grass outside the Main Hall. Who on earth would be writing letters in the middle of term? Today was a Tuesday; Dad's airmail letters usually turned up from Persia on Thursdays.

He went to the green baize letter-rack on the door of the Main Hall. There was only one letter in the rack, and even from ten feet away he recognised the familiar handwriting on the envelope. 'Wonder what Dad can be writing about?' he muttered to himself. He opened the envelope with care; he could always find somebody still willing to swap something for Persian stamps. There was only a single sheet of paper inside, and when he unfolded it he found the letter was only a few lines in length. 'Dear Johny,' it read, 'Just a hurried line to say I'm off to Washington in a few days, and will be at London Airport for an hour on Saturday from five o'clock. Meet me if you can. Yours, Dad.'

Gosh, what luck! There'd be a train about four o'clock which would get him there in time, and old Bramby, the Head, couldn't very well say no. Bramby knew he hadn't seen Dad for two years, and that it might well be another eighteen months before he was able to get home on leave. That was the trouble about working on an oilfield; leave came round only every two or three years, and if somebody went sick it meant everybody's leave got held up for a while.

An hour wasn't much, he thought ruefully. Still, it was better than nothing. He went back across the grass, and arrived in the corridor outside the Fourth Form just as the bell rang for afternoon school — and also just as Mallory came out of the Prefects' Room to pin the notice about the cricket team on the Events Board.

'Hi, Johnny — you've got a surprise coming!'

Johny remembered just in time to look astonished. It wouldn't do to let Mallory realise that Ted Ruthers had already spilled the beans. 'Surprise?' he repeated. 'What kind of surprise? Don't tell me — I can guess. You've put me in charge of the gang to roll the cricket pitch. That's the only kind of surprise that ever happens to me.'

'Take a look at the notice, and see.' Mallory pushed in

a drawing-pin with his thumb, and started back towards the Prefects' Room. Johny went to the notice, and let out a loud yell of triumph. He reckoned that was the right kind of noise for the occasion, and Mallory turned his head to grin at him.

Then, suddenly, Johnny's heart sank. So much had happened in the past few minutes that it hadn't struck him until now that the match agains Redvers Hall was next Saturday. And he couldn't possibly be in two places at once.

But there was no chance to do anything about seeing Mallory now — not until after school.

By then, though, so many things had taken place that it seemed impossible. At the mid-afternoon break, when the rest of the Fourth Form had their first chance to see the notice, he was immediately surrounded by a dozen friends who pounded his shoulders, and then chaired him back along the corridor to his desk.

'Hey!' he yelled. 'Let me down. What's all the fuss about?'

'Fuss, you great goon? You bet there's a fuss. You're the first Fourth-Former in Larchmont history ever to get into the First Eleven.'

If that wasn't enough, they chaired him again after school was over and carted him down to the tuckshop for a free tea. It was five o'clock before finally he was left to recover — and by then it wasn't so easy to go up to the Prefects' Room and ask Mallory to take his name off the list. He collapsed. stuffed to the brim and exhausted, on a seat looking out across the playing-fields. and closed his eyes to shut out the view.

'What's the matter, Johnny? Feeling sick from too many cream cakes?'

'Uuh?' He opened his eyes, and saw Ted Ruthers standing in front of him. 'No, not cream cakes. Nothing as simple as that.' He stood up. 'Where can I find Mallory?'

'He's down at the nets. Hey, what are you scowling about? Nobody'd think you'd just been given a place in the First Eleven. You look more like a man who's been left out.'

'Mmm. You're not far from hitting the truth, Ted. I'm going down to see Mallory to get my name dropped.'

'*What?*' Ted Ruthers stared at him as though he'd gone crazy. Well, maybe he had — from everybody's point of view except his own. But how many people knew that it was two years since his father had been home?

He stood up.

And then, suddenly, it came to him what this decision was going to mean. He'd be ringed round by all his friends, and no amount of explanation on his part would make up for the fact that the only Fourth-Former ever to get into the First Eleven had backed out.

He sat down again.

Saturday took a long time coming. The days in between should have been packed either with exciting thoughts of the meeting at London Airport, or the thrill of batting against Redvers Hall. But because the two events clashed, and a choice had been forced on him against his will, both turned to dust and ashes. Gloomily he sent a short cable to Persia which said simply, 'Sorry, can't meet you,' and even more gloomily he turned up for net practice each morning and evening.

But the moment Larchmont took the field on Saturday his gloom vanished. Cricket was in his blood, and at the first sharp catch in the slips he dived hard, grabbing the ball out of the air to break the Redvers Hall opening partnership with only ten runs on the board.

There was a roar from the grass banks beside the pavilion, on which a crowd of nearly a hundred was seated.

He settled down again in the hope of a similar catch. But the Redvers Hall batsmen were wary. There were no slip catches; runs came by smartly deflected strokes on the leg side, and there was a look of triumph on the visitors' faces as the total climbed into the forties.

With the score at seventy, and only one more wicket down, Johnny heard the school clock strike four. The strokes sounded the death knell to his hopes. In the back of his mind, right through from Tuesday, had been the thin thread of hope that rain would come pounding down all through Saturday, ruling out cricket altogether. Even as late as midday there could have been a violent summer storm, a cloudburst, an earthquake, or some other kind of last-second miracle.

But now, at four o'clock, the axe came down on his hopes. There was no longer any chance at all of reaching London Airport by five.

He hardly noticed the sudden tumble of the Redvers wickets, until suddenly they were coming off the field for tea, with the score at eighty-eight all out.

Eighty- eight! It wasn't a big total, but it was enough to put the wind up Larchmont College. For the Redvers Hall bowling was renowned as the toughest of any in the whole summer fixture list. And thanks to Mallory's experiments as captain, the strength of the Larchmont batting was a wide-open question.

It wasn't open, however, for more than the first ten minutes. By then, four wickets were down for a paltry eighteen, and Johnny was hurriedly buckling on his pads in readiness to go in at the fall of the next.

The sun had gone in, and it felt quite cold and damp as he walked out to the wicket. It would be just like fate to send a deluge now that it was too late.

'Come on, Alban! Let's see some runs!'

The first shout came from Ted Ruthers, sitting halfway up a tree which overhung the pavilion, but a second later it was taken up by most of the crowd, in a wave of sound that almost pushed him along towards the crease. He took centre and watched the Redvers Hall bowler walk back for the start of his run. It was a long walk; the bowler was tall, lanky, and obviously very fast. Certainly he was fast enough to skittle out the Larchmont batsmen who'd already gone back to the Pavilion, so there was no reason on earth why he shouldn't go the same way.

The ball shot down and pitched almost on the tip of his bat, and first slip missed it by only a matter of inches. Johnny's eyes opened wide. This was going to be every bit as difficult as he'd feared.

The second ball seemed even faster, but what it gained in speed it lost in accuracy. It went past on the leg side, and he was able to deflect it for a two.

At least it was a start. At the other end was Mallory, more a bowler than a batsman, but stubborn enough to defend if he found a partner who could do the scoring. Huh, thought Johnny, banging the tip of his bat down on a loose lump of turf, it's going to need a real batsman to do anything in the spot we're in now. A really seasoned batsman, with a keen eye and shoulders like an ox. Not me!

But he managed a sneaky single off the final ball of the over which gave him the bowling again. And this time, instead of facing speed, he faced cunning. A small, wiry bowler sent down deliveries in which the spin was craftily concealed. Johnny discovered that before half the over was completed. The arm came over in such a manner that it was impossible to tell whether a leg-break or an off-break ball was being sent down. It kept him on the alert, and not only was it a maiden over but on the last ball he survived an appeal by the skin of his teeth.

In spite of the grey sky, and the damp, chilly air, he felt sweat breaking out on his face. He settled down to watch how Mallory handled the fast bowler, and gave a great sigh of relief when a lucky stroke on a no-ball sent the fieldsmen scudding away in the forlorn hope of stopping a boundary. Off the next ball Mallory scored a single, and once again Johnny faced the bowling.

Crack! It was a beauty — certainly the best stroke he'd ever hit in his life. It went far over the bowler's head, too high to carry over the boundary for six, for it lost its speed and began to drop well inside the ground, but also too difficult a catch for the Redvers man who raced towards it.

*Crack! It was a beauty — certainly the best stroke he'd ever hit
in his life*

Missing the catch, the fieldsman couldn't recover in time to stop the ball rolling gently over the boundary line.

There was a loud yell from the direction of the pavilion, and as Johnny glanced across he saw the numbers on the scoreboard changed to thirty.

Fifty-nine to win. Whew! He opened his shoulders to the next one, exultantly, trying to repeat the stroke he'd just made, but had a narrow escape when the ball shot away off the edge of his bat, missing his chin by inches and barely escaping the outstretched gloves of the wicket-keeper.

He wiped his forehead. So much for getting above himself! He played out the over with grim caution, hoping to snatch a single off the last ball which would give him the bowling again; but the fast bowler gave him no chance, sending down a vicious ball which was completely unplayable.

Mallory faced the spin-bowler. His face was set in a confident grin, and he raised his bat for a safe, defensive stroke to the first ball of the over.

There was a yell from behind the wicket: 'How's that!'

Johnny watched in dismay as the umpire signalled Mallory back to the pavilion — caught at the wicket off a ball he'd barely touched.

The next batsman was out first ball. Thirty-seven! Johnny knew what the tail-end batsmen were like. It was no use defending, and trying to play for a draw. In spite of the murky light the only possible chance he had was to hit out at everything, and hope to keep the bowling away from his partners.

He began his new resolution at the start of the next over. The fast bowler's speed seemed to have faded a little, and the first ball was a gift — a gift which he sent sailing past cover-point for four. The second ball gave him a two; and then, to his surprise, the Redvers wicket-keeper failed to hold the throw-in, the ball went out on the other side, and his partner, too anxious for runs, called for an overthrow. Johnny hesitated, then saw to his horror that his partner was too far down the wicket to get back. Sprinting feverishly, he just managed to reach the crease as the ball came to the hands of the bowler.

The next ball lost him another partner.

And so it went on: a nightmare of trying to shield one partner after another from the bowling. He saw the total reach forty-five for eight. At least that meant that they were past the halfway mark, but the forty-four still needed for victory seemed like a thousand. He heard the school clock strike six, and thought of his father disappointedly climbing into the aircraft that would take him on to Washington. Had the cable reached him in time — or had he spent a miserable hour hanging about the airport waiting-rooms expecting Johnny to arrive?

Ah well, it was no use worrying about it now. He squared up in readiness for the next over, and sent the ball crashing away on the leg side for four. That was a boundary for Dad!

He looked across the field, following the path of the ball as it crossed the line.

And then, unbelievingly, he saw him. Saw the Old Man right behind the ball — waving like mad, across the grey expanse of worn turf, towards him! Hardly knowing what he was doing he raised an arm in reply, and then, knees weak from the shock, turned and took up his stand for the next ball.

It should have got him. Moving swiftly to avoid being l.b.w., he stumbled; but by sheer chance, stabbing outwards with the tip of his bat to keep from falling, he placed it right in the line of the ball and deflected it along the ground towards the slips.

The close shave took him out of his trance. He clouted the next ball clumsily but powerfully along the line it had come, too fast for the bowler to reach down and recover it, and they ran two, to bring the score into the fifties.

And then, almost without effort, it was in the sixties! He was now batting cautiously again, taking not a shred of a chance, blocking every dangerous ball, and running only when there was not the faintest possibility of a fast throw-in catching him napping. Up went the total to seventy! Redvers Hall were now changing their bowling almost every over, in a desperate attempt to unsettle him and stop the complete change of fortunes. In one costly experiment they put on a slow bowler, whose first ball sailed for the only six Johnny had ever hit in his life. He took two twos off the rest of the over, and then, to his dismay, failed to snatch the necessary single to keep the bowling for the next over.

But, surprisingly, his partner rose to the occasion. A huge blundering sweep of the bat swung the ball away somewhere on the leg side for four, and a single brought Johnny back into position again, facing the fast bowler, who'd now returned for another spell.

He glanced yet again at the scoreboard, carefully guarding his eyes from twisting round in the direction of his father. Eighty-five. Crumbs! This was it, then — the mighty four that would win the match.

He opened his shoulders, crashed the bat down to meet the oncoming ball — and then from behind him heard an unbelieving, exultant shout of 'How's that?'

There wasn't a shadow of doubt about it. The stumps were almost lifted out of the ground by the speed and force of the ball, and one bail had travelled ten feet behind the wicketkeeper. Johnny grinned ruefully, and began the journey back to the pavilion to a roar of applause that almost deafened him. As he walked, the last man in came towards him white-faced and trembling at the awful responsibility of having to make those four vital runs to win. Johnny caught his arm. 'Take it easy,' he whispered. 'Don't rush it.'

Then he was on the pavilion steps, being mobbed by every Fourth-Former there was, and with Mallory hammering on his back with great ham fists, shouting: 'Well done, Johnny! You'll wear a First Eleven Cap from this day on.'

And then, in a little oasis of silence beside the pavilion, he found the Old Man. He hadn't changed: still burned deep brown by the tropical sun; still tall, lean, thin as a rake. His hair was greyer, though, and long hours of hard work in the blistering heat had etched new lines round eyes.

'Hullo, Dad.'

He felt awkward for a moment. Two years was a long time.

'Hullo, Johnny. There was a fog at London Airport, so we came down at Gatwick and I missed the Washington connection. That means I don't have to fly on until tomorrow.'

'That's great, Dad.' He tried to sound enthusiastic, but it was difficult. It was always difficult to be grateful for just one day, when everybody else he knew had four whole months of life at home every year. 'Will you be coming back this way after Washington?'

'That's what I wanted to talk to you about, Johnny. I'll be coming back this way — and coming home to stay. I've got a home job now.'

Far off, Johnny heard a tremendous yell, and out of the corners of his eyes he saw the jubilant Larchmont supporters swarm on to the ground. Someone, out there in mid-field, had scored the four runs needed to win.

He opened his mouth to say something, but nothing came. Then he laughed weakly. Back on Tuesday it had looked like a pretty rotten kind of Saturday. But life was like that — you never really knew what was coming.

THE UNEXPECTED
TREASURE

This is going to be tough,' said Harry Barnes. 'The toughest thing we've ever tackled. It'll need brain as well as brawn.'

Jim Halton checked the pressure of his tyres by a firm pressure of his thumb, then put him pump back in its holder. 'Phooey!' he muttered. 'It's just a matter of common sense. The clues will be easy enough; all we've got to do is solve them, and then ride faster than anybody else.'

They'd been chosen by the Cycle Club of the Jordan Road Secondary School as the two riders to compete in a treasure hunt organised by the County Cycle Club for riders from all the schools. That meant they had to do well, or be thoroughly unpopular for the rest of term, for Jordan Road had been boasting in advance about how certain they were of success.

'Line up, everybody, please!' A veteran cyclist from the County Club had appeared at the starting-point, holding a bunch of white envelopes. He waved them in the air. 'I'm going to hand these out, but they mustn't be opened until I blow the whistle. Is that clearly understood? Right, then.' He selected an envelope. 'Rawsthorne Grammar School? Here you are. Hillside School? Here's yours. Jordan Road Secondary? Here's one for you.'

Harry Barnes fingered the envelope impatiently as he waited for the remainder to be handed out. It felt as if there was only a single sheet of paper inside.

The whistle blew. Hurriedly he tore open the flap, and opened out the piece of paper inside so that Jim Halton could see it too.

From around them came a mounting chorus of groans.

On the sheet of paper was written: *Aspire to see five counties plain, Embrasure cuts this view to twain.*

'Crumbs!' exploded Harry. 'Didn't I tell you this was going to need brains? What on earth does it mean?'

Jim Halton beckoned him away from the others. 'The first thing to do is to get out of sight. Then if we manage to find the answer we shan't get dozens of others following us. I learned that when we had a treasure hunt last year at a Christmas party.'

They moved behind some bushes, and then Harry looked at the paper again. 'Golly!' he said. 'What does "aspire" mean?'

Jim frowned. 'Hope, I think — or try to do something. Try to see five counties, I suppose. Now where would you try to see five counties?'

Harry shrugged his shoulders. 'Haven't a clue!' He looked glum. 'Hey, Jim, this is going to be far too difficult. Let's go back and see where everybody else is heading.'

Jim shook his head. 'Don't forget, they'll be crafty too. Nobody's going to head straight for the spot. No, we'd better try to solve it ourselves. Look, Harry, surely the place to see five counties would be somewhere pretty high up. Where's your map?'

'In my saddle-bag. Here you are.'

'Mmm! Now, here's where we are at the moment, in this green bit of lowland just outside Rawsthorne. There aren't many hills, except that bit marked in brown just north.' He paused, the added excitedly: 'Look, Harry, here are the five counties — none of them are very far from the hills. Let's go up there and see.'

'Better that than hanging around here, I suppose,' said Harry doubtfully. 'All right, then. What road is it?'

'B9008, then a left turn marked "Crostleigh". The road peters out after that, and it looks as though the rest of the way it'll be only a hill track.'

'Huh! Why did they pick on us for this lark? Think of it, we could be watching cricket, or just riding around comfortably on our own, taking our time about it. Okay, come on.'

They rode for twenty minutes along the flat surface of B9008, then Harry shouted: 'This must be it! Bear left.'

Immediately the road started to climb. It was only a narrow lane, barely wide enough for a car; and once, when a tractor came towards them, they had to dismount and ride back fifty yards to a gate to get out of the way.

The sun blazed down from a cloudless sky. Harry wiped the sweat off his forehead. 'D'you think we're being mugs?' he asked. 'I don't see anybody else heading up this way!'

Jim shrugged his shoulders. 'Maybe they're coming by another route, or they weren't so quick with their maps. Don't be so pessimistic, Harry — we're doing our best.'

Round a sharp bend the road came to an end. An open gate led on to open moorland, with a grass track running steeply up towards a ridge of hills.

Harry came to a stop, panting. 'There's nothing up there, Jim. Nothing but rocks, and that old broken-down ruin of a castle with a spire on top.'

Jim swung round. 'What did you say?'

'Nothing but rocks and and old ruin.'

'No, not that. The other bit.'

'Oh, crumbs — all I said was that it had a spire on top.'

'Give me that bit of paper, quick. Look, Harry — "aspire". A spire! D'you get it?'

Harry scratched his head. 'Phew, that was brainy. Right — let's get up there double-quick.'

Standing on the pedals, they forced the bikes up the steep slope and parked them carefully so that they could not be seen from the road below. They scrambled over fallen masonry into the ruins, and up a twisting stone staircase to the top of the spire.

'Gosh, what a view! This must be the place. You can see for miles and miles in very direction.'

'Cut the cackle, Harry. Quick, what's an embrasure?'

'I dunno. It sounds like a sort of bruise.'

'Don't be an ass! Look, there's a kind of window, with just a narrow slit for shooting arrows if anybody attacked this place. Could that be an embrasure?'

'No harm looking,' said Harry, and clambered across the broken stone flags towards it. 'No luck — there's nothing here. But it does cut down the view. What's "twain"? Does it mean two, because if so I'd reckon that's just about what I can see from here, and ...' He paused.

'What it is?'

'Nothing. Just that somebody's left an old tobacco tin here, wedged in the corner.'

'Well, open it quickly.'

There was a gasp from Harry. He stood up triumphantly, waving another white envelope, and started to return across the top of the spire.

'Whoa!' said Jim. 'Put the tin back where you found it. Don't leave it lying out there; we don't want to make it any easier for the others.'

Then they raced down the stairs back to their bikes. Harry tore open the envelope. He scanned the second clue briefly then handed it to Jim.

'*Post, if you can but afford to stamp here.*' Jim said the words slowly, then frowned.

'*Jim!*' It came urgently from Harry. 'Look down there!'

The two boys stared down towards the valley. Coming up from the point where the road ended were at least a dozen boys, riding steadily up the route they had taken themselves.

'Quick!' ordered Jim. 'Duck down out of sight.' He grabbed his bike and wheeled it round to the far side of the ruin, then looked along the range of hills. 'Head over there — but keep on the far side of the hilltop. When you get to that cairn of stones stand up as if you hadn't seen the chaps down below, and shout hooray. Then run down the far side and meet me in those trees. I'll wheel the bikes down there.'

'What's the idea?'

'Bluff, you ass. I'll explain later. Hurry up — off you go!'

While Harry raced along, dodging lumps of rock and slippery slopes, Jim manoeuvred the two bikes down the hillside towards the small copse of trees at the foot of the hills. Before he reached it he heard Harry's yell from his position at the cairn of stones, and, turning, saw his partner race down to join him.

'You clever blighter,' Harry panted as he arrived and they pushed the bikes into the shelter of the trees. 'I understand now. The moment I shouted they all came to a halt. Then they changed course and started heading for the cairn. It'll take 'em ages before they realise that they've gone to the wrong place.'

Jim grinned mischievously. 'Doesn't do any harm to catch the unwary in a trap. They'd do it to us if they had the chance. Now, where's your map again? I've been thinking while we came down. I reckon this next clue is under a mile-stone, and if we stamp on the ground it'll show us where the tin is.'

Harry shook his head in a very superior way. 'Huh! So much for *your* brilliant brains. What's the name of the village where you live?'

'Butterford. You know that as well as I do.'

'Well, keep thinking about it while you read the clue again.'

'Are you crazy? What d'you mean?'

'Just do as I ask, Jim. Quickly — we don't want to waste time.'

Jim re-read the clue, then looked up in amazement. 'Gosh, Harry, that's smart. Butterford Post Office, of course. Come on, let's go.'

Through a gap in the trees they could see figures and bicycles moving along the ridge of the hills. Jim chuckled to himself as he rode cautiously along a bumpy path between the trees.

The path grew broader, and then brought them to a road

they both knew well, with a ride of only two miles into Butterford. Suddenly round a bend appeared the Hillside team, pedalling furiously.

'Quick, Harry,' whispered Jim. 'Look discouraged.'

Slumped over their handlebars, they rode towards the Hillside boys. 'Any luck?' asked Jim.

'Us? Why ... er ... we're doing fine!' The words were bold, but the voice lacked confidence. 'How about you?'

'Huh,' mumbled Jim. 'Don't ever talk to me of treasure hunts again.'

They rode on, and, looking back over his shoulder, Jim saw the Hillsiders were now riding with less determination.

'That's slowed *them* down. Maybe, when they get to the hill, they'll meet the others and tell 'em how discouraged we were. That should help to add to the confusion.'

Harry grinned. 'Whew! I'd hate to have you for an enemy.'

The first houses of Butterford appeared just ahead, and they free-wheeled down the village street. As they passed Jim's house he licked his lips. 'What wouldn't I give for a long drink of iced lime,' he groaned.

Harry glanced at his watch, then shook his head. 'Not yet. I'll stand you one at the first café we reach. How's that?'

'Fair enough, I suppose.' Jim swung off his bike outside the post office, and went in. It was a general store with a post-office counter hardly visible among the mountains of tinned fruit, cereal packets and baskets of vegetables, and the owner was Jim's uncle. 'Hullo, Uncle Pete,' he said. 'Am I right in thinking you have a treasure-hunt clue for us?'

'You've come to the right place, Jim. Here it is. I expect there'll be lots of others along in a minute. D'you want a cup of tea while you're here? The kettle's on the boil.'

Jim shook his head. 'We daren't stop, Uncle. We're well ahead, and we don't want the others to catch up. Thanks all the same.' He waved goodbye, then ran out to where Harry was waiting.

'Well?'

'I've got it! That was a good guess of yours, Harry.'

'*Guess?*' Harry was indignant. 'That wasn't guesswork — it was pure brains. Hurry up and open that envelope.'

Jim stared at the next clue in perplexity.

'*Potter about in the summer and winter, with a constant daily round.*'

'Huh,' he growled. 'Try to make a village out of that.'

Harry said the words over to himself quietly, then shook his head. 'This one's a tough one. Who potters around in the summer and winter?'

'Everybody does, I reckon. Why *potter*, though? Unless... hey, could it mean a bloke who makes pots?'

'But why the constant daily round?'

Jim's face lit up. 'Because a potter uses a wheel — and that's going round all the time. But I don't know of any potters, do you?'

'What about the Arts and Crafts shop in Rawsthorne? There's a funny old woman who runs it, and she has a notice outside about home-made pottery.'

'Mm, it's worth trying.' Jim looked up, just as a group of cyclists came through the village. He sat down, promptly, at the edge of the road, and cupped his chin in his hands. Harry, who by now was getting used to his friend's tricks, caught on immediately, and leaned against a tree. Both looked as if they'd long since given up in despair; but they shot to their bikes in alarm a few seconds later, when the cyclists dismounted at the post office and streamed inside.

'Quick, let's get out of sight before they come out again.' They pedalled hard, in the hope that their rivals wouldn't be able to guess which direction they'd taken. Both were shaken to discover that, in spite of all their efforts, they were still such a short distance in front.

And then Harry, glancing back over his shoulders, burst out laughing. For the cyclists had come out with ice-creams, and were hurrying off in the opposite direction.

'I don't believe they went there for the clue at all,' he laughed. 'I think they just wanted ice-cream. They're not the lot we saw in the hills, anyway.'

The road from Butterford into Rawsthorne was mostly downhill, and it took them only a few minutes to reach the High Street. 'There's the shop,' said Harry, putting on his brakes. Then, a moment later: 'Oh, crumbs, I'd forgotten. Today's Wednesday, and it's early closing in Rawsthorne. The shop's locked up.'

'Does the old lady live over the shop?'

Harry shook his head. 'It's a lawyer's office up there. Crumbs! I don't even know her name.'

'It's there in the window, staring you in the face. Miss Elinor Fairbanks — on that bit of cardboard.' Jim's eyes lit up. 'There's a phone-box. Maybe she's on the phone, and we can get her address from the directory.'

Harry reached the phone-box first, flipped open the directory, and ran his finger down the rows of names beginning with F. 'Here it is!' he shouted gleefully. 'Brendan Cottage, Manston Marshes.' Then, less enthusiastically: 'Oh gosh, that's miles and miles away. Can't we ring her and ask if she's got the clues?'

Jim shook his head. 'She'll have been told not to say. Come on, it's not all that far away. We can do it in twenty minutes, if we pedal hard.'

Once again they swung back on to their bikes and pounded along the road. Jim's tongue was hanging out with thirst, and once, when they passed a small village shop with a sign which said Ice-Cold Drinks he had to fight to keep from pulling up.

Then they were out on the marshes, with only a few scattered houses. The road crossed over creeks, skirted ponds, and ran between huge banks of deep green reeds.

'Phew, what a place to live!' exclaimed Harry. 'It must be bleak in winter.'

'It doesn't look any too wonderful to me right now,' replied

Jim. 'I bet this cottage is tucked away down a path, and it'll take us half an hour to find it.'

'No, it won't. Look, Jim, there it is — right ahead.'

It was a tiny place, with solid timbers showing among slabs of white plasterwork, and the roof sagged in the middle with age. In front, a small garden was ablaze with flowers. Beside the cottage was a shed, half hidden by a rose trellis, and in front of this, in the open, was a potter's wheel and a stool.

They dismounted. Jim pushed open the gate, and they went up the path.

'Gosh — I hope this is the right place,' whispered Jim. 'We'll look awful fools if it isn't.'

Harry knocked on the door. They waited, expecting to hear footsteps inside, but none came.

'Go on, knock harder.'

Harry rat-tatted for all he was worth, but there was still no reply.

'Let's try round the back.'

They walked along a narrow path between rose bushes until they came to the back door. Harry knocked again; there was not a sound from inside the cottage, but the door swung slowly open.

'What was her name?' asked Harry. 'Fairbanks, wasn't it?' He cupped his hands and called: 'Miss Fairbanks!'

From somewhere inside came a faint whisper of reply.

'Gosh,' exclaimed Jim, 'it sounds as if she's ill. D'you think we'd better go in and see?'

But Harry was already across the threshold. Jim followed, and they went through the tiny kitchen into a small front room.

Miss Fairbanks was half in and half out of a chair. Her face was white. One hand held the telephone receiver, but there was only a yard of wire attached to it.

'Doctor...' she murmured faintly. 'Fetch a doctor. ... I've broken my leg.'

'I'll ride to get the doctor — you stay here with her,' said Jim.

'But the treas—?'

'Forget about that, Harry — this is urgent. I'll be as quick as I can, but while I'm gone see if you can wedge a cushion under that leg.' He shot out of the door, leaving Harry squatting on the floor beside Miss Fairbanks, with a cushion in his hand.

'What happened, Miss Fairbanks?'

Her eyes opened, and she looked at him with curiosity. 'Who are you? And how did you know my name?'

Harry explained about the treasure hunt. 'But tell me what happened to you.'

'I fell downstairs.' Miss Fairbanks managed to lift her body an inch or two while Harry pushed the cushion into place. 'I crawled in here... and tried to phone for an ambulance... but I had to stand up to reach the phone. I was too weak, and I... fainted.'

'You broke the telephone cable as you fell,' said Harry. 'Never mind, my friend has gone to get help.'

The wait seemed to last hours, but it couldn't have been more than twenty minutes before an ambulance bell in the distance signalled the arrival of help. As the ambulance men opened the rear doors Jim lifted out his bike, and joined them indoors.

When it was all over, and the ambulance had gone, Harry turned to him gloomily. 'Well, that fixes the treasure hunt. We haven't a chance in a million now.'

Jim stared at him: 'Have you gone off your chump? Nobody else has turned up yet for a clue — and there are the envelopes on the mantelpiece. If we take ours, and leave the others on the front doorstep, then all's well and we're still in the lead.'

It was an easy clue this time, and it brought them straight back to the starting-place, just outside Rawsthorne, where a group of members of the County Cycle Club were waiting to award the prizes. The 'treasure' was a new saddle-bag, with tools and waterproof cape, for each of them.

But that wasn't all! A stranger came hurrying up to where they stood and shook hands firmly. 'My name's Fairbanks,' he said. 'I've just heard how you helped my sister. D'you like going to the pictures?'

'You bet we do!'

'Well, I'm the manager of the Rawsthorne Cinema. Come along and see me tomorrow, and I'll give you each a year's free pass.'

As Harry often said later, when they were watching a thrilling show from the centre stalls, it was the *unexpected* treasure that completed that triumphant day.

TOO EASY FOR TIM

'Come on, Tim! Hurry up, Tim!'

It was a shout from all round the playing-fields, but it wasn't needed. Tim was already ten clear yards in front of his nearest rival as they came into the home straight, and he swept on past the cricket pavilion to the thin white tape, flinging up both arms as he forged through.

A mob of boys crowded round him, slapping his back and shouting that it was the fastest mile in the history of the school, but Barney hardly noticed. He was sitting high up on the grass bank overlooking the scene, his chin cupped in his hands. He didn't need to cheer. He'd known in advance that Tim would win, and set up a record. Tim always did. It had been the same when they went climbing at the scout camp: Tim was first at the top; Tim led the rescue party when somebody hurt an ankle. It was Tim who topped the cricket averages; Tim who scored the vital goal when a soccer match was at stake; Tim who captained the school boxing team; Tim who could outrun, outcycle, outplay and outswim anybody in the whole town.

And Barney was his brother.

It wasn't much fun being the brother of a hero. 'Why can't you be more like Tim?' said his father, throwing a ball across the lawn at home. It was Tim, of course, who leaped in front of him and grabbed it out of the air before it even reached him. And Barney's mother said: 'Tim's *always* ready for a run with the dog. Why aren't you?'

Barney just didn't know why. He'd tried everything, of course, but he was never as good as Tim. If he ran, he finished last; if he scored a goal, it was against his own side; if he batted, it was to score a duck as last man in, with only one run needed for victory. He'd even tried new sports that Tim had never tackled — only to find Tim joining in and beating him straight away.

Barney got up and stood with his hands in his pockets, looking down at the long-jump competition, in which Tim was already through to the finals. There was no need to watch — Tim would win.

He turned away. Tim would always be first, fastest, bravest — and that wasn't all. Tim was head of his form, secretary of the School Science Club, and all sorts of other things which needed brains.

What a chap to have for a brother! It wasn't fair that all the brains and muscles had gone into the making of Tim, and none into himself. He went to the tea-window beside the pavilion and stretched out a thin arm for a cup of tea.

'Hullo, Barney. Bet you wish you were Tim.'

It was a friendly enough greeting, with no hurt intended, but it made his blood boil. Outwardly he grinned cheerfully. 'Sure I do. What wouldn't I give...'

He didn't finish the sentence. He turned away and wandered off into the crowd, sipping the cup of tea to prevent it slopping into the saucer as he went.

There was a sharp crack of a pistol as the half-mile race started. Barney merely glanced over his shoulder to reassure himself that Tim was safely in the lead, then sat down again to finish his tea.

The next time he looked up the crowds were streaming down to the big marquee in the centre of the field for the prize-giving. He got up slowly. He wasn't in any hurry to watch Tim collect yet another row of cups for his bedroom mantelpiece. It was like a silversmith's shop already.

He stood at the back of the crowds, listening to the usual speech by the Headmaster, the usual praise for the winners.

And then, from somewhere in the distance, there came

the most peculiar sound he'd ever heard. It was an eerie, high-pitched, echoing sound which carried right across the playing-fields and almost drowned what the Headmaster was saying. Faces turned in the crowd, and Barney spun round completely, looking towards the far side of the field and the ruins of the old factory beyond the school grounds.

He was still looking in that direction when the sound came again: a long-drawn-out wail, with an oddly *metallic* noise about it.

He left the crowd and began walking briskly towards the old factory buildings. Before he was even halfway there the sound came yet again, and this time there was no doubt in his mind at all about where it was coming from. Somewhere in the gaunt ruins ahead was something — a human being or an animal — desperately in need of help.

But by the time he stood at the foot of the factory wall there were others beside him, who'd run from the crowd when they saw him heading so purposefully across the playing-fields.

The howl came again. This time it was only a few feet away. Barney jumped down into a ditch beside the wall.

'What is it?' came a shout from above.

'I don't know yet.' He pushed his way through scraggy bushes which grew out of the sides of the ditch, and then stopped short.

'There's a whacking great drainpipe down here,' he called out. 'I've just uncovered the entrance. It's a sort of...'

His words were drowned by another loud, echoing howl. He dropped quickly to his knees at the entrance to the pipe. 'It's coming from in here,' he shouted. 'It's a dog, I think.'

Behind him came a crash of feet landing in the dry weeds of the ditch. It was Tim. 'The Headmaster's dog's been missing all day. Must be him.' Tim pushed past. 'Here, let me have a look. Hey, Rover, come on out, there's a good boy.'

The only answer was another howl from far along the

drain. Tim looked round blankly at Barney. 'Why doesn't he come out?'

Barney frowned. 'Maybe he's stuck?'

'Stuck? How could he get stuck? It's a huge drain — why, I could get in there myself.' He bent down, thrust his head and arms into the muddy opening, and began wriggling his shoulders. He went on wriggling for nearly a minute, but no more of him disappeared. His head came back into view, covered with dark grey dust, and there was a look of surprise on his face. 'It's narrower than I thought. What do we do now?'

'Where's the other end of the drain?' called out somebody from above.

'That's an idea,' muttered Tim. He scrambled to his feet and shinned up the side of the ditch, leaving Barney on his own just as the wail from inside the drainpipe cames again.

It was a piteous sound. Barney found his hands were shaking, and he felt sick inside, but he knew what he had to do. There was no choice about it. Tim's shoulders were too wide to get into the pipe, and so were those of everybody else he could think of. It had to be someone thin, weedy, undersized.

In fact it had to be *him!*

He knelt down, took a deep breath, and thrust his head into the hole.

Pushing both arms out in front of him, he wriggled his shoulders into the pipe, with a bare quarter of an inch to spare on either side. Ahead, once his body blocked the entrance, it was pitch black. He reached out, searching for cracks in the piping which would give him leverage, and then wriggled his body in until he felt his shoes touching the rim of the pipe. Once his feet were in, movement was a little easier, and he thrust himself forward inch by inch until he felt he must have travelled at least six feet. From behind him, muffled, he could hear the voices of those outside; then suddenly the howl came again, ahead of him, deafeningly loud, almost cracking his ear-drums.

As soon as it ended, he called gently into the darkness, 'Rover, quiet now. Good boy! Just wait there until I come.'

There was an answering whimper. He tried to gauge how far away it was, but found it impossible. Again he wriggled forwards, his fingernails clawing at the loose dirt in the bottom of the pipe, and the rubber soles of his shoes thrusting behind him.

'Barney!' It was a very distant voice from behind him, sounding little more than a whisper because of the blockage in the pipe made by his body. 'Barney, come back, boy. It isn't safe.'

It was a voice he recognised — that of the Headmaster. He closed his eyes as his hair brushed a cloud of dust from the roof of the pipe. Not much sense in going back now, not when he'd come so far.

The air in the pipe was foul, and he stopped, gasping for breath. He coughed, almost choking with the smell, and at the sound there came another whimper from the darkness ahead.

It spurred him on. He moved forward a few more feet, more slowly this time, for his arms were growing tired. His mind swam dizzily, and he wondered if he would ever get there; then, suddenly, one clear thought came to him. He rolled slowly over in the tube until he lay on his back, and wriggled his arms over his head, down to his sides. With his elbows he thrust his body along; it was easier, quicker — and though he felt the rough surface of the pipe skinning his arms it was no worse than had already happened to his knuckles and fingertips.

Every bone in his body now ached from the awkward method of progress, and his breath was coming in short gasps. He heaved again — and felt his head bump against something warm and soft.

'Rover!'

The low whimper of reply came from only a few inches away. He wriggled over on to his stomach again, reached out, and found the dog's head. Tickling his ears and neck, he muttered: 'What's the matter, boy? Scared to come out?'

The dog panted, and whimpered again. Barney's hand travelled along its back, then down to the rear legs.

And then he understood.

Just beyond, the roof of the pipe had collapsed and he could feel the outlines of a huge boulder blocking it. At the base of the boulder, trapped between it and the floor of the pipe, was one of Rover's back legs.

His mind wasn't working very clearly, but he was still able to guess what had happened. Maybe the pipe had been a regular playground of Rover's; but this time, obviously, as he came through it the top had fallen in, pinning the leg as he tried to escape.

Barney caught hold of the leg and tried to move it. Rover gave a low whine of discomfort. With his other hand Barney tickled the dog's ears again, and rested for a moment while he tried to think of a way to free the paw.

Then he remembered his penknife. It was a big, heavy knife with two blades and one of those curious old-fashioned things that people said were once used for levering stones out of horses' hooves. He'd never had the chance to prove it; horses were a rarity, and modern tarred roads were free of loose stones.

Was there a chance that, by wedging the lever under the boulder, he might be able to prise it up without bringing down another cascade of stones, which might easily trap him just as the first one had done Rover? He felt perspiration burst out all over his body at the thought of lying trapped in the pipe, slowly suffocating in the foul air.

He reached down to his pocket and found the penknife. With difficulty, in the confined space he opened it and felt the outline of the lever, then reached his arm out past the dog. He could just stretch far enough to force the tip of the

344

lever into the space between the boulder and the bottom of the pipe.

He heaved, but nothing happened. From his awkward position, stretched out at full length, it was impossible to exert much force. He heaved again, until his shoulder muscles cracked, but still nothing happened. Lying flat, with his head against Rover's front paws, he concentrated grimly on the word 'leverage.' There'd been something about leverage in science lessons, but his whirling brain refused to recall it clearly. Something about long handles, he felt certain.

And then it came. Of course! What he had to do was wedge a small stone under the lever, as far down its length as he could, so that when he forced down the long handle of the penknife the short piece of lever at the other end would lift the boulder.

Groping to get his other hand past the dog he searched for a loose stone. The first few he picked up were loose and crumbly, then came one which by its sharpness was evidently a piece of flint. He jammed the penknife into place again, and then rammed the stone in below it.

By this time he felt his lungs would burst at any moment. What little air there was in the blocked pipe had been used up by Rover and himself.

He rested for a moment, and then, with every remaining fragment of muscular strength and will-power, he forced down the handle of the penknife.

There was a sudden sharp cry from Rover, then the dog's whole body shot forward against him as the paw came free.

'Quiet, boy!' Almost suffocated by lack of air, he now had to push the dog away to keep from being strangled by the wild attempts Rover made to clamber past him. Rescuing his penknife, he began wriggling back the way he had come, sustained more by instinct than any clear idea of what he was doing. The pipe seemed smaller, tighter like an immense stiff collar pulled round him; and he had to fight down panic, for the moment he began moving his lungs demanded more air, and there was no air left to give them. He concentrated on keeping his breathing as calm and even as he could, but it was almost impossible when every breath was a battle. Thrusting forward with his elbows he pushed his body back down the pipe, lifting its weight each time by pressing downwards with the toes of his shoes. In front of him the dog panted, shoved, struggled, and from time to time made frantic dashes as if by sheer weight it could force its way past him.

And then, just as he felt that another yard would be the limit of his endurance, he felt his foot go free at the end of the pipe. Strong hands seized one ankle, then the other, and like a cork from a bottle he was drawn out into the fresh air and unbelievable daylight. He sat down dizzily, staring at the grey dust and mud which covered every inch of him, and gulping huge breaths of air that tasted as sweet as if they'd been perfumed. He felt the dog rubbing itself against his legs, and reached down to examine the paw, which seemed unhurt.

For a long time he was hardly aware of the Headmaster's voice close beside him, or of the circle of boys grouped on the bank above the ditch. Then two or three words caught his ear: '...another hero from the same family as Tim.'

He didn't realise who they were talking about at first — not until strong hands lifted him out of the ditch, and he found himself carried shoulder-high back across the playing-fields towards the marquee. From a few yards ahead Tim turned to give him an enormous grin; and, as they neared the crowd, there was a burst of cheering.

He blinked at the sea of faces. *Another hero from the same family.* He scratched his head. There was no doubt about it — that was what the Headmaster had said.

It proved that you didn't have to be brainy and brawny to be a hero. It didn't matter what Tim did in the future — now that he, Barney, was a hero too!

THE SCHOOL IN OUTER SPACE

'Hey, Tim!' came the sudden urgent whisper, and a paper pellet was launched across the class in his direction by Harry Crowther.

It was Harry's bad luck. He'd been the slowest of them all to get used to life cooped up in a space-ship; the slowest to realise that there was no gravity, so that anything moving through the air would go right on moving until you put out a hand to stop it. The pellet shot over Tim's head, hit the curved wall of the classroom, and bounced straight back towards Harry. It was at that moment that Captain Bill Marsden, of the Outer Space Teaching Service, spun round from the blackboard.

'Who threw that?' he demanded.

Slowly Harry Crowther raised a reluctant hand.

Big Bill Marsden grinned at him. 'Bring it out here, Crowther. Let's have no secrets in this space-ship. Bring it out here and read it to the class.'

Crowther stood up, and Tim watched as he shuffled cautiously to the front of the class, his weighted boots thumping on the metal companionway between the desks. It was only the weighted boots which kept him from sailing up above the rest of them every time he lifted a foot to step forward, and once again Crowther had been slowest of them all in getting used to walking with care. Tim hid a grin behind his hand. Poor old Harry! He'd never really wanted to come; he'd only volunteered for the journey because Tim was going, and already he'd landed himself in more trouble than all the rest of them put together.

'All right, Crowther. Now you can undo that paper pellet and read out what it says.'

The chorus of laughter echoed back from the curved metal walls of the classrom. Tim saw a red flush spread up Harry Crowther's neck and into his cheeks; slowly, as if every movement was an agony, he unwrapped the paper pellet.

'Well?' Big Bill Marsden raised one eyebrow in patient amusement.

'Do I *have* to read, it, sir?'

' 'Fraid so, Crowther. As I said — no secrets here. A space-ship isn't big enough for secrets.'

'All right then, sir. What I wrote was...' Harry Crowther paused, and looked uneasily round the class until his eyes rested on Tim. 'The note was to Tim Richards, asking him to join me in going back on an escape-projectile.'

There was a roar of laughter, in which Bill Marsden joined. Then he put one hand on Crowther's shoulder. 'That's a crazy idea, Harry. To begin with, we're too far out — you'd never have enough fuel to take you back to Earth. We're nearly halfway to Crostal, and you can't juggle with the time factor on an escape-projectile. Surely you know that — they must have told you while you were still in ground-school?'

Tim felt sorry for Harry Crowther, and a bit guilty, too. When the Orphan Volunteer Scheme had been launched three years earlier, to take youngsters with no family ties on Earth to the newly discovered Outer Planets, he'd been excited from the very start, and hardly able to wait until his fifteenth birthday when he'd been allowed to volunteer. Harry hadn't been so sure, even at the beginning, and Tim felt certain he'd finally put his name down only because he didn't much care for the idea of being left behind after Tim had gone.

They'd been friends all their lives. Harry had made desperate attempts from time to time to talk him out of the whole idea; and almost every week, when on television they'd

Harry's right leg splayed out in front of him

watched the interplanetary telecast, he'd kept up a running commentary about how grim life must be in the new pioneer zones. 'It's all right if we get tickets for Venus,' he'd said. 'They've got proper towns on Venus, and you can have a bit of fun. But imagine getting sent to Volgar, or Pengal — or even worse, right out to that awful new place... what's it called? Crystal?'

'Crostal,' Tim had corrected him. And now here they were, nearly halfway there, with not a chance to get back. Through space the great blue-black hull of the ship raced on, with not a sound except the occasional sustained hiss as one of the steering-rockets was used to correct course. Escape-projectile? It just showed how little Harry knew about space-travel. Nobody but a tenderfoot would imagine you could cut back that far in anything but a fully equipped space-craft.

'All right, Crowther, you can sit down.' Captain Bill Marsden was already turning back towards the blackboard — but he stopped suddenly. 'Wait a minute, Harry! I suppose I've got to punish you for flicking pellets. Off with your right shoe.'

Harry looked at him in puzzlement.

'Come on, don't waste time. Off with it, and leave it here with me at the front of the class. You can have it back at the dinner-break.'

Mystified, Harry Crowther took off his weighted shoe and placed it beside Big Bill. Then he put out his leg to plod back towards his desk.

The look of bewilderment on his face during the next few seconds set the whole class in an uproar. His right leg splayed out in front of him, touched the floor, then bounced gently off again. Thrown off balance he fell to his knees, and promptly sailed upwards again, canted over on his left side by the weighted shoe still on his other foot. His arms windmilled as he strove to find anything he could hang on to, but it was his left shoe which finally anchored him, by hooking under the edge of his desk. He hauled himself down to the floor; then, hand over hand, worked his way down the space between the desks until he reached his own.

'That's standard punishment,' said Captain Bill Marsden. 'An hour of that and you won't flick any more pellets. Now, back to what we were talking about. Minerals on Crostal, wasn't it? Richards, can you tell us about the minerals on the planet we're heading for?'

Tim closed his eyes for a moment, trying to recall the coloured television diagrams he'd seen over and over again of the surface structure of the distant planet. 'Uranium?' he said hesitantly.

'Oh yes, but we can get that on almost any planet. What about useful up-to-date minerals?'

Gosh, there were so many new ones nowadays that it wasn't an easy question. What was that rare plastic metal found on only one planet in any of the universes yet explored? He frowned, then suddenly the name came to him. 'Viviform, sir. That's the important one, surely?'

Big Bill grinned. 'That's right. You can mould it by hand into any shape you like, then harden it by ray treatment to any degree, and it'll stand up to any amount of heat. In another twenty years a space-ship like this will be as obsolete as the Ark. We'll be travelling in ships made of viviform, wearing viviform space-suits, and firing viviform rockets. At least, you will — I'll have retired to grow flowers in a quiet corner of some planet.' He reached down to a box on the desk beside him. 'Here, I've got a few bits of unmoulded viviform you can look at.' He held up a handful of small pellets of material that looked like grey modelling-clay. 'Catch!'

The pellets sailed across the class quite slowly. Tim reached up and caught one, and so did several of the others; two pellets bounced off the rear wall and sailed back again. Harry Crowther grabbed one; and the other returned straight to Big Bill's hand.

Tim examined the pellet with interest. New metals meant

big changes. He knew that from talking to his grandfather before the old man, his last living relative, had passed on and left him with no choice but admission to the orphanage. The old man had remembered right back to the first discovery of uranium and plutonium — the original metals used in the old days of atomic fission — and had told him of the enormous changes they'd made in life on Earth: how at first they'd been used for making bombs; and then, after the Great Peace, for industrial purposes which had brought comfort and prosperity everywhere.

Now, perhaps, this little pellet and millions like it were going to have just as startling an effect. He pressed it, and the imprint of his thumb remained when he'd taken it away. He rolled it between the palms of his hands, until it was a long, thin, flabby rod, then moulded it into a tiny fat elephant, just as he'd done with modelling-clay when he was small.

'You get the idea?'

He looked up as Big Bill Marsden spoke.

'You've all seen how easy it is to mould this stuff. This bit which came back to me is now flattened by my fingers into a thin sheet. Does everybody see? Fine — so now we'll complete the job.' He pointed to a small container on the desk. 'That's the ray-box. All I have to do is to hold the sheet of viviform in front of it, and then turn on the ray — like this.'

He pressed a switch on one side of the box. There was no sound or flash; but a second later, when he switched off again and held up the sheet of viviform, it was rigid. He grasped the edges with both hands and strained to bend it, but the sheet held firm.

'Now you see how viviform works. And there's plenty of it on Crostal. Already there are five thousand miners and their families camped there, and by the time we arrive there'll be huts for a school. Take my word for it, Crostal is going to be the planet of opportunity.' He swung round to face Harry. 'Far more opportunity, Harry, than you'd ever find on over-crowded Earth.'

But there was no answering grin from Harry Crowther. He sat slumped at his desk, his face filled with gloom.

He was still sitting there when the lesson ended. One or two other boys laughed at him as they passed on their way through to the canteen, but Tim stayed behind and planted his heavy shoes down firmly beside Harry's desk.

'Harry.'

'Oh go away! Can't you see I want to be left alone?'

Tim shrugged his shoulders and left. It was no use arguing with Harry Crowther when he was in one of his moods. He'd known that ever since they'd first met at the orphanage; he was a stubborn ox, and any persuading that had any effect had to be done by himself. You couldn't tell Harry anything: the only way was to make him find it out.

He went into the canteen, and collected his glass of concentrated fruit juice with the small packet of tablets which provided a balanced diet on the journey. There were no ordinary meals on a space-ship. Tim had attended the lectures beforehand and knew all about the weight problems during take-off, and why even the weights in his shoes had to be something which would be useful at the other end of the journey.

He saw Harry go up to the serving-counter for his glass of fruit juice, and then pick up his tablets.

But what happened next made him sit up with astonishment. For Harry looked swiftly from side to side to make sure he was alone at the counter, and then scooped up a handful of tablets from the bowl in front of him. Before the Canteen Officer noticed he crammed them into his pocket.

Great snakes — what could Harry be up to? Tim watched as his friend manoeuvred his way cautiously to a seat, using his one weighted shoe as a brake while he propelled himself along by one hand, and slopped fruit juice out of the glass held in the other.

Why pinch food tablets? It wasn't as if there was any pleasure to be got out of eating them, for they tasted like dry flour, and you certainly didn't feel afterwards that you'd had a hearty four-course meal.

And then it struck him. At first he couldn't credit it; even Harry couldn't be such a fool — not after what Captain Bill Marsden had said. Only an absolute idiot would still think of trying to make a getaway in an escape-projectile. But if that wasn't what Harry had in mind, why take the tablets?

He grinned to himself. Poor old Harry. Only a day-dreamer like Harry would try to set out with only a quarter of the fuel he needed, and nothing but a handful of food tablets, to last through a journey which would take months or even years if it *had* been possible. Even the best escape-projectiles were slow, and, as Big Bill had said, there was nothing you could do with them to alter time factor.

He watched Harry carefully all evening. Three times his friend left the main schoolroom compartment. The first journey was to regain his weighted shoe, but on the other two Tim noticed that the only purpose seemed to be to check whether the escape-projectiles were under guard.

But he wasn't certain of Harry's plans until bedtime. They all slept in their clothes, removing only their shoes before lying down. Harry, he noticed, kept his on.

He waited, struggling to keep awake. Sleep came easily on space-trips. Big Bill said it was because of the extra strain caused by moving about all day in such entirely different conditions; whether that was correct or not he didn't know, but certainly every night he'd dropped off as soon as his head touched the pillow.

But not tonight. He listened to the snoring from the other beds, and wondered if he was imagining all this — whether Harry had pinched the tablets for some other reason, and the trips to the escape-projectiles were just a coincidence.

No — it was too much of a coincidence. But, gosh, he certainly felt sleepy. He'd give Harry just five more...

He opened his eyes wide, and stared across the room, in

which the lights had been dimmed. Harry was sitting up in bed, climbing out — and now heading for the door.

Tim waited just long enough to be sure Harry wouldn't hear him and turn round. Then he followed.

His friend moved slowly along the corridor towards the escape-projectiles — and then stopped. Hurriedly Tim flattened himself in a doorway. It was obvious what had happened. Somebody was standing near the projectiles, and Harry had pulled up just in time to avoid being spotted.

And now he was heading back — straight towards the spot where Tim was concealed. Tim held his breath, and drew himself a futher half-inch into the recess, but he needn't have bothered. Harry's eyes were looking straight to the front, and he was moving down the corridor at top speed, back towards the dormitory.

Five minutes later Tim cautiously opened the dormitory door and glanced towards Harry's bed. Either Harry was fast asleep, or he was a better actor than Tim had ever dreamed. He walked over and stood by Harry's bed, scratching his head in puzzlement. He didn't know what was the best thing to do. Wake him up, perhaps, and argue — try the old hopeless game of persuasion? No, it would only be a waste of time; and, moreover, it would warn Harry that Tim knew what he intended to do. That might make him panic and do something even more stupid.

If only he could make Harry understand that life on Crostal really would be full to the brim with opportunity. If only he could hammer it into that day-dreaming head that going back to overcrowded Earth had no future in it — even if it were possible to *get* back.

He stood there with his hands in his pockets. And then one hand encountered a small soft lump the size of a marble. For a moment he couldn't remember what it was.

Then it came to him. The viviform, of course! And with that realisation came also the answer to his problem.

Noiselessly he left the dormitory and went along the corridor to the classroom. On the table, just as Big Bill had left it, was the ray-box. He wedged it under his arm, and returned to the dormitory.

Sitting on the edge of Harry's bed he rolled the small lump of viviform between his fingers until it was a long, thin, flexible rod.

Harry lay on his stomach, with his legs flung out at the end of the bed. His big toe rested on the bedrail. Swiftly, grinning as he did it, Tim looped the piece of viviform round the big toe and the bedrail, then held the ray-box towards it and pressed the button. Soundlessly the ray did its work. He got up, returned the ray-box to the classroom, went back to bed and fell asleep.

It was a yell from across the dormitory that woke him. The lights were already on, which showed that Big Bill Marsden had been round to call them for breakfast, and everybody else was rolling sleepily out of bed except Harry. Harry was sitting up in bed, staring in amazement at his big toe, chained to the bedrail by a ring of viviform harder than toughened steel.

A dozen boys ran across the room, bumping and colliding because they hadn't yet put on their weighted shoes, and there was a hoot of laughter as they saw what had happened to Harry.

'How did it happen?' bellowed Harry. 'Hey, someone, get Captain Marsden along here to take it off me. I want my breakfast!'

'I'll go,' said Tim. He buckled on his weighted shoes and went down the corridor to the officer's quarters. Big Bill was shaving, but Tim interrupted him with the words, 'Come and look at Harry Crowther, sir. He's trapped.'

'Trapped? What d'you mean, Richards? How can he be trapped?'

'You'd better come and have a look, sir.'

Mystified, Big Bill followed him back to the dormitory and stopped at the end of Harry's bed, staring down at the thin loop of hardened viviform which imprisoned the big toe against the bedrail.

'Get it off me, sir, please — I want my breakfast!' Harry lay propped up on his elbows, looking anxiously at his foot.

Big Bill shook his head. 'I'm afraid I can't. There's nothing on a space-ship that will cut through viviform. You'll have to wait until we reach Crostal, and then we can use an oxidiser to break it.' His face darkened. 'What lunatic did this!'

There was absolute silence for a few moments. Tim swallowed hard, then opened his mouth.

'I did, sir,' he croaked.

Big Bill spun round to face him. 'You? You of all people, Richards? I'd have credited you with more common sense — and knowledge, too — than to do such an unbelievably stupid thing. Do you realise that this means Harry is chained to his bunk for the next month or more — until we reach Crostal?'

'Yes, sir.' Tim swallowed again. He couldn't imagine what kind of punishment lay ahead, but it was bound to be severe. Last night, when he'd done what he thought he had to do, it had seemed like a sensible idea. Now he wasn't so sure.

'You'll be confined to your quarters, Richards, for the rest of the voyage. And when we reach Crostal...'

'Just a minute, sir.'

Both Tim and Big Bill turned towards the bed. Harry was sitting bolt upright, waving his arms urgently.

'Don't do anything to Tim, sir. I know why he did it.'

'There can't possibly be any reason for doing a thing like that, Harry.'

'There was, sir. You see, I was planning to get away last night in an escape-projectile. I had a feeling Tim suspected. He must have done this to stop me.'

'Is that true, Tim?' Big Bill Marsden looked at him sternly.

Tim nodded. 'I was scared he'd get away while I was asleep, and that he'd kill himself trying to reach Earth.'

'You certainly *would* have killed yourself, Harry.' Big Bill looked grimly at Harry Crowther. 'You can thank your lucky stars that Tim was quick-witted.' A brief smile flickered at the corners of his mouth as he looked down once again at the captive big toe. 'At least there's one thing we know for certain. You won't be able to try it again.'

Tim stayed behind with Harry when the others had gone to breakfast. 'Sorry,' he said. 'Does it hurt?'

'Sorry my foot!' Harry burst out laughing. 'I should say sorry my *toe*. I suppose you're all quite right — it was crazy.'

It was later in the day, when Tim returned between lessons to keep Harry company for a few minutes, that he found his friend sitting up in bed with a look of excitement on his face. 'Look!' cried Harry. 'Come and look at this.'

On the bed in front of him Tim saw a small square object. 'What's that?'

'Take a closer look, Tim.'

'It's just a sort of tall box. Made of viviform, isn't it?' Tim stared at it dully.

'Don't you understand?' burst out Harry excitedly. 'With this stuff there isn't anything you couldn't build. Once it's hardened it can't bend, so you could put up skyscrapers as thin as paper, and bridges with struts no thicker than cotton thread.' The excitement died out of his face. 'Tim, I've got to get back to Earth! I want to use this stuff — spend my life designing buildings and bridges to be made with it.'

'But, Harry, there's no room left on Earth for more bridges and buildings. That's why people are leaving — because there's hardly room to sit down, let alone build more houses.'

'True enough,' said Harry gloomily. 'I wish it wasn't like that.' He looked at the model lying on the bed in front of him. 'There *had* to be a catch in it somewhere. What I need is a place where there's room enough to build.'

'What about Crostal?' said Tim quickly.

Slowly the excitement came back into Harry's face. He held up the little model, and then grinned at Tim. '*Crostal!* You're right, Tim. Earth's no place for me. Big toe and all — Crostal, here I come.'